MW00805547

THE

DOLLHOUSE
ACADEMY

ALSO BY MARGARITA MONTIMORE

Acts of Violet

Oona Out of Order

Asleep from Day

THE
DOLLHOUSE
ACADEMY

MARGARITA MONTIMORE

FLATIRON
BOOKS
NEW YORK

This is a work of fiction. All of the characters, organizations, and events portrayed in this novel are either products of the author's imagination or are used fictitiously.

THE DOLLHOUSE ACADEMY. Copyright © 2025 by Margarita Montimore. All rights reserved. Printed in the United States of America. For information, address Flatiron Books, 120 Broadway, New York, NY 10271.

www.flatironbooks.com

Designed by Omar Chapa

Library of Congress Cataloging-in-Publication Data

Names: Montimore, Margarita, author.
Title: The dollhouse academy / Margarita Montimore.
Description: First edition. | New York : Flatiron Books, 2025.
Identifiers: LCCN 2024020007 | ISBN 9781250320650 (hardcover) |
    ISBN 9781250320667 (ebook)
Subjects: LCGFT: Novels.
Classification: LCC PS3613.O54898 D65 2025 | DDC 813/.6—dc23/
    eng/20240510
LC record available at https://lccn.loc.gov/2024020007

Our books may be purchased in bulk for promotional, educational, or business use. Please contact your local bookseller or the Macmillan Corporate and Premium Sales Department at 1-800-221-7945, extension 5442, or by email at MacmillanSpecialMarkets@macmillan.com.

First Edition: 2025

10 9 8 7 6 5 4 3 2 1

For Larry David—and by Larry David, I mean Terry Montimore
(they are basically the same person).
With love and extra pickles.

We cast away priceless time in dreams, born of imagination, fed upon illusion, and put to death by reality.

—Judy Garland

Reality is something you rise above.

—Liza Minnelli

THE

DOLLHOUSE

ACADEMY

CHAPTER ONE

Ivy's Diary

JANUARY 11, 1998

I'm living a borrowed life on borrowed time.

It took me a while to realize this. Years of denial and blind compliance. By the time it finally dawned on me that my life wasn't really my own, the bitter truth of their mantra really sunk in.

You are replaceable.

Yesterday we wrapped filming on the three hundredth episode of *In the Dollhouse*. Camera crews and press agents from various media outlets swarmed to capture the milestone, along with representatives from the *Guinness World Records*, who brought framed certificates that officially declared *In the Dollhouse* as the longest-running prime time TV drama. They surprised us by announcing another world record: after nearly sixteen years on air, Tabitha Noelle as played by me, Ivy Gordon, was now the longest-running character on prime-time television. The cast and crew cheered as I was handed a second certificate.

A giant cake was brought on set, and a TV wheeled out to play a montage of celebrities and fans raving about the show and about me. All these people who adore me, who think they know me, who even want to be me.

Nobody should want to be me.

As I stared at the cake, 300 emblazoned in red icing, a thought popped into my head:

I've been living in the Dollhouse for more than half my life. Pouring my heart and soul into stories that were written for me, yet I've never truly reflected on my own.

For a long time, I've been too afraid to share my story.

I can't afford to be afraid anymore.

I'm thirty-four but I feel like I'm a hundred.

I'm so tired. Always so tired. They don't warn you about how you'll never get enough rest, always pulled in different directions. You'd think the more successful you get, the more powerful you'll become, the more autonomy you'll earn, but it's not true. You get so used to somebody else advising you and calling the shots, your inner compass gets warped; you put all your trust in others and forget how to trust yourself. As you become more recognized, you become a reflection of something bigger than yourself, and as your image grows more important, so do all your decisions. It gets so you can no longer make them on your own. The more eyes you have on you, the more crucial it is for you to say the right things, look and behave the right way.

If only I wasn't so taken in by them. *You will have everything*, they say, but when you do, you feel like you have nothing.

Whoever ends up reading this, above all else, I ask that you believe me.

I'm putting my life on the line telling you what I'm about to tell you. If that sounds like an exaggeration, let me share a little story to illustrate my point.

Before I discovered how many bigger, darker, scarier things the world contains, my greatest fear was flying. Since I was a little girl, despite the countless times I was shuttled between coasts for auditions and tapings, every time I set foot on an airplane, terror wrapped around me like a boa constrictor. I'd calm down long enough to let myself be buckled into my seat, but the second the plane began to taxi, I'd start to wail. The other passengers would throw dirty looks at my mother and me, mistaking my hysteria for an unruly child's tantrum.

After enough disapproving glares, I learned vocalizing my emotions was something to be ashamed of, no matter how much distress I was in. It's a lesson I'm still trying to unlearn.

My phobia didn't get any better with age. No matter how many hours I spent in the sky, I was gripped by fear until the wheels touched down on the ground, even in first class after I booked more jobs, even in Dahlen's private jets after I became a top earner and "precious cargo." People tried to comfort me with statistics, as if logic could magically flip my brain's panic switch. Nothing short of alcohol or medication curbed my irrational sense of doom, but I usually avoided drinking or taking the prescribed pills—in the event that the plane did go down and there was any chance of survival, I wanted to keep my wits about me.

So, I white-knuckled it, certain that every bit of turbulence would send us plummeting, or that engine failure was looming, or a bolt of lightning would strike us down at any moment.

You probably know about the 1988 bus accident in which I almost died. And I'll get into that, of course I will. But very few people know I almost died the previous year, not on a bus but on an airplane.

It was early September, and I was on a Dahlen private jet, returning from Rome after doing a European press tour for the movie *Colorbound*, the only non-Dahlen project I was allowed to work on. For most questions, my responses were riffs on statements my publicist had prepared for me and were far from controversial. I praised the film's writer and director, heaped compliments on the cast and crew. But a couple of times, when asked about the contract negotiations around renewing *In the Dollhouse* for several more seasons, I'd expressed ambivalence toward continuing to play Tabitha Noelle. Nothing controversial, I just added a throwaway line that happened to reflect my genuine feelings, about how refreshing it had been to take on a new character in *Colorbound*, and how after six years, I wasn't sure whether I could still make a meaningful contribution on the show.

Anyway, I was exhausted from the press tour—four countries in six days, answering the same questions over and over, feeling like I had to smile the entire time, because if I let one unpleasant expression slip, that's the photo they'd use. It's not like I got to visit the Eiffel Tower or the Trevi Fountain; I spent most of the time in hotel conference rooms and suites set up for reporters. It was a privilege to be on that junket, sure, but a privilege that drained every ounce of energy from me. My costars on *In the Dollhouse* (or ITD, as we all called it), the closest thing I had to friends, would be sympathetic about that when I returned. Except for the ones who might be jealous because they weren't allowed to shoot any outside projects. Probably I'd just keep my mouth shut about my exhaustion, just as I've grown accustomed to keeping my mouth shut about most things that distress me. I save those negative emotions for when I'm reading lines to a camera.

It was too bad my fear of flying kept me from sleeping on planes, because as soon as we landed in New York, I would have to return to the compound to begin ITD rehearsals. Fortunately, going over the show's latest script helped distract me somewhat from my obsessive worry that the giant metal bird I was encased in would drop like a stone and sink to the bottom of the ocean.

Several hours into the flight, the plane dipped abruptly. The downward lurch felt like being in an elevator whose cables had snapped. The other passengers on the flight—a group of middle-aged men in suits I assumed were Dahlen lawyers or finance guys—seemed unfazed, and the flight attendants assured us it was only a little turbulence, so I did my best to suppress my apprehension. By that point in my life, it had become one of my strongest skills.

Suddenly a piercing alarm echoed through the cabin and oxygen masks dropped from the ceiling. Bile burned my throat.

"Sorry folks, we've experienced a drop in cabin pressure. Just to be on the safe side, keep your seat belts buckled and go ahead and put on those oxygen masks. Crew, please strap in and do likewise."

The businessmen glanced at each other, shrugged, and put on their oxygen masks. I did the same, wondering how they could be so nonchalant, my hands shaking so badly, it took a few tries to adjust the straps of my mask.

I asked what was wrong with the plane, looking around for one of the flight attendants, who I imagined were donning parachutes, about to abandon the aircraft altogether. This couldn't just be turbulence. Were we going down? We were going down, weren't we? I pressed my lips together, teeth sinking into them from the inside until I tasted blood.

Nobody answered me and the plane continued to judder in the sky for what seemed like hours but must've only been a minute or two.

Then things got even scarier.

A high-pitched beep bellowed through the cabin, like a sadistic alarm clock through a megaphone. The overhead lights began to flicker, and the floor's emergency strip lights blinked on.

Too petrified to speak, I tried to catch the eye of one of the business-men.

But they all stared off into space, not speaking to each other, still looking disturbingly calm.

Finally, the pilot came over the loudspeaker. "We're going to be mak-ing an emergency landing in the Azores. Nothing to worry about, folks, just need to get a few things checked out before we continue on to New York."

An emergency landing was nothing to worry about?

I screwed my eyes shut and tightened my grip on the armrests until my nails punctured the leather.

The alarm kept shrieking and my brain kept repeating three words in time with its piercing rhythm: *we're going down, we're going down, we're going down, we're going down.*

It's impossible to say how much time passed before the wheels jolted against the tarmac and the plane shuddered to a stop.

I opened my eyes and pulled up my window shade but could only see the silhouette of dark hills and a smattering of lights in the distance.

The men in suits removed their oxygen masks and unbuckled their seat belts while I remained too stunned to move. Before I could make any sense of what was happening, the group of them formed a circle around me. To this day, I can't remember what they looked like.

I shrank down in my seat.

One of the men yanked off my oxygen mask. They took turns speaking.

"You look like a scared little girl."

"You thought it was the real thing, didn't you?"

"Next time it can be."

"Next time it might be."

"This is how easy it is to get rid of you."

"Nobody would even miss you."

"We have your replacement lined up."

"Do you want to be replaced?"

I shook my head no, tears streaming down my face.

"We don't want to replace you, either."

"But we will, if we have to."

"Be a good girl and watch what you say to the press."

"Be a good girl and sign that new contract."

"Or next time you think the plane is going down, it'll be the real thing."

"Are we clear?"

I nodded my head, tasting salt in the corners of my mouth. The seat of my jeans was cold, wet with urine. My teeth chattered.

A stack of papers was put in front of me and I was handed a pen.

Once I signed the contract, one by one, they patted me on the head like I was an obedient dog and disembarked the plane.

A minute later the pilot announced we would be continuing our flight to New York.

I was the only passenger left.

That's what they did to me when I made vague noises about wanting to leave the Dollhouse.

Imagine what they'd do to me for telling you what it's really like to be one of their dolls.

CHAPTER TWO

The sun is rising as our taxi crosses the bridge from Brooklyn into Manhattan, and the skyscrapers' dark silhouettes look as if they've been cut out of paper and set against an amber and indigo ombre background. The city skyline only ever looks this breathtaking on film, and I can't help but hope it's a sign of good things to come.

"Don't be nervous, Ramona," Grace says to me.

"I'm not nervous. You're nervous." I steady my jittering knee.

"You're right, I'm totally freaking out." Grace clutches at my hand. "Is this really happening?"

"Yes, it's happening and breaking my fingers won't make it any more real." I gently extricate myself and crack open a window to let out the cloying Royal Pine air freshener permeating the inside of the car. The driver has four little trees dangling from his rearview mirror, which is four too many.

"I've never done live TV before. What if I freeze? What if I fuck it up?" Her eyes go cartoonishly wide. "What if I say 'fuck' on air?"

I force myself to take slow even breaths—I've never done live TV before either. "You and your sailor mouth will be fine," I reassure her. "You were great in the preinterview with that assistant producer, and I'm sure you'll be great today. Plus, I don't know what you're doing to your face, but your skin looks luminous." An extra compliment is the fastest way to calm an uneasy Grace.

"You think so?" She pats her cheekbones with her fingertips. "I feel like it looks waxy today."

You know those women who are gorgeous but don't believe it, no matter how many times you tell them? Grace is like that. Has been since we were kids. Despite her flawless olive complexion and dark voluminous hair that would make a Disney princess jealous, I still had to bolster Grace's self-esteem regularly. I didn't mind. My uncles / de facto fathers, Reed and Alonso, lavished me with positive reinforcement, so instead of focusing on my blemishes and frizzy yellow hair that would make a scarecrow jealous, I grew up appreciating my dark teal eyes, the strong V of my eyebrows, and the fullness of my mouth. By some miracle, I made it through my gawky teenage years and into my early twenties with a healthy self-esteem. Unfortunately, the same couldn't be said for Grace, whose series of foster homes left her reserved and distrustful, which was sometimes misconstrued for snobbery. For the dozen years we've been friends, I've tried to show people they have the wrong idea about her, and that she has the wrong idea about herself.

Grace begins to gnaw at a cuticle, and I give her wrist a gentle swat. "Look how pretty the city looks," I say to distract her.

Rays of sun glint off glass and steel, the buildings blindingly beautiful, doubly so as they're mirrored in the river.

"Yeah, so pretty you almost forget how polluted the water is and how many people are slaving away inside those skyscrapers." Grace's tone is wry. "That's probably the real reason they make all those windows tinted."

I turn, and she cocks an eyebrow, challenging me. I look back to the window as our car enters the concrete maze of lower Manhattan.

"Don't pout," she says.

"I'm not pouting." I am, a little.

"Can we go back to how exciting it is that we get to be interviewed on national TV? Who knows who might see us?" The role of optimistic cheerleader doesn't suit her as well as it does me, but I still take the bait.

"I know, right? Like, what if some hotshot agents or managers are watching, or some big-time director, or even someone at the Dollhouse?"

"Don't say the *d* word."

It's such a cliché for an aspiring performer to dream about joining the Dollhouse Academy, but Grace and I can't help it. You don't hear anything about what goes on inside the Dollhouse—it's *that* elite and secretive—but the star power that's come out of Dahlen Entertainment's compound, from actors to singers to dancers to multi-hyphenates, is jaw-dropping. If you can get in, you have a better chance of finding your big break there than anywhere else, and Dahlen is responsible for some of the best television shows, movies, and pop music of the last fifteen years. There are annual statewide cattle calls, auditions open to anyone and everyone, and Grace and I have gone for the last six years straight, but neither of us has ever made it past the first round.

"Forget the Dollhouse. I'd be happy to land another commercial. My credit card debt is getting out of control, and my CrisisCrux money is already gone." Grace's biggest acting role so far had been in a national ad for a medical alert crucifix in which she played a helpful phone operator.

Our excited chatter peppers the rest of the drive to Midtown until we pull up to a building that looks like a repurposed factory. A slender bald man with a walkie-talkie and clipboard greets us at the curb and takes the garment bag, which contains our alternate wardrobe options (we were told no all-black or all-white clothing and no patterns). He ushers us inside, down an empty hallway into a brightly lit dressing room.

Hanging our garment bag on a wardrobe rack, he says, "There's water in that minifridge and coffee and Danish next door. One of the producers will be with you in a few, so just sit tight. Have fun!" He leaves as his walkie-talkie crackles to life.

It feels like we wait for hours in that room, during which time I have to distract Grace from gnawing her fingers to the bone as I gulp down water that does nothing to soothe the desert in my mouth. Finally, a producer who looks like she graduated high school yesterday comes in, waist-length blond ponytail swinging. She approves the black pleather miniskirt and fuzzy baby blue sweater Grace is wearing and my plum velvet T-shirt dress without looking at the other clothes we brought, runs through the interview questions with us, and sends us down the hall to hair and makeup for finishing touches.

A stocky man in a hot pink furry vest and matching lip gloss receives us, a bottle of water in each hand. "Welcome to *AM/USA*. Sit. Hydrate," he commands.

I thought I had my nerves under control, but my hand is trembling when I take the bottle.

He leans against the counter facing us and points first at Grace—"*You* look like you should be the sixth Spice Girl, Sassy Spice"—then at me—"and *you* should wear that shade of purple every day of your life. I've got an eye shadow that's gonna match it like a dream." Swiveling his head between both of us, he finally shakes it and says, "Look at the two of you making my job so easy. I barely need to do anything to your perfect faces, but those set lights can wash you out, so let me work my magic. Now tell me all about what segment you're here for."

We chat as he dabs and brushes and blends bits of color first on my face, then on Grace's.

Between the run-through with the producer and now this guy, I start to relax a bit, until—

"We're ready for you."

Grace and I are ushered through a series of corridors onto a soundstage that's far smaller than I expected, over to a set decorated with a crescent-shaped tawny sofa, fake fireplace, circular blond coffee table, and potted plants. I can't help but touch one of the plants—the leaves are tender, real, which is oddly reassuring.

Once we're seated and mic'd up, Pavani Chandra, one of the cohosts of *AM/USA*, comes out and introduces herself, as if we don't know who she is, as if we haven't seen this stunning woman on morning television for the last decade. She's taller and leaner in person, and her kelly-green column dress and halo of curly black hair make me think of a flower personified. She even smells like lilies (and hairspray), and when she shakes my hand, her skin is petal soft.

"Don't worry about the lights or cameras, pretend it's just the three of us having a conversation," she says.

A conversation with millions of people eavesdropping.

Beside me, Grace must be thinking the same thing because her body tenses up; I give her shoulder a quick squeeze before clasping my clammy hands in my lap. It feels like a tiny helicopter has taken flight in my stomach. Before I know it, a red light above one of the cameras announces we're on the air and I paste a smile on my face, hoping I don't look stiff and crazy-eyed.

"Welcome back to *AM/USA*," Pavani says. "Now we've got a fun story for you about a New York City movie theater that's put a new spin on their coming attractions. Owned by Reed Holloway and his partner, Alonso Rojas, Brooklyn's Cinema Magnifico—or the Mag, as it's affectionately nicknamed—is a local institution, screening independent, experimental, international, and classic films. For the past few months, every Friday and Saturday night the theater has hosted live coming attractions, in which these two young women sitting beside me, Grace Ludlow and Ramona Holloway, put on comic minimusicals highlighting upcoming films. The performances are causing quite a stir, with locals lining up just to see them. *AM/USA* was at the Mag recently to catch Grace and Ramona in action. Let's see what the buzz is all about."

I wonder if this is what jumping off a cliff feels like as, behind us, a large TV bearing the *AM/USA* logo goes dark and the image is replaced by one of Grace and me onstage in the Mag's main screening room. She's in a black three-piece suit with a tie tucked into the vest, hair slicked back, while I'm in a classic tuxedo with a red rose boutonniere, my hair also slicked back but edged with silver pomade, a fake mustache affixed to my face. The theater is filled with the plaintive score from *The Godfather* as an edited montage from the movie plays behind us.

On-screen, Grace and I begin to dance as we take turns singing. She takes the first verse:

Save your drama for your mama? Don't even bother.
Meet the Corleones in The Godfather.
They put the fun in dysfunctional family.
And they put bullets into traitors—literally.

We execute perfectly synchronized spins as I pick up the second verse:

Murder can work up an appetite.
Just ask Rocco and Clemenza as they leave the site.
What's for dessert? The main course is ravioli.
Leave the gun. Take the cannoli.

Back in the studio, Pavani offers an appreciative laugh as the clip concludes. "I can see why people have been going wild over the two of you. You've been profiled in the *Village Voice*, and you've even had the cast of Broadway's *Rent* come see you perform. New York City is a tough place to stand out, but you've managed to capture a lot of people's attention. Now let's get into these live coming attractions. They're so inventive! Do you both write the songs?"

"Ramona writes all the songs. She's way funnier than I am," Grace says, her voice surprisingly steady.

"But Grace does the choreography," I say, my own voice high and tight. "She's the best dancer."

"And how did the idea for these minimusicals come about?" Pavani asks.

"It started when my uncle Reed read in the paper about *One Flew Over the Cuckoo's Nest* being turned into a Broadway musical," I say, relaxing a little.

I leave out the part about how Reed ranted at the idea of this adaptation. "What are they gonna do next, a Broadway musical about the Vietnam War? *Apocalypse Now, Apocalypse Wow?*"

That was when Alonso reminded him, "Hon, they already did a musical about the Vietnam War. *Miss Saigon.*"

"I hated that show."

"You saw it three times."

I smile at the recollection of their playful bickering. "I thought I'd try writing lyrics, just for fun," I say. "I started with *Reservoir Dogs*—'*Mr. Blonde, Mr. Orange, Mr. White, Mr. Pink / Your diamond heist won't go as smoothly as you think*'—and when I had a whole song, I showed it to Grace, who said we should do it as a musical number."

Grace jumps in. "So I added some choreo, and we started rehearsing it. We showed it to Reed and Alonso, and they loved it so much, they suggested we perform it at the theater before some of the movies. Suddenly we were doing weekly live coming attractions."

The shows started to pull the theater out of the financial slump it had been in. My uncles never tell me how dire it is, but I saw plenty of bill envelopes marked PAST DUE over the years. Hopefully, all this press we've been getting will keep us in the black for a long time.

"Ramona, your uncle Reed and his business partner, Alonso, have been running the theater for nearly two decades," Pavani continues. "Did it feel like you grew up there?"

I hold back a frown at the way Pavani tiptoes around their relationship. "Actually, I think of Reed *and* Alonso as my uncles, considering they both raised me, and they've been together even longer than they've been running the Mag. And yeah, I do feel like I grew up in that theater. Grace and I both did—we've been best friends since the fifth grade. We had a tradition for a while where every Sunday morning, my uncles would make breakfast burritos and then screen any movie we wanted."

"Though they regretted that after we became obsessed with *Splash* in sixth grade and they had to play it for us every Sunday for like three months," Grace adds, and the three of us laugh.

"What was it that drew the both of you to performing?" Pavani asks.

"*In the Dollhouse*," Grace and I say in unison. She continues, "It's been our favorite show pretty much forever, and it's how we became friends. When we were ten, we both dressed up as Tabitha Noelle for Halloween. We *worshipped* Ivy Gordon." We giggle, remembering our twin black-and-white plaid skirts, white shirts, and red ties, Grace's silly blond wig. "Of course, Ramona made a better Tabitha because she was already blond."

"We were addicted to that show," I add.

"Did you do anything special for the record-breaking three-hundredth episode?"

"Oh yeah, we convinced my uncles to host a viewing party at the Mag. Grace and I even tried to rewatch all the older episodes beforehand, but there were just too many and we ran out of time."

Pavani tilts her head. "With all the movies you grew up with, what was it about *In the Dollhouse* you found so compelling?"

"We were definitely influenced by movies, too," Grace says, "but there's a lot less quality TV, so when a show like ITD comes along, it stands out. Like how it didn't fit into a specific genre—it was technically a drama, but it was also funny and weird and had a big musical number in every episode. And it's still great after fifteen seasons."

I think of the weekends we spent watching *In the Dollhouse* marathons while eating bowls of Cookie Crisp cereal, going through the shelf of VHS tapes in my room with episodes we'd recorded. Every Sunday night, we'd record new ones, with me pausing during commercials and Grace labeling the tapes because she had better handwriting. The show was an escape for both of us. For Grace, it was a respite from whatever foster family was currently making her life hell. For me, it was a break from the money problems and tragedies my uncles tried to shield me from as bills piled up and the AIDS epidemic swept through their group of friends. For forty-five minutes at a time, we could set aside real-world problems and become immersed in the world of Otus, New York, ITD's fictional town. We never wanted to leave.

Back in the studio, I say, "I think Ivy Gordon is a big part of that. She keeps finding new layers for Tabitha."

"*And* still recording great music and touring," adds Grace.

"Exactly," I say. "I don't know how she does it all."

"You should've seen our rooms growing up, Pavani," Grace says. "They were shrines to Ivy Gordon. Our walls were *covered* with pictures of her, and we played her albums nonstop."

"It's true." I give a bashful shrug. "I used to always say, when I grow up, I want to be Ivy Gordon. I still kinda worship her, to be honest. She's been a huge inspiration for me."

Pavani continues, "I guess it's safe to say you'd be interested in joining the Dollhouse Academy."

Grace's eyes flash. "The Dollhouse? Are you kidding? It's only been our dream since we were little girls. We haven't had luck with the open auditions yet—only one in, like, a thousand people even make it past the first round—but we won't stop trying until we're old ladies." Which, by Dahlen's standards, is age thirty, at which point it's rumored to become nearly impossible. We're lucky we look young for our age, but even so, at twenty-two we're already at the higher age range of new trainees.

"Grace, Ramona, I have a surprise." Pavani gestures to the television behind us. "Somebody you may be familiar with has a special message for you."

I give Grace a searching look, but her face mirrors mine as we turn to the screen.

My mouth falls open as the legendary Genevieve Spalding appears on the monitor, sitting in a director's chair, an *In the Dollhouse* classroom set behind her. Heir to the DahlenRex pharma fortune and a former child star, Genevieve founded Dahlen Entertainment and the Dollhouse Academy, now serving as the latter's president and director of operations. She's dressed in a black-and-white Chanel houndstooth tweed suit with her signature diamond owl brooch (rumored to be worth over a million dollars) pinned to the lapel. Her oversize cat-eye glasses, silver-white bob, and distinct red lipstick are immaculate.

"Hello Ramona and Grace. I've been told you're fans of Dahlen Entertainment. After reviewing tapes of your live coming attractions and sharing them with some of our talent scouts and casting directors, I must say the feeling is mutual. I think the two of you have tremendous potential, and I'd like to personally invite you both to join the Dollhouse Academy."

My body feels like it's simultaneously levitating and being zapped with electricity. I lock eyes with Grace, whose mouth hangs open. This must be a joke. Yet Genevieve sounds sincere as she tells us to keep an eye out for our acceptance packets. Dizzy and cotton mouthed, I think about the numerous rehearsals Grace and I did for that *Godfather* number in preparation for the *AM/USA* film crew. It took countless tries to get it perfect, and every time Grace messed up a line, she wanted to give up, but I wouldn't let her. Finally, I got through by reminding her how this TV appearance could transform our lives. By the time the film crew showed up and we got up on that theater stage, I buried my desperation and used it as fuel, let it give my voice and body extra heat. Seeing me take it up a notch, Grace followed suit, and a flying feeling took over. It was phenomenal, *we* were phenomenal, every second, right through the final two lines of the song:

> *They'll go to the mattresses, but they won't snooze.*
> *They'll make you an offer you can't refuse.*

CHAPTER THREE

In her *AM/USA* recorded message, Genevieve Spalding said to expect welcome packets for Grace and me, but she didn't specify when we'd get them. As giddy and eager to celebrate as we are, we tell Alonso and Reed to put away the champagne until we receive official paperwork from the Dollhouse Academy.

The first week that passes with no word is uncomfortable but not excruciating. Neither of us have any auditions lined up, so we throw ourselves into our respective acting classes and take extra shifts at the Mag—business has picked up even more since our *AM/USA* appearance.

It's a good thing we started doing the live coming attractions because, outside of acting classes, it's the only performing I've done in nearly a year, when I booked a role in a mayonnaise commercial (Sandwich Girl #2). And Grace has been through a longer dry spell than I have, a year and a half, since she had a minor part in an off-off-Broadway show called *Oh, Schiele!*, a musical based on the life of tortured Austrian Expressionist painter Egon Schiele.

The *AM/USA* appearance and subsequent invitation from the Dollhouse is by far the biggest break we've ever gotten, so we've been in a state of increasing hysteria for the past week.

"Why haven't we heard anything yet?" Grace moans over Chinese takeout on the eighth night. "What if Genevieve changed her mind about us?"

"I'm sure she didn't, and you'll get something any day now." The sleeve of Alonso's turquoise kimono flutters as he stirs duck sauce into his fried rice. My uncles have a ridiculous collection of silk robes, which they share freely; one of the house rules is to remove our shoes and change into comfy clothes as soon as we get home, which they call getting into "the Kimono Zone."

"Maybe it takes some time to get the paperwork together?" I say, spooning sticky pieces of sesame chicken onto my plate. "Or it got lost in the mail?"

"I would think documents that important would probably be FedExed or sent by registered mail," says Reed, followed by a thump as Alonso kicks him under the table.

Using our own made-up logic, Grace and I decide that if we don't hear anything by the end of two weeks, it means we won't get to join the Dollhouse after all. We continue doing the live coming attractions, and our performance for *The Silence of the Lambs* is the best one yet ("*If a serial killer traps you in a well / lure his little dog away and you'll be swell / Don't panic and don't fret, don't show too much emotion / just follow his instructions when he gives you the lotion!*").

On the morning of day twelve, I wake up extra upbeat and optimistic, sure this is the day. But when I come home that afternoon to an empty apartment and no mail from the Dollhouse, my mood nose-dives.

It's not going to happen.

I take a long shower and sob my guts out.

I thought the Dollhouse would be my escape from a life stuck in my uncles' struggling business, tearing tickets and filling popcorn buckets and always feeling like I'm on the wrong side of the screen.

Maybe an ordinary life is the only thing I'm cut out for. After all, before living with my uncles, how many times had I been told as a little girl that I wasn't special? When did I start fooling myself into believing otherwise? I should've known the Dollhouse invitation was too good to be true.

I remain in the shower until my voice is hoarse from crying, my skin goes pruney, and the water turns cold.

On day thirteen, Grace and I come home within minutes of each other in the late afternoon. Shortly after we arrive, the downstairs buzzer rings. It's a messenger carrying two glossy white boxes wrapped in a red velvet ribbon from the Dollhouse Academy. The boxes look like they're holding giant sheet cakes.

We sign for our respective packages, set them down on the dining room table, then Grace and I scream and jump up and down and run around the apartment.

I feel like a wayward train that's finally been put back on its correct track.

This is exactly what's supposed to happen.

I touch my face and find my cheek wet with tears I don't remember crying.

"This is it. Our lives are about to change forever," I say, waiting for Grace to tease me for being so dramatic.

Instead, she nods. "Big-time. Let's just hope it's for the better."

We fall into a reverent hush as we stare down at the boxes.

"On the count of three?" I ask.

"Fuck that, we've waited long enough." Grace yanks at the ribbon and pulls off the top of her box. I follow suit.

Inside is a nest of red tissue paper, beneath which is—

"No way! An actual uniform from *In the Dollhouse*! I'm putting mine on right now."

While Grace sifts through the clothes in a frenzy, I unfold each item carefully: the red tie, white button-down shirt, black blazer with its crimson crest, and black-and-white plaid skirt.

Beneath the uniform is a thin stack of papers held together with a binder clip, the upper left-hand corner bearing a stylized owl forming a capital *D*. Woven into the thick and creamy stationery is faint lettering. When I hold one sheet up to the light, I see "Ramona Holloway" water-marked throughout it.

"Damn. Dahlen doesn't mess around."

There's a welcome letter declaring we are among the chosen few and that great things are expected from us. Then things get real.

The letter goes on to say that we must sign a contract committing us to living and training at the compound in Owls Point, New York, for a six-month probationary period, during which we'll have minimal contact with the outside world. Room and board will be provided, and we'll receive a modest stipend, which we'll gradually pay back as we book jobs for Dahlen productions. The Dollhouse Academy can dismiss us for any reason during the first six months, but if we voluntarily leave before the time is up, we have to pay a ten-thousand-dollar "early dropout penalty fee" (ouch). At the end of the six months, the academy will determine whether to extend our contracts.

Incoming trainees are to make no significant changes to their appearance prior to arriving at the Dollhouse, including no plastic surgery, no cosmetic dental work, no tanning (fake or otherwise), no haircuts or dye jobs. We aren't required to wear the provided uniform, but "the Dollhouse Academy values a unified overall appearance among its trainees," so we're asked to only bring clothing that's black, white, and red (being New Yorkers, over half our wardrobes are already black, so that's not an issue). We can bring two suitcases and one small backpack or duffel, and there's a detailed list of what we're required to pack (mostly activewear and other practical items of clothing) and what's forbidden (candles, incense, microwaves and other small appliances, handheld electronic games, recording devices, any jewelry apart from wristwatches, all drugs except for prescription medications, all food and alcohol).

"It's like we're packing for summer camp, college, and the army all at once," Grace says.

To me, it feels more like I'm packing for the moon.

That night, Grace and I finally celebrate with my uncles. Reed splurges on a bottle of Chambord, finally breaks out the champagne and makes us Kir Royales, and we all get into the Kimono Zone. I put on ABBA's greatest hits while Alonso prepares Linguini with Shrimp Fra Diavolo, the smell of garlic and oregano wafting from the kitchen to the living room, which are separated by a half wall.

"You know Alonso is the original dancing queen, right?" Reed quips, his cherry blossom–festooned kimono fluttering as he spins. "You should've seen him at the Pyramid back in the day."

Alonso pauses peeling shrimp and struts into the living room to vogue for us, his limbs alternating between fluid and angular as he twists his body into a series of stop-motion poses. We clap and cheer for him as he catwalks back into the kitchen.

We sit down to eat just as "Money, Money, Money" comes on, which makes Grace and me fantasize aloud about what we'll do once the Dollhouse makes us rich and famous.

"My first big purchase will be a house for you guys," Grace says to Alonso and Reed. "It's the least I can do after you let me live here rent-free for so long."

Grace has been living with us since she was sixteen, when things became untenable with her latest foster family and she showed up at our apartment with a broken arm. Reed and Alonso said as long as she stayed in school and followed their guiding principle ("don't be an idiot or an asshole"), she could live with us. The four of us have been cohabitating modestly but happily in the small three-bedroom apartment above the Mag ever since.

"Aw, come on, I want to buy them a house," I playfully counter.

"Who says we want to move? Alonso and I like living here just fine," Reed says.

"Just fine? That's what we're settling for? As if you wouldn't trade this place for a West Village town house or Tribeca loft in a heartbeat," Alonso admonishes him before turning to Grace and me. "Girls, there's no need to argue. You can each get us a house. Ramona, you can find us something lavish but tasteful in the city, and Grace, you can buy us a beach house on the coast of Spain."

"I'd rather we fix up the Mag before we go spending money on new homes," Reed says as he twirls his pasta. "Get some new carpets, maybe expand the concession stand to be more of a café, like the Angelika."

"Except, unlike the Angelika, we could have seats that don't feel like medieval torture devices," I say. "New seats should be the top priority."

"I second that emotion." Alonso raises his champagne glass.

After dessert, which Reed prepares—a silver tray artfully adorned with Stella D'oro Swiss Fudge cookies dusted with powdered sugar ("What I lack in baking skills, I make up for in presentation")—Grace offers to relieve the manager working overtime downstairs.

"It's no big deal." She shoos away our protests. "Let me enjoy my final days with everyday people before I go off to be a big star."

After she leaves, Alonso and I clear the table while Reed washes dishes.

"You guys want to watch *Mystery Science Theater 3000*?" I ask. "I taped the last few episodes so we could fast-forward through the skits and just watch the good stuff."

"Actually . . ." Reed switches off the water. "We'd like to talk to you."

Alonso shoots him a look. "Do we have to do this right now? Can't tonight be about celebrating?"

"I wish it could, but who knows when our schedules might overlap and . . ." Reed sighs. "Look, the truth is, I don't want to wait."

"Oh god, what's wrong? Is somebody sick? Is one of you sick?" The pasta and liquor roil in my stomach. "Whatever it is, please just tell me."

"Nobody's sick, honey," Alonso says. "Nobody new, anyway." A pointed glare at Reed. "See, this is why I didn't want to get into it tonight. But if we must. Let's all sit and have a little chat."

The living room reflects my uncles' love of art nouveau, the furniture curved and the accents ornate, with filigreed mirrors and standing candelabras and Tiffany lamps—all thrift store finds that they painstakingly refurbished. Reed ushers me over to the canary-yellow velvet sofa. He takes a seat beside me while Alonso perches on an emerald club chair a few feet away.

"What's all this about?" I ask.

Alonso looks to Reed, who says, "The Dollhouse."

"Oh." Before relief can settle over me, suspicion prickles my skin. "Wait. What about the Dollhouse?"

"First of all, you need to know how proud of you we are," Alonso says. "This is a tough business, and for you to make it this far is tremendous."

"I haven't made it anywhere yet. Let's talk in six months and see where I am then." Though I'm being modest. Getting admitted to the Dollhouse is the single greatest accomplishment of my life.

Reed puts a hand on my shoulder. "We know the Dollhouse seems like the thing you want most in the world—"

"It is."

Undeterred, Reed continues. "But we want you to consider exactly what you're signing up for."

"That if I work really hard, I can actually have a career with one of the most revolutionary and prestigious entertainment companies out there?" My voice is tight.

"Sweetie, Dahlen is a brilliant organization but hardly revolutionary," Alonso says. "They're doing exactly what old Hollywood's studio system did, when studios owned the writers, actors, producers—even the theaters. They'd create a Joan Crawford or Marilyn Monroe, then sell her persona through the pictures she starred in. Dahlen has been trying to replicate that, only across television, music, *and* movies."

"Yeah, I know all about the studio system. You've railed against it a zillion times." I hate how much I sound like a bratty teen. "And yet, despite how evil it was, some of the best movies of all time came out of that era. Just like some of the best TV, music, and movies are coming out of Dahlen today."

"You're not wrong," Reed concedes. "But the whole reason that system broke down was because stars wanted to be more independent. Their careers—their entire lives—were restricted and controlled. And that seems to be what the Dollhouse does, too. Rumor has it, Dahlen stars can't join any unions and don't even have outside agents or managers."

"That doesn't mean they're being restricted or controlled," I say. "But it does me... hey don't have to pay dues or share their earnings with agents or managers. And if you consider how many big stars have come out of the Dollhouse, I'd say doing it this way has worked out pretty well for them."

"What about the ones that don't make it? How can you know the truth when everyone who lives at the Dollhouse Academy is kept away from the rest of the world?"

"You're making it sound like I'm about to join a cult."

"I mean . . ." Reed catches a warning look from Alonso. "There's no telling what really goes on there. Their whole operation is shrouded in secrecy."

"Oh god, please tell me you don't believe that stuff in the tabloids."

"We're not saying we buy into *all* the gossip," says Reed. "But some of the rumors . . . come off as more than rumors. There are a lot of performers whose careers never went anywhere after Dahlen. If you do something they don't like, they could make sure you never work in the industry again."

"Is this about the early dropout fee? Because I'll last the full six months no matter what."

"Six months is a long time," Reed says. "We'd be lying if we didn't say we were concerned."

"Wait, so you don't think I should go to the Dollhouse at all?" I let out a harsh laugh. "Why didn't you raise these *concerns* before?" A sour taste fills my mouth. "You didn't think I'd actually make it. I thought you supported me on this."

"You know we do," Alonso says. "We've always believed you had something special, a star quality. You shouldn't let that go to waste."

Reed sneaks a frown at Alonso and says, "We just want you to consider what you're giving up and what you might be risking. You may not be where you want to be in your career right now, but you have the freedom to work on any project you want to. If you go to the Dollhouse, you'll only be able to work within the Dahlen Entertainment system."

"Which is fine. Because that's what I want."

"Maybe today, but it may not always be what you want," says Reed. "And if they lock you into a multiyear contract . . ."

"Then I might end up rich and successful and happy. What a curse that would be."

"There's no guarantee the Dollhouse will give you any of the things you want." Reed's voice is soft and solemn.

"Of course not." I lower my voice, too. "But it'll give me a better shot than if I stay here. You have no right to try to talk me out of going."

When Reed tries to put his hand over mine, I pull away and give Alonso a beseeching look. Surely he's acting at the behest of my overly cautious uncle and doesn't share his paranoia.

"We just want you to go with your eyes open," Alonso says.

"And what about Grace? Are you going to have one of these little chats with her, too?"

"We *are* going to talk to Grace about this—"

I don't bother letting Alonso finish. "Yeah, good luck with that."

Reed nods, acknowledging my sarcasm. "We don't expect to make much headway with her."

"Because you think she's tougher than me. Well, I'm pretty tough, too."

"Grace is more closed off," Reed corrects me. "That doesn't make her tougher."

"So what kind of headway did you expect to make with me? Did you think you could keep me home, chained to the two of you and this apartment and the Mag for the rest of my life?" The bitter torrent coming out of me is unwarranted but involuntary.

"You know better than that, Ramona." The skin between Reed's eyebrows pinches. "Grace is more reckless and headstrong. If she's set on something, it's hard to reason with her. But you actually listen when someone has your best interests at heart because we raised you to know you can always count on us. Grace can, too, but she's been through a lot, and it's harder for her to trust." He leans over and gives my hand a squeeze. "We want you to go out there and be bold as you pursue all your goals . . . but be careful."

"Maybe all this worry is for nothing, and you'll flourish at the Dollhouse. That's what we're hoping. But whatever happens, you can always come home—anytime—if it doesn't feel right there." Alonso smooths the silk of his robe's sleeve like he's petting a cat. "Or we'll come get you. One call and we'll be on the next train to Owls Point—"

"In a matter of such urgency, we really should rent a car," Reed reasons.

"How we get there is beside the point." Alonso turns back to me. "Just know that you always have an out. If they try to coerce you in some way or make you compromise your values or—"

"I get it," I say, trying to sound more compassionate. "If things get creepy once I'm there, I'll leave."

A few days later, I arrive home before anyone else, so I bring up the mail. Among the packet of circulars, bills, and yet another AOL free trial CD is a small square envelope with my name and address written in tidy angular script. There's no return address or postal mark.

I use my house key to tear into the envelope and pull out a piece of plain white cardstock. The note is written in the same handwriting:

Whatever you think you want, you won't find it at the Dollhouse Academy. Don't come.

CHAPTER FOUR

A high involuntary laugh bubbles out of me as I stare at the note. What the hell is this? I drop the card onto the dining room table and walk circles around it, my stomach in knots. Who could have sent this to me and why? The simplest explanation: it's a prank.

If I show the note to my uncles, it'll only make them double down on trying to keep me from going (for a millisecond, I wonder if it could've come from one of them, then immediately shun the thought). If I show it to Grace, she'll dismiss it as a practical joke, sent by some jealous person who saw me on *AM/NYC*, and then spend ages speculating which former classmate or castmate was the most likely culprit. Either way, I'll be pulled into an exhausting debate for which I don't have the mental energy.

The best thing to do is keep the note to myself. I want to look forward to attending the Dollhouse, and I don't want that anticipation to be soured any further, or risk souring it for Grace.

In the ensuing days, I feel like I'm fighting a current as we make preparations to leave. Much as I try, the note nags at me, which makes it hard to match Grace's enthusiasm. For a while, things are busy enough that she doesn't notice as we take turns training the new hire that will replace us at the Mag (I try not to worry about whether business will dip without our live coming attractions) and finish out our notice periods at our other jobs. But we leave ourselves a few free days at the end of the month to pack and shop for last-minute items.

Two days before our departure, we spend the morning traversing the record stores and bookshops of the Village, first West, then East, splurging on new music and books to bring with us to the Dollhouse.

"A new adventure calls for a new soundtrack and reading material," Grace says, though we hardly need an excuse. Forget clothes or makeup—we've been haunting the city shopping for CDs, cassettes, and novels since we were teenagers. Each of us is bringing a Discman *and* a Walkman, and since there's no limit to how much media we can bring, we're dedicating a single suitcase entirely to music and books: paperbacks only, several CD wallets, cases of mixtapes, and a small boom box.

On our music shopping spree, Grace goes for experimental and electronic albums, whereas I favor Britpop and trip-hop. We have a quick lunch at Dojo on St. Mark's Place and then stop at the bookstore around the corner, where she buys copies of *Fight Club* and *The Beach*, and I get *Dangerous Angels* and *Bridget Jones's Diary*.

It isn't until later that afternoon, when we're at a shoe store in Union Square trying on sneakers, that Grace finally comments on my preoccupation.

"Am I crazy or are you way less thrilled than before?" Grace laces herself into a pair of white Adidas with a purple squiggle across the side.

"Black, white, and red only, remember?" I offer her the same plain white pair I just tried on, in her size.

"Thanks. So, what's up with you?"

"I don't know. It's been hard to be excited with everything that's going on." Truth by omission. "I'm nervous more than anything. I don't know what to expect. If it's gonna be like some kind of performance boot camp or something weirder and sketchier."

"Don't let your paranoid uncles spook you. I already promised them that if the Dollhouse turns out to be a crazy sex cult, I'll leave and take you with me."

"Thanks?" I give her a pained look. Does nobody trust me to leave a crazy sex cult of my own volition? "I'm sure it'll turn out to be legit, but . . . it might be, I don't know, *impossible*. Like we'll work our asses off and still not measure up." I take a wedge of balled-up tissue paper out of the toe of a black-and-white Reebok.

"That's exactly how I think it'll be. In which case, we'll have to work our asses off until we *do* measure up." Grace slips out of the white Adidas and returns them to the box.

"What if I can't hack it?"

"Then you go back to temping and working at the Mag, still auditioning, and maybe you'll get your big break somewhere else . . . or maybe you won't and you'll be happy doing something else."

"That's your idea of a pep talk? I give it a D-minus." My toes begin to tingle. I've tied my laces too tight.

Grace slides over next to me, and places her fingertips on my wrist, which, considering she's not the warm and fuzzy type, is the equivalent of a bear hug from her. "Ramona, chill. You're going to be amazing. We both know you can sing and act circles around me."

"Oh, come on—"

"It's totally true, don't even. You'll wow everyone at the Dollhouse." Grace points and flexes her foot. "I, on the other hand, probably won't last a week."

"That's so not true . . ."

Somehow, we end up swapping places and I return to my usual role of reassuring Grace, which feels better, more natural. And in the process of calming her nerves, I manage to calm my own.

CHAPTER FIVE

Grace and I wake up at dawn and say goodbye to my uncles as our suit-cases are loaded into a white Ford Econoline van.

"I snuck a phone card and a hundred-dollar bill behind your Elastica CD in case of an emergency," Reed says as he hugs me goodbye. "And Tower Records doesn't count as an emergency."

"I doubt there's a Tower Records in Owls Point," I say.

"Seriously, though, if anything doesn't feel right, get the hell out of there, call me, and we'll come get you," he continues. "Remember, you've grown up to be an outstanding woman, and whatever you do from here will only build on that. Whether it's on a stage, a screen, or anywhere else." The last few words catch in his throat. "Be careful out there. Don't break anything." He finds "break a leg" distasteful, so this is his way of wishing me well.

"He's just being paranoid, don't mind him," says Alonso when I hug him. "Go be your fabulous self. Chase those dreams. Call us when you can."

"I will." I kiss his cheek, sad to leave but unable to resist the promise that I'm finally *going somewhere*.

Our driver is a burly, bearded man with an Eastern European accent.

Once Grace and I are in the van but before he drives off, he says, "Let me know if you need rest stop." Though it sounds more like a warning not to need one.

I wave a final goodbye to my uncles, unsure if they can see me through the tinted glass.

It's overcast as we set out, and the gray skies give way to heavy rain that pounds on the van's roof and windows. Between the weather and several road accidents, we have a slow start out of the city, and the tedium puts Grace and me to sleep. I wake up before she does as the van winds its way along a mountain road bordered by fir trees. Owls Point is at the edge of the Catskills, and we've been on the road for over two hours, so I'm hoping we're almost there.

But the ride drags on, Grace snoring softly as our driver laughs at Howard Stern on the radio. I wish she'd wake up, just to have some company, but I leave her be. Instead, I take out my Discman and listen to a Portishead album the rest of the way, Beth Gibbons's moody wailing providing a suitable backdrop to the stormy drive. My own mood is at odds with the sullen weather and music. I nurse a hopeful excitement, the Dollhouse a magnet pulling me toward it.

It's another couple of hours until we reach a fifteen-foot-tall security gate, flanked by stone walls extending from both sides as far as I can see. How lucky am I, that I get to be one of the select few invited past these gates? But it feels bigger than luck, it feels fated. This was meant to happen. I am exactly where I need to be.

We pull up to a tiny cottage beside the gate, which turns out to be a guard booth. The guard hands the driver two clipboards, which he passes to Grace and me. Each one bears a thick stack of papers flagged with SIGN HERE stickers.

"Nondisclosure agreement," says the driver. "Standard protocol."

Grace begins scribbling her name on all the indicated pages with barely a glance at their contents. I skim through the dense text, the gist of which is clearly "keep this shit a secret or else." Or else what, though?

Even if I had more time to go over the NDA, I'm not sure how much of it I'd fully grasp without the help of an attorney. Something tells me if I asked for more time, I wouldn't make it past these gates.

I sign the NDA and return the clipboard to the driver.

Moments later, the gates open. Just then, the sun comes out with impeccable timing, a warm spotlight as our van winds up a tree-lined gravel path, which opens to reveal vast manicured acres of sloping hills.

"Are you kidding me with this?" Grace points at the sky. "A motherfucking rainbow? This can't be real."

The driver chuckles. "Is good omen."

Grace and I sit up in our seats, grinning like maniacs.

I grasp her hand and give it a squeeze.

We're here.

She squeezes back and whispers, "Can you believe it?"

We pass quaint ivy-covered brick houses, candy-colored Victorians, and a series of stone mansions that look like they should house mad kings, with arches and spires and towers. In the distance, there's a sprawling series of warehouses, presumably the Dahlen Entertainment soundstages.

"Damn," I say with hushed reverence. "It's like something out of a movie. Like *Dead Poets Society* meets *Clue*."

"Yeah, hopefully with less suicide and murder," Grace deadpans.

The van pulls up to one of the redbrick houses, its two-story columns and shutters gleaming a flawless white. Our driver brings our bags to the curb.

"Good luck, ladies," he says, before he drives away.

The front lawn has an immaculate hedge border, pastel flower beds, and stone birdhouses. Steps lead to an expansive patio with rocking chairs, porch swings, and wrought iron tables and chairs.

The front door swings open and a tall broad-shouldered blonde says, "I presume you are Ms. Ramona Holloway and Ms. Grace Ludlow. Welcome to the Gale House dormitory." She also has an accent, though hers is more subtle. Swedish? Finnish? "Come in and I will show you around. Leave your bags where they are, someone will bring them to your rooms."

We join her in the foyer and introduce ourselves, even though she already knows our names.

"I'm Solveig." A polite nod. "I'll be your orientation coordinator today." She gestures to a shelf divided into cubbyholes, each labeled with a name. "This is where you will receive your mail and important academy correspondence. Blue notices signify your class schedule. Yellow notices signify medical appointments, which take precedence over classes. Green notices are call sheets. Larger packages will be left outside your rooms."

"What if someone tries to steal our mail?" I ask, ever the paranoid New Yorker.

"We operate as a family at the Dollhouse and value trust here. That is why there are no locks on the bedrooms and no mailboxes. If an individual proves untrustworthy, they are immediately expelled." Solveig motions to either end of the hall with two fingers, like a flight attendant pointing out emergency exits. "There is also a console with a panic button on each floor in the event of a fire, medical emergency, or other crisis needing immediate attention. Your safety is assured at the Dollhouse Academy." She leads us down the hall. "The dorms are coed, though not the bedrooms themselves—you'll both have female roommates. Ms. Holloway, you will be residing on this floor, whereas Ms. Ludlow, your living quarters are on the second floor."

Growing up, Grace used to come over every weekend for sleepovers, and even when she moved in with us and we had separate rooms, we'd lay out sleeping bags on the floor of my room every Friday and stay up talking half the night. I guess we'll have to forgo that now.

Solveig opens the door to a large sunny room with blond wood furniture. Each side is a mirror image of the other, with a four-poster bed, wardrobe, dresser, bookshelf, and desk on either end.

"Yours is the left side," she says. "I will show you the common areas on this floor before we go upstairs to Ms. Ludlow's room."

Solveig points out the bathrooms, the kitchen, and a living room in the back filled with overstuffed sofas and armchairs, which make the room feel cozy despite being spacious. "You are expected to pick up after yourselves and there is also a rotating cleaning schedule. Now let me show you the second floor."

Upstairs, Grace asks, "I don't suppose there's any way Ramona and I could share a room?"

If Solveig is irked by the question, she doesn't show it. "You were put in separate sleeping quarters intentionally. You are better served to focus on the training program, not social activities. In fact, if being in the same dormitory proves too distracting, one of you may be moved to a different house."

"Training is our top priority," I say, disliking how obsequious I sound. "Nothing will distract us from that."

"Very good." Solveig's smile is warm. "You must be hungry. Let me show you to the nearest dining hall."

On our way there, she gives Grace and me a brief history of the Dollhouse Academy.

"You may not be aware of this, but Ms. Spalding has always been partial to owls. She considers them good luck. Which is why, when she came across a town called Owls Point and saw it housed a stunning boarding school campus that had long been abandoned, Ms. Spalding knew this would be the place to set up the Dahlen Academy and Dahlen Entertainment studios. And if you're wondering why it wasn't Spalding Academy and Spalding Studios, she needed a certain amount of family money to spearhead the ventures, and her father offered the necessary funds on the condition that both bear the family name."

"When did Dahlen Academy become the Dollhouse Academy?" I ask.

"In the early eighties, 'the Dollhouse' became a nickname given to the school by the students and teachers. Nobody is sure who came up with it, though many like to take credit. In turn, that nickname inspired the show *In the Dollhouse*. Once that program became popular, everyone referred to the academy as the Dollhouse. Ms. Spalding thought officially changing the institution's name after her father passed would be a nice way to recognize its evolution." We turn a corner and to our left is an enormous tiered fountain, behind which is a hedge maze.

"Oh my god." A panicked whisper from Grace as she tugs the back of my shirt. "Do you see who that is? Don't be obvious." She gestures surreptitiously at the fountain. Perched on the bottom tier is Vanessa Sanchez, a bold and darkly funny actor who starred in several of Grace's favorite films before joining the cast of *In the Dollhouse* a few years ago. Vanessa is smoking a cigarette, a breeze blowing her flame-red hair around her shoulders, as if she's at a fashion shoot. "I might die."

"Good afternoon, Vanessa." Solveig waves and turns to us. "Would you like to meet her?"

Grace opens and closes her mouth without saying anything.

"Definitely," I say, nudging Grace with my hip. "She's just a person, don't freak out."

"She's not a person, she's a goddess walking among us mortals. I'm going to puke," she whispers as Solveig leads us to the fountain.

"No, you won't, you'll be charming as—"

"Vanessa, I'd like you to meet two of our newest trainees, Ramona Holloway and Grace Ludlow."

Vanessa stands and hides her cigarette behind her back. She's way more petite and slender than I expected, and her tawny skin glows like it's lit from within. "Sorry you caught me like this. I'm trying to quit." She throws a regretful look over her shoulder then offers a dazzling smile. "Welcome to Owls Point. It's lovely to meet you both."

I wait for Grace to speak first, and when she doesn't, I say, "It's so awesome to meet you. I'm sure you're sick of hearing people say how much they love you, but—"

"Are you kidding? I never get sick of that! I love being adored," she says with her trademark playful arrogance.

Throwing an arm around my mute friend, I say, "Grace was just raving about your performance in *Transient Visitors* the other day for the millionth time."

Cocking her head, Vanessa turns to Grace. "That movie means a lot to me." Her face grows serious. "I don't talk much about my own experiences in the foster system, but it was important for me to be part of that project, and to be a consultant to make sure they got it right."

Finally, Grace finds her voice. "Oh, you did. You got *everything* right. I was a foster kid, too."

"Then I'm guessing you went through some shit." Vanessa offers a sympathetic smile. "You and I should trade war stories sometime, Grace."

We resume our walk to the dining hall. Once we're out of earshot, Grace says, "She knows my name. Vanessa Sanchez knows my name." Her voice is quiet, reverent.

"That is something you will need to get used to," Solveig says, a gleam in her eyes. "It is not uncommon to see Dahlen stars on Main Street or elsewhere in Owls Point. Sometimes, they'll even drop in on classes." At this, Grace and I exchange a can-you-believe-it look. "Before long, you may even be working alongside them."

To our right, a massive running track emerges with a dozen trainees jogging laps.

"Why do we have to dress in black, white, and red?" Grace asks Solveig.

"Because Ms. Spalding wishes to promote a sense of unity without strict uniformity, and black, white, and red are strong colors . . . they also happen to be Ms. Spalding's favorite colors," says Solveig. "Any other questions?"

There's so much I want to ask, but I go with the first thing that springs to mind. "Is it true Genevieve Spalding had a shade of red named after her?"

Solveig looks impressed. "Yes, as a matter of fact, it is. In her twenties, Ms. Spalding worked with a makeup artist to create a unique red lipstick for her. The color, a blue-tinged ruby, always received compliments, but Ms. Spalding and her makeup artist refused to share the formula. In 1978, the Pantone Color System added the shade to its palette under the name 'Genevieve,' and in 1981, Max Factor began manufacturing a lipstick very close to the shade called 'Very Vermillion,' which became one of their bestsellers. Ms. Spalding was not contacted by Max Factor about re-creating her signature shade of lipstick, but she did provide MAC Cosmetics with the original formula when they approached her in 1993, which was then used to create the 'Diva Doll' lipstick shade. It remains MAC's second-most-popular lipstick, just behind 'Ruby Woo,' which it sometimes gets mistaken for."

We round a corner to reveal a stunning stone church with countless arched windows and buttresses, along with a bell tower.

"If this place doesn't have at least one vampire or hunchback, I'll be disappointed," Grace whispers, and I stifle a giggle.

"It's gorgeous, isn't it?" says Solveig. "This chapel and some of the academic buildings, the ones you see in gray stone with buttresses and stained glass windows, are in the Collegiate Gothic style. The ones with the multiple spires, front-facing gables, and steep rooflines, are in the Tudor style. The marvelous multihued Victorian houses up ahead are primarily used as private residences for senior staff and more established performers who wish to remain on campus. Then you have the dormitories, with their white columns and shutters, which are Georgian. I have an impromptu quiz for you." Her eyes narrow and voice deepens with mock seriousness. "Can either of you tell me what the dormitories and certain other key buildings are named after? I will give you a partial list as a hint: Fisher, Mayberry, Gale, Hansen, Bowman."

Grace and I grin at each other and answer in unison, "Judy Garland characters."

"Well done, Ms. Holloway and Ms. Ludlow." Solveig offers us a pleased nod. "Ms. Spalding wanted to honor her favorite performer, and this is one way she chose to do so. You may encounter other tributes to Ms. Garland and her daughter Liza Minnelli, who Ms. Spalding is also very fond of, throughout the Dollhouse campus, but I will leave the discovery of those up to you."

We cross an intersection and to our left is a charming street dotted with colorful storefronts. "Down there is Main Street, where you will find various quaint shops and cafés," Solveig says. "Owls Point was a veritable ghost town when Ms. Spalding first arrived, and it took years of painstaking construction and rehabilitation to turn it into the impressive enclave you see today." She stops in front of a brick building. "Ah, here is the dining hall. This concludes my tour. Take the rest of the day to unpack and familiarize yourself with your new home. Classes will not begin until next week, and over the next few days, you'll engage in a series of orientation activities meant to relax and delight you. You will receive daily schedules in your mailboxes."

We thank Solveig, and after she leaves, Grace and I look at each other, expectant.

"You want to hold off on lunch and wander around some more?" I ask.

"Hell yeah."

Grace and I spend the next few hours exploring the vast Dollhouse campus. We stroll up and down Main Street, barely keeping our cool when we spot Dahlen stars out and about. We weave through the historic buildings and vast fields, some of which are being used for outdoor group classes—martial arts, meditation, boot camp drills. We peek inside the windows of several classrooms and studios, glimpse dance rehearsals, overhear acting workshops and individual singing lessons, but our curiosity quickly turns into intimidation.

We listen outside one window as a group does a dynamic rendition of "America" from *West Side Story*, and Grace gives me a sidelong glance. "So, um, don't make a whole big thing of this, and don't make me repeat it, but . . . I'm really glad we're here together. Even if it gets so chaotic we never see each other, just knowing we're both *in this* . . . I mean, I don't know if I could do it without you." She scratches the back of her head and turns away to discourage any outward physical affection from me, but I'm touched all the same.

"I don't think many people here get to go through this with their best friend. We're lucky."

"Now if we could only be that good." Grace nods toward the window.

"Just wait, that'll be us in a few months," I say, a quaver in my voice.

In my head, Genevieve's voice runs on a loop, telling us we have tremendous potential. As we stroll the vibrant lawns past picturesque architecture, I believe it.

CHAPTER SIX

Ivy's Diary

APRIL 2, 1998

The new recruits are here. When I saw them on that orientation tour, a wave of pity swept through me. If they only knew what was in store for them. If only I could tell them everything, right now.

Whatever catharsis I expected from writing this has eluded me so far. Instead, it feels like clawing at scars, undoing any healing as the old wounds pulse with fresh pain.

This is going to be harder than I thought.

Still, I must get these words down. I set aside this journal for months, but I can't avoid it any longer.

I need you to know who I was, what happened to me, and who I became.

I'll try to spare you the boring parts.

I grew up in suburban Ohio, in a house shadowed by grief. My father was an X-ray technician, my mother was a dental assistant, and I had a brother, Stevie, who was two years younger than me. Stevie died when he was seven. He had this condition, pica, which caused him to eat random items: buttons, crayons, rubber bands, once even a small toy car, which resulted in him needing emergency surgery. The doctor was able to save him that time, but not a few months later when Stevie ingested an icicle-shaped Christmas ornament. The glass icicle broke inside him and caused too much internal bleeding—there was nothing the doctors could do. I remember Stevie complaining of a stomachache and, after much pleading from my parents, telling them what he ate. The hospital smelled awful, like rubbing alcohol and old dirty socks and mint chewing gum. Eventually, the doctor came out and told us the news. You'd think my mother would've been the one to scream and cry, but it was my dad. Mom just crumpled to the floor like a marionette whose strings had been snipped.

I don't remember crying, but I must have, because I'm one of those people that find tears contagious. And there were a lot of tears in the months that followed. Our house was filled with emotional land mines: Stevie's favorite stuffed dolphin wedged in the sofa cushions, a jingle he always sang coming on the radio, a boy on TV who looked just like him and was eerily also named Stevie.

There's a special helplessness that comes with watching your parents break down over and over again. These were the people who were supposed to watch over me, be stronger than me, and here they were, falling apart over a tiny sneaker hidden under the ottoman.

It was around this time when I discovered my special power: if I tried really, *really* hard, I could get my parents to stop crying.

The first time it happened was while they were watching *The Carol Burnett Show* and I was tying new ribbons onto the ends of my baton. A commercial for a train set Mom and Dad had intended to buy Stevie for Christmas got them going. I grabbed a shawl out of the hallway closet, put the baton across my shoulders, and draped the shawl over the baton. Then I swanned into the living room, stopped in front of my parents, and said, in an exaggerated southern drawl, doing my best Carol-Burnett-cum-Scarlett-O'Hara, "I saw it in the window, and I just *couldn't* resist it."

My parents burst into confused laughter. No more crying.

From then on, I took it upon myself to be the family cheerleader and entertainer. Armed with years of gymnastics and dance classes, whenever I saw my mother's or father's mood start to falter, I'd put on a show, singing and doing a soft-shoe—depending on what room we were in, I'd throw in some tumbles or a cartwheel. Or I'd act out a funny scene from *All in the Family*, their favorite sitcom. I had a talent for remembering lines and a knack for picking up accents and speech patterns, so my impressions were pretty spot-on (my squawky Edith Bunker got especially hearty laughs).

I rehearsed routines with the fervor of an ambitious Broadway starlet. I slept with my ballet shoes on, wearing my leotard under my nightgown, just in case I heard one of my parents crying in the middle of the night (*"Showtime!"*). Never mind that my fifth-grade teacher wondered why I kept falling asleep in class. Never mind that I gnawed at the insides of my cheeks until they were raw and bit my nails until my fingers bled. Never mind that my pediatrician expressed concern about my being "frightfully underweight." It wasn't until our family doctor pointed out that I might be experiencing undue stress as a result of my brother's death the previous year that my parents finally took a closer look at me.

Mom and Dad decided we all needed a break. When I finished out the school year, we'd go visit Mom's sister Janet out in Miami. The day before we flew out, Aunt Janet's husband dropped dead of a heart attack. So instead of a vacation, we headed south for a funeral.

There was something knowing in the way Mom comforted Aunt Janet, maybe even a little smug, like Mom was playing tour guide in the land of desolation. She advised Aunt Janet to pack up her dead husband's belongings to get them out of sight, but not to get rid of them until she was absolutely sure what she wanted to keep. Mom warned her the first year would be the hardest, the first birthday without him (hers and his), the first Thanksgiving, the first Christmas. And when Aunt Janet cried, Mom nodded as she cried along.

Meanwhile, I gained a new audience member. My parents encouraged me to show off my songs and impressions and twirls and cartwheels for Aunt Janet, who was effusive in her praise. Plus, I had all new performance venues: the bungalow's open-plan living/kitchen/dining area, the terra-cotta-tiled lanai, the beach. The physical elements of my routines were trickier on sand, and I didn't enjoy sweating under a hot sun, but I relished the challenge, an attitude that would suit me well in my acting career.

"What a darling little girl you have," Aunt Janet would gush to my parents, dabbing at her drying tears. I would smile, more pleased at curbing her sobs than being complimented.

I also discovered books around this time. Aunt Janet left what my parents called "trashy novels" all around her house. Unsure whether I'd get in trouble for reading such adult material, I removed the dust jackets and subsequently received praise from my parents and aunt for sitting quietly for hours on end. Little did they know I was reading about sex and revenge and rape and murder.

A few weeks into our trip, the four of us went out for ice cream. We were sitting at a picnic table outside when a broad-chested man with mirrored sunglasses came up to us.

"You're my Jenny," he said, pointing at me.

He was a TV commercial director, shooting a national ad for an ice-cream company headquartered in Florida.

"How old is she, eight?" he asked.

I told him I was ten, just small for my age, offended that he would see me as less mature.

"Even better. Has this girl ever done any acting?" he asked.

And so it began.

"You ever get sick of people telling you how lucky you are?"

Those were the first words Timothy Boyd ever spoke to me, and they instantly cemented our friendship.

We were on the set of a commercial and he was playing my older brother. I was twelve at the time and he was thirteen, and we did look like we could be siblings. Our blue eyes had the same feline tilt at the outer corners, we both had chin dimples, and our hair was the same shade of white-blond (there were some *Children of the Damned* wisecracks I wouldn't understand until years later).

The set was a re-creation of a park bench by a lake and we were shooting the ad for Double Dippers, a packaged ice-cream cone with various flavored shells. It was the same product I was scouted for two years earlier and my sixth commercial for it—I was now frequently recognized as "the Double Dippers girl" in Miami. The previous ads were with me and my fake mother, but this time I was getting a fake father and brother, too. We would be enjoying ice cream on a sunny day in the park, each of us with a different flavored cone. I don't remember which one I was assigned, but it didn't matter, because my character, an impish little girl with a sweet tooth, was supposed to go around the park bench and steal a bite out of everyone else's cones when they weren't looking. Then I was to deliver a big grin to the camera, call out my signature line, "you gotta try 'em all!" and take a big bite out of my own cone.

Timothy and I were in the makeup trailer sitting next to each other. He was reading a comic book while a stylist put Brylcreem in his hair, and I was rereading *Valley of the Dolls*, waiting for my hot rollers to set.

"You sure that's something you should be reading at your age?" the stylist asked me. "Wouldn't a Nancy Drew book be more appropriate? My daughter is about your age, she loves those."

Irked at having my reading interrupted, I told her I'd already read this book before, twice, and that I found Nancy Drew boring. I said it's more interesting when you don't know who the good guys and the bad guys are because everyone's a little good *and* a little bad.

"I see . . ." She gave me a funny look and plastered a smile on her face. "Aren't you kids so lucky you get to spend the day eating ice cream!" Before we could answer someone called her away.

That's when Timothy won my heart forever with that single question: "You ever get sick of people telling you how lucky you are?"

He didn't wait for me to respond, continuing with, "You know who's actually lucky? Kids whose parents let them play outside without worrying they'll bust up their face and ruin their next callback."

He was right. The more people called me lucky, the less sure I was of actually being lucky.

As much fun as acting was, it was also work. Admittedly, it was my idea. But I was ten when I started out. When a kid tells you they want to be an astronaut, it's one thing to support them by buying a science book or two, maybe taking them to Cape Canaveral on vacation, but it's another thing to put them in a rocket and launch them into space. After that first Double Dippers commercial, when my parents asked, "Are you sure you really want this?" I was adamant in my desire to be an actress. But that was the first and last time they asked me. The swiftness and intensity with which they dedicated themselves to helping me succeed was astonishing. Within months, we moved to Miami, where my father found a job as a radiographer, while Mom decided to forgo her career and transition into being a full-time stage mother.

For the past two years, I'd spent afternoons, weekends, and school breaks being shuttled off to classes (acting, singing, and three forms of dance: tap, ballet, and jazz), auditions, callbacks, and commercial shoots. Since then, I'd wondered many times whether this was something I still wanted, but it felt like it was too late to change my mind. While kids my age with more normal lives were spending their Saturdays going to real parks and eating ice cream with their real families, I was spending the day in a fake park with a fake family, where I'd either have to pretend to eat ice cream or eat so much of it I'd never want to look at it again (to this day, I can't stomach Pizza Wheels after a sadistic director made me stuff my face with them until I projectile vomited). Quite frankly, I didn't need any kind of park or family; I would've rather spent today, and any day, alone, curled up on one of Aunt Janet's lanai loungers reading, or walking three blocks to the local library to replenish the stacks of books I kept all over the house. I was starting to think I'd rather read than do pretty much anything else.

Even today, I still think about that hairdresser calling me *so lucky*. Are you actually lucky if you don't want the thing you're so lucky to have?

All I ever felt truly lucky for was the time I spent with Timothy, beginning with that first day in the hair and makeup trailer.

"You know about spit buckets, right?" Timothy asked, barely glancing over at me while he flipped the pages of his comic.

"Yeah, but this director doesn't like using them."

"That's bogus. He's not gonna like it if you barf in the middle of a take, either."

This thirteen-year-old kid went to a production assistant first, then the director himself, demanding I get a spit bucket for the shoot. That's the kind of thing that could get you fired, but somehow, Timothy convinced the director. I got my spit bucket.

I wouldn't see Timothy again in person for four years, when I joined the Dollhouse Academy, and it would be like no time had passed, like we'd always been close, even though we didn't say much to each other on that Double Dippers shoot. Until then, I'd see him in other commercials from time to time, and in a few made-for-TV movies. His breakout role on the big screen, not long before the Dollhouse came calling, was as one of the teen misfits looking for buried treasure in *X Marks the Spot*, a late '70s spiritual predecessor to *The Goonies*. I made my parents take me to see that in the theater three times. If you're wondering whether I had a crush on him, I did, but it was more than that. Whenever Timothy appeared on-screen, I remembered the boy who stood up for me.

Timothy would become my best friend and the love of my life. And, as they did with everything else, the Dollhouse would take him away from me.

CHAPTER SEVEN

The next few days are so ludicrously fun, I have to keep reminding myself that this isn't a dream.

On Thursday, we have brunch with the new trainees in one of the dining halls. It's definitely a step up from our former high school cafeteria, which had brown peeling paint and harsh fluorescent lights and always reeked of old grease and Lysol. This place has a tin ceiling and wall sconces and bay windows, and it smells of ginger and fresh herbs and frying bacon. There's a juicing station, an omelet station, and platters of fruit and baked goods so artfully arranged, I hesitate to fill my plate for fear of disturbing the displays.

There are at least twenty people already at the long table reserved for us, a mix of young men and women, all bright-eyed and attractive. (*More attractive than me?* I banish the question from my mind. I know better than to open the door to insecurity.) At least half appear to be teenagers.

Will I be able to compete with them?

Again, I quiet my doubts. I wouldn't be here if I wasn't up to standard.

Somebody suggests going around the table and saying our names and where we're from, and when it becomes clear the table is too long for those at one end to hear those at the other, we decide each person should walk around the entire table introducing themselves, the shared awkwardness of which creates a bonding moment.

The thirty or so of us represent various physical types and races, with most of us from the United States, but a few from farther abroad: South Africa, Singapore, the Netherlands. Yet despite our different backgrounds and outward appearances, we're all here for the same reason, and what starts as an exchange of our performance histories quickly becomes a passionate discussion of our favorite plays, musicals, movies, and Dollhouse stars.

"Did you hear Riley Price's new album? It's her best one yet."

"That trailer for the new movie with Austen Martell and Malika Daniels looks amazing."

"This is supposed to be the last season of *Overruled*, but I'm hoping that's just a rumor."

As I eat the best Eggs Benedict I've ever had in my life, I look around the table and feel like a rapidly inflating helium balloon.

These are my people.

After brunch, Solveig ushers us onto a tram car, and we're taken on a Dahlen studio tour, visiting familiar back lot streets, soundstages, sets, and props and costume departments. I have to keep reminding myself I'm more than a fan, that I may very well end up performing on these sets or others, wearing costumes made especially for me.

Toward the end of the tour, we visit an *In the Dollhouse* back lot and actually get to watch a scene being filmed.

I'm dumbstruck when Ivy Gordon walks past our tram, wearing a suit made of a shimmery gray fabric and a pearl choker, her white-blond hair up in a chignon. She smiles and waves at us and my breath catches when she briefly looks right at me.

"Do you think it's the real Ivy?" a female voice murmurs behind me.

A male voice laughs. "What do you mean?"

"There was a wardrobe lady who said Ivy's shoe size had gotten smaller. You have to admit she looked a lot different after the accident. And there were rumors her personality changed, too," she says.

"If I had my face smashed in after my tour bus, like, drove off a cliff, I'd look and act different, too. Please don't tell me you believe those conspiracy theories."

"I mean, it's possible," she says. "Just look at Paul McCartney. He died in a car accident and was replaced by a guy who won a Paul McCartney look-alike contest."

Another laugh. "I can't even with you."

Grace and I exchange bemused smiles and roll our eyes. From time to time, I've come across wackos who believe those wild rumors about Ivy, but I didn't expect one of them would be a Dollhouse trainee.

"Quiet on set!" someone calls out.

Later in my room, while unpacking, I come across the white envelope with the warning note in a side pocket of my suitcase. I don't know why I brought it with me. Feeling a flash of annoyance and defiance, I take out the card.

Whatever you think you want, you won't find—

Wrong. I *will* find what I want here. I already have. Even so, I can't bring myself to throw out the note, hiding it in a drawer instead.

On Thursday night, there's karaoke, which at first feels like everyone is auditioning and trying to outdo each other but eventually turns into a giant sing-along. When we return to our dorm, I briefly meet my roommate, Nicole Chau. She gives me a quick bio as she's getting ready for a midnight call time for a two-episode arc on a new medical drama, *Standard of Care*.

"Daughter of Vietnamese immigrants, raised in San Francisco, was a gymnast until I was fifteen. Then I grew boobs and my gymnastics career was over, so I tried out for the school play, got bitten by the acting bug, et cetera," she says, tying her hair in a ponytail and grabbing her bag. "Gotta run. I'm nice, I keep things neat, and I'm hardly ever around, so pretty much the perfect roommate."

On Saturday, there's a field day with an obstacle course, relay races, tug-of-war, and other lawn games. The team Grace and I are on comes in first, thanks in part to the two of us dominating the three-legged race, and we each win a tote full of Dahlen swag—a branded T-shirt, baseball hat, mouse pad, an umbrella, a sterling silver replica of Genevieve's owl brooch, and a fifty-dollar gift certificate to Chapter and Verse, Owls Point's surprisingly well-curated bookstore/record store. That night, there's Dahlen trivia at the Sterile Cuckoo, the local pub, and our team comes in second.

The following day, there's a scavenger hunt, which familiarizes us with the vast campus, though our team is last this time because we get lost in the hedge maze, which we find more funny than frustrating. On Saturday night, we're treated to a fancy dinner at Vincente's, an upscale restaurant on Main Street, before Solveig leads us a few doors down to Talk of the Town, a dimly lit lounge with fuchsia suede banquettes and fringed lamps.

"You think the name of this place is a Judy or Liza reference?" Grace asks me as we file in. "I doubt it's named after the Pretenders song."

A lanky Black guy in front of us turns around. He was on our scavenger hunt team, but I forget his name. "Talk of the Town was the London club where Judy did her comeback performances before she died," he says. "Doesn't everyone know that?" He widens his eyes before breaking into a laugh. "Just kidding. Major Judy nerd here."

Grace's eyes twinkle. "Did you know she was originally cast in *Valley of the Dolls*—"

"As the aging theater legend Helen Lawson," he interjects. "Of course I know that. Even though she was fired from the movie, she kept the beaded suit designed for the character and performed in it for years after. It's Grace, right? And Ramona?"

"Yup," says Grace. "And you're . . . Dion?"

"*C'est moi.*" He gives a little bow. "And before you go thinking I'm a gay cliché for being such a Judy fan, let the record show, despite my love of show tunes, my favorite band is Metallica." That's when I notice his fingernails are painted black.

"Nice," Grace says. "I listened to them a lot in high school, until I discovered Nine Inch Nails and KMFDM, but I still put on *Master of Puppets* when I'm having a bad day. Let the record show, despite my respect for Judy and Liza, I hate most show tunes."

Dion laughs, and the three of us select a banquette to the left of the stage, which is occupied by a baby grand piano and a microphone stand.

"Who do you think will surprise us tonight?" Dion asks. "I heard Ivy might be putting on a little cabaret for us."

"That would be unreal," I say. "I've seen her live three times, but always in stadiums."

"Her *Little Doll Blue* tour was my first concert, when I was twelve," Dion enthuses.

A waiter comes by for our drink order. Once we get our cocktails, the lights darken and a spotlight illuminates center stage. A middle-aged man in a tuxedo comes out and sits at the piano. He begins playing a song that's familiar but takes me a moment to place because I'm used to hearing it as a grungy guitar line. It's a Riley Price song.

Moments later, Riley herself comes out onstage, and the room erupts in cheers.

Whatever mild disappointment I feel that it's not Ivy is immediately swept away as Riley launches into an acoustic version of one of her biggest hits. She's swapped her usual leather pants for a black cocktail dress, though her dark curly hair is wild as ever as she growls into the microphone. Grace and I were more into her angsty confessional music in high school, when it matched our own angst, but hearing her in such an intimate setting, her voice stronger than ever, makes us remember why we were fans in the first place.

"Can you believe this is our life?" Grace shouts into my ear as the audience applauds Riley's second song.

"Not really," I shout back. I've never seen Grace smile as much as she has in the last three days, and I've never smiled this much either.

Despite all this, the doubt creeps in.

You know this can't last.

You'll have to work like hell.

Are you sure you'll measure up?

I try to quiet the nagging thoughts pulling me out of the moment.

Focus on the music.

Forget everything else.

Enjoy the show.

And I do.

CHAPTER EIGHT

Sunday is our last day before classes start, and there's only one thing we're scheduled for: lunch with Genevieve Spalding.

What do you wear to meet one of the most important women in show business? I go with a red-and-black kilted skirt, white turtleneck, opaque black tights, and chunky loafers. It's humid out, so taming my curly hair takes some effort.

Grace is already by the front entrance when I meet her.

"Do I look like an electrocuted Cowardly Lion?" I smooth down my hairline.

"No, you look more like the Cowardly Lion post–Emerald City make-over," Grace assures me. "We better get a move on if we're gonna be on time."

And we would have been on time, but we have to navigate using the outdoor orientation maps, and our less-than-stellar sense of direction takes us down a few wrong paths until we finally reach Genevieve's house. It's a sprawling sage-green Victorian with yellow trim, set at the top of a hill, with a wrought iron gate enclosing the multiacre property.

As we approach, Grace utters a low whistle. "Damn, this is more of a manor than a house."

"Maybe it's one of the things rich people do to downplay their wealth, like how they call yachts 'boats,'" I say.

"You think it'll be a big deal we're five minutes late?"

"Probably, but what can we do about it now?"

Grace rings the security intercom.

"Who's calling please?" a crisp male voice with a British accent asks. I imagine a creaky butler in an ascot and white gloves.

We give our names and a moment later, he follows up with, "You're late."

I stutter out an apology at the same time Grace quips, "Traffic was a nightmare."

There's a long pause, during which I expect us to get sent away at any moment, from the property, if not the Dollhouse itself. Finally, the intercom emits a dry chuckle and the gate swings open.

We climb the stone steps to the house's front door.

Instead of a creaky butler, the man who greets us looks like the hero in a Jane Austen adaptation. He's young and roguishly handsome, dressed in a black turtleneck and jeans that manage to look simultaneously casual and expensive.

A gasp catches in my throat as we step into an entryway that opens into a domed foyer two stories high with a stained glass ceiling, an octagonal parquet wood floor, and a grand carved wooden staircase branching in two separate directions like the arms of a tree. I've never seen a foyer this breathtaking, even in a movie.

"You're the last to arrive," the man says, a sadistic gleam in his bright blue eyes. "Genevieve won't be happy about that."

"Is there anything we can—"

Grace cuts me off. "Should we get on our knees and beg for forgiveness? Or turn around and go home? We fucked up, but we're not actually capable of turning back time to undo our fuckup."

"That kind of feisty attitude might just propel you to stardom," he tells Grace. The corners of his mouth flex as he holds back a smile. "Or it could be the ruin of you. Perhaps both."

I find myself trying to catch his eye, but he keeps his gaze trained on Grace and gives me only a passing glance.

"Mason? Mason, have you seen—ah, here are exactly the two Ms. Spalding was asking about." Solveig appears from one of the foyer's multiple entrances. "She is not pleased."

We follow Solveig into an enormous room dominated by a bone-white tree, its delicate branches and multitude of tiny leaves so meticulously rendered, it takes me a second to realize it's a sculpture. Surrounding the tree is a royal-blue velvet banquette and a horseshoe formation of tables with matching velvet armchairs, the room's only splashes of color.

And here comes Genevieve Spalding in a black Chanel suit with white braided trim, the diamond owl pin on her lapel catching the light. She's much more petite than I expected her to be, and while she's in her sixties, she looks at least a decade younger.

I can't believe I'm standing in front of one of the most influential entertainment icons of the last twenty years. And she's looking at me with utter disapproval.

"The lateness is my fault," Mason says, giving me a soft nudge between my shoulders as he steps back. "They were here bang on time, but I delayed them by asking about those musical skits they did for that movie theater. Apologies we kept you waiting, but do please put the full blame on me."

"I will." Genevieve gives him a look that is menacing but flirtatious at the edges. "You and Solveig are dismissed. And you"—she turns to Grace and me—"can find your respective place cards and take your seats."

As Mason leaves he looks over his shoulder at me and winks. Only at me. How did he know about our live coming attractions? Did he see us on TV? Does he know about every incoming trainee?

We find our tables, which are on opposite sides of the tree, and I stop myself from waving at all the people I know. I offer a flustered smile to the three young women I'm seated with, which melts into relief when I recognize them all.

We grin and exchange whispered hellos.

Two of them are wearing Diva Doll lipstick. Do they really think such an obvious gesture will help ingratiate themselves? Then again, maybe I should be trying harder to ingratiate myself.

Genevieve takes a slow lap around the tables, saying nothing, her high heels *clack-clack*ing on the white marble floor.

"Jocelyn Ross." She stops beside a table a few feet away from me, examining a girl with shoulder-length auburn hair.

"That's me," the girl replies, her eyes glazed with awe and intimidation.

One step closer, then two, then Genevieve has a handful of the girl's hair cascading through her fingers. She gives it a little tug. "Your hair was longer when we recruited you. And a different color. Ash brown. Is that not correct?"

"Y-yes, it was," Jocelyn sputters, her hands fluttering to her hair. "But my aunt's been a professional hairdresser for, like, ever, and she said I can't go to the Dollhouse with a million split ends, and once we got rid of those, she convinced me that, like, my color washed me out and something warmer would be more flattering."

"I see . . ." Genevieve spins back toward the dining room's entrance. "It's a shame you and your aunt thought you knew better than the instructions we provided, which explicitly stated not to alter your hair." She pushes a button on an intercom camouflaged among the white moldings.

Moments later, two beefy men enter the room and head straight toward Jocelyn, who shrinks down in her chair. "I'll dye it back! I'll grow it out!" Each man grabs one of her arms and begins pulling her out of the room.

I fight competing urges, to reassure her and turn away from her. I remain in my seat, eyes trained on Genevieve. She regards the scene coolly, one eyebrow rising above the rim of her glasses. "You can do so in the comfort of your home, because your invitation to the Dollhouse Academy is hereby rescinded." She addresses the rest of us. "Two things we value highly here: paying attention and following directions."

Jocelyn bursts into tears as she's dragged out of the room, arms and legs flailing, and a lump forms in my throat. It's hard for me not to cry when I see someone else cry, and my heart goes out to this girl. I lean around the tree to see Grace, but when she meets my eye, her face is impassive. She's always been better at hiding her true feelings than me. Maybe that's what makes her a good actor. Then again, maybe keeping my emotions so close to the surface is what makes *me* a good actor. Maybe even a better one.

"Now then." Genevieve claps her hands once, as if to say, *all eyes on me.* "If you think you're all here because you're exceptional, think again. You're here because you have the *potential* to be exceptional. What you do with that potential remains to be seen." She does another slow lap around the tables as she speaks. "For every one of you, there are hundreds waiting to take your place. You think you're good-looking, talented, charming? There will *always* be someone coming up behind you, likely better in every respect. Did you have the lead in school plays, win dance competitions, pageants, or talent shows? Maybe you even did a few commercials, sang backup for a famous singer, or got parts in shows or films. None of that means anything here. Consider this ground zero for your career as a performer. If your precious egos are hungry to expand, if you're here looking for endless positive affirmation, look elsewhere. If you're here because you think the Dollhouse Academy will prove you're as great as you think you are, get out of my sight. But if you want to be something bigger than your paltry self, if you want to be part of an entertainment revolution and are willing to work yourself to the bone, you are welcome to stay."

She casts a look around the room, like she's challenging us to protest. "Let me tell you a little something about Dahlen Entertainment and the Dollhouse Academy. People thought I was out of my mind when I proposed setting up a facility to train performers and create our own show business microcosm. They said it was archaic, it would make performers feel like indentured servants. They said there was a reason the old studio system and star system failed, and this would fail, too. I told them they were wrong. I said if we built an entertainment empire where excellence took priority above all else, if we hired the finest producers, directors, writers, choreographers, then trained an army of performers to top standards, we would develop a brand allegiance unlike anything. We didn't need to hire established stars—we'd grow our own. And not only that, we'd make sure they, and the work we produced, reflected society, physically, emotionally, and culturally. As long as we provided a competitive wage, anyone part of the Dahlen family would remain loyal in order to participate in the most prestigious projects." She pauses, hands on hips.

"And you know what? I was right. I built a star factory from the ground up and now everyone is clamoring to be part of it." Her expression hardens. "I pride this organization on being a family, but it's also a business, and everyone must play their role. I've been in this industry for over fifty years now, and I wouldn't have gotten where I am today without learning from people smarter than me. The Dollhouse Academy instructors, consultants, counselors, doctors—we are all smarter than you. Listen to us. Do as we say. Learn from us. There are a lot of rules to follow here. There is a rigid schedule. You will be tested in ways you could never imagine. You'll feel like your time is not your own, your body is not your own, and your mind is not your own. You are nothing more than raw clay and we are here to mold you. Surrender yourself fully to the Dollhouse Academy and we will shape you into something truly exceptional.

"We want to make you stars. But it's not easy. Out of the thirty young men and women in this room, maybe one of you will make it into the highest stratosphere of fame and success. Right now, every one of you is thinking you'll be that one, but reality will prove most of you wrong. However good you may be, there's limited room to be the best. Fortunately, there are numerous other opportunities right here at Dahlen that may become available to you. A handful of you may become character actors, background singers and dancers—professions that will keep you in show business, but at a modest level. A few others may still end up above the line, but behind the scenes, as writers or producers or casting directors, or below the line, which can also be fulfilling—a good makeup artist or prop master can work on hundreds of projects over the course of their career. The trainees who wholeheartedly believe in the work we're doing will want to be part of it in any capacity, even if that means working in the Dahlen offices or in one of the Main Street establishments. Alas, approximately half of you will not rise to the standards and level of dedication the Dollhouse requires. Which is fine. If you're as attractive and smart as you think you are, you should still find your way in the world."

Genevieve completes another lap, her steps perfectly in sync with her speech.

"Whatever you think you know about your craft and this business, get ready to unlearn it. Your education begins here. Now." She walks over to the intercom and pushes a button. "Bring out the first course."

Around me, jaws are unhinged. I close my own open mouth.

When I tilt my body to steal another glance at Grace, she's already staring at me, bug-eyed. She mouths, *Holy shit.*

We both whip our heads in Genevieve's direction to make sure she didn't see our exchange. But she has her eyes trained on the dining room doorway, where several servers appear bearing large silver trays.

A small plate is set down before me and the odor hits me like a rock between the eyes. A cross between rotted fish and bleach. The dish itself is comprised of black gelatinous cubes stacked in a wobbly pyramid. It looks like squid ink Jell-O.

"It's lutefisk marinated in squid ink," Genevieve explains. At least I was half right. "Lutefisk is a Norwegian delicacy made of dried and salted cod cured in lye. My chef believes the squid ink adds a bolder flavor, and I agree. Eat up."

Around the room, hands hesitate over utensils. Fork or spoon? Most of us settle on a soup spoon. As people around me take their first bites, I hear coughs and suppressed gagging noises.

Here goes nothing.

I scoop up a cube of goth fish Jell-O and shovel the whole thing into my mouth, swallowing quickly and drowning it with several big gulps of water.

For the next ten seconds, I clench every muscle in my body to keep from vomiting what is truly the most horrific thing I've ever put into my mouth (and I once bit into a dumpling with a cockroach inside).

As Genevieve begins yet another circle around the room (it's amazing the marble doesn't have a grooved path from all her pacing), something dawns on me: it's not enough to keep the food down. I need to make her believe I'm enjoying it.

You will be tested in ways you could never imagine.

This meal must be one of those tests.

"Come on, everybody eat." Genevieve claps her hands, examining faces and plates as she walks.

I know my weaknesses as an actor. I can cry on cue, but I struggle with laughing authentically. I'm fine with the Greeks, but I struggle to master the cadence of Shakespeare. At the same time, I also know my strengths. While my uncle Alonso is a fine cook, Reed is a nightmare in the kitchen, his specialty being bland yet painfully salty casseroles with noodles that are bafflingly both under- and over-cooked. I've eaten plenty of those gross casseroles, retching on the inside but convincing Reed it's the most delicious thing I've ever tasted. That's what I need to do now.

Across the room, a guy exclaims, "I'm gonna hurl," and then he does, the splash of vomit on marble causing a few others to follow suit. At the next table, a pixie-haired brunette glances down at her plate and bursts into tears.

How ridiculous. Who cries over fish Jell-O?

The girls at my table are faring better, trying to cover up their grimaces as they spoon the lutefisk into their mouths. Across the way, Grace is eating with gusto, like each spoonful contains chocolate mousse, her favorite dessert. When Genevieve stops at her table, Grace gets a curt nod out of her. That's my girl.

I'm determined to secure one of those nods for myself, and I save the last bite for the moment Genevieve approaches our table, spooning it neatly into my mouth with a single "mm."

"How was it?" Genevieve asks me.

"I've never tasted anything like it," I reply with an appreciative smile.

She lets out a single snicker and moves on to the next table.

After the first course, Genevieve calls out, "Grace Ludlow, Yachi Tao, Jude Smolenski, and Ramona Holloway, please join me." She motions to a table off to the side of the room.

CHAPTER NINE

I can't imagine what awaits the four of us as we as we make our way to Genevieve's table, dodging envious glances.

Much as I appreciate the personal attention, being in such proximity to the head of the Dollhouse Academy is nerve-racking. What will she ask us to do next? Eat a live octopus in front of her?

I sit between Yachi, a willowy girl with a shaved head and a nose ring, and Jude, a cute guy about my age who looks like a surfer.

Once we're settled, Genevieve unfolds a linen napkin onto her lap and regards us. "Everything here is a lesson. When I said there's limited space for the best, I meant it. When I saw recordings of your performances, I saw something special in each of you."

Behind us, a waiter appears and sets Cobb salads in front of us.

Genevieve regards our hesitation with amusement. "Don't worry, they don't contain any unusual ingredients."

Even so, we pick at the salads as Genevieve does most of the talking, barely touching hers at all.

"Your first impression of me here may be that I am intimidating and harsh, but I also have a nurturing side. I never had children of my own, so I view all the Dollhouse Academy trainees as my children. As you probably know, I worked in show business for over thirty years—as an actor, singer, and dancer, then later as a producer—until I decided I wanted to usher in younger generations of talent and help them develop their careers. I also wanted to create a safe space for them to work where they'd be spared the horrors I personally experienced, particularly as a child star." She briefly removes her glasses and rubs the bridge of her nose. "Hollywood is a cesspit, and there are a lot of powerful men taking advantage of young and naive performers. It's disgusting, and I was determined to run my school and studio with more integrity."

My stomach churns and I put my fork down, unsure of whether I'm unsettled from what Genevieve is saying or from the fish Jell-O.

"Is that why you chose to open the school so far away from Hollywood?" Yachi asks.

"In part," Genevieve says. "I was also tired of the sprawl of Los Angeles and wished to settle on the East Coast, but away from the bustle of New York City. My husband, Harold, was originally from New York, and we often spent summers in the Borscht Belt."

"The Borscht Belt?" Jude echoes.

Genevieve chuckles. "That's the nickname for a section of upstate New York in and around the Catskill Mountains, which, back in the day, was full of hundreds of summer resorts favored by Jewish families. Harold was Jewish. Anyway, we loved it there, and after his sudden death in 1968, I wanted to honor his memory by creating an entertainment empire where we were both happiest." Her eyes grow distant for a moment, then snap into focus. "What would your ideal careers look like?"

"Ivy Gordon's," I answer immediately.

Jude shrugs. "I'm still figuring that out. Depends on what opens up for me."

"I want to be the first Asian to win an Oscar for Best Actress," Yachi asserts.

"I'd love a career like Vanessa Sanchez's," Grace says. "I'm not cut out for the America's-sweetheart thing like Ramona is. I tend to go for edgier roles."

"Don't limit yourself," Genevieve admonishes. "You have yet to scratch the surface of what you're capable of. All of you."

I catch a whiff of chocolate and vanilla as our desserts are brought over along with cups of coffee.

"My chef Jean-Luc makes the most divine chocolate soufflés."

It's all I can do to stop my eyes from rolling into the back of my head as I eat a few spoonfuls. Not wanting to pig out in front of Genevieve, I stop after a few bites. Grace, noticing I set down my spoon, does the same as Jude and Yachi devour their desserts.

Genevieve pauses with her spoon in midair. "What, you don't like it?" she asks Grace and me.

"Oh, it's only the best thing I've ever eaten," says Grace. "But I'm sure we're expected to be, like, really skinny."

"Nonsense." Genevieve spoons the soufflé into her mouth with relish. "I hate what society—and this industry—has done to women's relationships with their bodies." She sighs. "In my day, they demanded we be positively waifish, and they didn't ask nicely." Her voice hardens. "Those studio doctors should be hanged, the way they dispense toxic pills to young performers, then leave them fending for themselves when they're inevitably wrecked with addiction. The studio heads are no better. I barely got out alive, and when I started my own studio, I swore I'd protect my stars from such cruelty. If your work requires you to lose or gain weight, the Dollhouse is committed to helping you do so in a healthful way, with an emphasis on nutrition. Your body is your instrument, and you need to have love and respect for it. Discipline has its place, but so does the occasional indulgence." She takes another bite of her soufflé.

Considering her stern diatribe earlier, this is refreshing to hear. At her encouragement, Grace and I resume eating. While I'm not as nervous as I was earlier, there's still a turbulence in my stomach. I'm about to ask where the nearest restroom is when Genevieve lays her palms flat on the table and leans forward.

"In the same way I personally chose you all to join the Dollhouse Academy, every couple of years, I handpick a performer to personally mentor, and they almost always go on to great success. Ivy Gordon, Vanessa Sanchez, and Austen Martell were all past mentees." She pauses. "As much as I believe you four show promise, I can only mentor one of you, and it's too early to say which one of you that will be. It will depend on how you do these next few weeks."

Sweat breaks out on my forehead as a waiter comes by to take our dishes.

Genevieve stands and gives each of us an assessing look. "I expect big things from you."

Just then, as he's clearing my plate, the waiter drops a spoon. "I'll get it," I say. In the process of reaching down to retrieve it, the downward motion causes a pressure on my stomach.

No.

Keep it together.

Don't you fucking dare.

But it's too much.

Not only do I puke, I do so all over Genevieve's shoes.

Bile burns at my throat, but it's nothing compared to the shame searing through me.

From now on, no matter what I manage to accomplish at the Dollhouse, Genevieve will remember me as the girl who threw up on her shoes.

Genevieve gingerly steps away from me as another waiter rushes over to clean up the mess I made.

Once her shoes are wiped clean, Genevieve addresses the room. "I hope you enjoyed this orientation period. Now the real work starts. You'll receive your schedules and begin your training regimen tomorrow. After a month, if you last that long, you will each be assigned a counselor who will guide you on both personal and professional matters. You are dismissed."

I can't get out of the house fast enough and Grace hurries to keep up with me.

"But apart from that, Mrs. Lincoln, how did you enjoy the soufflé?" she jokes.

Gritting my teeth, I say, "I'm sure I'll be able to laugh about this someday, but not two minutes after it happened."

"Sorry."

My throat burns and skin prickles as we walk back to the dorm. "I guess we know which one of us Genevieve *won't* be mentoring."

"We don't know shit," Grace says. "I mean, the woman is terrifying, but she did seem . . . weirdly nurturing."

"Genevieve Spalding is the least nurturing woman I've ever met."

"That's only because you never met any of my foster parents. But yeah, we're in for a rough ride."

"As she pointed out in that monologue, which totally reminded me of Debbie Allen's *'Fame costs. And right here is where you start paying'* speech from *Fame*," I say.

"See, I got more Mamet vibes from it. It reminded me of the *'always be closing'* monologue from *Glengarry Glen Ross*. When they brought out cups of coffee at the end of the meal, I was sure she'd yell at someone to put theirs down."

"*'Coffee is for closers only,'*" we sternly quote Mamet in unison, and break into laughter.

When we return to Gale House, before we head over to our respective rooms, Grace lightly punches my shoulder and says, "Don't be bummed. You'll be so awesome, nothing that happened today is gonna matter."

As I head down the hall, I glance over at the mailboxes and look for my name on one of the cubbyholes. There it is. And there's mail for me. A blue class schedule and a square white envelope, "Ramona Holloway" spelled out in that familiar spiky script. Not wanting to open it in the hallway or possibly in the presence of my roommate, I take the envelope into the nearest bathroom.

I sit on the closed toilet seat, steady my trembling hands, and open the envelope, which contains the same white card as before. This note bears a single sentence:

Go home while you're still nobody.

CHAPTER TEN

Show her.

Just show her already.

An inner voice pesters me to tell Grace about the notes, but I resist.

Instead, I privately, endlessly obsess over who might have sent them. There was no postmark or return address on the second envelope either, so it had to be from someone here. But how did the first note get to me? Could one of the trainees be someone I crossed paths with before? I didn't recognize any of the new people I met, and none of them were from New York. Of course, Grace had access, but there's no way in hell she could've . . . she couldn't have, right? No way, absolutely not, and suspecting her is almost as bad as suspecting my uncles.

It could be Solveig, or someone else, working at Genevieve's behest to test me—the Dollhouse Academy is all about testing its trainees in unexpected ways. Regardless, I can't afford any more failure, so I need to set aside these speculations and turn my attention toward my classes.

The first two weeks feel like the sweet spot on a treadmill: just challenging enough. The days begin with an early rise and ninety minutes of rigorous exercise classes, everything from aerobics, yoga, and weight training to martial arts and army-style drills. After a quick shower and breakfast, there's a three-hour class, after which the rest of the day is free.

So far, I find the exercise classes far more challenging than the classroom ones. Acting Techniques mostly covers things I already know. On-Camera Scene Study is taught by Geoff Shepley, a former Dahlen character actor who specialized in playing weasels and double-dealers, and I find it similar to other workshops I've taken, though I welcome the refresher. The Alexander Technique, an alternative therapy centered around improving posture, seems like it's mostly standing and doing small body movements. And Film and Television Theory's curriculum is familiar, thanks to my uncles. We're told there won't be any tests or grades in the academic sense, but by now we're starting to realize the Dollhouse Academy has its own ways of testing and grading trainees.

"The first weeks aren't bad, because they're still easing you into it," Nicole warns me during a brief moment I run into her on Tuesday. So far, she's lived up to her claim of being the perfect roommate. "Enjoy it while you can because it'll get a lot more intense. And god help you if you get a dance class with Lady Edna—she's brutal."

But I'm sure I'll be able to handle that, too. Since there's minimal homework, most of our afternoons and evenings are free, so Grace and I spend them further exploring the campus and browsing the Main Street shops, particularly Chapter and Verse.

"I better start booking jobs soon, because I've already blown through my gift certificate and there's a new Boards of Canada album coming out soon," Grace says one afternoon while we're checking out the new releases. "If my TV and Film Acting teacher isn't bullshitting me, that might even happen. By some miracle, I seem to be doing okay in her class, though I'm sure that's not gonna last." She glances out the front window. "Is that Dion? I've got to talk to him about a scene we're doing together. Be right back."

She rushes out of the store, the bell above the door signaling her departure. When it rings again and I feel someone beside me, I assume it's Grace, so I don't look up from the Pulp CD I'm examining and say, "What is it about a British accent that's so damn sexy?"

"I haven't a clue, why don't you tell me?"

Mason's own sexy British accent startles me. Heat immediately floods my face. Speechless, I glance over and do a double take because he looks different from when I met him at Genevieve's house. There's stubble dotting his cheeks and chin, and his wavy hair looks more rumpled than intentionally tousled. He's more attractive with rougher edges.

I point at the CD and stammer, "I was talking about Jarvis Cocker."

Mason raises an eyebrow. "Of course you were. In any case, how have you been since Sunday's lunch? Keeping food down a bit better?"

It would be in my best interest to get along with anyone in Genevieve's inner circle, but I can't help glaring at him. "I normally have an excellent gag reflex." A fresh blush creeps over my cheeks as he smirks.

"Good to know," he says. "So are you a fan of other Brit-pop, like Blur and Oasis?"

"More like James and Radiohead. And trip-hop. Portishead, Sneaker Pimps, Massive Attack."

"Tricky?"

"I know I need to try his stuff, too, but I haven't gotten around to it."

"Put that down and come with me." Mason leads me to a back corner of the record store. The CD cases clack against each other as he sorts through them until he produces one with an orange-red cover, TRICKY stenciled across the front in capital letters. "This needs to be the next album you get. You better start catching up, his third one's out next month."

"Okay, okay," I say, examining the liner notes.

"'Hell Is Round the Corner' is a brilliant track. And appropriate, considering what you're about to go through."

"Everyone keeps warning me about how I shouldn't get used to things the way they are now, how much harder it's going to get," I say. "I'm not scared off that easily."

"I'm not trying to scare you off, only prepare you. A lot of people think they can handle it but break down after the first few weeks. The commitment it takes, the toll it takes . . . You don't know until you live through it."

"You don't know what I can live through," I retort.

Then again, neither do I.

Back in the dorm, I grab my Discman, lie back on my bed, and put on the Tricky CD I just bought. I cue "Hell Is Round the Corner" and am surprised it uses a sample from my favorite Portishead song, "Glory Box," a wistful tune about a woman frustrated with love. This song sounds dirtier, more like a dangerous seduction. When it ends, I play it again. And again.

I continue to breeze through my classes, and I earn especially effusive feedback from Geoff Shepley, who says I'm a natural in front of the camera. Once in a while, Genevieve stops by our classes to watch. Even her presence doesn't throw me off, and I earn two separate nods of approval from her for my scene work. Maybe I've still got a shot at being mentored by her, despite what I did to her shoes.

The Saturday before the third week begins, I receive a yellow flyer in my mailbox notifying me of a series of medical assessments the next day.

Hungry and caffeine-deprived (we were instructed not to eat or drink anything past dinner), Grace and I make our way to the Dahlen Medical Center, a large network of brick buildings at the edge of campus. Our appointments are in different wings, so we agree to meet in the dining hall later.

Things start out like a typical doctor's visit: there's a waiting room, and paperwork to fill out and sign, including several consent forms agreeing to participate in "emerging and experimental procedures and treatments" and a variety of waivers, which I'm assured are standard. Even so, the implication is that I have to agree to be a guinea pig, but if something goes wrong, neither my family nor I will have any legal recourse. I remember Reed's and Alonso's concerned faces, their words of warning, which I dismissed as so much paranoia. What am I really agreeing to be part of here? The latest warning note echoes through my mind.

Go home while you're still nobody.

Maybe the notes are a test, or maybe a genuine attempt to save me. What the sender doesn't realize is, for me, nothing is worse than being nobody.

"Ramona Holloway, the doctor will see you now," a receptionist calls.

My pen hovers above the clipboard for a moment, then I scribble my signature on the requested forms and hand them over.

The Dollhouse is my home now.

Moments later, I'm ushered into a waiting room, asked to undress, and put on a paper gown and plastic flip-flops.

"You will receive your clothes at the end of the day."

The end of the day? How many exams can there possibly be?

Quite a few, it turns out. I become a human pinball, passed around various departments as I get a full-body exam while being asked for a detailed medical history, then get vial after vial of blood drawn. This is followed by a CT scan followed by an MRI. There are other tests with acronyms I've never heard before that involve electrodes trailing wires attached to various parts of my body, which takes us past lunchtime, though nobody offers me food or even a break to regroup, leaving me lightheaded and wishing I'd brought a snack. Instead, there's an eye exam (after all the needles, a puff of air in my eye is nothing), then a hearing test, then a dental exam during which I'm told I need to floss more (doesn't everybody?).

"I'll be taking you to the level zero tanks next," says a big-bosomed woman in scrubs.

We're the only ones in the elevator and the woman inserts a key beside a button marked LZ and pushes as she turns the key. When we start to move, she says, "Apparently, they needed something that sounded fancier than 'basement.'"

Damn, it must be a rough day, considering how stiff my face feels when I smile. "Level Zero sounds like the name of a band I saw play at CB's once," I say.

"Sounds like the name of a band whose drummer I dated one summer. Their music was god-awful."

We share a laugh.

Hoping to extend this moment of camaraderie, I say, "Hey, I don't know if it's cool to ask this, but . . . why so many tests? I'm young, I'm healthy"—I wave a hand up and down my body—"I don't get it."

The doors open as we reach level zero, and the woman stiffens. "The Dollhouse Academy values your health and wants to be thorough in checking for any conditions that may impair your performance." She casts a glance down the hall and lowers her voice. Her hair smells like artificial kiwi and grazes my cheek as she leans in. "Look, this place is careful about who it invests its time and money in. Sure, you may be pretty and able to recite your lines, but if you've got something festering in you that'll threaten your career, they want to know about it now so they can either treat it or cut their losses. You'd be surprised how many seemingly healthy-looking young people come through here and end up leaving with a diagnosis. Lots of dreams have been dashed, but lots of lives saved, too."

So in addition to worrying I might not be talented enough, now I also have to worry about carrying some hidden disease. Lovely.

We end up outside a door with a keypad. As the woman punches in a series of numbers, she says in a subdued voice, "I shouldn't be telling you this but . . . They're going to demand a lot out of you. You better decide early on how much of yourself you'll give and how much you'll hold on to."

A beep, then a click as the door is unlocked. Before I can respond, she shoos me into a room painted entirely black, locking the door behind me.

The center of the room contains a giant water tank with a portable metal staircase beside it, and against one wall is a massive console of buttons, switches, and lights that looks like it could launch rockets into space.

A middle-aged man in a lab coat with a beard that looks like a Brillo pad tells me to undress and get into the tank. While I was naked for some of the other scans, too, this is different. This immediately reminds of me of the scene in *Splash* where the mermaid is being held captive by the evil scientist, chained in a water tank, the colors of her tail fading.

"What is this for?" I ask.

"This is part of a new research and development branch of Dahlen-

Rex in which they're pioneering a revolutionary new scanning technology called aquatic imaging." He follows with more scientific jargon that sounds legitimate but does nothing to put me at ease.

"I've already gotten a bunch of different scans. Is there any way I can skip this one?" No harm in asking, right?

"No, you may not. Please disrobe and get into the tank."

My body tenses, resisting. I take a long breath.

I've made it this far. What's the alternative, being removed from the Dollhouse? There's no way I'll let that happen.

My bare skin breaks out into goose bumps when I take off my hospital gown. I clench my jaw and get into the tank. The water reaches my neck and isn't so cold as to be distressing but not warm enough to be comfortable (not that any water temperature could make me comfortable right now).

"Position yourself right at the center of the tank—right there, yes."

There's a mechanical whirring above me as a device that looks like a colander with wires coming out of it is lowered down, stopping a few inches in front of my nose.

"Place the transmission helmet on your head. It will adjust automatically."

I grasp the device gingerly with my fingertips and hesitate. "Is this going to hurt?"

An impatient sigh from behind the console. "There will be some mild discomfort, which most people get used to after a few minutes."

A few minutes? "How long will I be in here?"

"Half an hour. We really need to begin." The edge in his voice says he's done answering questions.

I put on the helmet and a thick metal band inside automatically tightens around my forehead, pressing into my skin. From within the contraption, a visor is lowered over my eyes.

"There will be flashes of bright light. You may prefer to close your eyes. Hold your arms outstretched while your feet are hip distance apart. Remain as still and quiet as possible for the next half hour. We will begin in ten seconds."

I use the time for a few quick fidgets and stretches, then reach my arms out like I'm Da Vinci's Vitruvian Man.

Another mechanical whir, then there's a flash of light brighter than anything I've ever experienced, so intense I have to keep from staggering backward. My eyelids clamp together involuntarily against the blazing assault. More flashes of light behind my closed eyes and I cry out as a series of needles emerge from the metal band encircling my head and prick my skin.

"Try to refrain from making any additional noises."

I press my lips together to contain a stream of profanity.

The next half hour is hardly excruciating, but "mild discomfort" definitely undersells the experience. Aside from the flashing lights, there's a persistent high-pitched metallic clang that makes the MRI machine sound like a lullaby, and the water grows increasingly hotter. At first, the warmth is pleasant, but by the end of the half hour, it feels like I'm being boiled alive. Even so, after that first shriek, I remain silent on the off chance that this is yet another twisted test.

"You may exit the tank. A towel and fresh gown are in the changing room to your left. Your final appointment is in gynecology, on the fourth floor."

Awesome. After a day of having my naked body poked and prodded and dunked in a water tank, I can't think of a better way to finish things out than having my lady parts examined.

It's dark out by the time I leave the medical facility, feeling like I've been sapped of blood, water, vitality, everything. The walk to the nearest dining hall should take only a few minutes, but it's like moving through cement, my feet barely able to lift off the ground and shuffle forward.

I finally make it to the cafeteria, but after I pile my plate high with food and make my way to the tables, I see no sign of Grace, which makes me want to cry.

I take a seat by a window, eat quickly, and return to Gale House.

In my mail cubby is my training schedule for next week, which looks much busier than the prior weeks. There's also a note from Grace. She met some people from Hansen House and they're having a small party tonight; she'll be going, and I should come, too. I check to see what's first on my schedule tomorrow: circuit training at 6:00 a.m. It's just past nine, and I'm bone-tired, but also lonely.

I take what I hope will be an invigorating shower. Instead, it drains me of what little energy I have left.

I just manage to set an alarm for the morning before I climb into bed and fall asleep with a towel still wrapped around my head.

CHAPTER ELEVEN

"Stop! Stop!" yells Lady Edna, switching off Cole Porter's "Anything Goes." "I thought you'd finally make it all the way through without being a total embarrassment, but I was wrong."

After two easy weeks at the Dollhouse Academy, the treadmill was turned up full tilt and this past week has been . . . relentless.

As Genevieve promised, every aspect of my physical and emotional self is being pushed to the limit.

The class stands in place, arms at our sides, waiting for the torrent of criticism, and I try not to flinch as it comes spewing forth.

"Shirley, you're supposed to be in sync, not an echo—you're still a second behind everyone. Dion, you look like a crazy windmill during the world's-gone-mad verse. Rein it in a little. And Ramona." She swivels to face me, and I bite my lip. "Dear god, your movements are so stiff, if you don't loosen up, I'm getting an oil can for you. And you need to work on your breath control. You're huffing and puffing over your singing like a fat little boy chasing an ice-cream truck. Everyone take five and then we'll try it again."

Lady Edna storms off, her dark waist-length braid swishing back and forth like the tail of an agitated horse. We don't know if "Lady Edna" is a nickname or if she's actual royalty, but anyone who neglects to address her as such is swiftly corrected. What we do know is that she's fifty-nine years old but still as flexible as she was at twenty—which she frequently points out during warmups—and that she favors giant cocktail rings and animal print tunics over leggings. We know she has a sweet tooth, but only for candy canes, which she indulges in year-round, frequently sucking one to a such a fine point during class, we could lose an eye if we piss her off. We also know that she was a Broadway dancer and worked with Bob Fosse and Gwen Verdon on several stage productions, and she could've had an affair with Fosse but turned down his multiple advances. And we know that our collective work as dancers is "barely adequate" on good days and "appalling" on bad days, with the bad days outnumbering the good.

I never considered myself more than a passable dancer and didn't expect to become one of Lady Edna's favorites, like Grace has (and rightfully so), but I didn't think this class would kick my ass so completely. It's rare that I make it through a session without being singled out for my ineptitude.

"Are we ready to go again? No? You don't want to be on the number one television show in the country? Funny, that's what I thought at least some of you were here for." Lady Edna rounds us up and motions for an assistant to cue the music.

In addition to being an instructor at the Dollhouse Academy, Lady Edna choreographs some of the big dance numbers for *In the Dollhouse*, including one for an upcoming episode revolving around a school production of *Anything Goes*. According to Lady Edna, it'll be one of the biggest and most ambitious musical numbers the show has done to date, and she's looking to cast any new students who can handle the choreography.

Most of us cannot.

But there's still a week to go before Lady Edna makes her final selection, and even though Grace is a shoo-in and I'm a long shot, it won't stop me from getting this routine down. I can't practice at Gale House (there's an unspoken rule about not filling the dorm with the clatter of tap shoes), but there are various rehearsal spaces on campus available to reserve, and Grace and I have spent many nights in them going over the "Anything Goes" routine.

In my nightmares, Cole Porter's words haunt me, the lyrics set to a metallic *rat-a-tat-tat* that sounds more like machine-gun fire than tap shoes.

Gone are the days when I had afternoons and evenings free. My new schedule is crammed from six in the morning to at least six at night. My course load has doubled, with additional classes after lunch (voice, speech, daily dance lessons, music theory, and cold reading, in which we learn to perform a scene with little to no advance preparation). While there was minimal homework assigned during my first two weeks here, now the instructors are piling it on. After dinner is for rehearsing monologues, practicing choreography, and doing assigned reading.

Every time I look at my schedule, I marvel at the sheer volume of activity. My muscles ache and my head throbs from all the new information I'm cramming into my brain, and at night in bed, it's hard to switch it off. My body is in shock from so much movement and so little sleep. I'm like a sponge, absorbing and absorbing, but also being wrung out over and over again.

The instructors are exacting, and while some still offer a bit of warmth and support, they all make it clear that the honeymoon period is over and shit's getting real.

Given my promising start, I thought I'd at least be able to excel in singing and acting, but now even that's a struggle. Geoff Shepley, previously so supportive, called my latest scene work "contrived" while my cold reading instructor found my monologue delivery "flat and dry." Meanwhile, a vocal coach has been on me for my "inconsistent tone" and "intonation and phrasing issues" due to my poor breath control, a problem Lady Edna seems to delight in pointing out. Meanwhile, when Genevieve stops by one of my classes, it only turns the screw on my nerves. I've gone from earning nods to looks of disdain.

I expected it to be strenuous, but I didn't expect to be corrected for the way I do every little thing: walk, talk, sing, dance, emote, even the way I hold my body when I don't move at all. At this point, I wouldn't be surprised if I was told I blink incorrectly. Sometimes it makes me feel like everything I learned about being a human is wrong and now I have to relearn it.

The biggest adjustment this past week has been feeling like nothing is my own anymore. My mind and body are being molded by the instructors. My time is being dictated by the Dollhouse. Despite Nicole not being around much, I don't even have the full privacy of my own room. And though I'm often surrounded by other people, there's little time to socialize. Grace and I share two classes, but our new schedules allow for only one or two meals a week together.

"I get what everyone's been warning us about now," I tell Grace at dinner in the middle of the fourth week. "This place is no joke. I still can't get over how insanely busy and competitive it's become. It's like we've been thrown into a showbiz Thunderdome—"

"Two trainees enter, one trainee leaves," Grace intones.

"Exactly." I impale a piece of roasted potato and hold my fork aloft. "The one thing that's helped me keep it together as a performer—and a person—is not comparing myself to anyone else. This place makes it impossible."

"Hey, so far we're keeping up with the rest of them."

"So far."

Aside from this tidal wave of stress, there are some bright spots. We've spent nearly a full month at the Dollhouse, which will qualify us to participate in Dahlen auditions, on top of which, many of the classes are full of potential opportunities. In addition to Lady Edna and the dance routine for *In the Dollhouse*, instructors are constantly scouting backup singers, dancers, and day players. And there are always Genevieve's pop-up visits. If someone shows real promise, there's no telling what kind of spotlight awaits them. I just need to keep pushing and honing my talents, which admittedly feel diminished right now. I don't know if it's the workload or the intimidation of all the gifted people around me, but instead of shining, I feel tarnished.

As if sensing my self-doubt, Grace goes on about how we can't let ourselves get intimidated, how we've been chosen for a reason, etc. It's the type of pep talk I'd normally be giving; being on the receiving end makes me wonder if it always sounds so hollow.

Grace and I return to the dorm to change into our dance clothes before meeting Dion in a rehearsal room. As we walk by our mail cubbies, a yellow sheet catches my eye.

On top of the classes, every few days a yellow note arrives in my mailbox, summoning me to the medical wing for more tests, taking up much of what precious little free time I have left. Sometimes it's a brief visit for more bloodwork; sometimes it's for tests involving physical activity while being hooked up to electrodes; one time it was a full Sunday—the one day we get off—for psych evaluations. Fortunately, I haven't had to face that awful water tank again, but I still dread it whenever a yellow memo turns up.

Except this one's not for me, it's for Grace, who has the mailbox below mine.

Snatching up the paper, she gives it a scan and groans. "Looks like we'll need to do our rehearsal another time."

"Tonight? Seriously?"

"I guess they must really *vant to suck my blood, ah-ah-ah.*"

"Are you trying to do Count Chocula or the Count from *Sesame Street*?" I hide my disappointment by teasing her.

"His name is Count von Count, Ramona. A little respect for puppet royalty, please."

"In which case, shouldn't you be counting things?"

Grace huffs but concedes. "*They vant to suck my blood one time, two times, three times this veek alone!*" Switching back to her normal voice, she adds, "Sorry I won't be able to go over those steps with you guys tonight. Alas, the Dollhouse needs their favorite pincushion."

I change into my dance clothes and head over to the rehearsal room, hoping Dion has a better handle on the routine than I do. A sheet of paper is pinned to the bulletin board:

R/G: Sorry but I can't make it. I got scouted for a show and the audition is tonight!—D

Wow, good for Dion. I take down the note, snuffing out the flash of jealousy that flares up in me.

I have no desire to rehearse on my own. So where to now?

Something tells me I may veer off course tonight.

CHAPTER TWELVE

A balmy evening breeze ruffles my hair as I walk across the campus, and antique gas lamps illuminate the old buildings and manicured lawns.

Since I unexpectedly have a few hours free now, a restlessness whips up in me.

I walk down Main Street, past the boutiques that sell nothing but black, white, and red clothing, past Chapter and Verse and all the other darkened storefronts. A handful of restaurants are still open, as is the Sterile Cuckoo (I question the thought process that went into naming a bar after a Liza Minnelli movie when she famously battled alcoholism). There are small clusters of people drinking and laughing on the front patio, and seeing them makes me feel suddenly homesick.

If I were back in the city, it's the kind of night Grace and I would've spent in the garden of an East Village pub, getting tipsy but not drunk, flirting with boys and maybe handing out a number or two. Or if we wanted to stay local, we'd walk down to the Italian ice place, two scoops of coconut for me, two scoops of cherry for Grace, and do a slow meander around the neighborhood, past the barbershop that never seemed to close, the Chinese take-out place with the best shrimp fried rice, the stationery store with two fat tabby cats roaming around, the diner with the cranky waiters, and the pharmacy that always smelled like baby powder.

I've been so preoccupied these last few weeks, I haven't had a chance to really miss New York City or my uncles until now.

Even though it's dark and I still don't know the expansive wooded areas of the campus—to say nothing of what lies beyond them—I can't resist the urge to explore farther. Unsure of how far I'll let my spontaneous wanderlust take me, I set off down the long quiet road that leads to the Dollhouse Academy's main gate.

The path is well-lit but free of vehicles and cuts through a forest, making it feel remote. Despite our assured safety on campus, I'm uneasy. What if the sender of those notes is stalking me? A rustle in the bushes makes me pause in my tracks. This could be the premise of a horror movie, in which case I'd be yelling at my cinematic counterpart to turn around and run home before something jumps out of the darkness. But just like my fictional misguided heroine, I continue forward.

I'm so caught up in my apprehension and curiosity, I don't notice the golf cart until I hear the screech of its brakes.

"What are you doing out here?"

It's Mason. He's clean-shaven and in a suit, hair gelled back. I hate how my breath quickens at seeing him.

"I'm taking a walk," I say.

"Alone? On a Sunday night? In tap shoes?" He motions for me to get in the cart. "Come on, I'll drive you back to your dorm."

"I don't want to go back to the dorm. Hence my being outside, walking around."

"Where do you want to go then?"

"Somewhere . . . else. Am I really not allowed past those front gates?" I'm not sure if I'm more uneasy at the idea of being trapped here or what might happen to me if I continued on alone.

"You can't leave without a special pass, which you definitely do not have . . . but even if you did, there's not much to see. The closest town to Owls Point is miles away and makes this place look like a thriving metropolis. You'd more likely get lost in the woods or run over or worse." He gives me a look that begs me to be reasonable. "Would you please get in? I can't take you off campus, but if you don't want to go back to the dorm, I can take you somewhere else."

"Where?"

"You'll never find out if you stand there pulling faces."

I get inside the golf cart.

"How much do you love that Tricky album? You bloody love it don't you?" he asks.

I bloody do, but I reply, "It's fine."

"I was right about 'Hell Is Round the Corner' wasn't I?"

"The song or my life at the Dollhouse?"

Mason flashes me a grin. "Exactly."

Instead of making a U-turn, he continues toward the gate, then veers down a side path that takes us through a wooded area of the campus I haven't seen before.

"So did Genevieve's Spidey sense tingle? Did she send you out to fetch me?" I ask.

"No, it was a nice night, so I decided to go for a drive. Having access to this"—he pats the cart's dashboard—"is one of the perks of the job."

"What exactly is your job?"

"I'm a PA."

"A production assistant?"

"Personal assistant. To Genevieve. Though not her only one."

"How many does she have?"

"Three."

"Do you all live with her?"

"Yes, in the staff quarters. One handles Dahlen matters, one handles Dollhouse matters, and then there's me."

"And what do you handle? Personal matters?" It's hard to keep the innuendo out of the question.

"Odds and ends." Mason keeps his eyes on the road. "There's always plenty to keep me busy." Is that annoyance in his voice?

"I'll bet there is."

"You can knock it off with the insinuations." Yep, definite annoyance. "I don't fuck Genevieve."

The unexpected candor jolts me. "I didn't say you did."

"Maybe if you weren't so quick to judge, you'd be showing more promise in your classes."

Yeah, that one stings. "How the hell do you know how I'm doing in my classes? Is snooping around in trainee files another one of your job perks?" Am I flattered that he was interested enough to snoop on me in particular?

"It hardly gives me pleasure to read about someone wasting our resources."

"Stop driving. I'm getting out."

"We're here anyway." Mason pulls into a small paved lot, parks the cart, and gets out before I do. He begins going down one path but points me to another. "Follow that and it'll eventually connect to Francine Road, which will take you back to your dorm."

My anger and curiosity duke it out, and the latter wins. "Wait. What is this place?"

"Parliament Lake. I like to come out here whenever I need to clear my head. They intentionally don't include it in the orientation so trainees can discover it for themselves. You looked like you could use a moment somewhere out of the way. But then you got all stroppy with me."

I weigh my options. Trudge back to the dorm on my own or hang out at a lake with an asshole.

"Okay, let's see this lake," I mutter.

A short path gives way to a pebble beach edged with willow trees. Low outdoor lights cast a hazy glow over the area.

"I try to make it out here every day, even if I can only spare a few minutes," Mason says. "Puts my mind right."

There's a large log a few feet from the water, which is where he chooses to sit. After some hesitation, I sit beside him, and he takes a flask from the inside pocket of his jacket, offering it to me.

I unscrew the top of the flask and whiff the contents. "Whiskey?"

"Johnnie Walker."

"Red or Black?"

"Blue. Does it matter?"

"Nope." I take a swig, the liquid tracing a delicious burn down my throat, leaving a smoky aftertaste.

"I'm going to tell you a couple of important things now." Mason takes the flask back and nips from it. "First of all, you don't chug high-end whiskey, you sip it. Second of all, when someone tells you the truth, don't get mad at them. The more you do that, the more likely they'll start lying to you."

This time when I hold the flask, I take a dainty sip and taste flavors I hadn't noticed: honey, orange, and ginger. When I hand it back, our fingers brush.

"So are you a failed actor?" I stare at the lake ahead of us, a full moon cutting a slice through the still, navy water.

"Indeed I am." His voice is matter-of-fact. "As 'damn sexy' as my British accent is, not being able to master an American accent limited my roles at Dahlen."

"Why did you stay here? Why not try your luck in NYC or LA?"

"I knew I didn't have that *thing*, that x-factor and the dogged tenacity you need if you have any chance of making it. But I really loved Dahlen's movies and shows—even if the music's a bit bland—and I wanted to stay on and make some sort of contribution. Being Genevieve's assistant, I get to see so many sides of the business, and I haven't been able to narrow my focus to one thing, like producing or marketing. It's been seven years and I don't know if it should bother me that I haven't figured out my next move." He tips back the flask and passes it to me.

"Do you think I have that *thing*?" I brave a look at him, my hand tightening around the flask.

He leans in, searching my face, taking the question seriously. "I think you're lovely to look at, and you have the x-factor, but your dedication to the Dahlen vision is still in question. As is your tenacity. You may be too fragile for this place."

What a bittersweet response, a compliment with a threat hidden inside, like the apples with razor blades they warn kids about every Halloween.

"I'm not fragile." But the words come out in a ragged whisper. I drain what's left in the flask. The whiskey warms my belly but the rest of me is cold. "Can we go back now?"

I say nothing on the drive other than a quick thanks when we reach Gale House. It isn't until I'm inside and see the familiar white envelope in my mailbox that I realize I'm still holding Mason's flask.

CHAPTER THIRTEEN

Ivy's Diary

APRIL 20, 1998

This is around when the trainees start struggling. I can always spot the new ones by the way they don't hide their awe when I pass them on campus, and by the way that awe is quickly subsumed by strain. Of course, their desperation to make their dreams come true will keep many here for some time yet. They don't know how easy it is to become trapped by your desires. To lose yourself.

It's hard to describe what it's like to have your identity stolen from you. Especially when that identity is familiar to millions of people around the world. It's like simultaneously being kidnapped and dying. The you that's left behind is empty, a shell, going through the motions. You become familiar to strangers while slowly becoming a stranger to yourself.

It could also be argued that the Dollhouse didn't steal me away from myself, but only took what I gave them of my own volition. Maybe I started giving myself away years before I even entered the Dollhouse.

After I became the Double Dippers girl and got a few other commercials, my mother and I took our first trip out to Los Angeles, where I quickly got an agent. For the next couple of years, she and I flew back and forth during summers and other school breaks to go on auditions. Despite all the hours I spent on airplanes, my fear of flying didn't improve. If anything, it got worse. It may have eclipsed my genuine feelings about acting for a while, because after the trauma of air travel, reciting lines in front of a camera was far less painful. Anything was better than flying. Getting my eye poked with a mascara wand by a careless makeup person. Being moved around sets like I was a piece of furniture. Having an adult costar scream in my face because she was going through a divorce and I kept missing my mark. Being called "sexy" by a male director while shooting a scene in a swimming pool when I was eleven. All of these things were preferable to getting on a plane.

Eventually, I told my parents I'd quit acting if I had to take so many flights.

My father, who'd just purchased a new car with the money I'd received from a Barbie commercial, and my mother, who'd developed a taste for Pucci dresses and Missoni knitwear, were quick to protest. Aunt Janet, who was living comfortably off her late husband's estate, said if I wanted to stop flying, I should stay put in Miami.

But my parents didn't listen to Aunt Janet, and they didn't hear what I was really trying to say: I not only wanted to stop flying, I wanted to stop acting. Instead, they heard me say I wanted to move somewhere I could pursue acting more seriously.

So we picked up and moved from Miami to Los Angeles a couple months shy of my thirteenth birthday.

My father decided to take a break from being an X-ray technician and try his hand at entrepreneurship. My mother remained at my side, now more focused than ever on my burgeoning stardom.

According to child labor laws, if you're under fourteen years old, there are only three ways you can work legally. You can have a paper route. You can work in a family-owned business. Or you can be a child actor, taking part in productions that can cost millions of dollars, in which you must shoulder adult responsibilities and pressures. What a preposterous loophole this is.

And if you're one of the rare child actors who finds continued success, you might have the added burden of being a key source of income for your family.

Before long, I became the sole breadwinner. That put a different kind of pressure on me. Whether or not I liked acting, now I needed to keep doing it. I was paying our family's rent before I got my first training bra.

While I was ambivalent about performing, it came easily to me, and I was good at it. When we first got to LA, my agent told me it was an advantage that I was petite and looked younger than my age, because I'd be able to go out for little kid roles, but I should expect to go on dozens of auditions before landing a decent part. It took me only ten. I got cast in *Sharp Teeth, Pretty Teeth*, a horror movie, with fourth billing. The director was Italian, making his American debut. I played a nosy little girl who suspected her next-door neighbors were vampires. Despite reassurances from my parents, agent, and other actors that not looking my age was "a good thing" for my career, it bothered me that I was entering my teen years and still playing a child. Of course, my protests were mild, and I quickly booked several more parts as a young girl.

I was usually the only kid on set, and more often than not, the adults were decent to me, at a bare minimum polite. But there were some who regarded me as a nuisance. I tried not to get offended whenever somebody on set cracked the "don't work with animals or children" adage, but what was that supposed to mean? That I was so wild and difficult to work with? That I was a thing to be managed?

The ironic thing about the business was that even though I was cast to play roles younger than my true age, I was expected to behave like an adult. I was rewarded for being on time, knowing my lines, standing in the right place. After a long day of shooting, a director once said, "What a tough little girl you are, not complaining once. And you don't even look tired." I began to equate being compliant with being a good person.

How much of my childhood did I sacrifice during that time? I was often told I was wise beyond my years, but sometimes I wish I'd had the luxury of being foolish.

Sharp Teeth, Pretty Teeth came out in 1977 and was a modest hit. It didn't make me a superstar, but I got recognized a lot more when I was out and about, which I wasn't entirely comfortable with. I've never gotten used to strangers acting like they know me intimately because they've seen me pretend to be someone else on a screen.

My newfound fame didn't only get me attention from strangers, but also from industry professionals, who sent over scripts with characters calling for a cute and clever young girl.

At this point, I was earning enough from my acting work that we were able to buy a house in Los Feliz, an old LA neighborhood in the hills. There were a lot of fitness-oriented businesses opening up at the time, and my father tried to jump on the trend. Over the next several years, he'd alternately own a bike shop, a martial arts dojo, and an aerobics studio, all of which he ran into the ground. Mom once said he was the opposite of Midas: "everything he touches turns to shit." In the meantime, he needed more money to fuel those failures, just as my mother needed more to decorate our big new house and fill her big new closets.

Fortunately, I soon booked a role as a series regular on *Fish Out of Water*, a second-rate sitcom about a family of Martians who move to San Francisco and try to pass as human.

When the first season wrapped, there was a party at a hotel in West Hollywood. My mother was off schmoozing, and I was standing around with a glass of champagne, trying not to feel awkward, when cool fingers encircled my arm.

"Ivy Gordon, my dear, you are quite a talent." The woman was tiny and impeccably groomed, her dark bob threaded with silver, the panes of her eyeglasses reflecting a light I mistook for warmth in the large brown eyes behind them. "My name is Genevieve Spalding and I have a serious proposition I'd like to discuss with you. It may very well propel you to the heights of stardom."

I told her I didn't want to be a star, politely detaching myself from her grasp.

"If it isn't stardom you want, what is it?" she asked. "Why don't we find a quiet corner so you can tell me."

The two of us stepped out onto an empty balcony. I searched for the right words and finally told her I wanted something I couldn't get back.

She smiled sadly. "I'm afraid I can't return your childhood or innocence to you. Barring that, how about a proper education and late adolescence spent among your peers? I run a boarding school in upstate New York alongside a television and film studio. You're obviously bright and a talented performer. Come to the Dahlen Academy and find out exactly what it is you want to be." She produced an ivory business card from the breast pocket of her Chanel suit and pressed it into my palm.

I told her I was on a hit show and it wouldn't make sense to leave now. Besides, my parents didn't want me to go to school, they wanted me to work. Yet the thought of moving east to a more academic environment made me feel electrified. I gazed down at the cars darting across the Sunset Strip, each one zipping by with such purpose and freedom.

"*Fish Out of Water* is a moderate hit, but it won't stay that way. The writing is flat, and the premise won't hold past a second season. Forget about what your parents expect of you. If you're mature enough to support your family, you're mature enough to leave them and support yourself. You're what—fifteen? You can get legally emancipated."

I knew all about that from one of my costars, a fifteen-year-old who planned on getting emancipated as soon as our season two contracts for *Fish Out of Water* were negotiated and she got a place of her own. This way, she wouldn't need a guardian on set and could work longer hours, which would make her more appealing to casting directors. How marvelous it must be to love your job so much, you willingly signed up for more hours. That side of legal emancipation held little appeal for me. What did entice me was being granted personal autonomy.

Whether I stayed with this show or moved east or did something else entirely, the thought of having control over my life's direction was more intoxicating than the champagne I was anxiously gulping.

I told Genevieve I'd think things over and went searching for my mother. I found her on a different balcony, in the arms of an assistant director. Before either could spot me, I slipped back out.

This was my wake-up call.

My parents kept pressuring me to sign on for a second season of *Fish Out of Water* and I told them I'd only do so if they consented to my getting emancipated. At first, they balked at the idea. I said I wanted them to continue to manage my finances and career, I just didn't want my work schedule to be hampered by child labor laws. This convinced them. They offered their consent, which speeded up the legal process. A few months later, in the spring of 1980, the day after my sixteenth birthday, a judge accepted my petition, and I was legally emancipated. That same day, my parents told me they were separating.

As soon as I was an adult in the eyes of the law, I finally took my life into my own hands. I turned down the second season of *Fish Out of Water*. Then I called Genevieve Spalding and told her I'd like to attend the Dahlen Academy.

Despite their separation, my parents presented a unified front in their attempts to convince me to stay in LA and continue acting. They were appalled by what they saw as me "demolishing my career." But not as appalled as I was when I found out how much was in my Coogan Account. Based on the Coogan Law, which was named after child actor Jackie Coogan, whose parents robbed him of every penny he made, 15 percent of all a young actor's earnings are required to be put into a blocked trust until that child reaches maturity. I barely thought about my Coogan Account until I was emancipated and granted access to the money. There was less than five thousand dollars remaining. Apparently, my mother had been paying herself a hefty manager's salary out of my earnings and my father found other loopholes that allowed him to steal my money to fund his business schemes.

Add it to the stack of betrayals. I fumed for days, threatening to take them to court, but then we received a call from Florida. Aunt Janet had died after a brief but pervasive battle with pancreatic cancer. After the funeral, I ultimately decided I would not pursue legal action, though I told my parents I wanted nothing more to do with either of them ever again. Now that Aunt Janet was gone, I felt like I had no real family left. All I wanted was to get far away.

I had enough money to get me to Owls Point, New York, which was all that mattered. Dahlen Academy would be my perfect escape. I dreamed of spending hours poring over books in ivy-covered buildings. Forget on-set tutors and learning in short increments. Education was such a low priority in Hollywood that sometimes I got the feeling they preferred us stupid as long as we hit our marks and said our lines correctly. Dahlen Academy would be different. I'd finally have the opportunity to study with my peers, be around more people my age.

The irony of it all is so rich, I can't help but laugh now.

Here I was, a young girl, finally unshackled from her parents and the industry's demands, moving to the other side of the country, determined to embrace my freedom and assert my hard-won autonomy.

Yet the first major step I took in securing my independence would ultimately rob me of it.

I moved to Owls Point, New York, in the summer of 1980.

Prior to my accepting Genevieve's invitation, I stressed how important it was for me to continue my education. She promised I'd be assigned a curriculum tailored to my needs and interests and assured me that I'd adore the collegiate atmosphere of Dahlen Academy. I was given a full load of academic classes, which I took in the mornings: Classic Literature, Intro to Sociology, Eastern Religions, and a class that straddled the line between science and philosophy called Interpretations of Time. In the afternoons, I had various dance, singing, and acting classes.

Much as I appreciated the knowledge I cultivated in my morning classes, I absolutely adored my afternoon classes. Perhaps because those were the areas in which I showed the most natural ability. It was easy for me to pick up choreography, learn accents, and memorize lines. I could cold read a scene and instantly get a sense of my character's internal and external goals or perform a well-known monologue and find new layers and nuances within the text. I was a mezzo-soprano with perfect pitch and a three-and-a-half octave range, comfortable adapting my voice to a variety of musical styles. But more than that, I fell in love with drama. I had never analyzed scenes and characters in such depth before or studied such sophisticated material, whether classic texts or contemporary Dahlen scripts. My passion for performing was there, it had just never been nurtured properly until then.

When I had been at the Dollhouse exactly one month, I was assigned a counselor who encouraged me to talk about my life, the happy times as well as the hardships. I thought you had to be crazy to see a headshrinker, but my sessions with this woman made me see otherwise. She helped me understand that the tragedies in my life had shaped me into the strong young woman I was. When she expressed support of my decision to focus on academics, I told her I'd be open to auditioning for some Dahlen projects, provided they were of the same quality as the scripts I'd read and that I'd have the final say over which roles I accepted. Neither one of those conditions was an issue, so I went on a handful of auditions, invigorated by the idea of playing more mature and multifaceted characters. I booked supporting roles in two movies, a teenage romantic comedy and a lighthearted coming-of-age story about camp counselors. The scripts were well written, and both productions were a joy to work on. I felt like I was finally carving my own path, steering my career in the direction I chose. How exhilarating, to command full agency over my life. In the process, I found I didn't miss my academic work falling to the wayside as much as I thought I would.

When I had been at the Dollhouse for a full year, Genevieve summoned me for tea.

We met in her Victorian mansion, in what she called her "owl room," a cozy chamber with small round windows, antique furniture, and black velvet flocked wallpaper festooned with dozens of portraits of owls in gilt frames. The resulting effect was lovely but eerie, like being watched from every side of the room.

A handsome young man served us tea at a small table set with fine china and a tiered tray of finger sandwiches and pastries. I was struck by how immaculately tailored Genevieve's suit was to her petite frame and how perfectly it matched her red lipstick, which didn't leave a mark on her teacup when she drank from it.

"How has your first year at Dahlen Academy served you?" she asked.

I told her I was enjoying the dramatic aspect more than I expected, how the curriculum was rigorous and informative, the instructors knowledgeable and exacting, though not unfairly so, and the other trainees proficient and bright.

"Ah, but you are the brightest," Genevieve said. "Others spend years gaining mastery of certain skills that come so naturally to you. I can understand why you wanted to expand your education. You must have been so bored in your previous career. And no wonder. The roles you took back then barely scratched the surface of what you are capable of achieving as a performer."

I had never considered my boredom and frustration with the industry was rooted in not taking on work that was challenging enough.

As if hearing my thoughts, Genevieve said, "You have yet to find a role that is truly worthy of your abilities. I believe Dahlen Entertainment can rise to the challenge. We are currently developing a series called *In the Dollhouse*, which we believe will be groundbreaking. It's set in a boarding school in upstate New York—not unlike this one. The creators took 'write what you know' a bit *too* much to heart, but there's no denying this show is something special. I think you'd be perfect for the lead role of Tabitha Noelle. I'll have the sides sent to your dormitory, but I'd also like you to read the first episode's full script." She produced a bound script and set it between us on the table. "I think you'll agree that it's extraordinary. The protagonist, Tabitha, dreams in musicals, so every episode will feature at least one big song-and-dance number. Given the glowing reports from your instructors, I'm surprised you never pursued a career in musical theater. Had you grown up in New York instead of Los Angeles, perhaps you would have."

Or had I been raised by parents who wanted me to fully develop all my talents and interests, instead of being greedy and throwing me toward the biggest paychecks.

"We have the rest of the show cast but have yet to find our Tabitha Noelle. I think you could be her. In fact, I'm going to have you bypass the initial auditions and move straight to the chemistry read with our male lead, a promising young actor named Timothy Boyd."

"I love Timothy!" I went bright red. "I mean, I love his work. We did an ice-cream commercial together years ago."

"Marvelous. He's been shooting films for us on location in Europe and Asia, but he's eager to settle down stateside. I'll be curious to see how the two of you play off of each other now. There's one more thing," Genevieve said. "Once in a rare while, when I see a trainee with tremendous potential, I offer myself as a personal mentor. It has been years since I've come across someone as naturally charismatic as yourself, and I'd love to help shape your career. However, that would mean committing yourself fully to the performing arts and eventually dropping your academic coursework. I can only extend my offer of mentorship—and this possible role on *In the Dollhouse*—if that's a commitment you would be willing to make. Of course, I also want you to make the most informed decision, so take this script, read it over, and think about everything we discussed today."

After our meeting, I went to the library with the script tucked under my arm and thought about Genevieve's proposal. Could I fully commit to being a performer? I loved learning across multiple subjects, stretching myself in so many directions . . . though I had to admit I was beginning to stretch myself a bit too thin. Weariness was seeping into my bones from all the late hours I spent reading to keep up with my academic courses. This left me with little time to read for pleasure, an activity I sorely missed, though one I could resume if I dropped my coursework and ended up on this show, since I'd have enough downtime on set. Of course, that wasn't a strong enough reason to abandon my education. I had to choose being a performer above all else. It seemed too soon to make such a big decision. Perhaps there was a way I could buy myself more time. Surely other good roles would come along if I turned this one down.

In the library, I found a quiet corner and opened the script. I devoured the pages in half an hour and then read through the entire thing again, this time more slowly and purposefully.

It was the best script I'd ever read. There was so much nuance, detail, observation, and insight about the Dollhouse Academy's students and staff, as well as the other residents of Otus, New York, the eccentric town they all inhabited. It was like turning a magic trick over in my mind, unsolvable and dazzling. How had the writers been able to convey so much in so few pages? It was nothing short of astonishing, the way they painted a detailed portrait of this fictional town, this school, and at the heart of it, two teenagers, Tabitha Noelle and Hayden Close, navigating adolescence, parental expectations, and different class systems. Tabitha wasn't a precocious little girl who liked ice cream or a precocious preteen with vampire neighbors or a precocious Martian teenager. Tabitha Noelle was a fully realized human being, one who I desperately wanted to inhabit on-screen.

I was only seventeen but not so naive as to believe another role like this would come along anytime soon. I not only wanted to be Tabitha Noelle, I also felt in my very bones that it was my destiny to play her.

This certainty was only magnified when I showed up for the chemistry read a few days later and set eyes on Timothy Boyd. His formerly blond hair had been darkened to a chestnut brown, which made his blue eyes even more pronounced and piercing. The roundness of his face had given way to a square jaw and chiseled cheekbones. Now eighteen, he had become a breathtaking young man.

I always found it silly whenever girls would say a boy took their breath away, but Timothy had that effect on me.

A casting assistant introduced us, but Timothy remembered who I was and wrapped me in a hug.

"This'll be way better than eating ice cream," he murmured in my ear.

When actors do a chemistry read, it's not necessarily to see if they have a romantic spark. It's to see how actors interact, connect, and complement each other, visually, temperamentally, and otherwise. The relationship between Tabitha and Hayden would start out antagonistically, evolve into friendship, and eventually become romantic, so our chemistry needed to work on multiple levels.

When Timothy and I did our scenes together, the rest of the room melted away. I had never felt so fully present in the company of a single individual, and so lost in a scene.

We read three different scenes together several times. After we finished, everyone at the casting table looked stunned. When I glanced toward the corner where Genevieve stood, she nodded at me.

Outside, Timothy suggested we get some burgers to go.

"I know a quiet place," he said and led the way to a brick cottage nestled at the edge of the woods near a Tudor mansion. "It used to be servants' quarters but was left off the campus maps, so not a lot of people know about it." The only furniture in the house was a dusty old cot, a nightstand bearing an oil lamp, and a wooden table with picnic-style benches.

Timothy sat beside me instead of across from me, which made me too nervous to eat. We spent the next several hours talking and ignoring our food. It turns out our ice-cream commercial was memorable for him as well, and he'd been following my acting career just as I'd been following his.

"Are you ready for your life to change?" Timothy asked. "Whatever little fame or success we've had up to now won't compare to what's coming next."

"You don't know for sure that I'll get the part."

"I do know. And you know it, too."

He was right. I did know.

"This is your last chance."

"For what?" I asked.

"For a normal life."

"I never wanted a normal life."

"Good. Me neither."

And with that, he leaned over and kissed me.

I had been kissed before, but never like this, where the earth felt like it split apart and swallowed me, where I was both plunged in darkness and bathed in bright light, simultaneously plummeting and ascending.

The next day, I called Genevieve and told her I would quit my academic classes.

"You'll need to quit all your classes. You'll be too busy being Tabitha Noelle."

I would, in fact, be so busy being Tabitha Noelle, I'd forget what it was like to be Ivy Gordon. Even today, I have trouble remembering.

When I accepted the role on *In the Dollhouse*, I felt like I was being given the greatest gift, the role of a lifetime. It all comes at a cost, though. The price for Tabitha wasn't only giving up my normal life, my privacy, my very identity. Sooner or later, it would also cost me the only man I'd love with all my heart.

When I look back on that moment in the cottage, I wish I could take it back.

I wish I could convince Timothy a normal life would be just fine.

CHAPTER FOURTEEN

Usually, Grace can deduce when I have a crush, sometimes before I even know it myself. That's why it's surprising that in the days following my encounter with Mason, she doesn't pick up on it. Maybe it's for the best. Despite my attraction, I don't know what to think of him, and I don't want Grace's opinions shading my own before they have a chance to fully form. It's probably better to put Mason out of my head.

Still, a heavy uneasiness builds inside of me. I'm too full of secrets. It feels unnatural keeping so much from my best friend. If I can't tell Grace about Mason, I need to tell her about the notes.

It's tough to find a gap in our schedules but we finally do, grabbing coffees during a shared stretch of time between classes (I've had yet another one added to my schedule, something called Breaking Down Barriers). I lead us to a quiet gazebo.

"Did you hear Yachi went home?" Grace asked.

"I didn't. What happened?"

"Nobody's sure if it was a family thing or if she lost her shit. Apparently, she was sobbing as she left."

"Didn't somebody else drop out last week?"

"Yep. This place is no joke. But it's not all bad. Dion booked a three-episode arc on *Overruled*."

I feel a bittersweet twinge. "Holy crap, that's amazing. Isn't it, like, impossible, to book something so fast?"

"Not *impossible*, just not typical." Grace squirms in her seat. "So what's up?"

"There's something I need to show you." I sit on the weathered bench, set my drink down, and pull the cards out of my messenger bag. "But before I do, I need you to not give me a hard time about why I didn't show you sooner. It's not that I didn't trust you, it's that I didn't want to burden you."

"But you decided to burden me now? When we're both under this much stress?" She takes the cards with a wry smile. "Gotta love your timing, Ramona."

I blink away the mild sting of her comment. "It's more that I wanted to get your take on this, see if you think I'm worrying over nothing."

"All right then."

It only takes a few seconds to read the notes, but she takes longer poring over them.

The first two left me uneasy, but it was the third one that triggered real fear:

You can't trust anybody here.

Eventually, Grace looks up at me, her mouth scrunched to one side, her expression inscrutable.

A pause before she speaks. "I can't believe you didn't show me these sooner. That's pretty fucking lame."

"I thought you weren't going to give me a hard time about that."

"Since when do we keep secrets from each other?"

The hurt on her face makes my insides crumple. Grace is the closest thing I have to a sister. In grade school, when I wanted to dress up as Cyndi Lauper for Halloween, she spent two full days helping me make a skirt out of newspaper, meticulously cutting and gluing scraps from the

New York Post. In high school, when I earned the nickname "Zitler" during a particularly unfortunate acne breakout under my nose, Grace accosted anybody who dared to use it and drew a mustache with permanent marker on them, until everyone stopped. And just last year, when I got dumped a few days before Valentine's Day, Grace canceled the romantic dinner she had planned with the guy she'd been dating, brought home a sausage and olive pizza (my favorite), and spent that Friday night with me watching the first three *Nightmare on Elm Street* movies. "Pretend it's him," she said whenever Freddy slashed up a victim in a particularly gruesome way.

Grace may not be the most emotionally effusive person, but she always shows up for me. Why have I been shutting her out?

"I don't know, I guess the whole idea of being in the Dollhouse and then *actually* being here has been messing with my head," I say. "But you're right, we shouldn't keep secrets from each other. I'm sorry. I owe you a rose and gummy bears." This is how we offer each other a little pick-me-up and, in the semirare cases we get into a fight, how we say we're sorry. (She gets me a sunflower and Skittles.)

"It's fine, I'm off sugar right now anyway." She smirks. "We're good."

The tense breath I let out is audible. "In which case, you *need* to tell me what you think of these." I gesture to the cards between us.

"Obviously somebody is trying to fuck with you. Maybe one of the trainees? Someone who saw you on *AM/USA* and felt threatened?" Grace takes a long sip of coffee. A soft breeze makes her hair ripple as if it's under water. "Or who knows, maybe it's one of the older stars trying to scare off the new talent. Though that seems less likely."

"Why single me out, though? And why be so vague and use such perfect penmanship? If they wanted to freak me out, they could've done letters cut out of magazines or a scary serial killer–looking scrawl." A final glance at the notes and I tuck them into the back pocket of my messenger bag. "Do you think it might be one of the weird ways the Dollhouse tests us?"

"Could be . . . but I don't think it's a serious threat or anything. More likely someone being jealous and petty." Grace nibbles on her lower lip, which she only does when something is nagging at her.

"What's wrong? What aren't you telling me?" Dread tickles the back of my neck.

"So . . . um . . ." Grace fidgets, traces a wavy pattern along the gazebo's railing. "Lady Edna won't officially announce it until tomorrow, but she told me a few days ago that I'll be in the dream sequence."

"Oh wow, that's awesome! I knew you'd get it." I want to be thrilled for her except . . . "Why didn't you tell me sooner? What happened to not keeping secrets from each other?"

"I know, I'm a hypocrite, and I owe you Skittles and a sunflower. But I didn't say anything because I know you've been struggling. I didn't want to rub it in."

"Yeah, but we both know you're a great dancer and I'm mediocre on my best day. Acting is more my thing."

"Right, well that's the thing." Grace stares at her Mary Janes and turns her toes inward. "When Lady Edna told me I'd be in the dance number, she also said she thought I'd be good for a small speaking role in that episode. So I did a chemistry read with Ivy and I got the part. I'm going to be on ITD." When she looks up, her face is bright with awe.

"Oh my god." Tears prick my eyes and something sharp twists inside me. Not only did she get to meet my idol before I did, but she'll also get to work with her. "Grace, congratulations. That's so great." No wonder I'm not making any strides at the Dollhouse. I can't even pretend I'm genuinely happy for my best friend. "Do you think this means Genevieve will choose to mentor you?" The look on her face tells me she's already been chosen. I can't keep the wobble out of my voice as I say, "Holy shit, you're on a hot streak. Wow."

"I know it hasn't been easy for you, so I kinda feel bad."

"No, no, please don't feel bad. Forget about my bullshit. If roles were reversed, I'm sure you'd be happy for me."

She raises an eyebrow. "Don't be so sure. If all this happened to you, I wouldn't be surprised, but I'd still want to kill myself. We know you're the nicer one."

I turn away. I don't feel like the nicer one. "Look, I need to get to whatever this new Breaking Down Barriers class is, but tell me more about it later? Maybe at dinner?"

"Yeah, of course," she says as we stand. "Forget about the notes. I think somebody is trying to psych you out, and it's working. Don't let this creep get the better of you."

The notes are suddenly the last thing on my mind. I'm still reeling from Grace's news. "You're right. They're not important. What *is* important is how much you're kicking ass. This could be your big break. There's a reason you're getting mentored by the great Genevieve." I hate how hard it is to keep my bitterness in check.

Grace waves a dismissive hand. "Eh, I'm sure I'll do something to fuck it up and get fired on my first day . . . And I'll find some way or other to disappoint Genevieve." She gives a bashful shrug. "But who knows what might come of all this, right?"

"Right. And you won't fuck it up. I'll do a character breakdown with you, run lines, make Epsom salt baths for you after rehearsals, whatever you need." I swallow down the lump in my throat.

"You're the best, Ramona."

At the corner, she gives me another hug as we head off in separate directions.

CHAPTER FIFTEEN

After the conversation with Grace, I don't want to go to my next class. I'm queasy with disappointment, both at her news and my reaction to it, and I want to go hide under a blanket and cry. This is a new low for me, experiencing such ugly feelings toward my best friend. I've never been jealous of Grace before.

She's never given you a reason to be jealous before.

I shake off the hideous thought.

Breaking Down Barriers is held in a massive stone Tudor house, on the second floor. The room looks like a dance studio, with one wall entirely mirrored, though instead of bare wood, the floor is covered in gym mats. Folding chairs are piled up in one corner, but the other fifteen or so trainees already here have chosen not to make use of them. Instead, they've spread themselves out all over the room, some sprawling fully on the mats, some sitting cross-legged. A few are reading, one girl is meditating, another is doing crunches, and a guy near her looks like he's napping.

Great. This is probably a wacky movement or dance class, no doubt yet another thing I will suck at.

Barely anyone glances at me when I enter the room. I select a spot near the door that'll give me a decent bubble of personal space and a quick getaway if things go sideways.

A fortysomething woman comes in, closing the door behind her. She has deep-set eyes like raisins pressed into cookie dough and is wearing black stirrup leggings and a bulky white fisherman's sweater.

"Good afternoon, everybody," she says in a booming voice with a hint of a rasp. "I'm Sofia Stenning and this is Breaking Down Barriers. The first thing I'd like you all to do is stand and form a semicircle facing away from the mirror." She waits while we get to our feet. "Good." Sofia runs a hand through her short curly hair, tilting her head as if expecting it to be much longer. "Now let's go around the room and introduce ourselves."

Once that's done, she begins her spiel. "So, if you're here, it's because one or more of your instructors felt like you could use a bit of help getting in touch with your physicality and vulnerability, or what I like to call your inner rawness. One of the keys to being a good performer is to make your material personal. Whether a song, a dance, or a scene, there needs to be genuine emotion underpinning it. In your case, something is holding you back. Some barrier. We're going to find a way to break down those barriers."

The polite smile I was holding slides off my face, and I notice others around me looking solemn and uncomfortable; a few are downright pissed off.

So we're all here because we've been found lacking. This is some kind of remedial class. As Sofia blathers on about how we shouldn't be bothered that we're in need of such a course, and how this in no way reflects our level of talent, my hands slowly tighten to fists at my sides. This is the last thing I need right now.

"The Dollhouse Academy is a challenging place, and every day you make it through, you should applaud yourself," she says, twisting a silver band around her thumb. "Now, this class will have its own set of challenges, which I hope you'll embrace as an opportunity to learn and improve. I'll be asking you to move beyond your comfort zone in various ways, starting right now." She crosses her arms over her hips and in one swift movement removes her sweater and tosses it aside. Then she slides her thumbs into the waistband of her leggings and wriggles out of them. She stands in a beige T-shirt bra and bikini brief underwear, her ample belly and upper arms threaded with stretch marks, her thighs dimpled with cellulite. Shoulders back, head held high, she regards us with the confidence of a supermodel. "Being vulnerable means revealing yourself. We're going to begin by revealing ourselves in the most literal way possible. I'd like you all to strip down to your underwear." When none of us makes a move, she adds, "Now. Please."

To my surprise, everyone around me begins taking off their shoes, then removing layers of clothing. Is this really happening?

I'm the only one not getting undressed.

As she surveys the room, Sofia's gaze lands on me. "I know this'll be difficult for some of you, but this industry requires you to be in touch with your bodies. It's not about showing off or assessing whether we adhere to a certain standard of beauty. It's about being comfortable in your skin. Maybe some of you will find it easier to bare your souls than your bodies, but in this class, we'll be doing both."

I still don't move. My hands remain clenched into fists, nails now digging into my palms.

A moment later, Sofia comes over to me, speaking in a low voice. "Ramona, I really need you to complete this exercise. Otherwise, I'll have to ask you to leave."

I think about that woman in the elevator the day I got all those medical exams. This is one of those moments where I need to decide how much of myself I'm going to give.

The thing is, I'm comfortable with my body. When I tried to stand up for myself about getting into the water tank, I wasn't uneasy about taking my clothes off, I just didn't want to be naked at that moment.

That's how I feel now. Not shy or squeamish about my bare body, but protective of it. And even though I'm only being asked to strip down to my underwear, even though it wouldn't take much to make myself do it, it's still more than I can show of myself right now.

"Ramona, this is the last—"

"No, I get it," I interrupt, grabbing my bag.

Before she can say anything else, I leave.

If I go back to Gale House now, I'll spend the rest of the day crying, so I try to shake it off by walking around campus.

As if guided by some masochistic inner compass, I end up across the street from Genevieve's house. Though she's nowhere in sight, who should be coming out of the front gates but Mason.

It's annoying how my heart starts pounding out a big drum solo in my ears the second I spot him. Shut up, stupid heart.

My first instinct is to turn around and put as much distance as possible between us. Instead, I walk right toward him.

"Hello, Ramona."

"Hi, Mason." I face him like we're squaring off in a boxing ring. "You were right, okay? About the Tricky album, about my life becoming hellish, and probably other things."

"You being too fragile for this place?"

"No, fuck you. Not that."

A sardonic smile flickers across his face. "Just trying to be helpful."

"If you want to be helpful, tell me where I can go to scream my head off without anyone hearing me."

Mason scratches his chin, which bears a fresh coat of stubble. A quick glance at his watch, then at me, and he says, "If you're serious, I can take you there myself. It's a five-minute walk."

"Fine." Seeing as he's trying to help me, I ease up on the bitchiness. "Thanks."

We start walking. "Does this need to make like an Edvard Munch painting have anything to do with Genevieve mentoring your friend?" he asks.

"That's part of it."

"It may be better for you not to have this mentorship. While Genevieve can fast-track you to success, her close scrutiny can be unbearable. I couldn't bear it."

I give him a sidelong glance. He's less irritating when he opens up. "What was it like? What was she like?"

"At first, it's exciting. You meet for tea every week and she tells you what a big star you're going to be and what you need to do to get there, and you go along with it. But then you start to let her down in all these small ways, because her standards are so exacting, and then you start to let her down in bigger ways—"

"Like not being able to do an American accent?"

"Not being able to do *any* accents, not being able to sing or dance or do comedy—Genevieve scouted me when I was the lead in a touring production of *Hamlet* that was about as hilarious as a heart attack."

We turn a corner and walk along a park, empty except for one middle-aged man flying a kite, grinning up at the sky. Must be nice.

"For what it's worth, I suck at Shakespeare," I say. "So if Genevieve is so demanding and impossible, and if you failed as a trainee, why stay on and work for her all these years?"

"She's demanding, but she's not impossible. She has a good sense of what people want and what they need, and she could see I wasn't cut out for acting but had a broad passion for the business, which could possibly take me far enough to run the film or television division of Dahlen, or even be her successor one day." He leads us down a tree-lined path to a house that looks like a miniature castle. "Genevieve said, *'Loyalty is a choice, not an obligation bound by blood. The strongest families are the ones we choose to be part of.'* She said if she could cherry-pick her own son, it would be me. When you're a twenty-year-old whose only family is a pair of emotionally distant parents who don't hide their relief when you decide to move thousands of miles away, that's a powerful thing to hear."

It must've been powerful for Grace to hear something like that, too.

"We're here." Mason opens a side door that leads to a set of steps, waving me to follow him downstairs. "A recording artist who shall remain nameless used to live here and had the basement converted into a studio." He unlocks another door at the base of the steps and flicks on a switch, illuminating an empty room covered entirely in tan carpet. "It's soundproof. Nobody's living here at the moment, so you have the place to yourself, but I do have a meeting at four. Will ten minutes be enough screaming time for you?"

"Sure. Thanks for this."

"You're welcome." Before he leaves, Mason gives me a pained look.

"What?" I ask.

"It's only . . . I wish I could say something that would truly cheer you up, and I know I can't, and that's a bloody awful feeling."

Once I'm alone in the room with my own awful feelings, I open my mouth to scream, but no sound comes out.

It isn't until I'm back at Gale House that the tears threaten, though before I can let them loose, I'm distracted by a phone message in my cubby from my uncles asking me to call. It dawns on me that I forgot to call this past Sunday for our usual weekly catchup. There's nobody in the kitchenette, so I perch on a barstool in there, grab the cordless, and punch in the PIN assigned to me followed by our number in Brooklyn.

"*Hola!*" Alonso's upbeat voice comes across the line. While Reed's phone greeting is apprehensive until the caller proves not to be a telemarketer, Alonso favors exuberance for all.

His warmth brings fresh tears to my eyes, but I can't let him know I'm upset. Despite tanking my classes, the least I can do is put on a believable performance here. "Hey, Alonso! It's Ramona. I got your message. Everything okay?"

"We didn't hear from you yesterday, and you know Reed, he started worrying."

"Sorry I didn't get a chance to call. Rehearsals with my scene partner ran late." And I had more tests in the medical wing. "There's been so much going on!" Not too perky, just enough energy to convey *I'm good, I'm busy, you have nothing to worry about.*

"Anything exciting you can dish about?"

"Nothing personally, but my friend Dion booked a part on *Overruled*. And Grace got a small role on *In the Dollhouse*. Plus, she'll be personally mentored by Genevieve." I wince, unable to stamp the news with an exclamation mark, fresh pain slicing through me.

"Oh, honey. I'm sure she's thrilled." Though there's a hint of sadness in his tone and a hesitance. "You know, that's not a reflection on what you're capable of. This business is so random. It takes some people longer to break through."

"Yeah, of course." I hold my voice steady, though it's threatening to crack. "It's so rare for trainees to be cast in anything during their first month." And to be taken under the wing of the woman in charge. "I should see it as inspiration."

"Absolutely, baby doll. You'll be the next one." His encouragement wraps around me like an embrace. "You're only getting started. Just keep going and it'll happen for you. As long as you don't give up, you can't fail."

"You're right." Except he's wrong. I could absolutely fail and am well on my way to doing so in a multitude of ways. In fact, I probably just failed my newest class by walking out in the first ten minutes.

I chat a bit more with Alonso, relieved that Reed is busy working at the theater because he'd pick up on how upset I was, coax out more of my dark feelings, and reiterate his offer to come get me. Not that I'd take him up on it, but it would make him worry more about me, and it would make me more homesick than I already am.

"I miss you," I say as we get off the phone.

"We miss you so much," Alonso says. "But I know you're strong enough to get past whatever bumpy road you're on right now. If you're having a hard time breaking through, it's only because they don't see the Ramona that Reed and I know so well. Let them see that Ramona, because she's a badass."

Later that night, a shriek wakes me up from a dead sleep. I scramble out of bed and squeeze in beside Nicole, who's already listening at the door in the dark. I wish we had a peephole.

The incoherent screaming moves down the hall before a door slams.

"Gino? Gino, come out. Whatever it is, it can't be that bad," a girl calls.

"Should we go out there in case somebody needs help?" I ask.

"I wouldn't," says Nicole. "Better to stay out of other peoples' business."

"I'm going to make sure everyone's okay." I grab a hold of the doorknob and let myself out.

A small crowd has formed in the hallway and a petite Black girl is pounding on the bathroom door. "Gino! Come on, open up. Don't do anything stupid in there."

From within the bathroom, Gino shouts, "It's not her! You all think I'm nuts but she's someone else now! They're gonna make me someone else, too!" There's a sound of breaking glass and he lets out a strangled cry. This is followed by a string of obscenities and two words he repeats over and over, though I can only make out the first one: Project Something.

The girl pounding on the door casts a frenzied look down the hall and locks eyes with me. "Call for help," she bellows. "His name is Gino Rinaldi."

I rush over to the emergency console and push the panic button.

"Gale House, do you need police, fire, or medical assistance?" asks the operator.

"Medical, I think," I say.

"What is the nature of your emergency?" The woman's concerned-yet-neutral voice reminds me of Grace in that CrisisCrux commercial.

"Gino Rinaldi needs help. He's locked himself in the bathroom and . . ."

"He's losing his shit," Grace calls over my shoulder. I hadn't seen her come downstairs.

"Help is on the way," says the operator.

Soon after, two paramedics carrying a stretcher storm into the dorm and tell us to clear the hallway. When they can't coax Gino out of the bathroom, they break down the door. A brief struggle ensues, but they get him strapped down and carry him out. Gino continues to scream and thrash about on the stretcher. There's a gash on his forehead and blood trickles down the side of his head.

"Fuck Project Understudy and fuck all of you," he shouts. "We're all in a prison here and none of you even know it."

CHAPTER SIXTEEN

The following day marks a full month that Grace and I have been at the Dollhouse. To celebrate, we have lunch at Maybe This Thyme, an upscale bistro on Main Street.

We order quiche and, despite busy afternoons ahead and Grace still shunning sugar, indulge in a glass of champagne each.

As we raise our glasses, the mood feels off.

"Here's to you ruling the school already," I say. Is my smile genuine? Was it too much to add "already"?

"Nope, I don't accept that toast," Grace says. "Here's to *us*. *Both* ruling the school. Perpetually."

We clink glasses, and when I take a sip of champagne, it goes down the wrong way.

"Are you okay?" Grace asks when I'm done coughing. "I mean big picture okay. Something's clearly bugging you. Is it the notes? My recent—and sure to be temporary—streak of good luck?"

Yes, all of those things. "It's not good luck, you earned it." But I don't want to dwell on that. "I can't stop thinking about what happened to Gino.

I couldn't fall asleep after they took him away." I shudder, thinking of the way he panted and writhed, the foam at the corners of his mouth, the piercing look he gave me as he was wheeled out of the dorm.

"It was pretty disturbing," she says, reaching for the salt.

"And what was all that about Project Understudy? What do you think he meant, 'she's someone else now'? You think there's something shady going on?" I recall the girl on the studio tour spouting the theory that Ivy Gordon was replaced with a double. Could there possibly be any truth to it?

"Who knows? Dude was obviously out of his mind." Grace jerks a shoulder up partway, like she can't even be bothered with a full shrug. "I heard his girlfriend back home dumped him or boned his best friend or something. Maybe the 'understudy' refers to whoever she cheated on him with. I guess girlfriend drama plus Dollhouse pressure equals . . ." She makes the sound and gesture of a head exploding.

Grace is probably right—it was all the pressure that broke him. With our personal treadmills now turned up to full speed, some of us are bound to fall off, while others will build up an endurance to run longer and faster. I refuse to fall off like Gino did. For one thing, I can't afford to pay a ten-thousand-dollar penalty fee for leaving early. But also, I can't help but believe that if Grace can flourish like this, I should be able to as well. Shouldn't I?

Heading into the second month at the Dollhouse Academy means I'm free to go on auditions and I'm assigned a counselor. That afternoon, I have my first session with him, which is held inside a fuchsia and powder-blue Victorian that looks like it's made of gingerbread. There are multiple entrances, and it takes me a full lap of the wraparound porch before I find the correct one.

A shaggy-haired thirtysomething man answers the door. The unlikely combo of his leather pants and argyle sweater says rock star trying to dress up for a job interview.

"Hi, I'm here to meet Dr. Milligan," I say.

"Please, call me Devon." He extends a hand.

His grip is firm, on the verge of painful.

"Have a seat."

The room looks like an English professor's office, with overflowing built-in bookshelves, an antique desk covered with piles of papers, and a couple of beat-up leather armchairs amid stacks of more books. It should smell musty, yet a clean scent fills the room, like someone just folded fresh laundry in here.

"Pardon the clutter." He takes an armchair across from me. "I just switched offices and I'm still settling in." A tape recorder is on the table between us, and he gestures to it. "I'll be taping our sessions but rest assured, whatever you share stays between us."

You can't trust anybody here. The third note's warning echoes in my mind. "You're kinda sounding like a shrink. I thought you were here to help steer my career, advise me on which auditions to go on and stuff like that."

"I'm here to do all those things. The Dollhouse Academy looks at us as more than career counselors. I'm also here to be your personal counselor." Devon crosses an ankle over his knee and steeples his fingers. "So, Ramona. Tell me how you're settling in."

This guy is already grating on me. "I'm sure you have access to my file and can see how crappy I've been doing."

"Crappy is relative."

"Well, relative to the other trainees, I'm probably doing the worst. Setting aside dance, which has never been my forte, my singing and acting has been sucking, too. I did well the first couple of weeks, but as soon as they added more classes and more pressure, it's like I can't set foot into a class without getting really self-conscious. I rehearse all the time, do all the exercises, but still don't seem to be improving. Meanwhile, everyone around me is getting more talented by the minute. I know I'm not measuring up." I point down at myself. "How do you solve a problem like Ramona?"

Devon doesn't say anything, waiting for me to say more. So I do.

"Aren't you supposed to give me a spiel about how I need to get out of my head and get me past whatever is making me sabotage myself before I get kicked out of here?"

His eyebrows flick upward. "All right, then let's lay it out as it is. You were personally invited to the Dollhouse Academy by Genevieve on the strength of various performances at Cinema Magnifico, a tape of which was provided by *AM/USA*." Damn, he must've memorized my file right before this meeting. "Since arriving here, as you mentioned, you started off strong, but the last two weeks, you've fallen short in nearly all your classes."

"Hey, I thought I was doing okay in Film and TV Studies."

He gives me a look that says *cut the crap*. "If you need a little pat on the back, yes, Ramona, your Film and Television Studies instructor reported no problems with you. Neither did your Music Studies instructor. And your progress in the Alexander Method has been adequate. Are those enough gold stars for you? Can we move on to the classes where you're stinking up the joint, the ones that'll have more bearing on your career?"

My head snaps back as if he hit me. "Wow. Isn't sarcasm supposed to be a counterproductive form of communication or something?"

"Depending on how it's wielded and who its recipient is." He shrugs. "I took a calculated risk."

An invisible vise squeezes at my throat. "I thought counselors were supposed to be nice." Before I can hold them back, two hot tears spill down my face.

Devon sighs. "Damn it. I'm sorry, I didn't mean to—I went about this all wrong. Some of the shit they put you through, it's too much. I'm new at this, too, still figuring out when I'm supposed to play good cop versus bad cop." There's a click as he turns off the tape recorder. "Can we start again?"

I nod, both confused and touched by his sympathy as he rewinds the tape. "Let's both try to do better here," he says and pushes the record button again. "So, Ramona, it seems like you're having a tough time at the Dollhouse. Based on some of the reports from your instructors, you're not performing to your full potential. I'd like us to work together to figure out what's holding you back, determine what you'd like to achieve for yourself here, and devise a strategy for how to achieve it."

I still feel raw, but if he's willing to take a softer approach, so am I. "That's something I've had a hard time with. When I got here, I knew what my ideal career as a performer would look like, but it seems like this place wants me to be great at everything."

"The way the Dollhouse Academy operates, they like to throw a lot at you all at once to see where your true talents lie," Devon says. "It's taxing on the trainees—I don't envy what you're going through—but it's been an effective method of establishing consistent and disciplined practices as well as unearthing hidden talents while making the trainees more well-rounded."

"Sure, I get that. I want to be well-rounded, and I love the idea of unearthing hidden talents. Though at this point, mine have either all been discovered or they're hiding out in the Bermuda Triangle. The Dollhouse's approach—I mean Jesus, calling it taxing is an understatement. It's borderline inhumane." I rub the back of my stiff neck. "I don't know how to say this without sounding whiny, but I'm tired *all the time.*"

"That's something you'll have to get used to in this business."

"Yeah, I'm aware," I say. "I thought I'd get used to the pace by now, but it's been a month and I still finish each day physically and emotionally tapped out. Despite being exhausted, I have trouble getting to sleep—half the time, my brain keeps running through everything I did that day, every mistake I made, every new thing I need to remember, and it keeps me up for hours. On Sundays, I spend most of the day in bed, and that still doesn't get me ready for the week. I used to love all my classes, but now I dread going to half of them. Like, I'm happy to give dancing a shot—I could handle Grace's choreography for the Mag skits just fine—but I'm not a natural dancer, and it wears me down being told what I already know about my lack of grace and agility."

"Fair enough, but let's set aside your frustrations with Lady Edna's class for a moment. You've shown yourself to be a capable singer and actor, but you're having problems in those areas, too."

"I am." I stare at the carpet.

"Why?"

"I don't know. It's like, the more corrections I get, the more I start to second-guess myself and overthink everything I do. The instructors keep telling me I'm too stiff, and they're right, but I don't know how to keep all their directions in my head and also be natural. It's funny, before I came here, I was telling Grace how I was afraid I might end up working my ass off and still not be good enough. And that's exactly what's happening. I'm putting in the time and the work, I'm dedicating myself one hundred percent to this place, and I'm still falling short."

You may be too fragile for this place.

I try to shut out Mason's voice.

Devon uncrosses his leg and sits forward. "Instead of looking at your Dollhouse Academy experiences with a wide-angle lens, let's zoom in a bit. You started a new class yesterday, Breaking Down Barriers. Why did you walk out of it?"

"I didn't want to strip down to my underwear."

"Are you uncomfortable with your body?"

"Not at all. Grace and I did one of our live coming attractions—the one for *Jaws*—in bikinis. '*Better stay off the beach or stay afloat. / To catch this shark, you'll need a bigger boat.*'" I sing two lines of the song complete with the routine's arm movements, which Lady Edna would undoubtedly criticize.

"Right. So you had strangers in a theater looking at your body. Why couldn't you handle the same in a small classroom?"

"Performing at the Mag in a bikini was my choice. I had time to mentally prepare, get into character, do necessary grooming. That class didn't give me a choice. It didn't give me time."

"Neither do improv classes. The whole point is to get you out of your comfort zone."

"Yes . . . but . . ." I sputter, and any other justifications slip through my fingers.

"It says in your file, you lived on a commune with your mother in Oregon until you were ten, and your Uncle Reed came to see her shortly before she died and brought you back to New York with him."

This snaps me to attention. "Yeah, so?"

"Where was your dad in all this?"

"Out of the picture. Apparently, I was the product of a one-night stand. So romantic, huh?" A saccharine smile.

"What do you remember about this commune?"

"It was a farm. We ate a lot of bland food that made me gassy. I remember I liked feeding the animals, but they smelled bad and I was a little scared of them. It wasn't, like, Jonestown or anything. They were a bunch of hippies living together—ones who didn't believe in doctors, which is why my mom's kidney infection went undiagnosed until it killed her. But they definitely weren't into any creepy stuff." A sigh slips out of me.

"Does part of you wish they were?"

As much as I want to cross my arms, I keep them relaxed so as not to signal any defensiveness. "Of course not."

"Maybe it would make you more interesting, more distinct," he says. "It must be hard not to be able to distinguish yourself from the other trainees here."

"It's killing me." Tears spring to my eyes, which are still puffy from yesterday's crying jag. "Two people I know, Grace *and* Dion, booked jobs within their first month here."

"That's the exception, not the rule."

"Maybe they're exceptional and I'm not. No matter how hard I work, I can barely keep up and I definitely can't stand out—at least not for the right reasons. And the way Genevieve pitted me against three other people including my best friend, promising to mentor only one of us, that was cruel."

"This industry is competitive. Life is competitive. Why is what Genevieve did cruel?"

Because it feels like she drove a wedge between Grace and me. But I don't trust Devon enough to confide that much to him. Instead, I say, "I'm just crushed I didn't get the mentorship. And not only did Grace get that, she also got a speaking role on *In the Dollhouse* while I have to take a special class because I'm falling short. And I hate complaining about any of it because I can't stand how whiny and entitled I sound."

"Humor me for a minute and complain anyway."

It's shameful how little I hesitate before I begin. "I never expected her to pull ahead like this. I know Grace is a better dancer but . . ."

"But what?"

No, I can't. "But nothing. She's been working hard and deserves to see that work pay off."

Across from me, Devon looks to the ceiling and heaves a sigh. "Come on, Ramona, be honest. Grace is the better dancer, but what? You think you're the better actor?"

"And singer!" It feels gross to say it out loud, but also like a valve inside me has turned, releasing the pressure that had been building.

"And yet, so far you've gotten little validation for your talents, while Grace has received plenty. How does that make you feel?"

"Shitty. Obviously." I tug on a lock of my hair and wrap it tightly around my finger. "Extra shitty, because I can't set aside my own pettiness to be happy for Grace, and I can tell she's hurt even though she won't say it." The tip of my finger is red from the golden noose of my hair. "It's horrible, but I wish I got that mentorship, or at least got cast in something first, so I could cheer Grace on with all my heart. I've never felt this way before."

"Has Grace ever experienced more success than you?"

"Yeah, of course . . ." But is that true? When she booked that CrisisCrux commercial, I had just filmed an ad for a local car dealership and gotten a callback for an indie film. Even though I didn't get that part, I got cast in an experimental theater production around the same time. So I had a couple of small successes to buoy me when Grace had her biggest success, and any other time, I was usually the one faring better. "Okay, maybe not. She's just never been this good under pressure. I guess I'm not used to being the struggling one. Don't get me wrong, of course I'm happy for Grace. But part of me wonders if she just got lucky with this role. Which fills me with self-loathing. But also self-pity. It's the worst."

Devon taps his chin with two fingers, as if performing a tiny drum-roll. "Here's the problem. You were . . . underperforming as a trainee before Grace got this booking, which may have had a further negative impact. So how do we get you out of this vicious cycle?"

"I don't know. Up to now, no matter how rough things got, I always had enough small wins to keep me going. Not that I need to be coddled—I've had my share of rejection and brutal feedback in acting classes, and I've always been able to take it in stride." My body slumps. "It's gotten to the point that I even question the rare compliment I get from an instructor. I've never doubted myself this much before, but this place . . ." I throw up my hands. "It's making me wonder whether my best will ever be enough."

"Very good." There's a squeak of leather on leather as Devon stands and crosses over to the desk. "I applaud you for making it this far in life without letting your insecurity get the best of you. But now, we need to figure out a way for you to move past it. There are a few ways we can do this." He opens a drawer and rummages around in it.

"Does one of them involve me being in my underwear?"

"Not necessarily. In fact, I'll clear it with the Dollhouse for you to drop Breaking Down Barriers with no consequences. On two conditions." He comes back over, holding a couple of small cylindrical objects. "One, you continue your sessions with me and commit to building on the stark honesty you've shown today. And two, you take these as directed."

They're pill bottles. I take them from him and read the labels, which bear the names of drugs I've never heard of. Both are to be taken daily, one in the morning and the other at bedtime.

"What is this stuff?" I ask.

"The green pill, Dextrovigilax, will help with your energy levels, alertness, focus, and mood stabilization. The yellow pill, Profloxisom, will help you relax and prepare your body for rest and recovery. Both have been developed by DahlenRex and both have facilitated significant cognitive, physiological, and emotional improvements with minimal side effects." He sounds like a commercial.

The pill bottles rattle in my hand as I turn them over, holding them between my thumb and forefinger. I've never taken anything other than aspirin and antibiotics. "Are these some kind of amphetamines or barbiturates?" I think of *Valley of the Dolls*, how the characters took pills—"dolls"—to get through their ups and downs until they became addicted.

"Oh goodness, no." Devin is vehement. "Those drugs are much harsher on the body, can create a dependance, and come with stronger potential side effects. These are more akin to an enhanced herbal supplement."

"And what kind of side effects do they have?"

"A very small percentage have reported mild grogginess, headaches, and brain fog for the Profloxisom, though that's typically offset by the Dextrovigilax, which can cause dry mouth and loss of appetite." Devon regards me with patience.

"Right. Just so I'm clear. If I start taking these and keep meeting with you, I can drop Breaking Down Barriers? And I won't get put into a different class where I have to recite poetry naked or something?"

A stifled laugh. "No, you'll be free and clear of that class." He switches off the recorder. "I'll even let you in on some inside Dollhouse protocol. Should you make it past the initial six-month probationary period or get a significant role in a Dahlen production, you'll see many more classes cut from your personal curriculum."

"Good to know." I'm skeptical, but I do feel my apprehension lifting.

There's a click as the recorder comes back on. "You wouldn't be here if we didn't think you could measure up," he says. "Right now, a lot of negative thinking is getting in your way. We need to find a way for you to process and move beyond it, which we'll work on in our sessions. In the meantime, I think these supplements will really help."

"It's worth a try, I guess." With that, our hour is up.

I head back to the dorm, holding a pill vial in each hand, their contents rattling like miniature maracas as I walk. As much as I don't want to rely on something artificial, part of me hopes these are miracle drugs that will turn everything around for me.

Before I set foot in Gale House, I have a feeling there's new mail awaiting me.

I'm right. There's a white envelope in my mail cubby, as if I willed it into being.

If they offer you pills, DO NOT TAKE THEM.

CHAPTER SEVENTEEN

Ivy's Diary

MAY 10, 1998

Hearing what happened to Gino Rinaldi brought back terrible memories. I knew Project Understudy had never shut down completely, but I'm worried it's taken a sinister turn again.

Asking Genevieve would be pointless (she'd only tell me what I wanted to hear), so one way or another, I need to confirm for myself where things stand with Project Understudy. It's time for me to cultivate some new connections. There are people here who are overlooked, but who see more than they let on. I learned that from Timothy. I need to find someone like that now, someone I can build trust with, who will be able to access the sensitive information I need.

Until then, I must continue acting the role of Ivy Gordon, just as I do Tabitha Noelle.

It didn't used to be this way.

When I look back on the days of shooting that first season of *In the Dollhouse*, they were a kaleidoscope of experiences and emotions that left me in a constant state of exhilaration.

There was the bustle of moving out of one dormitory and into a Victorian house closer to the studio along with the rest of the main cast, ten of us total. I went from sharing a room with one girl I barely saw to sharing a house with nine other people with whom I'd regularly interact. This suited me fine because one of them was Timothy. He and I were put in rooms across the hall from each other but always ended up in my room. We loved the bay window facing an expansive backyard with trees whose leaves were turning shades of tangerine, amber, russet, and crimson. We'd sit on opposite sides of that window, our legs tangled together, and try to study our scripts, but we'd invariably get distracted by the outside scenery or, more often, the heat of our skin, the hungry looks and mischievous smiles we'd exchange until we threw aside our scripts and drew the curtain.

The cast was asked to participate in group activities for a week before rehearsals began in order to coalesce as a group. We went jogging and prepared meals and played board games and sat around a firepit in the yard, telling scary stories about working in show business. Four of us were teenagers, two were twentysomethings playing teenagers, and the remaining four were in their thirties and forties, but despite the age differences and our varied experience levels, we treated one another as equals.

As much as Timothy and I enjoyed getting to know our castmates, we were more interested in getting to know each other.

Timothy Boyd. What a bolt of lightning that boy was in my life. From the time we did that chemistry read, we were inseparable. I grew to know him better than anyone before or since, better than myself, even.

I loved learning about his quirks, like how he put too much salt and pepper on his food, how he sneezed like a cartoon mouse and always three times in a row, how he believed in ludicrous things like Bigfoot and aliens.

In some ways he was my opposite. I grew up, for all intents and purposes, an only child, whereas Timothy was the youngest of six, with three brothers and two sisters. While I got my start in television, Timothy got his in theater, at age seven, playing Tiny Tim in a touring production of *A Christmas Carol*. I was the only performer in my family whereas Timothy came from the world of New York theater: his father was a well-respected director, his mother a set designer, and all his siblings took to the stage before him. Unlike me, he never felt pressured to financially support his family. Sets and stages were his playground. Timothy was intrigued by the intensity with which I approached performance, whereas I coveted the levity with which he approached his craft. Perhaps this is why we played so well off each other on *In the Dollhouse*. And in our lives beyond the show.

The preproduction seemed to run like a well-oiled machine, which we were pulled into as needed. There were fittings for what would become the iconic schoolgirl uniform. Should the skirt be a solid color or plaid? Should there be a traditional necktie, a cross tie, or no tie at all? Should the primary school color be burgundy, navy, or something else? Despite pleas from the director and producers not to go with red or white, which are hard to film, Genevieve had the final say: the school colors would be red and black, naturally, and the uniform would consist of a black-and-white plaid skirt for the girls, black trousers for the boys, white button-down shirt, fire-engine red necktie, and black blazer embroidered with a red crest.

"Simple. Classic. They'll figure out how to make it work on-screen."

There were hair and makeup tests. Whenever possible, the show was to feel like it didn't belong to a specific era, to maintain a sense of timelessness. Feathered hair, heavy eye shadows, and shiny saturated lips were shunned in favor of Hollywood Golden Age glamour with a dash of French New Wave and '60s mod: winged eyeliner, matte lips, soft bobs, tousled bouffants and pompadours.

To get what would be known as the "Tabitha" hairstyle requested in salons by countless girls throughout the '80s, my long hair was bleached and cut just past my shoulders with long bangs layered around my face. Then it was set in hot rollers and tortured with a teasing comb to get soft waves with volume at the crown. Brigitte Bardot meets Barbarella. The hairstylist must've used a full can of Aqua Net every time he did my hair, and the sharp peppery alcohol smell lingered in my nostrils all day.

There were other smells distinct to that period of my life. Sawdust and paint from the sets being constructed. The amber and citrus-heavy Opium perfume our wardrobe designer doused herself in. Irish Spring soap mingled with the sweet tang of Timothy's sweat. The sulphuric cabbage soup my castmate Stacey ate for weeks to shed weight before we began shooting.

Due to a disciplined food and exercise regime set in place for me by my mother from the time I began acting professionally, I'd never struggled with my weight. However, during the months of preproduction for *In the Dollhouse*, when Timothy and I were falling madly in love, I'd relaxed my rigid rules around meals and workouts and had put on weight.

"My dear, we have six weeks until principal photography and you've gained fifteen pounds," Genevieve said. Ever since she'd become my mentor, we met weekly for tea in the owl room. "You have such lovely delicate features, such a perfect hollow to your cheekbones, you can't afford an ounce of extra fat on you, or they won't get captured properly on film. I hate to ask this of you, but I do need you to slim back down to your original size."

Fifteen pounds! I hadn't realized it was quite that much. I swore to Genevieve I'd go on the cabbage soup diet right away.

"I wish you wouldn't, and I wish Stacey hadn't, either." Her tone grew softer, more compassionate. "Fad diets aren't the answer. I offered Stacey a better alternative, but she turned me down. I hope you'll be more sensible. After the insults, threats, and crash diets foisted on me, I don't want you going to any unhealthy measures or developing a complex about food. That's why I've been working with the top scientists at DahlenRex to create a natural appetite suppressant that's safe and effective. I myself have been taking it for years."

I asked why, if there was a miracle weight-loss drug available, it hadn't been made public.

"It would be cost prohibitive for the general population—one of the key ingredients is found only on one island in Indonesia and is impossible to grow elsewhere, much as we've tried. We have the brightest minds working to re-create a synthetic version, but in the meantime, I control the limited supply of this supplement, and I believe you are worthy of being one of the select few to enjoy its benefits." With that, she removed a glass pill vial from her suit's breast pocket, handing it to me as if it contained precious gemstones.

How grateful I was to be in the spotlight of Genevieve's attention. But more than that, to be cared for in a way nobody in my family ever cared for me. It brought tears to my eyes.

"You're part of a new family now, Ivy. A better family, because you have chosen to be here, to be among us."

I took the pills. I began to lose weight. And when I developed problems sleeping, which I attributed to general excitement, I was given a set of second pills to take, which were also effective. If there were any side effects, they were sidelined by the pheromones coursing through me as Timothy and I became more infatuated with each other.

Our relationship grew physical quickly. It was more than an expression of lust; it felt like a natural extension of getting to know each other. I relished discovering every detail of Timothy's body: the smattering of freckles along his lower back, the birthmark behind his knee shaped like a tiny snowman, his unexpected tender spots—behind his ears, the insides of his forearms, right below his collarbone.

Rather than shooting a TV pilot for *In the Dollhouse* and waiting to see whether it would get picked up, Genevieve was able to secure a direct-to-series commission of thirteen episodes with a major network. There were whispers a top executive owed Genevieve a favor, or maybe blackmail was involved, but this is one time I believe in the simplest explanation, which is the strength of the writing. There's a reason *In the Dollhouse* has gone on to inspire so many other beloved shows, including *Twin Peaks*, *My So-Called Life*, and even *The X-Files*.

We began shooting in late October. Call times were at 6:00 a.m. and we usually kept going until 8:00 p.m., sometimes later. Typically, we'd spend eight days on each episode, with two days off before beginning the next one. There was always a sense of respect and camaraderie among the cast and crew. Angry outbursts were acceptable only if they were scripted. During read-throughs, we were encouraged to speak up if the writing felt off for our characters. Whenever someone kept fumbling a scene, we would be patient or try to lighten the mood. It was a refreshing change from some of the other productions I've worked on. Being treated like a human being with valuable input made me that much more dedicated to my craft, and to Dahlen. Despite the long days, it was a joy to arrive on set.

While the work was fulfilling, it still was a grueling schedule, and it's fortunate Timothy and I were working on the same show; otherwise we wouldn't have been able to spend much time together. During meal breaks, while we were encouraged to eat with the cast, we often snuck off somewhere to fool around, though we had to be careful not to muss up our clothes, hair, or makeup too badly. Despite our best efforts, we frequently got admonished for returning to the set disheveled, but we were too captivated with each other to care.

After the first month of production, Genevieve, impressed by my singing in the musical numbers, decided I should record an album.

"It will be marvelous, Ivy," she goaded when I expressed hesitation. "The show will propel your fame, which will make you sell more records, which will get more people watching the show. Ivy Gordon will become an unstoppable creative juggernaut."

I wasn't sure that was something I wanted to be, but I agreed to it all the same. I began spending my days off in a recording studio, performing slightly different arrangements of the songs I sang on the show, a mix of originals and covers, and was even encouraged to write a song of my own.

Timothy complained of seeing less of me and said I should tell Genevieve I was being overworked. I was, but music offered me a type of high that was different from acting, one that I didn't get enough of solely from ITD's musical numbers. Besides, if the album helped get the show picked up for additional seasons, we'd get to spend more time working together. As it was, after the first season of ITD wrapped, Timothy would be flying to London to shoot a movie, and while I intended to go abroad with him, I knew he'd be too busy working to see much of me. That was fine because I'd use those days to explore London's historic sights and catch up on my reading. Besides, seeing Timothy in a limited capacity would be better than not seeing him at all for four months.

The first episode of *In the Dollhouse* aired on a Sunday night in January 1982, while the season was still in production. On Monday we got the

ratings: twenty-two million people had tuned in to watch. It instantly became the number one show in America. The magnitude of that still strikes
me today. In 1982, the total population of the United States was around
230 million. Although there wasn't as much competition for viewers back
then as there is today with cable television, it still means nearly one in ten
people watched our show that night.

A few weeks later, the first single I recorded, "Class Act," was released
and knocked Olivia Newton-John's "Physical" off the Billboard charts'
top spot. Since MTV had debuted the previous summer, Genevieve
thought it would be a good idea to record a music video for "Class Act,"
which used some of the footage from the show as well as shots of me in a
library wearing a more provocative version of the uniform (skirt hitched
higher, blouse unbuttoned to reveal a hint of cleavage). MTV quickly put
the video on heavy rotation, which helped sell the single and promote the
show. Genevieve had been right.

A few days after we finished shooting, I found out I was to begin a
press tour for the release of my first album, *Dollface*, followed by rehearsals
for a series of concert dates in twenty major cities. I wouldn't be able to
join Timothy in London after all.

How did I not see that coming?

Of course, I tried to plead with Genevieve. Couldn't we delay the tour
by a few months?

"Certainly not, the venues have been booked and it's critical we get
you out there selling albums and concert tickets."

Was a press tour all that important? Couldn't I just do magazine and
radio interviews over the phone from London?

"Don't be naive. People expect to see you face-to-face, to photograph
you. It's time you began meeting your fans and courting the media. Building fame is a delicate dance, and you can't afford to miss a single step.
Listen, I myself despised the promotional side of the business when I had
to do it. Nevertheless, it's part of the process, a necessary evil. Getting the
press on your side will go a long way to ensuring your success and being
able to continue doing what you love. And after investing so much in you,

first as an actor, now as a singer, Dahlen is counting on you. I'm counting on you. While he may say otherwise, deep down I bet Timothy is counting on you, too. You and he are poised to be America's sweethearts, and embarking on this journey together will only make you stronger as a couple."

But how could Timothy and I embark on anything together if we had to spend the rest of spring and much of the summer apart?

"You know what they say about absence and hearts. Once in a while, you'll need to endure temporary separations in order to enhance your respective careers. It's better you learn to be mature about it early on."

Once again, I was expected to behave with a maturity well beyond my years. I was only eighteen.

When I lapsed into a broody silence, Genevieve tried a different tactic.

"How about this? We can't delay your actual tour, but I think we can move some things around to find an extra week for the two of you to be together before heading off to work on separate projects. You can spend that week in New York City and even stay at my apartment at the Gramercy Park Hotel."

This sounded like a generous offer. Timothy and I had often discussed visiting the city together. I'd only been there twice before, once to shoot a commercial and the other for a movie, both visits brief and with little time for sightseeing. Timothy was eager to introduce me to his family and show me his favorite spots around Manhattan. A number of Broadway theaters were set to be demolished that year, and he wanted to see them one last time before they were torn down.

The timing and setting for this trip could not be more perfect.

"Does that sound reasonable to you?" Genevieve asked.

The gratitude with which I accepted sickens me today. At the time, I saw it as winning another battle, whereas now I see it for the manipulation that it was.

"Of course," she added, as if coming up with the idea in the moment, "it will be quite an inconvenience reconfiguring your calendars and will involve calling in a lot of favors. As such, I hope you and Timothy would be willing to make some small publicity appearances for Dahlen. We could give you bodyguards if you'd be more comfortable. Either way, having you two seen together would get more people watching *In the Dollhouse* when it's in repeats this summer and get them more invested in the Tabitha/Hayden storyline. We could potentially draw out your on-screen romance over many seasons . . ."

Genevieve didn't need to spell it out for me. I readily agreed to the week in NYC, and when I told Timothy about it, he was also excited, though we declined the bodyguards. Surely we hadn't become *that* famous.

Before we left, a press agent at the Dollhouse gave us pointers on how to behave in front of the media, how to be humble and gracious, how to speak in catchy sound bites and steer the conversation back to what we were promoting. Genevieve advised me to assume someone from the media was always watching and recording when I was out in public, and to be sweet and effusive when fans approached me, especially young ones, no matter how tired or irritated I might be.

"Your reputation must be immaculate, and it doesn't take much to blemish it. You are not allowed to have a bad day. Treat the public warmly and they will embrace you. But they will look for every reason to knock you off your pedestal and move on to the next pretty young thing. Embrace and cherish being the golden girl as long as possible."

Who ever said I wanted to be put on a pedestal? Back then, all I wanted was to take a vacation with my boyfriend.

I was aware New York City could be gritty and dangerous, but I was unprepared for the reality of that. On my previous brief stays, work had shielded me from the worst of it, whisking me past squalid corners, keeping me contained on film and commercial sets. This time, with Timothy insisting we take in as much of the city as possible on foot, I had a close-up of the seediness and tumult. On our first day, we visited Times Square, where Broadway theaters were nestled among a thriving scene of pornography, prostitution, and drug dealing. After enduring numerous propositions, sneers, and several surreptitious gropes, we beat a hasty retreat back to Genevieve's apartment, only to discover that Timothy had been pickpocketed.

The two of us wanted nothing more than to hole up in the hotel after that, but we had promotional obligations to fulfill. What was supposed to be a relaxing week with a few minor publicity engagements ended up being a media circus. We did interviews with several publications and radio stations, as well as multiple TV appearances including *Late Night with David Letterman*, where a wildlife expert brought out a boa constrictor that Timothy and I wore around our necks like it was nothing. Dave called us good sports and said we were welcome back anytime.

The most disturbing part of the trip was the paparazzi. There was at least one photographer following us everywhere we went, including the private park off the Gramercy Park Hotel. We used Genevieve's key, hoping for a reprieve from the constant surveillance, only to hear a camera's shutter moments after we got cozy on one of the benches. Timothy lunged for the photographer, grabbed him by the lapels, and would've struck him if I hadn't pleaded with him to stop.

We didn't want paparazzi keeping us from exploring the city, though they did make it difficult. Sometimes the photographers would cause such a commotion, passersby would recognize us and begin to swarm us for autographs. I was caught off guard by such bold familiarity, with some people finding it acceptable to hug me, put their arm around me, even stroke my hair as they told me how much they adored me. Fortunately, Timothy would often step in and curtail the more touchy-feely fans.

While Timothy and I did enjoy moments of our trip, for the first few days, I didn't feel quite like myself. I had wanted to enjoy our vacation without any chemical interference, so I had stopped taking the pills for weight loss and sleep. In addition to all the unwelcome attention, I endured unpleasant withdrawal symptoms. I felt like the walls were closing in around me and became so ill, I was unable to meet Timothy's family on the one day all our schedules lined up. After a few horrible days of barely sleeping, overeating, and feeling like my head would split open, I resumed taking the pills, determined to wean myself off them later.

Much as I dreaded being separated from Timothy, the chaos of Manhattan paired with the sense of being exposed and unsafe made me desperate for the idyllic confines of Owls Point.

In hindsight, I'm sure Genevieve or someone else at Dahlen arranged for the photographers to follow us around, providing them with our schedules and even a key to the private park. I wouldn't put it past them if they hired some of the fans who approached us, maybe even the pickpocket. Timothy and I were now commodities, and Dahlen would make sure we were in high demand.

I returned to Owls Point after a week, still shaken up and prone to anxiety attacks. Genevieve promptly put me on a third supplement, which she promised would calm my nerves. With such a hectic schedule awaiting me, I scrapped my earlier plan of weaning myself off the supplements. I couldn't afford to be out of sorts when I had an album to promote and, later that year, a second season of *In the Dollhouse* to prepare for. At the time, it didn't cross my mind that I must've developed a serious dependence, if the withdrawal symptoms were so severe. I was merely relieved to feel like myself again, and to be home.

It wouldn't be long before I had to go back out there, to tour and promote, but I was given every assurance that next time, I'd have bodyguards and other protections put in place to shield me from the unwanted elements of the outside world.

In that way, I willingly let myself be led into a series of gilded cages.

CHAPTER EIGHTEEN

AUGUST 1998

I took Grace's words about the anonymous notes to heart. Somebody was trying to psych me out, and it was working. If I was already experiencing this type of interference while I was a nobody, it was merely a taste of what was to come as I attained more success and popularity. There'd always be something or someone standing in my way, trying to trip me up. If I was going to turn things around for myself at the Dollhouse—or get anywhere in life—I had to ignore discouragement, tune out my detractors, and power through all obstacles. I had to shut out those voices from my early childhood on the commune telling me I'm ordinary—I wouldn't be here if that was the case. And if I wanted to stay here, I had to minimize distractions, beginning with those notes, and embrace the Dollhouse regimen with fresh vigor.

So that's what I did.

It's now been a few months since I've received any new cards, which makes me think it was a joke that's run its course or a loyalty test that I've passed.

Even so, I still dread checking my cubby, though my other mail is less unnerving. Once in a while, there's a letter from my uncles, but for the most part it's blue slips dictating my class schedule or yellow slips demanding my presence in the medical wing. Ever since Grace's turn on *In the Dollhouse* was so well received, she's become a recurring character and spends countless hours on set, so I've been getting occasional brief notes from her promising we'd meet up soon and wishing me luck on my auditions.

It's been lonely seeing so much less of my best friend.

Grace's character is Juniper York, a sardonic transfer student who wears rhinestone cat collars and too much eyeliner, speaks in a deadpan, and whose signature move is a heavy sigh and sideways eye-roll. When she first tells me her part on the show has been expanded, I'm able to congratulate her sincerely, while feeling only a minor stab of envy and inadequacy (thanks to my sessions with Devon). I take my pills like a good girl, show gradual improvements in my classes, and receive a few callbacks on auditions, though I have yet to book even a walk-on part. Despite all that, I have to trust my time will come. And I have to support Grace. After all, she did the thing we both set out to do and now gets to act in our favorite TV show of all time. Go Grace!

Okay, so maybe, just *maybe*, the real reason I dread checking my mailbox is because of these notes Grace sends me. Despite her good intentions, when she writes something like "You're next!" I can't help but read "You're still failing!" which makes me feel like garbage on multiple levels, for interpreting a heartfelt message so darkly and believing my made-up subtext more than her sincere well-wishes.

Needless to say, I still have a way to go in my counseling sessions.

The supplements, though . . .

I considered not taking them after getting that last warning note. But I desperately needed to improve my performance at the Dollhouse. What if the other trainees were on a personalized cocktail of supplements, hence why they were doing better than me? What if Grace was taking them without telling me? (We *have* been keeping secrets from each other, after all.) The least I could do to balance out my mediocrity at the Dollhouse was to step up and show how committed I was to being here. If I was going to fail, I wouldn't do so without trying everything first.

So, I've been taking the pills, and I have to say, they're making things—not *better*, per se, but more endurable. If I were a video game character, the green pills would extend my energy bar, enabling me to fight longer and harder. And the yellow pills keep me from obsessing about the day's missteps as I try to fall asleep, letting me finally get some proper rest. Green for go, yellow to mellow. Thankfully, I haven't felt any negative side effects so far.

During the rare chats Grace and I manage to have these days, I don't bring up the pills.

One nice thing I've noticed since taking the supplements is that I don't feel as tightly wound and prickly all the time. I'm able to handle criticism from my instructors and rejection from casting directors with a level head. I'm able to endure the Dollhouse's invasive medical exams and Devon's invasive counseling without being too bothered.

Funny how nothing seems to bother me as much as it used to, but Grace's notes are still like thorns that find the most sensitive parts of my skin. How terrible that I dread getting encouragement from my own best friend. Is this how she used to feel about my pep talks?

Today, something brand-new awaits in my mail cubby: a green sheet. No fucking way.

I was starting to think this would never happen.

I pore over the paper in disbelief, triple-checking that it's my name written at the top. Finally, cautious elation trickles in.

It took four months and dozens of auditions, but I finally booked a part. It's a thriller called *Sisterhood* about a sinister college sorority. A small role, but that doesn't matter. Maybe I'm not a talentless hack wasting the Dollhouse's resources after all.

I have to tell Grace. She's probably out, but I take a chance and run upstairs to her room, anyway. As luck would have it, she's here, rummaging through the contents of her dresser.

"Grace! Oh my god, I'm so glad you're home, I didn't think I'd catch you." I wave the green flyer around then stop short when I see an open suit-case on the floor. "Are you packing? Where are you going? Is ITD shooting on location?"

A guilty look flashes across her face before she grins and rushes over to me. "Holy shit, you did it! Of course you did. What's the part?"

My mouth hangs open, unsure of whether to answer her questions first or demand she answer mine. Something about this doesn't feel right.

"What's going on?" I ask. "Where are you going?"

"I'm, um . . ." She gnaws at her lip. "I'm actually moving."

"To Fisher House? I guess that makes sense." That was the dorm that housed recurring characters on several Dahlen shows, including *In the Doll-house*. "Does that mean they signed you up for more episodes? We can cel-ebrate together!" It's so nice to feel genuinely happy for her, though there's a niggling twinge that she didn't tell me she's moving out. Also, it's not lost on me that I'm an asshole for needing my own personal success in order to applaud hers.

Grace shoves her hands into the back pockets of her black jeans. "Ac-tually, I'm, um, moving into one of the Victorians. And, um, I'm actually not going to be in this next season of ITD, actually."

"Jesus, if you say 'actually' one more time, I'm gonna lose it."

The guilty look is back as the words come pouring out of her mouth. "Juniper got a spin-off. I mean, I did. It all came together so quickly. I didn't even know they were working on a script. But they were, and the network loved it and gave us a thirteen-episode order. We go into prepro-duction next week."

It's not the news itself that saddens me, it's the way she uses "us" and "we," like she's now part of this big, wonderful other thing, like she's moved into another orbit and left me spinning on my own.

"When did you find all this out?" I ask.

Grace resumes throwing clothes in her suitcase, not looking my way. "A week ago, but of course I waited until the last minute to pack. I know, I totally suck for not telling you, especially after I gave you a hard time about keeping secrets from me, but Genevieve said it would be better not to say anything about it."

We've had an unspoken agreement that Grace wouldn't discuss her mentorship with Genevieve, so it's jarring to hear her speak the woman's name now, especially in this way that emphasizes their closeness.

"And why did Genevieve say that?"

"Because you've been . . . going through it and it might have a negative impact on you . . . And if I'm being totally honest, it's also been hard sharing good news with you."

My face grows hot. "I don't want you to feel like you can't tell me about all the awesome things happening in your career. No matter what's going on with me, I still want to know."

"I'm not sure that's true." Despite her tone being light, the words hit like a hammer. "I think it's easier for you when I'm a disaster and you're talking me off the ledge."

"I never considered you a disaster. If anything, I wanted you to see yourself the way I did." I'm not sure why I go for the past tense, but I don't correct myself; I don't know how I see her in this moment.

"Do you really think that's it? Isn't it easier to feel good when I'm your charity case, taking pity on the little orphan who thinks she's a piece of shit who won't amount to anything?"

"I never thought of you like that. You've always been like family to me."

But she doesn't hear me. "And now that I have a little more confidence and my career is starting to pick up, you can't seem to handle it." When I open my mouth to protest, she holds up a hand. "You say all the right things, but your face is a different story. Whenever I tell you about how well I'm doing, you look like I'm punching you in the stomach."

Because that's how it feels. "I'd be lying if I said I wasn't jealous, but I'm also proud of you. If roles were reversed, wouldn't you feel the same way?"

A flash of outrage as she bares her teeth. "Roles *have* been reversed.

For as long as we've known each other, you always got the better parts in school plays, you always booked more jobs, had more friends, you got a national commercial before I did, got a boyfriend before I did."

"Hang on, now you're mixing in the personal."

"It's *all* personal." She balls up a tank top and throws it into her suitcase.

"Are you seriously saying you resented me? All the boys thought you were hot, but you were so mean to them, they didn't want to come near you. And you weren't much better with the girls in school. I can't help it if people got sick of being around a pretty girl who wouldn't stop bitching about how ugly she is, someone who's pessimistic and sarcastic all the time—even I get tired of that shit."

"Well you won't have to hear me bitch about anything anymore."

"Right, because now that you have the Dollhouse telling you how wonderful you are, you don't need me." My windpipe narrows but I won't let my voice crack. "Meanwhile, when I was *going through it* these last couple of months, you barely showed up for me. You acted like none of it was a big deal while I was positively drowning and dealing with those creepy notes on top of everything." I feel shrill and out of control and before I can stop myself, I say, "For all I know, *you* sent me those notes."

Her mouth compresses into a thin line. "Are you for real?"

My mind is spinning in irrational circles. "I mean, that would explain how that first card got to me in Brooklyn with no postmark. And you were always good at copying Reed's handwriting on sick notes when we cut class and . . . well, maybe giving me a negative distraction was a good way for you to get ahead."

"You're disgusting for saying that—for even thinking it. I've always had your back."

"Not so much recently."

"I've been *working*," she roars. "And I tried to be there for you when I could, but there's only so many times I can say 'you got this' and 'don't give up' before it stops meaning anything."

A nasty laugh escapes me. "It's exhausting, isn't it." It's not a question.

"Yeah, being someone's emotional crutch *is* exhausting."

"Try doing it for years instead of months."

Something between a cough and chuckle comes out of her mouth. "It's funny, you spent all this time building me up, telling me that as long as I work hard, I'll achieve something. Yet now that my hard work is paying off, you can't handle it. I thought you'd at least be happy because of what this means for Reed and Alonso."

I feel like I'm in a car that's been sideswiped. "What do my uncles have to do with any of this?"

Her face flashes confusion then settles into resigned pity. "They didn't tell you. Of course not. They have to protect their precious Ramona from the harsh realities of the world."

Balling my hands into fists, I unclench my jaw. "What harsh realities? What the fuck is going on?"

"Business has . . . not been great since we moved up here. And it turns out they owe back taxes on the property. They're being threatened with foreclosure. I sent them some money from my ITD earnings, but I'll be getting a salary bump with this new show, and I was able to negotiate an advance because of extenuating circumstances. Genevieve was surprisingly understanding about it." In case her haughtiness doesn't come across enough, she actually raises her nose in the air.

All these barbs pierce me at different angles, but the one that hurts the most is that Grace gets to be the one to save my uncles, not me.

She gets to be the hero. I'm the disappointment.

There's so much more to say, words that we've been storing up for weeks, years, grievances begging for air. We face each other, hands on hips, breathing heavily, like two dragons about to spit fire.

I drop my arms first and take a step back. No point in both of us getting incinerated.

"Wait," Grace calls out as I'm stepping out of her room.

I turn around.

She holds out the green flyer. "Congratulations." The word is flat, perfunctory.

"Yeah, you too."

Back downstairs, I grab the cordless phone and head for the first unoccupied space I can find, which turns out to be the laundry nook. I call my uncles and Reed picks up.

"Yes, hello?" The familiar greeting, suspicious because the Dollhouse blocks its numbers on caller ID.

"It's me."

"Ramona." His tone brightens. "We weren't expecting to hear from you—wait, what's wrong?"

"How could you tell Grace about your money problems and not me? *Why* would you even tell her?"

"We weren't planning to, but she got it out of Alonso. We were going to fill you in eventually, just asked Grace to keep it on the down-low for now."

"And you thought that would work? Grace and I are best friends." *Were* best friends? "It'll always get back to me. How could you keep this from me? And don't say you didn't want to worry me—"

"But that's exactly it. Grace told us about what a difficult time you've been having, and we didn't want to burden you further."

"I'm sorry, she *what*?" The rancor I carried downstairs with me has been doused with gasoline and set on fire. How dare she talk about me behind my back?

"She was concerned about you and knows we do the warm fuzzy thing better than she does. Well, at least Alonso does. You know I try in my own way." A sigh. "It appears that we've all been keeping things from each other." Reed's tone is contrite but unperturbed. I want him to be a lot more perturbed.

"Except for Alonso. I can't believe he blabbed to Grace."

"Really?" he asks, dubious.

I sigh. "No, I can totally believe it. You'd have better luck keeping a secret taking out a full-page ad in the *Village Voice* than sharing it with Alonso." Despite my foul mood, when my uncle snickers, I can't help following suit.

"The last thing we want to do is take money from either one of you, but—and we're okay now, I promise—but we were faced with the prospect of losing our business and our home."

"No, I get it. I'm glad Grace is in a position to help." A dull ache spreads through me. "I just . . . I just wish it could've been me." I wipe a wet cheek with the back of my hand.

"Oh, Ramona." The pity in his voice makes me cry harder.

"I wish it could've been me," I repeat in a whimper.

CHAPTER NINETEEN

"Cut! Regina, you want to sound apprehensive, not hysterical. Just do it the way you did it in rehearsals. Let's go again," says the director, a scrawny middle-aged man with a toothpick sticking out of the corner of his mouth.

I don't correct him about my name and neither does anyone else.

I've spent hours with the script, creating a rich backstory for my character until I was able to lend nuance to the most innocuous line. The way I did it in rehearsals was natural and spot-on, just as it was in auditions. What happened between then and now?

It's the middle of the night and we're on the eighth take of this scene. A boom operator messed up the first take, but the other seven were all me. All I have to do is walk down a cobblestone street with two other girls as we talk about what might be going on in the mansion behind us (the mansion in question being Genevieve's house). When we notice the front gate is ajar, I accept a dare from one of the girls to go onto the property and take a closer look at the house. Once I slip around the back, I let out a shriek and am never seen again.

The scene itself will only amount to about two minutes of the movie, but we've been filming for over an hour so far. We're still on the master shot—a wide shot that will capture all of the action in the scene in a single, uninterrupted take—with a medium shot and close-ups to follow.

Here are the different ways I've fucked up so far: I've missed my mark, tripped on the cobblestones, forgotten my lines (twice), stepped on another actor's line, delivered my lines too calmly, and now too hysterically.

"It's not that complicated," mutters one of the girls in the scene with me as our hair and makeup is touched up.

My body tenses. I know it's not that complicated. I've done this before. I don't know why I can't get it right this time. Maybe it was the script revisions. I had my lines down cold but was given a new script an hour before shooting. Maybe it's these high heels that are a nightmare to navigate on the cobblestones. Though after all the movement techniques I've practiced these last few months, a pair of shoes shouldn't be tripping me up so literally.

Maybe it's me. Maybe they made a mistake casting me.

"Last looks!" calls the assistant director.

"Relax your mouth," says the makeup artist, brushing color on my lower lip.

We go again. This time I do something funny with my arm when I walk through the gate. Then I step on a line again. Then I forget another line. We finally get the master shot, but by the time we move on to the medium—where we're filmed from the waist up—I'm a nervous wreck and my lines are sounding too panicked again.

The director calls for a ten-minute break and asks to speak to me. He's known for being a good guy, so I'm hoping for a few words of encouragement to smooth out my nerves.

"Listen, Regina, we've got a tight schedule here and all these extra takes have put us really behind." The toothpick wiggles up and down as he speaks. "I hate to do this, but it's not working out."

A coldness envelops me.

Poor Regina. How awful for her to be getting fired from a movie in the middle of a scene, by the director himself.

It takes a moment for my brain to register what's happening.

"Oh." I am Regina. "Wait, please." My hands flutter like someone else is possessing them. "I know I can do this. You saw me do it in rehearsals. I promise I'll get it right this time. One more chance. I'll be perfect."

But the director isn't buying it; his toothpick droops like it's giving me a thumbs-down sign.

Before I know it, I'm changing back into my clothes and being escorted off the set like a criminal. I stand there across the street from Genevieve's house, shivering, and barely notice when a suede jacket is draped over my shoulders.

"Come on. They don't like it when you hang about."

It's Mason.

"Why? It's not like I'm going to ruin their movie more than I already have," I say. Even so, I let him lead me a few streets away, to one of the dining halls. He unlocks the front door.

"I'm not hungry." I feel like my body has been hollowed out and replaced with dry ice. A different kind of emptiness.

"Take a seat. Away from the windows. I'll make you some tea."

I nod to his retreating back, slipping into the arms of the suede jacket, which smells smoky and earthy, like it's been around an open campfire. The streetlights cast a soft glow through the bay windows, offering enough illumination for me to find my way to a corner booth.

Right now, more than anything, I wish I was with Grace back in Brooklyn. Whenever one of us had a bad day, we'd make boxed mac and cheese and watch reruns of our second-favorite TV show, *The Mary Tyler Moore Show*, which my uncles had gotten us into. ("Tabitha Noelle is fine as far as TV role models go," Alonso used to say, "but Mary Richards is a groundbreaking feminist *queen*.") Even though Grace talked over the episodes, I never minded, because we'd seen them all multiple times and her wisecracks made me laugh, sometimes more than the show itself. ("Why would anyone want a place with a sunken living room? It's like, 'You know what my home needs? More booby traps!'") Grace used to joke that she was the Rhoda to my Mary, the sassy self-deprecating sidekick to the sweet and steadfast star of the show.

Now she's the star of her own show, and I feel neither sweet nor steadfast.

I miss my sidekick.

Mason returns with two mugs of tea.

As he's about to slide into the booth across from me, I ask, "Can you sit next to me?" I cringe at how needy I sound.

"Yeah." His body doesn't touch mine when he sits but is close enough that I can feel the heat emanating from it. "I would've brought you whiskey, but my flask seems to have gone missing."

"I would've given it back, but I've kinda been avoiding you." I wrap my hands around the mug, wishing it would scald me, but it's not hot enough.

"Avoiding me? Did I do something to offend?"

"I didn't want any distractions," I say.

"I had no intention of distracting you. I know how important it is for you to be here."

"Did Genevieve send you as some kind of test?" I blurt out.

"What? No. She's out of town this week and asked me to keep an eye on the film shoot to make sure they don't damage her garden. What kind of test?"

"Everything here feels like a test. I'm getting really good at failing them."

"You wouldn't still be here if you were failing that badly."

"Let's see what happens when word gets out that I was fired from the one job I booked the entire time I've been here."

"Actors get fired from jobs all the time. Think of it as part of your origin story. When you make it, you could talk about how—"

"Please don't. I mean, I appreciate all this—the jacket, the tea—but there's nothing you could say that's going to make me feel any less shitty. Right now, I'd rather wallow."

"Wallowing it is, then."

I sip the tea. It's strong, a little bitter but also sweet. "Be straight with me. How bad is it? Will this get me kicked out of the Dollhouse?"

"It might. If you get called into a private meeting with Genevieve, that's when you should worry. She only has one-on-ones with those who are doing very well or very poorly. Which isn't to say you may not be given another chance—whatever you do, don't beg, she hates that—but . . ."

"So, it looks like I'm probably done here." A strange giggle floats out of me, like a child letting go of a helium balloon.

I go limp, resting my head against Mason's shoulder. He responds by putting his arm around me, and I nestle in closer.

I lift my head and he lowers his, and when our faces are just a few inches apart, he stops.

"Ramona, listen . . . I'm not going to kiss you."

It's all I can do not to burst into tears. "Who said I wanted you to kiss me?" I make a weak attempt to pull away, but he pulls me in tighter.

"I'm not an idiot. It's been a while since I've seen you, but the thing between us is obvious. This would be a terrible time to act on it."

"And why's that?"

"Because you're at a low point right now and you'd associate that with the start of . . . whatever we'd be starting. Plus, it might be taking advantage of your . . . precarious emotional state. Beyond that, should things between us develop, I don't want to be a reason you stay here."

"I'm not precarious. And I'm about to be booted anyway." I reach for my tea, needing its external warmth, but it's gone cold.

"Not necessarily. Genevieve might find your tenacity a worthwhile reason to keep you on. But even if she does extend your contract . . . think about whether you really want to be here."

"It's all I ever wanted. I've been giving it everything I have, but it's not enough. Not the blood, sweat, or tears, and they must've taken gallons of blood by now. Should I be worried about the medical stuff they've been doing to me? The supplements I'm taking?"

"I hope not. It's one aspect of this place I've always had reservations about." He takes a heavy breath. "I don't know what they're doing with all the scans and bloodwork and personal histories—I think it's to see how you do over time with the curriculum at the Dollhouse and the drugs they end up doling out to everyone."

"So, they're not just supplements?" I glance up and catch a pointed look from him.

"You know they're not. And you've made progress by taking them, but everyone reacts differently, and once you start, going off them is murder. It's like the argument for taking steroids—sure, they enhance your performance, but it's a form of cheating. These drugs dull certain things and sharpen others to help you be a better performer, but wouldn't you rather do that on your own merit?"

"Obviously, my own merit hasn't been enough. But the drugs haven't been enough, either."

"Or maybe, as much as I'd hate to see you go, you'll do better elsewhere."

"So you're saying I should leave even if I don't get tossed out? Take my chances somewhere else or maybe give up acting altogether?" I try to give my words an impervious edge, but somehow I end up sounding like a frightened little girl.

"I can't tell you what to do . . . but I'm not sure you're going to find what you're looking for at the Dollhouse."

My head jerks up. "Have you been sending me anonymous notes?"

"What, you have a secret admirer or something?"

"A secret stalker, more like. I got the first one before I even got here, and it said not to come because I wouldn't find what I was looking for at the Dollhouse."

Apprehension furrows his brow. "Anonymous notes aren't my style. If I send you something, you'll know it's from me."

I believe him. "So then why does everyone seem to think I don't belong here? Because I'm too fragile?"

"Not necessarily that. I worry this place might make you bend in ways you shouldn't have to. I . . . I don't want to see that for you."

We both go quiet.

"I thought you believed in Dahlen, and that's why you've stayed here all these years," I say.

"I believe in the work that comes out of Dahlen, but I'm starting to have second thoughts about the methods used to produce that work. They do find clever ways of trapping and keeping you. Perhaps it's time for me to consider whether I still belong here."

I bury my face in his chest, and he puts his other arm around me.

"Everything is terrible," I say, the words muffled.

"Yeah. But it can't stay that way forever." He strokes my hair. "Is there anything I can do, apart from the obvious, to make you feel better?"

I set aside my physical desire and consider what, within reason, might assuage my current despair.

"Maybe there's one thing," I say. "Could you get me Grace Ludlow's new address and phone number? I called the campus directory, and they said she's unlisted."

Mason sucks air through his teeth. "Yeah, they do that with performers that reach a certain level, to give them privacy . . . Let me see what I can do."

The next day I receive a red sheet of paper in the mail.

I've been summoned by Genevieve.

CHAPTER TWENTY

I show up at Genevieve's five minutes early, dressed impeccably (I'm even wearing Diva Doll lipstick). I'm hoping to hear Mason's crisp British accent on the intercom, but instead, a somber female voice asks me to identify myself before buzzing me through. The woman looks even more severe in person, with a pronounced V between her eyebrows and a mouth pressed so tightly closed, her lips are practically invisible.

She leads me to a room wallpapered in forest green, its curved walls cluttered with portraits of owls, photorealistic paintings of various shapes and sizes, lit by wall sconces.

It's hard not to feel like helpless prey in here.

Despite being asked to take a seat at the round antique table in the center of the room, which bears a tea set and place settings for two, I remain standing and slowly pace the perimeter, observing the owls and mustering my courage. I'm not overly superstitious but hope to borrow some of Genevieve's belief that these creatures bring luck.

My back is turned when she enters the room, and her voice cuts through the air like a whip.

"I usually do a proper tea, with pastries and sandwiches, but today I thought I should protect my shoes."

And so our scene has begun, but what does Genevieve want from me in this moment? If I take the meek route, I might as well return to the dorm and start packing. Being in this room means I'm on my way out. If I'm going to fight for my place here, I need to be bold.

"It's a shame there won't be any food because I was hoping to sample more of your chef's exotic cuisine." I try to match her haughtiness. "Monkey brains, bull testicles, maggot cheese. It's part of this new diet I'm on. There's no way I'll overindulge in foods like that, and if they cause me to puke once in a while . . . well, that's been known to help keep the weight off, too."

Genevieve narrows her eyes, then saunters over to the table and pulls out a chair for me. "You should know better than to suggest unhealthy weight-loss techniques, even in jest."

When we sit, she puts her elbows on the table and entwines her fingers, which are knobbed like pale twigs.

"I'm worried about you, Ramona. Your trial period is nearing completion and I'm still not sure what—if anything—you may be able to offer us." She makes me sound like an appliance that she's thinking of returning.

"I think I have a lot to offer . . ."

An uncomfortable pause as we both wait for me to continue.

"I-I just may need more time to find my niche. I've never doubted my talent as a performer." Not until I set foot in the Dollhouse, that is.

"Talent can be cultivated whereas star quality is inherent. Your friend found her niche. She has star quality."

Damn, this woman is a master of poking the tender areas.

"I thought Grace and I were invited here because we both had star quality."

"You wouldn't be here if I thought otherwise. But it's gotten . . . buried somewhere. You flicker inconsistently. Also, I don't know exactly which constellation you fit into. You're too pretty to be the girl next door or the intellectual or the quirky best friend." I half expect her to tell me I'm more of a Mary than a Rhoda. "You *could* be the bombshell, but something tells me you wouldn't go for the surgical intervention required there"—she draws a circle, first around her chest, then the lower half of her face—"or would you?"

I take a moment to consider. It's so common for stars to get surgery to enhance their appearance, going back to the early days of Hollywood. If icons like Joan Crawford and Marilyn Monroe weren't above getting nips and tucks, why should I be?

"I'm pretty happy with the way I look," I say. "But I'll do whatever it takes."

"I'm not entirely convinced." Her face hardens. "Which would also preclude you from . . . certain other Dollhouse initiatives."

"Like what?" I suddenly feel like I'm wielding a big heavy machine gun, with no idea of how much damage firing it may cause. I pull the trigger anyway. "Like Project Understudy?"

Genevieve sucks in her cheeks. "What do you think you know about Project Understudy?"

"Only that Gino Rinaldi was screaming bloody murder about it when he was carried out of our dorm on a stretcher."

"That young man had personal problems. He was in the early stages of participating in Project Understudy, but we misjudged his abilities. It's a shame when that happens."

I ignore her pointed tone. "What exactly *is* Project Understudy?"

"Exactly what it sounds like. We have a number of expensive projects on the go at any given time, and we need to secure potential alternates should our top performers not be able to see their work through."

"But why make it sound like some sketchy government experiment?"

"Much of our operations are confidential. It helps us retain a competitive edge."

There's obviously more to it than that, more than Genevieve would ever share with me. If she gave me that sliver about Project Understudy, I can only imagine the glacier of secrets beneath the surface.

Even so, I can't resist asking, "Does all the medical testing done on us have anything to do with it?"

"The medical exams are to ensure you remain in top form and can sufficiently handle the stress at the Dollhouse Academy. Which, in your case, I have some doubts about." Genevieve clears her throat. "Now that we've established what you aren't suited for, perhaps we could figure out where, if anywhere, you might fit in as a performer." The way her eyes scan me up and down makes me think of the Terminator. "You *could* potentially play the ingenue, but I can't say for certain. Something is missing. You lack . . . vulnerability."

Here we go. Tell me what I'm not so I can prove the opposite. "That's funny, because I've been told I'm too fragile. Now I'm not fragile enough?"

"Vulnerability is not the same as fragility. Exposing yourself can be a feat of strength if you do it correctly."

"I can be vulnerable." If need be, I'd get fully naked for this woman before I let her expel me from the Dollhouse.

A tinkle of silver on porcelain as she stirs her tea. "I need you to bear your soul, not your body. Not through tears either. Any good actor can cry on cue."

I tilt my head to the ceiling, willing my eyes to go dry.

Why am I so desperate to stay here? Why does it feel like it's the Dollhouse or nothing?

Because it is.

Because if Grace can do it, so can you.

I'm not sure if the thought is coming from a place of inspiration or unkindness.

I meet Genevieve's gaze head-on. The light glints off her cat-eye glasses, her irises a dark void behind them.

What does this woman want from me? At this point, I really don't know.

"Look, Genevieve, I've been working my ass off and doing pretty much everything that's been asked of me. I got fired from one movie, but up to that point I was showing improvement in all my classes. It seems like you're ready to cut me loose but also want me to figure out the secret code to convince you to let me stay. But I don't know what magical thing I can say or do here, so . . ." I'm practically panting by the time I trail off. No wonder my teachers complain about my breath control.

"See, here's the problem. Bravado suits Gracie, but on you it's ill-fitting."

I recoil at the name. "Are you talking about Grace Ludlow?"

"Yes, we're rebranding her as Gracie. No last name."

There's no way Grace didn't push back on this "rebrand."

Genevieve continues. "A certain cynicism and sarcasm have pervaded the pop culture of this decade, and while I am personally not a fan, I recognize its popularity and value. Gracie embodies this contemporary attitude, and her ethnically ambiguous look is also very now. You have a bit of edginess to you, not as much as she does, but enough that it's at odds with your Barbie looks and makes you difficult to pin down. Which brings us back to our original dilemma of where you fit in."

How do you solve a problem like Ramona?

She fingers the owl brooch on the lapel of her black silk suit and the bird's diamond eyes catch the light. "Have you ever considered the notion that you chose to become an actor and embody the personas of others because you haven't fully developed your own? Maybe I can't find a category for you because you yourself don't know where you belong."

"I know I've never felt like I belonged anywhere as much as I do here," I say with all the certainty in my heart.

Genevieve's pinched face relaxes a degree, fresh curiosity in her eyes. "Keep talking."

"I don't remember a lot of my early childhood. As you probably know, my mother and I lived on a commune in Oregon until I was ten. We all dressed the same, in jeans and white tunics, and we were taught to think and breathe and live as one, yada yada yada. Their motto was 'Alone, you are ordinary; together, we are extraordinary.' I hated it, and I knew I didn't belong there. Even as a kid, I wanted to be special, to stand out from the crowd. It's pretty easy to draw a dotted line from that to my being here."

A small "hmm" from Genevieve, but her unwavering gaze tells me to continue.

"When my mom died and I went to live with my uncles, I felt like they were my real family and Brooklyn was my real home. That changed when I started fifth grade—like a lot of kids, I didn't feel like I fit in, more like I had to be a certain version of myself in order for people to like me. Except around my uncles, who supported me unconditionally, and Grace, who was unapologetic when it came to being herself, even if that meant not getting along with the other kids.

"So there I was, feeling at home with my uncles and with Grace, but at odds with the rest of the world. I felt this way until I was a freshman in high school and started acting. The moments where I inhabit a character living in a fictional world, that's when I feel the biggest sense of belonging. And with each role I take on, I discover something new about myself while also imprinting a piece of myself on the character." I tilt my body forward and lower my voice. "I know how this industry works, how quick it is to pigeonhole a performer and demand they play the same 'type' over and over. I thought Dahlen was better than that. Maybe you think I'm too prickly to play America's sweetheart and too wide-eyed to play a femme fatale, but I think I have it in me to take on anything."

"You say these things, but your track record thus far hasn't demonstrated it."

"I'm starting to find my rhythm. The drugs Devon prescribed—"

"Supplements."

If you say so. "They're helping me improve. Yes, I got in my head too much and messed up on that movie set, but I did finally book a role. I'm more of a tortoise than a hare."

"Things move quickly in this business. This isn't a place for tortoises."

"Then I'll grow long ears and a fluffy tail. I'll evolve. Adapt."

A long pause, and I can practically see the scales as Genevieve weighs her options. "Let's try this. I'm not ready to extend your contract, but I'll let you work through to the end of it. That gives you a little over a month. I'll expect to see more than degrees of improvement from you in that time. I want to see you worthy of booking a substantial role in a Dahlen production. It's asking a lot, but in return, I'm willing to help you." She reaches into her breast pocket and retrieves a slender pill vial.

Not this again.

"It's a new supplement we're developing that helps with nervous conditions."

Jesus, she's making me sound like a Victorian lady sprawled across a fainting couch.

"Some people cope with stress better than others," she continues. "I have a hunch the workload here is taking a toll on your creative side, making you second-guess yourself. These tablets, in conjunction with your others, will enable you to . . . take things in stride better."

She extends the vial on an open palm.

Obviously, I have no choice. Not if I want to stay here. Relief and reluctance swirl inside me like opposing tides.

I take the vial. "Okay."

Her head is tilted at an expectant angle. More gratitude is called for. It's what I should be feeling, instead of this sudden riptide of suspicion that sweeps in, ready to pull me under.

But I say thank you.

"One more thing," Genevieve says as she stands to leave. "Mention Project Understudy out loud again, to *anyone*, and you will face immediate dismissal from the Dollhouse Academy."

Back at Gale House, I head upstairs to Grace's room.

Her back is to me when I cross the threshold, bent over the bottom drawer of her dresser, which is full of clothes again.

"Hey you. Are you not moving after all?" I say, hoping she'll reciprocate my friendly and casual tone.

The girl who turns around has dark hair and a similar slim-hipped build to Grace, but isn't her.

"I actually just moved in," she says, in a southern drawl. "Well, a week ago, but Bowman House is having plumbing issues, so they transferred me here. But I'm guessing you were looking for someone else. I'm Tia." She extends a hand.

"Ramona." I shake it weakly, hiding my disappointment. "My best

friend lived here before you, and from behind, you look just like her." Less
so now that Tia's facing me, though they both have golden olive skin and
heavy-lidded brown eyes (I can hear Genevieve's voice in my head calling
her "ethnically ambiguous"). "It's actually kinda spooky," I say.

Tia widens her eyes and fans out her hands. "You think that's spooky? I
had a lunch at Genevieve's house yesterday where a girl got kicked out just
because she got a spray tan before coming here. This girl was carrying on
and had to have security guards forcibly remove her! Can you believe it?"

"That happened at my orientation, too. I wonder if they put on a little
show for us to scare us straight." A confusing camaraderie settles over us.
"Did they serve you the black Jell-O?" I ask.

"Oh my god, yes! Some people puked!"

"I puked."

"No way!"

"Way. And that's not even the worst of it."

I recount the full story, and what they say about comedy being tragedy
plus time must be true, because we find ourselves laughing.

Tia gives me a grateful smile. "You're the first person I've met here
who I feel comfortable talking to. The other trainees are nice enough, but
they seem really . . . competitive."

"This entire place is competitive."

"Yeah, but friendship shouldn't be."

I wince. "Sometimes it seems like all anyone cares about here is pursuing their dreams. People don't have time for much else. Making friends
somewhere like this can be tough." Keeping them can be tougher.

"Why, I just can't imagine living that way." There's something about
the southern belle frill on her words I find endearing. Despite her physical
likeness to Grace, it's reassuring that once she opens her mouth, Tia hardly
sounds anything like her. "I'm one of those people who usually makes
friends wherever I go. I even befriended the driver, Ratislov, on the way up
here from the airport. What a difficult life that poor man has had."

"Where did you fly in from?"

"Kansas City, Missouri, but would you believe I'm originally from a small town called Fame? My aunt Ellie said it was a sign from the Lord above." She lowers her voice to a stage whisper. "But that whole church-and-god thing never really stuck with me. I believe you should be a good person because it's in your heart, not because some book tells you to, know what I mean?"

I nod. It strikes me that I haven't met anyone this sincere since I've been at the Dollhouse Academy.

"Hey, do you want to grab a coffee?" I ask.

"I would love that." She breaks into a delighted smile. "Can I get a half hour to finish unpacking and change?"

"Of course. I'll meet you downstairs."

After the last brutal few days I've had, making a new friend revitalizes me in a way I didn't realize I needed.

As I head back to my room, my mind drifts back to Grace. I wonder if Mason will get me her new address. Even though we both said hurtful things, I want to mend this distance between us. Especially before she becomes famous and even harder to reach.

Tia comes bounding down the stairs beaming at me. "You ready to go?"

"Let's do this." I return her smile, setting aside my broodiness for now.

CHAPTER TWENTY-ONE

Ivy's Diary

AUGUST 11, 1998

I've been so caught up in work these past months. My new fragrance, Forever Platinum, was launched earlier this summer and I was sent on a promotional tour of high-end department stores across the US and Canada.

When Genevieve initially told me of the plan, I balked at touring for a perfume of all things. Surely such a thing was beneath me.

"If Elizabeth Taylor can do it, so can you," she snapped. "Unless you want us to find someone else to do it?"

I was quick to capitulate. As always.

The tour helped distract me from my concerns about Project Understudy, but it also interrupted my tentative investigation. Not that I've gotten far with it. All the lower-level staff I've spoken with so far have politely stonewalled me, so I have nothing to confirm my suspicions . . . but I have nothing to refute them, either.

Then, last night, I heard a rustling outside my house. When I went to the window, there was a flash of white hair. A figure retreated into the darkness, but I swear it looked like . . . but it's not possible. I cannot let my thoughts derail. I must turn my mind away from the darker corners it currently occupies.

It helps to reflect on my earlier years at the Dollhouse, to remind myself that I've been bestowed a tremendous amount of privilege.

One of life's greatest tragedies is, you don't know you're experiencing your best days until they're behind you.

After that week Timothy and I spent in NYC, the rest of 1982 was a happy blur. There was choreography to learn, costume fittings, photo shoots, voice lessons, phone and radio interviews. "Class Act" continued to dominate the airwaves and MTV, so there was a lot of anticipation for the release of my album *Dollface*. Enough that some journalists made the trek up to Owls Point to interview me in person, with photographers in tow.

I'd be lying if I said I didn't love all the attention. Reporters hung on my every word. I was dressed in the finest clothes and made up to look more stunning than I could've ever imagined. Compliments rained down on me, for my acting, my singing, my beauty. I eventually suffered some vertigo from the altitude of my pedestal, but for a long while, I relished being lifted up so high.

There was talk of how to market me as a singer. I wasn't a diva or a rocker—it made more sense to craft a sexy-but-sweet image for me, along the lines of someone like Olivia Newton-John. And when I had "real" moments, like stumbling on a red carpet or accidentally saying "shit" on live television, it only made me more relatable.

The *Dollface* tour was a Tilt-A-Whirl, with swarms of screaming fans and bright lights and being rushed from one place to the next, onstage, backstage, on the bus, off the bus. In between, there were photo and video shoots for a makeup brand I was the new face of, a shampoo ad, and a line of blue jeans I was now endorsing. At least there was minimal air travel, at my request.

With everything moving so quickly, there were some aspects of my new life that were difficult to adjust to, like how tricky it was to coordinate my schedule with Timothy's for a daily phone call, which sometimes only lasted a few minutes, or being exposed to countless strangers but also kept in a protective bubble of bodyguards and handlers. It was disorienting, traveling from place to place so swiftly, forgetting where I was or what day it was until somebody handed me that day's schedule.

But despite all that, I loved being on tour. Whatever high I experienced singing in a studio was magnified exponentially while singing live.

I couldn't believe how many people came out to see me. The energy of thousands of adoring concertgoers was like a direct shot of adrenaline to my heart, a soaring sensation unlike anything else. Getting lost in the songs, meshing with the band, singing my heart out—when it all came together, I couldn't imagine a better high.

Whenever Timothy and I managed to find a couple of free overlapping days, we fought jet lag and work exhaustion to secure private time together. Dahlen always made us do some public appearances to keep the press happy, the paparazzi fed, and our fans' fervor stoked. But Timothy and I also insisted on at least twenty-four uninterrupted hours alone, which we typically spent in a hotel, sometimes not leaving the room at all. There was plenty of sex, of course, but so much more than that. We'd order room service and have a picnic on the floor. We'd watch *American Bandstand* and *Soul Train*, dancing to the songs. We'd play along to *The Price Is Right*. Or sometimes we'd switch off the TV and talk for hours, about our dizzying days, where we wanted our fame to take us, and what we wanted to do beyond stardom (create a children's hospital charity, open an animal sanctuary, have kids). And all these things, the dancing, the laughing, the talking, the dreaming, the lovemaking, all formed a protective shell from the rest of the world.

These visits were divine but over far too quickly. Why do the good things in life rush by like a train hurtling at top speed?

In any case, the *Dollface* tour also went by in a blur, and before I knew it, I was back in Owls Point, preparing for the second season of *In the Dollhouse* and reunited with Timothy.

Everything should have been blissful. But it wasn't, not quite.

I began to notice a change in Timothy.

While I'd been managing the hectic pace of my schedule with the aid of all my supplements, he had refused to take any. Once we returned to

Owls Point, as production began to ramp up, he slept poorly and became easily agitated.

I told him there was no shame in getting a little extra support.

"You forget what happened when you stopped taking the pills," he reminded me. "You're fine on them now, but you can't take them forever. And who knows what they're doing to your brain over time."

I hadn't told him that I'd begun taking a third supplement. But I did reiterate how much they helped me with energy, sleep, and a general sense of well-being.

"But what if the pills are dulling other parts of you?"

I assured him they were allowing me to be the best version of myself, just as Genevieve promised they would. As my obligations multiplied, the pills helped me stay on top of everything, and they would help him, too. Furthermore, it was unfair of him to judge without having taken the supplements himself.

In this way, I convinced him to give them a try.

That was one of the biggest mistakes of my life.

In the spring of 1983, we attended the Grammy Awards in Los Angeles, where I won Best New Artist, beating out the Human League and Stray Cats, two bands I still listen to today. While I'd won several small awards prior to this, for music and acting, this level of industry recognition felt different. I was proud.

By that summer, *In the Dollhouse* was still the top show after two seasons, and singles off my debut album were still making the charts and crossing over internationally, so I had to do a promotional European tour. That same summer, Timothy booked a film that would be shooting on location in San Francisco. When we were working on the show together, things were great, but as soon as production stopped, it seemed impossible for us to remain on the same continent. The distance put a strain on our relationship, but we endured it.

By early autumn, we were both back in Owls Point, drained but ready for the new season of ITD.

Timothy and I talked about moving out of the house we'd lived in with the other cast members and finding our own place, maybe somewhere outside of Owls Point, in a neighboring town. When I mentioned this to Genevieve, she took us on a tour of a quaint, out-of-the-way English-style cottage near Parliament Lake. It looked like something out of a fairy tale: ivy-covered eggshell stone with a false thatched roof, flower boxes in the windows, and periwinkle shutters. I couldn't have dreamed up a more perfect house.

Timothy had some reservations, but after we saw a few properties off campus, none of which had even a fraction of the cottage's charm, we agreed to move to Parliament Lake.

Maybe Timothy and I were too young to be playing house, but we were in a business that accelerates a person's maturity. From the time I was twelve years old, I had a career that supported a family of three. I showed up on set and did the same work the grown-ups did, and once I was emancipated at sixteen, I also worked the same hours they did. So moving in with Timothy and owning property before I turned twenty hardly felt too advanced.

That autumn, just before the show went into production, the medical tests began.

Initially, it was a matter of insurance and protection. Now that ITD was phenomenally successful and the main cast was under contract for two more seasons, Dahlen wanted to safeguard its investments and make sure we were in top health.

Aside from that, Dahlen Entertainment was interested in expanding their "creative medical synergy" with DahlenRex. They had already planted the seeds with the supplements, but this program promised to be more in-depth.

It made perfect sense. Rehearsals, production and touring schedules, and press junkets could put a lot of stress on a performer's mind and body, and show business came with added pressures of maintaining one's image, from both an aesthetic and reputational standpoint. The Doll-house Academy (as we all called it since the show aired) needed to give their trainees the best possible chance at becoming stars, and Dahlen Entertainment needed to keep those stars in top form for as long as possible.

On the Sunday before rehearsals were set to begin, Timothy and I were summoned to a building that had recently been expanded. What had once served as a clinic for minor injuries now appeared to be a full-fledged hospital and medical center.

While Timothy and I arrived together early in the morning, we were quickly directed to different sections of the building and wouldn't see each other again until after dinner.

That day, every inch of my body was examined, probed, and scanned. There were injections to remove blood and others to fill my body with god-knows-what. Many of the tests required partial or full nudity, which didn't bother me except when there were bright flashes of light that made me wonder if my body was being photographed. There was a test where I was interrogated about my life while being hooked up to various wires. Could it have been a lie detector? Oddly, when I provided certain answers, even when they were truthful, I sometimes received a mild electric shock.

Whenever I asked what the purpose of a specific test was, I'd get a dismissive response, like, "new Dahlen protocol."

The worst came toward the end of the day, when I was asked to strip down, put on latex thong underwear and a head covering akin to a swim cap, and stand in what appeared to be a square of wet cement in the middle of a brightly lit room with metallic walls. I was told a mold would be taken of my entire body, one section at a time. This way, if I experienced any injury, they'd have an original version of me to compare it to.

This sounded peculiar, but the reasoning was explained in such a convincing manner, I not only accepted it, I praised Dahlen for their ingenuity.

They started with my head, putting one straw up each nostril and another in my mouth, smearing Vaseline over my eyebrows, eyelashes, and hairline. Then they worked their way down my entire body, covering my skin in a cold gooey substance before it was wrapped in some type of bandage. I felt like I was being mummified.

As the casts began to harden, they felt heavier, but I was given strict instructions not to move my body even a millimeter or risk having to begin the entire process all over again.

Finally, somebody announced that the cast was dry enough. Once again, I was told to remain perfectly still as a metallic whirring filled the room. Bit by bit, pieces of the cast were cut off me, from the top down. It was surreal to see this plaster facsimile of me being removed in sections, like being simultaneously copied and dismembered.

Timothy was already there when I got home, pacing our living room.

"We need to get out of here. This place is dangerous," he said.

There was a feral look in his eyes I hadn't seen before. I told him we had to trust they had our best interests at heart. After all, look how far we'd gotten.

"Ivy, you can't possibly be that naive. All they care about is making tons of money off of us. Oh sure, they'll give us the VIP treatment and say all the right things to keep us happy, but that's just so we keep working and doing what they say. As soon as we stop . . . Nobody at Dahlen is your friend, not even Genevieve. Especially not Genevieve."

That wasn't true. She was more nurturing than my own mother had been. I told him maybe he took it for granted because he came from a supportive family, but her wisdom and kindness weren't lost on me. Genevieve wanted to protect us from the terrible things she was put through back in her day, the sort of abuse some young performers outside of the Dollhouse were still being subjected to.

"She isn't protecting us from anything!" Fear twisted his face. "I've been hearing about something called Project Understudy. Apparently, the Dollhouse is creating a 'shadow academy' to train replacements for its top stars."

Timothy stopped pacing, gripped both of my hands, and gave me a pleading look. "They're not training performers to replace our characters. The Dollhouse is training them to replace *us*."

CHAPTER TWENTY-TWO

SEPTEMBER 1998

After my blowout fight with Grace, being fired from *Sisterhood*, and then nearly getting expelled by Genevieve herself, I was in a dark place.

But I put my head down, kept pushing myself in all my classes, kept taking my supplements, and kept auditioning. Finally, yesterday, I got another green flyer. This was the one I've been waiting for. Not a movie, a TV show. *The* show.

I celebrate by treating myself to a little shopping spree at Chapter and Verse, debating whether to get the latest album by Tricky or Massive Attack (as if I won't end up getting both).

"Have you heard this one? It's smashing."

I look up to see Mason. It's the first time I've seen him since the night I was fired from *Sisterhood*, the night he refused to kiss me. The familiar galloping of my pulse pounds in my ears.

Shut up, stupid heart.

He's few feet away, holding out a CD with a close-up of a human iris on the cover, half blue, half amber.

"Visual Audio Sensory Theater?" I ask, reading the words across the front.

"VAST is the band—actually the brainchild of one guy. The album is experimental electro-rock with a dark, gritty edge and world choruses. You should hear it. Track four is my favorite."

Turning over the CD, I read the track listings and snort. "Yeah, you *would* love a song called 'Pretty When You Cry.'"

"Just for that, I'm going to buy you this CD."

Rolling my eyes, I head to the register, where I pay for the Tricky and Massive Attack albums.

Outside, Mason accompanies me back to Gale House. The buckles of his leather jacket jingle as he walks.

"You look more upbeat than I've seen you look . . . well, ever," he says.

"I made a new friend, and I just booked a three-episode arc on *In the Dollhouse*." I was playing an upper-crust transfer student named Skylar Vaughn. It was a small part, and I wouldn't have any scenes with Ivy, but there was potential for me to become a recurring character if I played this right, which I was determined to do. I was overjoyed to have this chance.

"Yes, I did hear something about that. Congratulations." There's a rustle of plastic as he switches his shopping bag from one hand to the other. "Something tells me we can't credit your new friend with your improved mood as much as booking ITD."

"Fair enough. But it's not like I'm one of those people who's entirely defined by my career."

We stop at a pedestrian crossing and Mason regards me, tilting his chin one way then the other, like I'm a picture frame and he's checking to see if I'm crooked. "In your estimation, what percent would you say being a performer *is* who you are?"

"I mean, it's a big part of who I am. Maybe . . . fifty percent?"

"And what's the other fifty percent?"

Something about this line of questioning doesn't sit well with me; it's like I've been thrown into a maze of thorny bushes, and there's no way I'll find my way out without getting scratched up. I get enough of this from Devon. "I don't know, a lot of things. There's more to my personality than acting and singing. I have plenty of interests—reading, listening to music, watching movies and TV shows." Those all seem too connected to performing, though, so I throw in, "I love to travel."

"Really? What are some interesting places you've been to?"

The light changes and we resume walking. A tang of freshly cut grass fills the air and I'm starting to think I'd enjoy this walk much more without Mason. "Well, I haven't had a chance to do much traveling yet other than some family vacations to the Adirondacks and the Jersey Shore, but I'm interested in seeing more places. What are you getting at?" I quicken my pace, but Mason is taller than me, with longer legs, so he easily matches it.

"I've seen a lot of young people come through here whose entire personal happiness becomes bound up in how well they're doing in this business, which is not a meritocracy. You can't allow a roulette wheel to dictate your self-worth and well-being."

"Wow, thank you so much for educating me about showbiz, I had no idea it was like that," I mock-gush. Switching back to a normal voice, I say, "What I don't get is, I'm finally seeing my hard work pay off, and instead of getting a moment to bask in that, I feel like you're saying I shouldn't feel *too* happy."

"That's not what I'm saying at all. I—"

"You're kinda trying to shit all over it."

"I'm really not."

"Or are you one of those guys who goes for the bird-with-a-broken-wing type?"

"That's preposterous. The fact that I struck a nerve is something you should think about. I've seen plenty of people develop a codependency toward this business, and quite frankly, you're headed in that direction. I'm sorry if that's unpleasant to hear, but I'm not very good at telling you what you want to hear, am I?"

We reach the block with Gale House and it's all I can do not to break into a run to the front door. "Right now, I don't need to hear anything from you. I already have one annoying counselor and I don't need another. I have to go study my lines."

"Ramona, hang on." Mason tugs on my plastic shopping bag from Chapter and Verse, and before I can stop him, he drops the VAST CD inside.

I return to the dorm seething. What a load of bullshit. Mason can't tell the difference between neediness and grit. No wonder he couldn't hack it. Maybe he's even a little jealous.

And there's something else tugging at me.

Is this how Grace felt when you couldn't be fully happy for her?

If so, maybe I deserve to have my own happiness deflated right now.

As it is, it's hard to fully enjoy this moment because Grace and I still aren't speaking. It's been over a month, the longest we've ever fought. Being on *In the Dollhouse* is something we dreamed about as young girls together; now that it's actually happening, her absence is making the experience bittersweet.

Mason was able to get me her new address and number, and at first, I didn't do anything with either one. In fact, I went out of my way to avoid the part of campus where she lives now. I didn't want to risk seeing her before I was sure of what I'd say. I picked up the phone countless times to call her, but every time I'd be overcome with indignation before I could finish dialing. Grace has my number, too, so why hasn't she bothered to call? Why should I be the one to break the silence?

When I initially recounted our argument to Devon, he said something that's stuck with me: "Do you want to be right or do you want to be in this relationship?"

So last week, I sent her a pack of gummy bears and a white silk rose. I tried to write an accompanying note but the right words still eluded me. Sure, something as simple as "I'm sorry" and "I miss you" would've conveyed what was in my heart, but it didn't feel like enough. And a darker part of me wondered if I was truly sorry, or if she was, or whether the things we'd said to each other needed to be said. If so, I hope it will clear the way for a new phase of our friendship, not end it.

It's been eight days and there's been no word back from Grace. However busy she is with her new show, surely she could've taken a minute out of her day to respond. She could've asked one of the PAs on set to send a message through the campus mail—hell, she might have her own assistant now.

Maybe she needs more time to stew before she comes around. That's preferable to the alternative, that our friendship means so little to her, she doesn't want to set aside any time to mend it. Or worse, she doesn't want to come around; she's done with me.

Ahead of me, there's a blur of dark hair as Grace rushes down the hall toward my room. She's not done with me!

I run after her and it isn't until I'm two feet away that I realize it's Tia, not Grace. I really need to stop doing that.

"Guess what, guess what?" Tia gushes. "Lady Edna said I wasn't a complete catastrophe! She said I was *almost* keeping time with the rest of the class today!"

I grin. "That's practically a hug from Lady Edna. The other day she said I danced like a gazelle—"

"A gazelle! That's a big step up from . . . what does she like to call you?" She snaps her fingers. "An arthritic Tin Man."

"No, let me finish. She said I danced like a gazelle being electrocuted." I hold out my palms, invisibly weighing the two options. "Though I guess that's still a step up from an arthritic Tin Man."

"Most definitely. Want to take a walk before we run lines?"

"Sure." I had promised to help Tia prepare for her Scene Study class and she, in turn, was going to help me rehearse my lines for *In the Dollhouse*.

It's not fair to compare Tia and Grace, I know it isn't, but I can't help it.

The truth is, having a friend like Tia is refreshing. Where Grace would grouse and nitpick and find the dark side of everything, Tia is upbeat and compassionate and wildly optimistic. Case in point, the first thing she says when we get outside:

"I bet you're going to be so great on ITD, they'll make you a series regular and you'll finally be able to drop Lady Edna's class."

"At this point, I just don't want to get fired," I say.

"Forget about what happened on *Sisterhood*. That was your first pancake. The first pancake is always a dud, so you throw it out. Your next pancake will be perfect, I'm sure of it."

"How can you be so sure?"

"When I was a little girl, before we settled in Fame, we moved around a lot. Daddy had a gambling problem, so we were always getting evicted or chased down by debt collectors. It seems like all my childhood memories are the four of us—Mama, Daddy, and my older sis, Nadine—crammed into a cheap motel room with my parents bickering. At night, after Daddy stormed off in search of another poker game, Mama, Nadine, and I would crowd around the television and watch *In the Dollhouse* reruns. It was my happy place. I'd see Tabitha Noelle, how she rose out of poverty and got away from her own troubled family, and all I wanted to do was be right there with her in Otus, New York. Mama said if I worked hard enough and wished hard enough, those wishes would come true."

A bittersweet nostalgia sweeps through me. "I didn't grow up with a lot of money, either, and even though my uncles tried to hide it from me, I'd overhear some of their conversations when things got tight and worry along with them."

"Isn't it awful? It's like being cold and trying to cover yourself with a blanket that's too small."

"Yeah," I say, remembering all the dinners where I was the only one with a plate of food while Reed and Alonso shared a bowl of stale popcorn and lied about eating earlier. "*In the Dollhouse* was my happy place, too," I say.

"And look where we are now."

As we walk through the campus in the late afternoon's golden light, Tia's encouraging words feel like cartoon birds landing on my shoulders.

"I'm telling you, Ramona, everything is about to change for the better. For both of us."

I hope she's right.

CHAPTER TWENTY-THREE

The makeup artist is saying something to me. I pause my Discman in the middle of the VAST CD I've been listening to ad nauseam since Mason gave it to me.

"Twenty-two? I wouldn't have put you a day past seventeen." She applies a light mauve onto my lips with a tiny brush. "No wonder they have you in uniform."

And how incredible to be wearing it. My right hand drifts up to check that the red necktie is still there, while my left sweeps across the lap of my black-and-white wool skirt.

Yes, this is real.

I sneak a feel of my hair, which I was commanded not to touch, my fingertips grazing the glossy ends. It's been curled in large rollers, slightly disheveled, then pinned at the sides. My makeup is simple but striking: white eye shadow, black-winged eyeliner, a trace of blush, and this lipstick.

Earlier in the week, during our first table read, I saw Ivy for the first time since the studio tour. She walked right by me as she made her way to the other end of the table, and I was dumbstruck. With her more relaxed posture and without makeup covering up the freckles scattering the bridge of her nose and cheeks, her aqua eyes electrifying and bright, she looked much younger than thirty-four. It's a testament to her acting that she plays the headmistress role with such maturity.

I was nervous during the read-through, since a lackluster table read can precipitate major script changes and, in some cases, cast changes. But my lines seemed to go over well, the humorous ones even getting laughs.

During the scenes I wasn't in, I watched Ivy. Even though I was seated far away from her, there was still something magical about her presence. Every time she spoke a line, the entire table became more attentive, laughed a little louder at her jokes, kept their eyes on her. It's astonishing how some people effortlessly exude charisma.

Sitting in this makeup chair, an effervescence sweeps through me, like I'm being carried away on a wave of champagne. Not only do I look like I belong here, I *feel* like I belong here.

"Ramona, hey." Jude, the actor I'm going to be doing the scene with, pokes his head in the door. "We just got some script changes. Do you want to run through them real quick while they're setting up?"

"She'll be done in five minutes," the makeup artist answers for me.

I hold up my arms helplessly and try not to move my face as I tell him, "Sure thing. Five minutes."

"Great. I'm gonna grab a bagel. Meet me by craft services?" he asks.

I give him a thumbs-up, put my headphones back in, and finish listening to the song, Jon Crosby's gritty voice alternating between scream-singing *where do I put the lies* and *where do I put the love.*

Five minutes later, I'm eyeing the craft services table, my stomach rumbling. Tempted as I am to have a bagel, I don't want to risk being chastised for messing up my lipstick or getting crumbs on my clothes, so I make do with tossing a few grapes into my mouth.

A strand of hair from Jude's pompadour falls perfectly across his forehead as he chews. He points at me. "You look great."

"Thanks. I like how you pointed at me when you said that, like we're not the only ones here." I pop another grape in my mouth.

"It's called emphasis, Holloway."

"Is that something you learned on the farm? I may need you to explain it to me."

Jude takes a step toward me, a sly glint in his hazel eyes. "I may need to explain a few things to you."

"You sure sound wise for a country boy."

Despite my first impressions at Genevieve's lunch, Jude Smolenski never surfed in his life; he actually grew up on a farm in Illinois. Our paths hadn't crossed again until this project and I've known him for only a week, but unlike my interactions with Mason, which always leave me confused and troubled, I know where I stand with Jude. Brimming with pure midwestern charm, he's made it perfectly clear.

"You know this is going to happen, right?" Jude said the other day while walking me back to Gale House after rehearsal.

"I have no idea what you're talking about," I responded, my voice high and full of faux innocence.

"I mean you and me. Isn't it fun to know it *will* happen, but not know exactly when?"

At that moment, he stopped and pulled me off the main path, behind a cluster of spruce trees that marked the entrance to Gale House.

"Like, it could happen right here, right now." He put his palms on my shoulders, which felt like being submerged in warm water, only from the inside. As he slowly brought his face toward mine, his pupils dilated like the aperture of a camera lens.

Mesmerized, I held my breath but couldn't resist a quick glance over my shoulder, which broke the spell.

"See, that's the problem, though," he said, stepping back. "Right now isn't the best time, because we're too out in the open."

I tried to play it cool and hide my disappointment. "Sure, I get that." Then a fresh boldness surged through me, and I took a step forward. "Though we *are* used to playing for an audience." This time I put my palms on his shoulders and his Adam's apple bobbed up and down as he swallowed hard. Jude was only a few inches taller than me and it would've been easy to stand on my tiptoes and . . . but no. I gave him a little smile and took two steps back. "Then again, I guess some things are better without an audience."

Is this how it was between Ivy and Timothy? More than a mere attraction, but an easy, almost familiar connection? An innate belief that you're both on the same side?

Just as it wasn't fair to compare Tia and Grace, I tried not to compare Mason and Jude, though once again I couldn't help it. Of all their differences, it was Jude's straightforward and unruffled congeniality I appreciated the most. Where Mason was a twisty road with a razor wire border, Jude was a straight, open path. Where Mason created friction, muddied the waters, and made me feel rudderless, Jude was smooth and clear and made me feel invigorated.

"Come on, we can rehearse over here." Jude leads us behind some bleachers that serve as part of the show's gymnasium set. "We won't be shooting here today, so there's no one else around."

"I see you're fully committed to this naughty teenager scenario," I say. "Are we going to go all the way with it, drink some beer, smoke a joint?"

"Do you want to go all the way?" he asks in a low voice.

It's quieter back here and the light creates thick stripes across our bodies. Part of me wants this to happen now. We're in our private bubble and it could be a perfect moment, except . . . "We don't have a lot of time to learn these new pages."

"Right. And we have more of them now, too." He hands me a sheaf of papers.

I start scanning them, muttering a few new lines out loud, then grin as I notice the scene hasn't only been altered, it's twice as long as it was before.

"Pretty sweet, right?" Jude says. "Genevieve saw a taping of our chemistry read and demanded the scene be rewritten. Apparently, she wants our characters to echo Tabitha and Hayden, only this time you're the rich snob and I'm the rebellious scholarship kid, and we both hate each other at first but there's also a thing between us." He motions at me then back at himself. "Like, everyone else sees it but we'll be the last to realize that we're into each other. Not at all like what we have here." He makes the same circular motion.

"Not at all."

"And if we kick ass on these next few episodes—which we will—we could have our storyline expanded and maybe even become series regulars."

A series regular on *In the Dollhouse*.

It's suddenly hard to get enough air into my lungs, even though I'm gulping in big breath after big breath.

"Ramona, whoa. What's wrong? You look like you're gonna pass out."

"This is only the second job I've booked here. The first one didn't go so well." In broad strokes, I tell him about my disastrous experience on *Sisterhood*.

"It doesn't matter what happened before." Jude takes my hand. "When I was a kid, all the guys would tease me about how much I loved ITD—I think they refused to watch it because it had the word 'dollhouse' in the title. But I didn't care. I was sure of two things. One, *In the Dollhouse* was the greatest show on TV. Two, I'd be starring in it someday."

"I was never *sure* I'd be on it. I just hoped harder for it than for anything else."

"Right, and look at us now. There's a reason why we're both here. In this scene. Together. This won't be like any small part you or I played before. This is its own thing. It'll be more than a few episodes."

And with that, he takes my face in his hands and kisses me long and slow. This time, when I can't find my breath, it's for all the right reasons.

"Cut! Jude, Ramona, you were perfection. Let's reset for the close-ups."

My head feels like it's floating ten feet above my body.

I can't believe I'm standing on one of the classroom sets that I've seen in countless episodes of *In the Dollhouse*, with its parquet floors, stained glass rose window, and antique school desks with wrought iron legs.

It had been a long time since I last felt that flying feeling. Not since before coming to the Dollhouse, when Grace and I performed our live coming attractions. But the rest of the world melted away when Jude and

I performed together. The feel of his kiss still lingered on my lips, and the promise of more to come flickered in his eyes as we brought our characters to life, verbally sparring, circling one of the desks as if in a choreographed dance.

Unlike last time, this director, a fortysomething woman with long fingers and tinted glasses, has been nothing but effusive about my performance.

And not just the director. When we're done with the close-ups, as we leave the set, several people stop to compliment us. One harried-looking PA, dragging a teddy bear larger than she is, pauses to say, "You guys . . . unbelievable," before licking the tip of her finger and making a sizzling sound.

Unbelievable is exactly right.

"I told you this would be different," Jude murmurs into my ear as we walk over to wardrobe.

It is different. How thrilling, to do what I love most in the world, and to be rewarded for it.

This is, without question, one of the best days of my life.

It's just past nine as we leave the studio, and it's warm out, the air still.

"I grabbed us some sandwiches from craft services," says Jude. "Want to have a picnic somewhere?"

"Yeah." An idea pops into my head. "I know exactly where we can go."

We take the shuttle to the other side of campus, and I lead us through the woods to Parliament Lake.

"Nice." Jude heads over to the same fallen log where Mason and I sat. "Now I'm wondering if I should've waited until we were here to kiss you."

"I'm glad you didn't wait." I take the sandwiches out of his hands, set them down on the log, and stand between his knees. Automatically, Jude wraps his arms around my waist and pulls me closer.

It's been weeks since I've seen Mason, since that argument we had outside my dorm, and even though I don't owe him anything, guilt plucks at me like I'm an out-of-tune guitar string. I shouldn't have brought Jude here.

But then Jude's hands slip beneath my T-shirt, cool at first, sending a shiver through me, but warming as they slide up my bare back, triggering more shivers, until I bend down, arms around his neck, and kiss him deeply.

When I return to Gale House, a white envelope awaits me.

Enjoy it while you can. It can all be taken away from you.

CHAPTER TWENTY-FOUR

OCTOBER 1998

After receiving the note, I had one shaky day on set, but my insecurity gradually grew into anger—I won't let some anonymous stranger sabotage me, not when things are falling into place. I returned to set the next day newly determined, and everything went smoothly shooting the rest of that episode.

Better than smoothly.

The chemistry between Jude and me is palpable, even more so now that we're a couple off-screen, and it sends the writers scurrying to beef up our roles in the subsequent two episodes. After we finish shooting those, we're offered contracts for the rest of the season as recurring characters on *In the Dollhouse*. It's just as Jude predicted.

And when my six-month probation period ends, I'm offered a two-year extension on my Dollhouse Academy contract. I'm also offered a room in Fisher House, but odds are low I'll get the perfect roommate twice in a row, so I choose to remain in Gale House.

Since I'll be in episodes throughout the rest of the season, I may finally get to act alongside Ivy Gordon. So far I've done a scene with Vanessa

Sanchez (trying not to be smug about the fact that Grace never got the same chance), but what a thrill it would be to get close to the woman I've idolized for so long. On the few occasions she's glanced my way at table reads or on set, she's offered little more than a smile. The opportunity has never come up to say anything to her, though if it did, I don't know where I'd begin. Grace had found it somewhat disappointing doing her scene with Ivy ("she's polite and professional, but kinda like a robot when the cameras aren't rolling"), but I'm sure I'll have a better experience if and when I get to shoot with her.

After what happened with *Sisterhood*, I hadn't wanted to tell my uncles about booking *In the Dollhouse* until I was sure I'd actually hold on to this job. Truth be told, I still thought about that last note from time to time, so I kept things vague during our weekly calls, saying I had some promising auditions, and I had a new boyfriend, who's also my scene partner (technically the truth).

It isn't until I'm offered a recurring role and new contracts that I'm ready to share the news with Reed and Alonso, so I call them one Friday night.

"We had a feeling we'd be hearing from you." Alonso's voice is sympathetic.

"It's perfectly reasonable that you'd feel upset," Reed adds from the other line.

I pull away the phone from my ear and stare at it, confused. "Why would I be upset? What happened?" A prickle of dread. "Is it Grace? Did something happen to Grace? Is she okay?"

"She's fine. She's . . . better than okay." Alonso's words are loaded.

"Then what would I be upset about?" It feels like we're trying to have two different conversations.

"We thought you saw the *Rock the Dollhouse* trailer. Starring *Gracie*." There's a disapproving note in Reed's tone.

"No, I . . . Gracie?" It takes me a second to remember Genevieve telling me about my friend's rebranding.

"They gave her quite the makeover. Girl got her nose *and* lips done," Alonso says, in full gossip mode. "They also gave her this red dye job—it really pops, but I'm not sure it works with her skin tone."

"I haven't seen it yet. The trailer." I walk back to the kitchen and grab a tangerine from the fruit basket. "It sounds like she's become a different person."

"Don't get me wrong, she's still a knockout," says Alonso. "Though perhaps a Bette Midler circa *Beaches* red would work better on her."

Reed is less diplomatic. "She's had too much work done, and she's gotten too skinny. I hope they're not starving you up there, too."

"Grace probably just stopped eating carbs," Alonso reasons. "That's how everyone is dropping weight these days. It works, but as far as I'm concerned, a life without bread isn't a life worth living."

"Are you eating properly?" Reed asks. "Are you eating carbohydrates?"

"Yeah, I'm eating fine. Carbs and everything." Though when I think about it, between the busy shooting schedule and the new relationship with Jude, I haven't had much of an appetite, and a wardrobe assistant recently had to take in the skirt and blouse of my uniform and swap my blazer for a smaller size. I've barely eaten anything today, and this tangerine I'm peeling is more for something to do with my hands.

There's a stilted silence.

"How are things with Jude?" Alonso asks.

"They're great. He's great." But the point of this call isn't to gush about my new boyfriend. "Actually, I have some news." In broad strokes, I tell them about Skylar Vaughn.

"Congratulations, sweetheart," says Reed.

"We knew you'd make it." Alonso sounds like he's on the verge of tears.

"I just wish they hadn't put you through hell first," Reed grouses.

"The best part is, they gave me a two-year extension on my contract with the Dollhouse Academy. A month ago, I thought for sure I'd get kicked out." I pop a tangerine segment into my mouth and bite down, its tartness flooding my tongue.

There's another pause. Was that a sigh on the other end of the line? If so, I bet it came from Reed.

"So, are we going to get to see you again anytime soon?" Reed finally asks. "Maybe before Thanksgiving? Or are they going to keep you prisoner there for—"

"Ignore him," Alonso interjects. "We both miss you—Reed just has a funny way of showing it. It *has* been a long time, though, and we'd hate to have Thanksgiving and Christmas without you."

"If they won't let her out for Thanksgiving, I'll drive right up there—"

This time I interrupt Reed. "Hey, calm down. I'm not a prisoner here, and you won't have to wait until Thanksgiving to see me. Jude and I don't have any scenes in the episode shooting next week, so they won't need us for a few days. We're actually going to come down to the city, now that my six-month probationary period is up, and I'm allowed off campus. Maybe we'll even swing by Brooklyn," I tease.

There's whooping from Alonso on the other end of the line. Reed, far calmer, says, "That's all wonderful news, Ramona. We can't wait to see you."

"Me, too," I say, but there's a sour note in my cheer, knowing there's no good answer to what I'm about to ask next. "So, um . . . have you talked to Grace recently?"

"Sure, she calls every week and sends us checks regularly," says Alonso, followed by a muttered exchange in which Reed admonishes him and Alonso retorts with, "She asked, why shouldn't I tell her?"

"Actually, now that I've started earning a decent amount, I was going to send a check, too, but since I'll see you soon, I'll bring it in person. It's probably not as much as Grace can give you, but hopefully it'll help with getting the Mag back on its feet." I don't mean to refer to the theater as a person, but it feels oddly appropriate.

"As long as it's perfectly clear that this is a loan and we'll be paying you back every last cent," Reed says.

I only agree to avoid a drawn-out debate, but of course I won't accept any money from them. Hopefully this is the start of me being able to support my uncles financially after all these years and they won't need any more money from Grace.

"So the last time you talked to Grace . . ." I hate returning to her, but I won't be satisfied until I get some sort of real update. "How did she sound?" The unspoken second question: *Did she mention me?*

"She sounded tired," says Reed, with compassion (toward me or her?). "She's been busy shooting *Rock the Dollhouse*, and since the show is a musical, she's also recording the companion album, which gives her barely any time to herself."

Alonso lets out a frustrated grunt. "I keep telling her it's not normal to work seven days a week, but she says she doesn't want to piss anybody off by speaking up. Which doesn't sound like the Grace we know and love."

"No, it's not," I say. But then again, apparently she no longer looks like the Grace we know and love, either. She's Gracie now, whoever that is. "I'm assuming she didn't say anything about me."

"I'm sorry, honey, she didn't," says Alonso.

That stings.

I return to the subject of my upcoming visit, wanting to end the chat on a high note, and by the time we get off the phone, the three of us are buzzing again.

After hanging up, as I head back to my room, a familiar voice calls out my name.

"I haven't seen you in forever, girl." Dion comes into the hall and hugs me. "Can you believe we made it out of Lady Edna's class alive? I thought for sure one of us would lose an eye." His breath comes out in a gush. "The first episode of *Overruled* I shot is about to air. Come watch with us?"

I follow him to the living room, which is filled with a handful of trainees. The opening credits roll and, a few minutes later, we whoop when Dion, who plays an idealistic first-year associate, appears on-screen. While I try to keep an eye out for Grace during the commercials, I get caught up in talking to Dion during the breaks. It isn't until the end of the show that the ad for *Rock the Dollhouse* comes on. Everyone in the room breaks into cheers.

"Go, Gracie!" Dion calls out.

I'm mesmerized as her face fills the TV screen, familiar yet not with the more prominent cheekbones and new nose, lips, and vivid hair, which has been cut into a shoulder-length bob with blunt bangs.

So, this is Gracie.

The picture zooms out and there's something hypnotic and vaguely disturbing about this version of my friend as she slouches, tosses her hair, and rolls her eyes for the camera, the Dollhouse uniform hanging off her newly gaunt frame.

"I'm not a dick for being jealous, right?" Dion asks in a low voice.

"No," I say. *And I wasn't either, right?*

"Even though we have it good, it's kinda hard to watch someone doing *this much* better. I'd do anything to have my own show."

It *is* hard to watch as Grace stomps out of frame, but not because she has her own show.

I'd do anything to have my best friend back.

CHAPTER TWENTY-FIVE

Ivy's Diary

OCTOBER 12, 1998

Every time I finish one of these entries, I can't imagine picking up the pen and writing another one. It hurts too much to remember.

Then I look at the calendar and I see the days speeding by. While I've developed a reluctant complacency over the years, these past few months, I haven't been able to shake the sense that things aren't right here.

There must be information in DahlenRex's medical records or the Dollhouse Academy's trainee files that would confirm my suspicions or put me at ease once and for all. Fortunately, I may have found a source to help me in my search for answers. I won't divulge any identifying details about him in case this diary falls into the wrong hands, but I'm hopeful he will become my ally. When I first began speaking with him, he was starstruck and confessed he's always been a big fan of mine. While he's become more comfortable around me, he still looks at me with great reverence. It pains me to exploit his adoration this way, but I tell myself it's for the greater good. Even from our few conversations, I can tell that he, too, is uneasy about the potential wrongdoings being perpetuated here, and he has access to areas that may contain evidence. Now it's a matter of convincing him to help me collect that evidence.

I haven't had any more lurkers around my cottage, but while hiking around Parliament Lake last week, I could swear I was being followed. I kept turning around and saw nobody until one time I caught a flash of that familiar pale hair twenty feet down the trail. Of course, by the time I retraced my steps, there was nobody there. I tell myself I was imagining things, that I mustn't let myself get carried away with paranoia and delusions; I've seen the bleak consequences of such thinking. I reassure myself that I'm safer here than anywhere else.

They make it so easy to stay, surround you with a beautiful town, beautiful people, beautiful words. And once you taste success, you get hungrier for it, and you give away more of yourself without even realizing it. I never imagined I'd remain here for over eighteen years.

At the same time, when I fantasize about leaving, reality swiftly creeps in: breach-of-contract lawsuits and having my reputation smeared by god-knows-what kind of manufactured scandals. If I get out of this whole mess alive—which is not hyperbole, considering the lengths they've gone to in order to keep me here—I could be left penniless and even more broken than I am now.

What would I do then? I'm only thirty-four. Would I go find a job in a library or bookstore? Then what? There would be daily reminders of who I used to be as people stop and ask, "Hey, aren't you . . . ?" and wonder out loud how I ended up where I did. What kind of freedom is that, where my prison bars follow me like a shadow?

It's better to be somebody than a former somebody.

It's better to have adoration than pity, even if that adoration is hollow and misplaced, aimed at a false projection of myself.

There's another reason I haven't been able to leave the Dollhouse, a big one. Timothy. His presence echoes through Owls Point: the soundstages, the candy-colored houses, the woods, the lake.

I always worried that if I left this place, I'd leave Timothy, too.

Now I'm more worried I'll end up like him.

In the autumn of 1983, after those first rounds of medical tests, it took ages to calm Timothy down.

He was already partial to conspiracy theories—he believed a UFO crashed in New Mexico in the 1940s, that the government ran mind control experiments, that Lee Harvey Oswald wasn't JFK's true assassin— but he'd never conveyed this level of panic and paranoia before. Probably because none of those other things directly affected him.

I don't remember what I said that finally got him to stop ranting, though I did keep asking what sort of proof he had. All Timothy could offer was the whispered warning of a lab assistant.

"He said, 'Beware of Project Understudy. They're creating a shadow academy to replace you.' Those were his exact words."

How he could put so much stock into that is beyond me, but he did. He said it felt true.

This man actually said "beware," like some cartoon villain? Maybe it felt true to Timothy, but it felt absurd to me, and I told him as much. In my mind, this was some mean-spirited lab assistant, perhaps jealous of Timothy's good looks and fame, trying to bring him down a peg. Surely he couldn't have expected Timothy to have taken the warning seriously, yet he had.

"Why would they make casts of our faces and bodies then?" he asked.

I repeated what I'd been told about having a model to compare ourselves to in the event of injury, adding that if he believed it was to make living replicas of us, he'd seen *Blade Runner* one too many times.

When I finally got him to calm down, I requested a meeting with Genevieve. We convened, as usual, in the owl room, the scent of jasmine tea permeating the air.

"We really need to do something about that boy's paranoia," she said. "Perhaps we should modify his supplement regimen." Genevieve tended to stir her tea endlessly and seldom drink it. "Regardless, there's hardly anything nefarious about those molds made of you. It *is* to protect your likeness in the event of any unfortunate occurrences. Additionally, Dahlen Entertainment is partnering with Mattel to create a line of *In the Dollhouse* collectible dolls, beginning with its two biggest stars. There's been secrecy around the project because the contracts haven't been finalized, and we

don't want the news to leak. I trust you and Timothy will keep that confidential."

Of course we would. We were good little soldiers.

"As for all the medical testing, that will become a more regular part of
your routine. I'll need you to smooth that over with Timothy. The research
and development team at DahlenRex has had some recent breakthroughs
with treatments that will only serve to benefit our performers."

She never used the word "drugs" or "medications." They were "supplements" or "enhancements" and now "treatments," which had never been
mentioned before.

"I cannot stress enough how much your well-being, and Timothy's,
means to me. How much I value the well-being of everyone here." She
laced her fingers together, her face earnest. "Ivy, you and I have something
in common. Just as you lost your aunt very suddenly to cancer, I lost my
dear husband, Harold. He often complained of indigestion and stomach
pains but saw it as the way his body handled the stress of running a movie
studio. No matter how much I pleaded with him, he refused to see a doctor. What limited free time he had, he wanted to spend with me. By the
time his stomach cancer was diagnosed, it was too late to do anything.
He was gone four months later." A tear ran down her face and she wiped
at it angrily. "How bitterly ironic, to be part of a family that pioneered
treatments that may have been able to save him, yet to lose him so unexpectedly. That man was everything to me. Can you imagine having to go
through something like that with Timothy?"

My eyes welled up at the thought. I shook my head.

"I don't want that for either of you." She sat up straighter. "I'm not at
liberty to divulge the specifics, but we are working on some radical new
screening procedures to detect physiological irregularities early on. And
there is a top secret project in the works."

Project Understudy?

"How did you hear about that?"

I detailed Timothy's encounter at the medical facility as Genevieve
scowled then forced a smile.

"I'm not pleased that any whisper of this project has leaked, but I can tell you a bit about it. In fact, I can show you."

Genevieve walked over to the room's entrance, pushed a button on an intercom, and spoke into it. "Please bring up Leonora."

Turning back to me, she said. "I was waiting until we were further along to tell you, but I suppose I can give you a little preview now." While we waited, Genevieve paced broad circles around the room. "You've grown enormously popular, but there is much further you can go, as both a performer and a celebrity. However, I've sensed your drive waning when it comes to the latter."

It was true. I was less interested in fame and found most publicity tedious.

"Nevertheless, maintaining that fame is essential to your career. I, along with some of the brightest minds at Dahlen Entertainment and Dahlen-Rex, have come up with a solution that should make all of us happy."

As if on cue, a man in blue nurse's scrubs appeared in the doorway with an apple-cheeked brunette about my age. She broke out into an astonished grin when she saw me.

Genevieve motioned for the girl to come into the room. "This is Leonora. Do you notice anything special about her?" she asked me.

It took a second but then it hit me all at once. "She looks like me. A lot like me."

"And we're not through with her yet," Genevieve said. "Once we lighten her hair and make some adjustments to her cheeks and chin, she will look exactly like you." She turned to the man. "That will be all, you can both go."

Once it was just Genevieve and me, she continued circling the room. "Body doubles are not as uncommon as you think, and not just on film sets. Did you know Stalin had at least two?"

I didn't know that.

"It's true. One named Rashid was said to have been used to replace Stalin in some public functions after World War II. Rashid studied for two years with a Russian actor who'd played Stalin in propaganda films and claimed there were other doubles hired by the Kremlin to appear at media events and government functions. And it wasn't just Stalin with the political decoys—Manuel Noriega and Fidel Castro had them, too. Sometimes the doubles even got plastic surgery to resemble their targets." She paused to let that sink in.

I could see where this was going but remained quiet, a bit unsettled that all of Genevieve's examples were dictators.

"After I left Hollywood and began to build a separate entertainment empire, I saw the necessity of creating my own decoys, which I still use today when I travel. As much as I try to foster a sense of community here, not everyone is capable of meeting my standards, and there are some disgruntled former Dollhouse trainees and Dahlen employees out there. The doubles add a level of security when I'm off the compound."

Genevieve sat back down across from me. "Whatever that lab technician told Timothy, there is no shadow army being created here. It would be impossible to replace either of you. But it's easy to burn out in this business, which is something I'm looking to prevent, especially when it comes to my top talent."

If Timothy and I would be substituted with body doubles, wouldn't they essentially replace us?

"Only in certain publicity opportunities, like staged moments for the paparazzi and red carpet events, on a superficial level. Leonora can be made to look like you, walk like you, and adopt your physical mannerisms, but she could never sing and act like you. We don't plan on having her speak."

But how could she attend events in my stead and not talk to reporters?

"Simple." She clapped her hands once, a devious smile playing upon her lips. "We tell the press you are experiencing problems with your vocal cords and are under strict doctor's orders not to speak. This will not only get you more sympathy from your fans but also create a bit of added mystique. It still means going out on press junkets and doing actual interviews from time to time, but whenever possible, I will require journalists to come to Owls Point to limit your travel. This way, you can focus on the aspects of your acting and singing career you enjoy the most. What do you think?"

What could I say? It was a preposterous idea, but brilliant. Could we really pull it off, though?

"Without question," Genevieve assured me. "Though I do have concerns about how agreeable Timothy will be to this arrangement. His own double *will* be required to speak and is taking longer to learn his mannerisms but should be ready in about a month. We'll test both decoys out informally first, getting snapped by the paparazzi in New York City, or perhaps farther afield in London or Los Angeles. I do worry Timothy will get it in his head that we're looking to replace him entirely, when that is not at all the case. However, I don't think I have the power to convince him as effectively as you could."

Of course, Timothy was instantly suspicious. But when I explained why there was so much secrecy surrounding Project Understudy and how much it would benefit us to be able to focus on the work we enjoyed most, and on each other, he eventually came around.

In the late autumn of 1984, our doubles made their debut during a weekend in Manhattan; they visited art galleries in SoHo, ate at trendy downtown restaurants, danced at FunHouse and Danceteria, and took in a matinee of *Dreamgirls*, with paparazzi following them at every turn. Timothy and I were given that same weekend off, which we spent making grilled cheese sandwiches and playing board games naked.

"I could get used to this," Timothy said.

And in the year that followed, we did get used to it. We marveled how thoroughly our doubles convinced the public.

In the fall of 1985, after we'd shot the first few episodes of the show's fourth season, Timothy and I were brought in for another round of exams, which began as the others did—more bloodwork, more scans, more psychiatric evaluations and interviews—until the end of the day, when I was brought into a room with a giant water tank. I was asked to disrobe and enter this tank, told it was a new type of imaging technique along with some medical and technical jargon. It was a peculiar test, but I put that and the entire uncomfortable day behind me the moment I left the medical building.

When I got home, Timothy was pacing around the living room, which immediately filled me with dread.

"Did they try to get you in a water tank?" he asked.

I told him they did.

"I didn't get in that thing, I got the hell out of there. You should have, too."

Why? He wouldn't say.

"You know that lab assistant who warned me about Project Understudy? I never saw him again. All the lab assistants were different after that. He was probably fired along with the rest of them."

I reasoned a large facility like that likely had a sizable staff, but Timothy wouldn't accept my rationalizations.

"Ivy, listen to me. We need to stop taking these pills."

I toed Genevieve's party line, reiterating how much the supplements helped me.

"You're delusional if you think they're harmless little vitamins." His eyes radiated hostility.

It was foolish not to have realized it sooner. Timothy didn't want *us* to stop taking the supplements, he wanted *me* to stop taking them. He had already stopped taking his. This explained his moodiness, his short temper, his neurotic behavior over the last few weeks.

Rather than deny it, he grew defensive. "They were affecting me in weird ways. Nothing bothered me anymore, which was fine at first, but then nothing excited me anymore, either. At first that didn't bother me, either. But it started bugging me that it *didn't* bother me, if that makes sense. Eventually, I couldn't take being in this wishy-washy *nothing* state. I didn't want it to affect my acting. I didn't want it to affect how I felt about you."

My head was spinning. The pills certainly hadn't tamped down the wild love I felt for Timothy, but there was also a sense of betrayal that he'd stopped taking his without telling me, and an encroaching horror that he'd done so because he'd become a zombified version of himself. Or maybe the horror was because I hadn't noticed, had even preferred the milder version to this erratic one.

I remembered what Genevieve said about tweaking the formula for Timothy's supplements and told him maybe he'd feel better on a different dosage, but there was no reasoning with him.

"I'll quit the show before I go back on those pills," he said. "I'll leave Owls Point."

Those words made me go cold.

"Maybe we should both quit," he said. "Aren't you sick of Genevieve and everyone else around here dictating every part of your life? Why are we still putting up with it? We're America's goddamn sweethearts, we should be able to go anywhere we want, do anything we want. Okay, we have a little more free time, but we're still working our asses off."

I said I was sure we could get a reprieve soon.

"I wouldn't be so sure. I miss my family. I've only seen them twice in the last year. Don't you miss your family?"

I had no family outside of Owls Point.

"Never mind family. Don't you want to have the freedom to shoot a movie outside the Dahlen complex? To take a break from recording albums and touring? To be able to visit the places our doubles get to visit without it turning into a media circus? It's not normal, the way they've caged us in, the way they're controlling us." He grabbed me by the upper arms and shook me once, hard. "Don't you see, they haven't just made dolls that look like us, they're turning us into their own dolls."

By that point, I was crying. I couldn't get past the fury in his voice, the desperate grimace twisting his face. Where was the sweet, optimistic, ambitious boy I had fallen in love with?

Timothy circled me like a shark, his eyes unfocused as he continued to rant. "You know what they're doing with those water tanks? They want to photograph every inch of us to create better replicas and zap our brains into being more compliant. Apparently, those body casts weren't enough.

First they stole our faces and bodies—how long before they steal our souls? Is that something you could live with? Not me, not ever."

Before I could reply, Timothy stormed out of our house.

I should have followed him, but I was afraid he might say more terrifyingly paranoid things or lash out at me. Instead, I stood in the middle the room, feeling like the walls were crumbling around me.

I tell myself I wouldn't have been able to change anything if I'd followed Timothy that night.

That's always been my problem: I make excuses for my cowardice.

I should have gone after him, but I didn't. Instead, I called an ambulance and remained at home, waiting.

He didn't come home that night.

It would be a long time before I saw Timothy again.

CHAPTER TWENTY-SIX

"Was it always this crowded?" I ask Jude as our car enters Times Square.

It's not only the streets that seem so densely packed but also the buildings themselves, with billboards and digital displays stacked on top of one another as logos fight for attention: Disney, Virgin, Coca-Cola, Kodak, Cup Noodles, Pepsi, MTV.

We're in the back seat of a town car—Dahlen arranged transportation to and from Manhattan for us as a little bonus for extending our contracts, along with two nights at the Marriott Marquis.

"You've been away for six months, not six years," Jude teases, leaning into me and peering out my window.

We step outside to an urban symphony of car horns, jackhammers, plastic buckets used as makeshift drums, and wailing fire trucks. I used to find these sounds energizing, but now they're giving me a headache. Maybe I've acclimated a bit too well to the Dollhouse's placid surroundings. Upstate, the only intrusive noises outside are lawn mowers. Otherwise, it's birds chirping, leaves rustling, the occasional *whoosh* of a plane overhead.

I expected my first urge when I got to the city would be to go exploring, take in the color and chaos. Instead, I can't wait to get up to our hotel room.

"This place is intense. Even Chicago was never this . . . claustrophobic." Jude did some theater in Chicago before getting recruited to the Dollhouse through one of the annual cattle call auditions.

In our room, we drop our bags on the floor and flop backward onto the bed, letting out synchronized sighs.

"So what do you want to do?" he asks. "Go sightseeing, shopping, walk around, visit a museum, find some authentic New York pizza, see a Broadway play, do one of those bus tours?"

Just hearing the list of options makes me want to burrow under the blanket and hole up here for the next couple of days. I want Jude to enjoy this trip, though, so I force an easygoing cheer and say, "We don't have to meet my uncles until five, so we can do whatever you want until then."

"Anything?"

I roll onto my side, facing him.

Jude and I have been having sex for weeks now, pretty much since we started seeing each other, and it's been great, but finding a place to be intimate when we both have roommates has been tricky. We've made do with our bedrooms when roommate schedules allow, along with prop closets, rehearsal rooms, secluded outdoor spots in wooded areas, and a few other locations where privacy is tenuous and the romance factor low. This is the first time we've been in a room with a bed where we don't have to worry about anyone interrupting us.

"Anything," I say.

We don't leave the room until it's time to meet my uncles.

"I don't care how touristy and overpriced this place is, I love it. Cheers," declares Alonso, raising his apple martini. "And remember to make eye contact when you clink glasses or it's seven years bad sex."

Jude and I exchange a naughty smile as we clink glasses.

We're at the hotel's revolving restaurant, forty-eight floors up, sitting at a table beside floor-to-ceiling windows. It takes an hour to make a full revolution and we're here at sunset, when you get the prettiest views of the city. Right now, we're facing a cluster of skyscrapers with the jagged spire of the Empire State Building peeking out behind them.

"No need to worry about prices tonight. Dinner is on me," Jude says.

"Killer dimples *and* a gentleman. You did good, Ramona," Alonso says, then looks between me and Jude. "Judging from your bedhead, I don't think *either* of you need to worry about bad sex."

"Alonso, seriously," Reed admonishes, though there's a playfulness in the way he swats Alonso's arm.

Jude nearly chokes on his gin and tonic, but I just chuckle and sip my mojito. This is nothing compared with some of the more outrageous things he's said in front of my boyfriends.

"So." Reed clears his throat. "I guess we won't ask what you've been up to today, but what do you have planned for tomorrow?"

"Besides restocking on condoms," Alonso adds. "Which you better be using." This earns him another swat from Reed.

Luckily, I've prepared Jude for this meeting. "Absolutely, sir," he says. "My father had three rules in our family. If you drive the pickup, you refill the tank. If it makes you happy and doesn't hurt anyone, it's okay. And if you can't keep it in your pants, wrap it up. You could say Dad was . . . direct."

"What did he think about you pursuing acting?" Reed asked.

"He would've rather I pursue baseball, but I blew out my shoulder at sixteen. And my older brothers were more interested in taking over the soybean farm than I was, so I got a pass on that. Dad wasn't much of a theater fan, but he said as long as I didn't pressure him to come to any of my plays and found a decent way to make ends meet, I could do as I pleased. Though he did attend my high school production of *Oklahoma!* and enjoyed it quite a bit."

We laugh, and Jude asks my uncles about running a movie theater. I sit back, content to sip my drink and watch two men I love and one man I really like getting along so well.

We face the Hudson River as the sun sets, the sky appearing streaked with fire. My face hurts from smiling so much. Our overpriced dinner arrives, and we order another round of drinks. It gets dark and the lights on the buildings outside surround us like geometric constellations.

While we're too high up to see most of the Times Square billboards, there's one that slowly revolves into our sight line. It's a large digital screen, and for a moment, it's showing nothing but a plain brick wall. I gasp as a twenty-foot-tall Grace walks in front of the wall, dressed as Juniper York in the Dollhouse uniform and Doc Martens. She crosses her arms, puts one foot flat against the wall, and sulks, blowing her cherry-red bangs out of her heavily lined eyes. Above her head, ROCK THE DOLLHOUSE appears in a graffiti font.

"Wow, she looks *awesome*!" Jude exclaims. "I had a TV acting class with her."

My uncles turn to me with matching puzzled looks, which I respond to with a subtle head shake. I had told Jude about having a best friend in general terms but said we lost touch when I started at the Dollhouse.

"She was so good in that class," Jude continues. "I can see why Genevieve chose to mentor her—at least over me."

"Don't you think Grace looks a little . . . I don't know, plasticky now?" I ask. "She didn't need to get her nose and lips done. And she looks emaciated."

"It's showbiz, that's what's expected." Jude's eyes don't leave the billboard as he speaks, as if this larger-than-life version of Grace is hypnotizing him. "I mean, she was cute before, but she looks *so good* now. Nowhere near as gorgeous as you, though," he's quick to add.

Our dessert arrives but I don't touch my chocolate mousse.

Reed and Alonso exchange glances but say nothing.

"You don't think she looks less special?" I press on. "What's the point of looking *so good* if you look like everyone else? Do you think I should get my nose and lips done, too? What if the Dollhouse asks *you* to get a bunch of plastic surgery?" I don't know why I'm jumping on him like this when I told Genevieve I'd do whatever it takes to stay at the Dollhouse. Hypocritical much?

Jude gets a look on his face like he just stepped into mud and realized it might be quicksand. "I think your face is beautiful the way it is. And I don't know what surgery I'd get if the Dollhouse asked. I guess it depends."

"It *depends*? What does it depend on?" Why am I lashing out like this? Even though we're barely moving away from the billboard, it suddenly feels like the floor beneath us is spinning faster and faster. "You'd give up your identity that easily in exchange for a little bit of fame?"

"If I don't do it, someone else will. Actors change their appearance all the time. We gain or lose weight, wear wigs, different costumes. And yeah, sometimes we get surgery. I don't see it as giving up my identity. I still know who I am on the inside. That's not gonna change."

"Even if you're unrecognizable from the outside?" I snap.

"I don't get why you're so upset, but I'm sorry if it was something I said." Jude cringes. "I promise I won't get any major work done anytime soon, okay?" The downward curl of his mouth breaks me out of my anger.

What is wrong with me?

You miss Grace.

You also have a funny way of showing it.

"No, *I'm* sorry," I say. "I don't know why I went off like that."

"It's a mystery for the ages." Alonso gives me a sidelong look.

The rest of the meal is subdued. I manage to take one bite of the chocolate mousse and it sits like a glob of mud on my tongue until I finally wash it down with water.

After dinner, I offer to see my uncles out of the hotel and tell Jude I'll meet him back in our room.

When it's just the three of us in the elevator, Alonso says, "I like that boy. He's got just enough hayseed in him to make him charming without being full-on 'aw shucks.'"

"He seems like a good kid," Reed agrees. "Speaking of good kids, are you okay?"

The delicate way he asks makes my eyes brim with tears. "I'm finally good, happy. It's just, you know . . ."

"Give it a little time, *chica*." Alonso ruffles my hair. "You and Grace will work it out eventually."

"None of our other fights have ever gone on this long."

"The two of you have history," Reed says. "She'll come around."

The doors open at the eighth-floor atrium lobby and we step out.

"We'll find our way out from here," Alonso says. "Go back upstairs and make up with your country boy."

As we say goodbye, Reed says, "You're looking a little skinny. I hope you're taking care of yourself."

"I've been so busy, sometimes I forget to eat," I say. "But I'll make a point to remember. Promise."

His face goes from dubious to resigned as he comes in for a hug. Afterward, I hand him a check, feeling a swell of pride. Reed takes it, albeit reluctantly.

On my way back to the room, I catch my reflection in the elevator glass. My cheekbones are more prominent, and my eyes look larger, but they also have faint purple shadows beneath them. I may be more camera-friendly this thin, but I look healthier with more weight on me.

Naturally I haven't told my uncles about the supplements. Considering everything about the Dollhouse they already find daunting, this would just add to their needless worry.

Is it needless, though?

Could there be side effects to the pills I'm not aware of? Could that have something to do with my irrational outburst at dinner? Jude's been taking them, too, and he hasn't had any problems. In any case, I'm able to think clearly now, and I have more immediate concerns.

I need to go make up with my country boy.

CHAPTER TWENTY-SEVEN

JANUARY 1999

The Dollhouse gives us time off for Thanksgiving and Christmas, but Grace doesn't come home for either.

Jude spends Thanksgiving with his family in Illinois, but I bring him home to Brooklyn for Christmas. Since we barely left the hotel the last time we were in NYC, this time I take him into the city, to some of my favorite bookshops and record stores. Walking down Eighth Street from west to east reminds me of how Grace would always comment on the number of shoe stores. ("No, but for real—why so many shoes? Why this street? Did all the shoe store owners come together and decide *this* is the street where we should all peddle our wares?") I tell myself I don't even know where she is, and it's crazy to think I might run into to her in such a big city, yet I can't help but look for her. One day when we're in the East Village, having lunch at Yaffa, I see a slender girl with cherry hair slide into a zebra-striped banquette and I gasp and knock over my glass of water. The girl glances over at me, and of course it's not Grace, but for a second my heart stops.

On New Year's Eve, Alonso cooks a feast using his mother's favorite recipes: asopao, Asado de Puerco, and tostones. Reed makes the usual Kir Royales ("use enough Chambord and you'll never notice the cheap champagne"), and I drink a few too many.

On New Year's Day, as a special treat, my uncles screen the movie of Jude's choice just for the four of us and he selects *Taxi Driver*. As we watch, all I can think of is the live trailer Grace and I did for it (*"cabbies and guns and city scum, oh my / if you're looking for a taxi, try another guy / is he talkin' to you, is he talkin' to me / is he gonna snap? / just you wait and see"*). Jude finds it touching that the movie makes me cry. I don't tell him the real reason it does.

As much as I missed Grace and hoped to run into her while in the city, when Jude and I return to Owls Point, I continue to avoid the section of campus where she lives now. It's easier to think about her less once I'm back at work.

At least, it's easier for a few days. In early January, *Rock the Dollhouse* airs as a midseason replacement and debuts at number three in the ratings, between *ER* and *Friends* (*In the Dollhouse*, even after all these years, still claims the top spot). The following week, Gracie's first single, "Whatever, Forever," hits the airwaves and comes in at number two, right behind Britney Spears's ". . . Baby One More Time." A week after that, both the show and the song are in the top spot. The music video becomes a staple on MTV and features Gracie in her Dollhouse uniform cutting class and stealing a school bus with some classmates as her passengers. In the final scene, Gracie stops the bus in the middle of a bridge and dances on top of it with the classmates, wearing a tight, sequined version of the uniform. The media, while citing Ivy Gordon as the original sexy schoolgirl, instantly dubs Britney and Gracie "the dueling schoolgirls" and creates a rivalry where there hadn't been one before.

It's astonishing to watch how swiftly Grace's star rises. The campus buzzes with excitement for her. Each dorm gets boxes of T-shirts, posters, and advance copies of her CD, and the Dollhouse Academy transforms into a Gracie fan club seemingly overnight. Everyone raves about how not since Ivy Gordon has a trainee made it this far this fast, in music *and* television.

If I was trying to avoid reminders of my friend before, it's pretty much impossible now with her face plastered all over walls and clothing, the life-size poster of her in Chapter and Verse, and her voice coming out of every stereo and TV in Owls Point.

I try to listen to her self-titled album, but only make it through a couple of songs. Even with her edgier vocals, it's generic bubblegum pop, the kind of music Grace would've snorted at and called "*so cheesy.*" Surely she can't think these songs are good?

As for the show, I can't speak to its quality because I can't bring myself to watch more than a few minutes of it. And when "Whatever, Forever" comes on the radio or MTV, which is all the time, I have to switch it off. I can tell myself it's because it makes me miss her or the music isn't my taste, but envy is also a factor.

It's shameful because everyone else here is rooting for her. I should be her biggest fan. I *was* her biggest fan.

How breathtaking it must be to achieve so much this quickly and this young.

At the same time, it must be overwhelming to sustain it. I wonder how Grace is handling everything. Maybe she needs a friend more than anything.

It's time for me to find out how she's really doing.

On a Monday night, I finally muster the nerve to call her, and this time I don't hang up before I finish dialing. I get an answering machine and leave a message for Grace. When she doesn't return my call by Wednesday, I tamp down my frustration (*she's a lot busier now, maybe she's had no time to call back*), try again, and get the machine again. She still doesn't call me back and I bury my frustrations further (*maybe she didn't get the messages*).

Her birthday is that Sunday. I was going to mail her a card, but since I have the day off, I decide to hand deliver it.

That afternoon I take a shuttle to the other side of campus and find the house that matches the address Mason gave me. It's a frilly Victorian, magenta with peach trim, snow dusting the turrets and gabled roofs like icing sugar.

I hesitate at the bottom of the steps then climb them deliberately, with purpose.

She's probably not home.

At the front door, I knock, wait, ring the bell, wait, then repeat several times. Eventually, a thirtysomething sleepy Black woman in a yellow bathrobe and slippers answers the door.

"Sorry, I didn't mean to wake you," I say.

"Is that why you rang the bell a hundred times? Or was that supposed to be a lullaby?" She clutches the robe at her throat.

"I'm looking for my friend Grace Ludlow." When the woman shows no signs of recognition, I add, "Gracie?" It takes me a minute to place her without makeup, but now I'm sure she plays one of Grace's teachers on *Rock the Dollhouse.* "You're on the show with her, right?"

"Right. And?" Fresh suspicion hardens her face.

"My name is Ramona. I grew up with Grace. She's my oldest friend. I've been trying to get ahold of her. Today's her birthday . . ." My voice wavers and I swallow the lump in my throat.

"Ramona . . . Are you the girl that's been leaving all those messages?"

"That's me."

"Well, she's not here." The woman regards me for a moment, as if deciding whether or not I mean harm. Finally, her shoulders relax, and she steps across the threshold, lowering her voice. "They moved her to a different house."

"Which one?" There's no hiding my desperation.

"There's a gated private lane, not far from Genevieve's place, where they put up their most important talent. Bowles Boulevard. You won't be able to get past the gate unless your name is on a list. But she's not even in Owls Point right now, she's in LA. Listen, honey . . ." She shuffles forward and drops her voice again, this time to a murmur. "Once they reach this level, it's hard to get near them. If you have any good sense, you'll leave it be. If you have better sense, don't try to follow in her footsteps. Go for the supporting roles. You'll have a nice life and get to do what you enjoy." Fixing me with a firm stare, she puts a hand on my shoulder. "I've been doing this a while and I've seen some people get badly burned by that spotlight. You're better off not chasing it."

"But what about my friend?" I sound like a little girl looking for a lost puppy.

"Let her go. Sooner or later, she'll be different from the person you knew. It'll be easier if you accept that now." With that, the woman gives my shoulder a pat, steps back, and closes the front door.

I walk back to Gale House in a daze. On the way, I drop Grace's card in the mailbox, hoping it will reach her, despite having her old address on the envelope.

I don't know what's more unsettling, the thought of Grace being pressured to cut ties with her old life or her doing so willingly. Either way, my earlier resentment and remorse morphs into something darker and stickier. I need to know she's okay.

Back in the dorm, I put away my winter coat in the hall closet and glance at my mail cubby. On top of a green flyer is a pack of Skittles and a silk sunflower. Holy shit.

"Surprise!" chirps a voice behind me. I turn around. Tia is beaming at me.

"Wait . . ." My bubble of hope bursts. "You did this? How did you know . . . ?"

"You told me your best friend used to get those for you when you were down, and you seemed sad since you got back from Brooklyn, so . . ."

As with Jude, I had only told Tia about the broad strokes of my friendship with Grace. I must've let this detail slip.

"The florist had run out of sunflowers, but I found this one in a prop closet." Uneasy but expectant, Tia looks like she's waiting for a judge's verdict.

"This is amazing. So thoughtful. Thank you. I don't remember the last time I had Skittles. I feel like I could eat this whole bag right now." Even though I'm still in the throes of emotional whiplash, I try to make my gratitude convincing as I open my arms for a hug.

Tia barrels into me. "I'm so glad you like it!" She drops her voice to a murmur. "I have some big news. It's a secret, but I'm gonna burst if I don't tell somebody. Can we sneak out and find a quiet place to talk?"

It's like I've been thrown into an improv game, where information is being fired randomly and I need to keep the scene moving. Pulling away, I say, "Yeah, of course." You don't say no in improv.

After we've walked far enough away from the dorm, she asks, "How about the hedge maze?"

"Let's check it out."

To be extra careful, Tia waits until we're in the center, which contains a small clearing with topiaries shaped into owls, and benches surrounding a large bronze sculpture of a leafless tree with more owls perched among its branches.

"What's going on?" I brush some snow off one of the benches so we can sit.

Sitting close to me and keeping her voice hushed, Tia says, "I finally got a part."

"That's great!" At my exclamation, she gestures for me to take it down a notch. I murmur, "Show or movie?"

"It's something else. It's . . . this superconfidential program. Like, I swear, you absolutely cannot—"

"Project Understudy?"

Her head jerks back. "You've heard of it?"

"Vaguely." I picture Gino Rinaldi being wheeled out of our dorm. "What's it all about? Tell me everything." My urgency seems to spook her, so I pivot to a more gossipy tone. "I've been *dying* of curiosity, but nobody has the scoop. I promise, whatever you tell me will stay between us."

Doubt clouds her eyes. "Okay, but I'm really putting my trust in you here."

I recall Genevieve's threat to expel me if I ever uttered the two words I utter again. "Project Understudy. What's the deal?"

"It's kinda what it sounds like." Fresh snow begins to fall as Tia speaks. "You know how everyone is going crazy over Gracie? Well, between *Rock the Dollhouse* doing so well and now her album going to number one, Dahlen expects big things from her. It's a lot of responsibility, and it might be too much for one person to handle. That's where I come in."

It's like my tongue is coated in sand. "What does that mean?"

"I'm learning to be like Juniper York. How she talks, sings, her body language, mannerisms. For example . . ." Tia slouches and scrunches her face into a wry smirk. "Why are we, like, *sitting outside*, in the middle of a *snowstorm*? That makes *zero* sense." Her delivery is uncanny. A moment later, Tia perks up and becomes herself again. "I think I'm pretty close to getting rid of my southern twang."

It feels like I'm back in the revolving restaurant, only this park bench is spinning around much faster. "I don't understand. Does the Dollhouse think it can replace Juniper like Darrin on *Bewitched*? Why would they need to? Is something wrong with Grace? And why all this secrecy?"

"I mean, I don't really know how they plan to use me or when. The instructors aren't big on details."

In my mind, I hear Gino's panicked voice shouting, *It's not her!* "And they're not making you get plastic surgery to look like Grace?"

A nonchalant shrug. "No, but I always thought my nose was too wide and I love Gracie's new nose, so . . ." Another shrug to bookend the thought.

"And how long are you supposed to wait in the wings? What if the original Gracie never needs an understudy? They're not making you do anything creepy, are they?" I don't know why I throw in that last question. I can't help but search for a nefarious angle to this program. Otherwise, why would Genevieve threaten to expel me for bringing it up?

"It's not that different from being an understudy in a play. And I don't know how long it's for, but they're paying me good money." Her chin juts up. "Maybe I should've kept my mouth shut."

I've slipped into tiger mode and put her off. "No, no, no, I'm glad you told me. It all sounds *so exciting*." Big smile. Bigger. Don't stop until she smiles back. There we go. "This could be your big break." Though it would be at the expense of Grace failing. "And if they don't need to replace Juniper, who knows what other roles might come up."

Tia's eyes flash with a conspiratorial gleam. "From what I hear, they're heaping so much on Gracie, she's already struggling to keep up, and they've been having some problems with her on *Rock the Dollhouse*. Showing up late to set, not knowing her lines, temper tantrums here and there." As if remembering her manners, she straightens up. "Mind you, I love Gracie, and I love that the Dollhouse has a new superstar. But it seems like it's way too soon for her to be burning out when she's just getting started." She frowns. "If it were me, I know I'd have the stamina to handle everything they threw at me. I don't intend on setting foot back in Missouri until I've made it." The twang returns to her voice. "There's no way in hell I'm going back to a dead-end town where all people do is work boring jobs, get married, and have kids. All my mom ever wanted was to have two daughters, so she feels like her life is complete. And my sister processes insurance claims for a living and doesn't even mind! They might be happy staying in Fame, but I want something more."

"I want more for you, too," I say. "And for me." And for Grace.

As we leave, the topiaries and hedge maze remind me of *The Shining*, which then reminds me of the live trailer Grace and I did for it early last year, dressed up like the twins with matching bloodstained blue dresses (*"Enjoy your stay at the Overlook Hotel / A little slice of heaven or maybe hell / 'Come play with us,' say the creepy twins / Find room 237, it holds many sins"*). After we performed at the Mag, we wore those bloody dresses out and laughed at all the strange looks we got on the subway and later at the dive bar on St. Marks Place.

I need to find a way to talk to Grace. I have to make sure she's okay.

CHAPTER TWENTY-EIGHT

The following day, when I step onto the soundstage, my nerves are humming, and my guts feel like I just ate a bowl of Genevieve's fish Jell-O.

Today will be the first time Ivy Gordon and I read a scene together.

"You'll be great, just chill," says Jude in the shuttle to the studio. He slips an arm around my waist and gives me a squeeze. "There's nothing to worry about. You're a recurring character now."

"That doesn't mean anything." I stare out the window, watching the snow-covered Tudor and Gothic mansions glide by, so perfect they look fake, like painted scenery you could punch a hole through.

Of course, I like to think being a recurring character offers a bit more job security, but having a contract through the end of the season doesn't mean I'll be featured prominently. Even though I've done well on the show so far, a bad interaction with its principal star could derail all my progress to this point.

All of which is to say, it feels like my entire career rests on nailing this scene with Ivy.

The script was sent over late last night, so I haven't had a chance to memorize my lines, but it's not worth being off-book this early, since there are usually tweaks made after the read-through. In this episode, a strange grapefruit-size metal orb has been thrown through the headmaster's office window, shattering it. Since Skylar was spotted on the grounds near Tabitha's office, she's brought in for questioning.

We're having the table read in a conference room near the soundstages. While everyone dresses casually for these, Ivy always looks polished. Today she's in a black velvet pencil skirt and crisp white button-down, tails out, the perfect waves of her platinum hair skimming her shoulders.

As we begin the read-through, during the early scenes in which I have fewer lines, I study Ivy for . . . for what, exactly? I once read an article about how babies will stare longer at conventionally beautiful people, and I believe it. It's no wonder Ivy had dolls made in her image—her face is flawless. As is her line delivery; she's able to imbue even the most innocuous dialogue with wit and personality.

The tabloids call Ivy the most eligible bachelorette in showbiz and speculate as to why she's never been married (she never got over Timothy, she's gay, she's barren, she's too much of a workaholic), as if that means there must be something wrong with her. That always drove me nuts. Here was a woman with a successful career—two, actually!—yet she's still judged for the absence of a romantic partner. Growing up, I did wonder whether she was lonely, but there was something powerful about seeing her stand alone on all those red carpets. Maybe that's one reason I never put as much energy into romantic relationships as other people. For me, it was more important to *be* somebody than be with somebody.

We get to Ivy's scene with me, which goes pretty well, though I do drop a section. It's embarrassing to have to circle back when it's pointed out, but it seems like she and I play well off each other. At the end of the scene, I look over at her again, and she offers me a small smile. Not a smile that says "you are going to be the next great actor of your generation," but one that says, at the very least, "not bad."

"That was awesome, babe," Jude whispers, squeezing my knee under the table. Apart from our fight in New York, things between us have been fine. Maybe not as wildly passionate as they were before, but that's natural, right? Besides, he's unfailingly supportive, like right now, when he says, "Go talk to her. You've been dying to, and now you have a reason."

That gives me the courage I need. I walk over to where she was sitting and try not to hover too closely as she talks to the director a few feet away. Instead, I glance at the table, where Ivy has left her script open. I'm curious about the notes she's made in the margins, but before I can read them, I hear her voice behind me.

"Nice job in that read-through, Ramona."

I turn around and stand face-to-face with my childhood (and adolescent and adult) idol.

The last thing I expected was that our first exchange would be *her* complimenting *me*.

"Wow, thank you. Coming from you especially that means so much." I try not to sound overly obsequious, but it's *Ivy Gordon*. "I'm sure you've heard it a million times, but I'm a great admirer of your work." Oh god, could I have said anything *more* generic? I basically told her "I'm a big fan," only I gave it a pretentious hat.

"That's very sweet." Her face glosses over with a perfunctory politeness.

"I was wondering—I, um, didn't see—it doesn't look like—" How mortifying to be stumbling over my words in front of her. "The director didn't schedule any rehearsals for us. I'm sure you're super busy, but I was wondering if you might have some time for us to rehearse our scene together."

The polite mask is back. "It's not a matter of being busy, though I am tied up with recording my next album. It's a matter of how I like to work. I prefer to go into the scenes fresh, so whatever dynamic develops between us does so organically."

"Right. Of course." I say it like I overlooked something obvious.

Just then, a PA comes over and whispers in her ear. "I need to take a call. Looking forward to working with you." She walks off.

Ivy and I shoot our scene a few days later. Working with my hero is so daunting, it initially throws me off my performance. I speak too quickly in the first take, too slowly in the second, and do something "stiff and pe-culiar" with my arms in the third. Naturally, Ivy is perfect in all the takes. Just when I think this is going to be a nightmarish repeat of my *Sisterhood* shoot, I force myself to stop spiraling and channel that urgency into con-vincing Headmistress Noelle that I, Skylar Vaughn, did not vandalize her office window. My fourth attempt is the Goldilocks take and earns a "we got it" from the director. Fortunately, I maintain my consistency for the subsequent shots.

The following morning, just as the sun is rising and I'm about to head back to the set, I spot a new piece of mail.

It's the script for the next episode of *In the Dollhouse*. I flip through it to see how many scenes my character has and who they're with, and I let out a gasp. It's a crossover episode with *Rock the Dollhouse*.

I was going to beg Mason to get me Grace's new phone number, but now I won't need to.

I'll be seeing her in person next week.

CHAPTER TWENTY-NINE

Ivy's Diary

JANUARY 29, 1999

My source has started collecting information for me. Nothing about Project Understudy's specific operations, but enough to confirm the program has been restarted. I confronted Genevieve about it under the guise of hearing rumors, and she finally admitted that yes, Project Understudy is active again but wouldn't go to the extreme lengths it did before. I'm so tired of feeling like I have no choice but to trust her.

Should I simply resign myself to my life here? After all, I have yet to find definitive proof that something sinister is going on. And while I still occasionally get the eerie feeling of being watched, it's possible I've adopted some of Timothy's paranoia.

At the same time, something is telling me to keep searching for the truth of this place, to keep writing down my story.

This is where it gets much, much more difficult . . .

That autumn day in 1985 after Timothy stormed out of our cottage, I gave him some time to cool off, sure that he'd return by morning. But morning came and he was still gone. In our mailbox was a notice telling us production on ITD was suspended. I was immediately filled with so much panic, I doubled over and threw up on an azalea bush.

I marched over to Genevieve's house, the first time I'd ever been to see her without an appointment. At first, her housekeeper refused to let me in, but I made such a racket at the security gate, I was buzzed through and Genevieve, still in her robe, came to the front door.

"She can come in," she said to the housekeeper.

Genevieve motioned me to follow her into a sunroom, which looked like a miniature greenhouse.

"I would offer you coffee, but you should probably avoid caffeine seeing the state you're in."

I was suddenly apprehensive to ask about Timothy directly, so instead I asked why production on the show was being halted.

"You know why."

I looked around the room helplessly, as if one its numerous sun-dappled plants would provide the answer I was seeking. But only Genevieve could do that.

I asked where Timothy was.

"He's been sent to an off-site facility to recover from extreme exhaustion."

Part of me recognized "exhaustion" for the obfuscation that it was, but a larger part of me wanted to believe Genevieve implicitly. After all, Timothy and I were worked to the bone at a pace that wasn't sustainable, even with miracle drugs. It made sense that he'd become dangerously worn down.

Then again, I was exhausted, too, but I didn't need to be shipped off somewhere to recover.

What kind of facility was this, anyway? A hospital?

"There are medical staff on hand, yes. But think of it more like an enriched health spa."

Sensing I needed her to say more, she relented. "It's obvious Timothy has been . . . troubled. We've been trying to help regulate his erratic behavior through the use of emerging pharmaceuticals DahlenRex is developing—not the supplements we have you on, what he was prescribed was more . . . robust."

I told her Timothy was certain the drugs were harmful, which is why he stopped taking them. After a moment's hesitation, I added that I had once tried to stop, too, then detailed my own dreadful experience.

"Don't you see, that speaks to the efficacy of these supplements and medications! Your body goes through withdrawal symptoms because it's no longer receiving the benefit of these enhancements. You were wise enough to understand you were better off taking them, whereas Timothy chose to continue suffering. I cannot fathom why he would do that. Fortunately, this facility will set him right."

I asked when I could visit him.

"It would be best if he received his treatment without any disturbances. I'm afraid this includes visits, phone calls, and letters. Even from you. Right now, he needs to focus on his recovery. I think you would agree?"

I asked how long he would be at this "health spa."

"That depends on Timothy. We're concerned his double may not be able to pull off acting in his stead, so our writers are developing a storyline in which Hayden Close gets into a car accident that leaves him in a coma. This will leave Timothy free to take all the time he needs to recover, the rest of the season even."

The rest of the season? I couldn't imagine shooting a single episode without him.

"Nonsense." Genevieve tossed her head. "You are a professional and you will do what the job demands of you."

And what if I was feeling exhausted, too? Maybe I could also use a few weeks recovering in a health spa.

At this, her dark eyes grew nearly black. "If you want to do that, we can rewrite the show so Ivy gets into the same car accident and doesn't survive at all. We can also rerecord your album with a new singer. In fact, I could have you escorted off the grounds right now."

I could go to the press and tell them everything about Project Understudy.

The sound of porcelain shattering caused me to jump in my seat. It was startling yet beautiful, like a tiny musical explosion. Shards of

Genevieve's cup lay scattered around the table, which was now spattered with coffee.

Her face was mottled. I hadn't noticed earlier, but it was the first time I saw her without lipstick. "If you dare breathe a word of this to anyone, I'll make sure you are painted in the press as an unstable lunatic, a drug addict, a nymphomaniac . . . I can get them to print anything, and get witnesses to back up the accounts, too."

I shrank back in my seat as Genevieve got up and stood over me.

"Listen to me, you spoiled, ungrateful little bitch," she hissed. "You have no idea how lucky you are to be here, to have the life that you have. All of that can go away in an instant. And if you're finished here, forget about getting another job in film or television, and forget the stage, too. You won't even be able to book a dinner theater gig. Now are you quite through with your little temper tantrum?"

Tears streamed down my cheeks as I nodded.

Genevieve looked stricken and put a hand to her chest. "I don't know what came over me, Ivy. I'm so sorry." Shaking her head, she returned to her seat. "The situation with Timothy clearly has us both upset. Whenever I've faced distressing situations in life, it's always helped me to throw myself into my work, so I assumed that would be best for you, too. I certainly didn't mean to lash out at you like that." She offered me a linen napkin to wipe my face.

Still reeling, I told her I hadn't meant to lash out, either.

"Let's forget this ever happened. Go home and take all the time you need to regroup. If that means both of you sit out for the rest of the show's production while you get back on your feet, so be it."

As I thought more about it, I knew she was right. After a couple of days, I would go stir-crazy in that cottage without Timothy. Returning to work was the best option.

"If you're quite sure . . ." Genevieve gave me a sympathetic look. "I'm worried sick about Timothy myself, but rest assured he's in good hands. In the meantime, use this as an opportunity to get lost in your creative work. Rewrites on the next episode will come in a day or two. And if you feel up to it, perhaps you would like to contribute some songs on your new album."

I did as I was told, as I always do. I showed up on set. I showed up at the recording studio. I did my job.

The cottage was lonely without Timothy, but after a few days, I stopped crying myself to sleep. Maybe that had something to do with the new supplements I was given. They made everything seem . . . tolerable. At first, it was ghoulish acting with Timothy's double, but when I imagined it was actually him in that hospital bed, it brought forth a new emotional depth to my performance (what a dreadful way to earn an Emmy). I channeled that same energy into writing three new songs for my album. I missed Timothy terribly, but I threw myself into my work, and when I wasn't working, I immersed myself in books, stocking up on novels by Judith Krantz, Sidney Sheldon, and V. C. Andrews. I got lost in the glamorous and tawdry lives of others to fill the void in my own life.

In late November, after Timothy had been gone a little over two months, I returned to the cottage one Saturday night, after a long recording session, to find the dining room table set for dinner, with a centerpiece of fresh flowers and two lit tapered candles emitting an inviting glow. The house smelled like something hearty cooking, a meaty soup or stew.

Timothy was at the stove, stirring a pot, with his back to me, not having heard me come in. I watched him with bated breath. He looked like a wisp of himself.

I called out his name and he turned around. His cheeks were more sunken in, his eyes distant and wary, but it was him. He gave me a smile full of relief and tenderness before rushing over and sweeping me up in his arms. There was a new frailty to him, and I was scared to hug him too tightly, but he squeezed me so hard it knocked the wind out of me.

What happened after he left our cottage that night? Where had he been taken?

He insisted we discuss things over dinner and dispatched me to open a bottle of wine while he dished out the stew he'd prepared. When I look back at us now, in our early twenties, sitting at a table set with lace place mats, fine china, and silver utensils, drinking wine out of crystal goblets, it feels like we were playing grown-ups. We should've been eating pizza off paper plates and drinking beer straight from the can.

Once we were seated and had taken a few bites of food, Timothy told me what had happened.

"To be honest, after I left here, the next thing I remember is waking up somewhere that looked like a fancy hospital room, strapped to a bed, hooked up to an IV. I had no idea where I was or how I got there, and I screamed my head off until a nurse came in. She said I was in a treatment center called Epiphany Bay and went to get a doctor, who told me I'd been found near Parliament Lake, 'behaving in a dangerous manner.'"

What did that mean?

Timothy didn't want to go into specifics, but I pressed him to tell me everything. "The doctor said I got ahold of a metal pipe and was waving it around, threatening to bash the skull in of anyone who tried to come near me . . . and also threatening to bash my own head in. Apparently, it took three people to restrain me. Since I was considered a threat to myself and others, I was brought to Epiphany Bay and put in a psychiatric hold. The doctor explained that I needed to be evaluated and treated for any mental disorders. All I wanted to do at that point was get out of there and come get you, so we could run away together."

Tears welled in my eyes then and they do again now, remembering.

"But the doctor said I was unstable, and that if they released me now, I could end up hurting myself, or worse—you. So, I stayed."

Timothy reached across the table and placed his hand over mine, his fingers ice-cold. "I'm so sorry for scaring you like that, for everything I put you through. I didn't know my mind wasn't right. All that stuff about zapping our brains and giving us drugs so we become complacent puppets—it was deranged. I didn't know I was sick, that the pills were treating that sickness. Now I realize it wasn't the pills that were making me lose my mind, it was going off them. I'm just glad they found me before I did something awful."

My mouth opened and closed, but I couldn't think of how to respond or what to believe. Who was the real Timothy, the nervous angry version or this benign regretful version in front of me?

"Please forgive me," he pleaded. "I was unhinged, but I'm better now. It took some time for me to understand my mental condition and how to keep it in check. I had to undergo a lot of treatment." Though when I asked what those treatments entailed, he was vague. "There were a lot of counseling sessions, nature walks, that sort of thing. Mostly I needed to give myself time to recover from my mental break and develop coping mechanisms to remain stable, especially in stressful situations. And I think I've done that. I feel much better. That guy who ranted about what an evil place this is, about Project Understudy, he wasn't me. We're both so lucky to be here, so lucky to have this life, and to have doubles that can take some of the pressure off. I was looking at things completely the wrong way before, but I see them clearly now. I don't want to do anything to damage our life together. From now on, I won't miss a single medical appointment and I'll take every pill I'm prescribed. I swear, I'll never put you in another situation where you're afraid of me."

As I gazed into his gaunt, earnest face, I wished I could tell him the truth, that I was afraid in *this* moment. There was something altered about him. The way he spoke had a mechanical cadence, like he was badly reciting lines. There was something missing behind his eyes, something that had been extinguished. I told myself it was a temporary loss, that the mischievous spark would return.

It never did.

Even so, having most of Timothy back was better than not having him at all.

I can say this with certainty, because not having him at all is excruciating. It's a pain that haunts me every day.

The rest of 1985 passed in a happy haze, as did most of 1986. After our separation, the love between Timothy and me was reignited and reinvigorated, and our quality of life continued to improve as Genevieve made press come to Owls Point for interviews with us, and our doubles were used more for public appearances. Both of us were attending regular medical screenings and taking the pills prescribed for us, concoctions that kept us alert, levelheaded, and jovial.

In the Dollhouse was unlike any show that came before it, and it was getting stronger with each season. We were equally engrossed in our side projects; Timothy kept finding compelling film scripts, and I wrote more songs. Our creativity blossomed in ways it never had before, and the gratification from our work spilled over into our relationship. When each person in a couple is happy separately, it's easier to be happy together.

In November of 1986, while we were filming the fifth season of *In the Dollhouse*, things took a turn.

It was a rare day off for both of us, and I was curled up with a book in the room of our house that I'd turned into a reading nook, while Timothy was out jogging around Parliament Lake. Without warning, he burst through the door, sweaty and wild-eyed.

"Did you see them?" he panted. "Did you see the new trainees?"

Periodically, we ran into new Dollhouse Academy recruits on campus, their fresh faces filled with hope and determination. Timothy and I would wave and say hello as we walked by, but the trainees often remained rooted in place, dumbfounded.

I told Timothy I didn't know which trainees he meant.

"You'd know it if you saw them." Though he was still catching his breath, he paced the small room lined with bookshelves. It gave me instant flashbacks to the last time he was this worked up. "There's four of them, two girls and two guys. The girls are both blond and pretty, like cheap knockoffs of you."

That was hardly something to get upset about. There were a lot of aspiring blond actresses out there.

"Okay, fine. But the two guys? Both look like me. Genevieve said we each had one double. Now they're training more? How many does the Dollhouse need? How long before we become disposable to them?"

At this, I felt a tremor of unease, less because of what he was saying rather than how he was saying it. After all, Genevieve mentioned she'd used multiple decoys over the years.

Cautiously, I asked whether he was still taking his meds.

"I am, but it's funny how you think I've stopped because I'm questioning things about this place. Doesn't that say something about what the pills might really be doing to us?"

A week later, after returning home from a recording session, I found him upstairs in the bedroom, throwing clothes into an open suitcase.

"Those new Project Understudy trainees? They're not going to be used as doubles like the others. They've been brought in to replace us if something happens to us or we start acting out. *Permanently* replace us."

How could he make such a radical assumption?

"There's a janitor in the medical wing I've gotten friendly with. He said Dahlen Entertainment and DahlenRex are becoming more and more interconnected, that they'll medicate top stars within an inch of their lives if it means making more money off them by keeping them in a chemical haze. He also said they're developing new protocols involving brain surgery."

At this, dread pooled in my stomach.

"I know it sounds crazy, but this guy said we couldn't begin to imagine some of the advancements DahlenRex has made."

He was basing all this on the word of a janitor?

"Nobody pays attention to the cleaning staff. They overhear things. They see things people carelessly throw away. Sometimes confidential things."

Even if that was the case, I didn't understand why this janitor would share any confidential information with Timothy.

"He's a good guy and he thinks I'm a good guy, too. I'm one of the only people who says hello to him, asks about his day. Who knows his name: Caleb. He wanted me to be aware of what was really going on here."

And did Caleb have any evidence to back up his claims?

"He did, but he has to find the right time and place to share it with me, so he doesn't lose his job—or worse." At this, his eyes went wild, and he held tightly to my upper arms. "Ivy, it's time for us to leave. We could wait around for Caleb to show us the evidence, but I trust him, just like I trusted that lab assistant who warned me about Project Understudy. At this point, we've made enough money that we can do whatever we want."

Except we'd have a lot less money if we were sued by Dahlen Entertainment for breach of contract. And we'd be blackballed. I felt like a broken record having to remind him of this all over again. Besides, I said, we love our work, we love our home in Owls Point, and we felt no adverse effects from the pills we were taking.

"What if we love it here so much *because* of all the pills we're taking?"

A darker, deeper chill passed through me followed by an unkind thought: Why couldn't he leave well enough alone and let us enjoy our lives? Instead, I asked again if he'd stopped taking his medication. I begged him to remember what happened last time he did, to not repeat past mistakes.

"What if it wasn't a mistake? What if I was sane all along but your precious Genevieve twisted the truth and made me out to be a lunatic?" He was gripping my arms so hard, I knew he'd leave bruises. As if sensing that, he let me go.

Once again, I paid less attention to his words and more to his actions and expressions. There was a tiny amount of spit foaming in the corner of his mouth making me think of rabid dogs. I threw a worried glance at the suitcase, then back to Timothy.

It took all my willpower to keep my voice from matching his fevered pitch. I reasoned, if Caleb had proof to back up his claims, we should wait to see it before making any rash moves. If that proof was legitimate, I'd have no qualms about leaving.

Timothy came to his senses and agreed that was a reasonable course of action. Once he was able to speak more rationally, I also pleaded with him to take his pills. He said he would, but I wasn't fully convinced.

A few days later, I was startled out of a dead sleep. The sun was just coming up over the horizon as Timothy pulled me out of bed and urged me to get dressed.

"Caleb showed me. It was a Xerox of a surgical record from September for one of the trainees. He said it was for one of your doubles. I didn't understand all the medical jargon, but I knew 'craniotomy,' because a cousin of mine is epileptic and had to have one. It's when they remove a piece of your skull so they can operate on your brain. Apparently, controlling us with pills isn't enough anymore. But they're not looking to zap our brains in a water tank. DahlenRex is pioneering a new type of lobotomy, a 'meta-lobotomy' they're calling it, which essentially turns you into a human puppet. They're using the trainees as their guinea pigs."

In my barely awake state, I fought to make sense of what he was saying while changing out of my pajamas. How did he know this one medical record meant that a trainee was undergoing some sort of dreadful experimentation? What if she was also epileptic, or had another condition that made it necessary to get brain surgery?

"That's what I asked Caleb. So he showed me a copy of a second medical record from last month for a different trainee. One of my doubles. What are the chances that two teenagers would need brain surgery within a few weeks of each other?"

My head was spinning. Why the early wake-up? Was he taking me to Caleb to show me these medical records?

"No, we're going to the lake. The trainees jog the track there every morning. We're going to find the two that were operated on and see for ourselves what was done to them. Then we're getting the hell out of Owls Point."

This did not sound like a good idea. I would've preferred to speak with Caleb and see this so-called evidence for myself.

"Are you saying you don't trust me? I'm doing this with or without you. If you don't want to come with me . . ."

But of course I would.

We arrived at the lake and followed the track counterclockwise. Since there were painted arrows on the path directing pedestrian traffic in a clockwise pattern, this ensured we'd meet the group face-to-face. Ten minutes later, four teenagers resembling us appeared, clustered in a rhythmic run.

Timothy put his arms out to the sides, blocking their way. Awe and confusion flashed across their faces. Why were the Dollhouse's biggest stars interrupting their morning exercise?

"Which of you two had the operation?" He craned his neck to examine their hairlines, then stepped toward them for a closer look. From where I stood, it wasn't obvious that any of them were wearing wigs.

The group exchanged baffled glances among themselves, followed by shrugs and headshakes.

"You're lying," Timothy said, weaving around them, getting in their faces. "Two of you had brain surgery, and I want to know which two. Was it you?" One of the young men cowered as Timothy reached out and touched his hair. "No, it had to be you. That's gotta be a wig." He lunged at one of the young women, grabbing a fistful of her hair and pulling on it. She cried out, and I ran over and pried her hair from Timothy's fingers. Before he could approach anyone else, the group took off, sprinting away.

As they fled, one of the blondes cast a fearful look over her shoulder and met my eye. "Get away from him, he's crazy!"

Timothy turned to me. "Is that what you think? That I'm crazy? This doesn't prove anything. I saw those records. Those surgeries happened. We might be forced to get them next. No way am I sticking around for that."

I told him to go home and start packing, offering to smooth things over with the trainees, so as not to raise any suspicions. I'd meet him back at the house.

Once he was out of sight, I went to the only person I thought could provide any sense and sanctuary: Genevieve. I'd known her for over six years at that point and she'd never steered me wrong. She had helped bring Timothy back from the edge before and would know what to do now.

Genevieve wasn't home, but when I explained the situation to an assistant, he paged her at the studio. I was brought into a sitting room and waited, my thoughts in a tailspin. Should I have stayed home and tried to reason with him? Would he leave without me? It never dawned on me to wonder if there was any merit to his wild claims; his volatile state made it impossible to believe him.

Genevieve finally appeared.

"Timothy is being taken to Epiphany Bay for another stay," she said. "He's going to be fine, Ivy, don't worry."

But he wasn't fine. Despite their security measures, two days after he arrived, he escaped his room, into to a wooded area on the grounds.

Timothy was found the next day, hanging from a tree by a bedsheet. He didn't leave a note.

CHAPTER THIRTY

FEBRUARY 1999

Anticipation twists me in knots. Today's table read will mark the first time I've seen Grace in nearly six months. The first time since our big fight. The first time since she's become Gracie.

Even with all the travel she's been doing to promote her new show and album, it's odd that it's been this long since our paths crossed. Or maybe it's more disturbing, that she's been so effectively hidden away from the rest of the world, and even from the rest of the Dollhouse.

But today there's no avoiding it: we'll finally see each other face-to-face, whether Grace likes it or not.

It wasn't until getting this script that I told Jude about my history with Grace. He was miffed that I hadn't confided in him sooner, but he's not one to hold a grudge.

Jude and I get to the conference room a half hour early so I can scope out the seating arrangement. I was fine to head out on my own, but he wanted to tag along. Sometimes I think he might be a little *too* supportive.

We all have assigned seats, and I'm curious to see where Grace's placard is in relation to mine. It's a long shot that I'll be seated next to her—we have no scenes together—but if I'm across from her, I'll be able to really study her and try to get her to make eye contact. As luck would have it, my chair is diagonally across from hers.

We take our seats, and I fiddle with the cap on my water, screwing and unscrewing it. Beside me, Jude studies the script and rubs absent-minded circles on my lower back, which is pleasant at first but then becomes inexplicably irritating. I pull away and stand up, selecting a Danish from the platter of breakfast pastries laid out on a separate table.

"You want one?" I take a bite and the burst of cloying pineapple filling makes me want to spit it back out.

"No thanks."

When I sit back down, he keeps his hands off me, which is a relief but also makes me feel a little guilty.

Sometimes I wonder if Jude is too nice for me.

Before we know it, the room fills up with actors, writers, Dahlen execs, and the director. When Ivy comes in, she smiles at me as she sits down, but even that does little to soothe my jitters.

"Does anybody know where Gracie is?" asks the director.

Only her chair remains empty.

She's been a star for five minutes and she's already commanding a dramatic entrance?

Unless something is wrong. A seesaw of worry and annoyance tips back and forth inside me.

Five minutes after we're scheduled to begin, Grace rushes in.

"Sorry to keep you waiting. Dance rehearsal ran late. You know how Lady Edna can be," she says with a rueful smile that earns sympathetic nods from around the table.

Grace scans the table, her gaze landing on me briefly before taking off like a skittish butterfly.

She's in all black: baggy cargo pants, a fitted spaghetti-strapped tank top, and a bulky cardigan that keeps sliding off one shoulder. Perched on top of her head are giant sunglasses she wears as a headband.

There's no question she's lost too much weight; her prominent collarbones look like they could cut glass, and her head looks too big for her body. But there's also something luminous about her. Upon a closer look, I may have been too hasty (or catty) in disparaging her hair. The bright crimson actually flatters her olive skin, which has a new glow to it. Even though I still think she looked better with her original lips and nose, she's irrefutably gorgeous. More than that, she exudes a true star quality.

How have I never noticed this about Grace before? Is it because I was too busy trying to cultivate my own star quality? Or is it because I was scared to look too closely?

My eyes bore into Grace's, willing her to look over at me again, but she's studying her script now. Which is something I should also be doing, since I still need to prove myself in every scene I'm in if I want to go from recurring character to series regular.

As the read-through begins, Grace's acting is the best I've ever seen it. I didn't want to admit it when I caught clips of *Rock the Dollhouse*, but I can't deny it now. As Juniper, she balances her caustic wit with moments of reluctant sweetness, a perfect mix of cynicism and heart (not unlike Grace herself). Seeing how good she is makes me want to up my game, and even though I have fewer scenes and am part of the B story, I play each line thoughtfully, as if I'm doing this for the camera.

In the entire time it takes us to get through the script, Grace never makes eye contact with me.

After the table read, we break for lunch. I have every intention of accosting my friend, but she's suddenly surrounded by other cast members, semi-bashfully accepting compliments, smiling and laughing, and I find myself rooted in my seat.

Grace is clearly thriving. What's more, she's doing so without me. Maybe she's outgrown me. Or it's possible she never needed me. All those years of giving her moral support might've been holding her back in some way; perhaps I didn't give her enough credit for her self-sufficiency and tenacity. The worst thing of all? Maybe Grace was right, and I was the one who needed her in order to feel better about myself. My cheeks burn at the thought.

"It looks like she's heading out," Jude says to me under his breath. "You sure you don't want to go talk to her?"

What would be the point? Why should I chase her down? If she holds me in such little regard that she can't even acknowledge my presence, maybe I shouldn't be fighting so hard for our friendship.

Then again, maybe Grace is one of the few people I know worth fighting for.

I slide back my chair a few inches, but before I can stand, Vanessa Sanchez accosts Grace, engaging her in animated conversation for a moment before pointing at the door. They leave together.

So on top of everything, Grace is now friends with her personal hero, too. Further reason she doesn't need me.

"She's obviously busy," I say, pretending to scrawl notes in the margin of my script. "Maybe another time."

Don't lose your shit here. Wait until you're outside.

"Jude, could I grab you for a few minutes?" the director calls out.

Oh, thank god.

A few minutes could be an hour with this director, so I tell Jude I'll meet him in the Dahlen cafeteria later. I'm actually relieved, because I don't want to unpack everything that just happened with Grace—or rather, didn't—in front of Jude.

Outside, I tell myself to breathe, to hold it together, but the tears come anyway, hard and fast.

"Need a ride?" Mason calls out from a golf cart a few feet away.

I use a knuckle to dab away my tears and get in the passenger seat. "Why do you always seem to catch me at my worst moments?"

"It's just your misfortune, I suppose. Or is it mine?" he muses. He smells faintly of coffee and cigarette smoke. "I'd offer you my handkerchief, like a real gentleman, but we both know I'm not that."

"Who even carries a handkerchief around anymore?" I say. "And you have your gentlemanly moments." Why am I defending him?

Because he's there during your worst moments.

"Shall I drop you off at Gale House?"

"No, I can't handle being around people right now."

"Good thing I'm not people then."

"You know what I mean. Is there anywhere quiet we can go?" I hope he doesn't suggest the lake, because I feel like I've sullied that place for us. "Close by, I need to get back for wardrobe fittings later."

"Quiet, close, no people. Got it." Mason makes a sharp turn and a minute later pulls up to a construction site at the edge of campus with a partially built six-story building surrounded by scaffolding.

"Are we going inside?"

"No, the site is closed until they figure out some electrical issues. We can hang out here. There's no reason for anyone to come around, so that fits your criteria: no people, no noise." At my less-than-enthused reaction, he asks, "What's wrong, were you hoping for somewhere more romantic?"

Something hot and prickly flares up in me. "Why do you have to be nice with a side of asshole?"

"If you want the regular kind of nice, go back to your boyfriend."

I probably should. Even though Mason and I are only talking, being so near him makes me feel like I'm being unfaithful to Jude. Maybe that's why my palms are sweating.

"So come on then, what's got you all worked up?" Reluctant compassion softens his tone.

Fresh tears spring to my eyes. "Grace acted like I was a piece of furniture—not even, she looked at the furniture more than she looked at me. And forget about talking to me. I was sitting across from her, maybe five feet away, and—zero acknowledgment." The cold is seeping into the golf cart, so I hug my arms across my chest.

"You sure this isn't about you being jealous?"

This is why I prefer to talk to Mason about such things. He's not afraid to ask unpleasant questions, whereas Jude would try to spare my feelings. "I mean, a little. I'd kill for either a hit show, *or* a hit album. Though her music isn't great. There's no way she doesn't hate those cheesy pop songs. Even so, the fact that she gets both the hit show *and* album at the same time—it's like winning the lottery twice in a row. So yeah, of course I'm jealous. But I'm also happy where I am now. Which makes it ridiculous that all these great things are happening, yet we're still not speaking to each other. I guess she'd rather be hobnobbing with other Dahlen stars, probably because she is one now."

"Yeah . . . you're better off cutting your losses with that one."

"She's not, like, some guy I went on two dates with who stopped calling. We've been best friends since fifth grade—more like sisters, really. I don't understand why she's letting one stupid fight negate all the history we have together."

Mason drums his fingers on the steering wheel. "I'm guessing it's not really about the fight you had. This place pushes you to your limits, breaks you, and then remakes you how it sees fit."

"How Genevieve sees fit?"

"Part of the star-making process here is limiting your ties to the outside world."

"But I'm not outside. I'm in here with her."

"Just because you're here, doesn't mean you can't still be an outsider. Your friendship is from the before times. Her loyalty to you can't trump her loyalty to the Dollhouse. It's easier if that loyalty is eradicated."

"What are you saying? That she's being brainwashed against me?" I think of the recent meetings with Devon, how he's been telling me to move on and leave Grace in my past. "Is that what those counseling sessions are really for, to turn us into obedient little dolls?"

"If that was the case, that would make this a rather sinister place, wouldn't you say?" he says with no trace of alarm.

"Here's the thing, though. Grace looked so . . . in her element. Her performance in that table read was so natural, I've never seen her that good." It's hard to say the next words aloud, but I need to try them out. "Maybe she's better with me out of the way."

"It's possible . . . but maybe not for the reasons you think. If your friendship was any sort of distraction or threat to Grace's career, they'd find a way to make her see it as such."

"Does that mean I'll also become a better performer without her? Or do I have to cut myself off from my uncles first?"

"You're being sarcastic, but you never know what this place will ask of you. Sometimes the ones who rise to the top aren't the most talented, they're just the most capable of making tough choices. They commit themselves fully to the Dollhouse."

I start to say I've been fully committed from the start, but hasn't a part of me always held some reservations? Whereas Grace's determination to be here never wavered.

"You've had one foot out since the beginning, haven't you?" Mason turns to face me, which is when I notice his blue eyes are faded and bloodshot.

Instead of answering his question, I ask, "Is everything okay with you?"

"Genevieve has me working overtime on . . . various projects."

"Which I'm sure you have no intention of telling me about." Could Project Understudy be one of them? I stop short of asking directly. I've already put myself at enough risk discussing it with Tia. While Mason has done nothing to prove himself untrustworthy, I can't be 100 percent sure asking him about Project Understudy wouldn't get back to Genevieve. After all, despite the kindness he's shown me, his allegiance is ultimately to her and the Dollhouse.

"Naturally. It's just been a bit more hectic than usual."

The haunted look on his face and the way he's clutching the steering wheel with both hands tells me it's more than long hours.

"Look, I have a good reason to be here," I say. "Maybe I had one foot—not even a foot, a toe—out the door before, but now I'm fully in it. Aside from the bullshit with Grace, which is out of my control, I'm doing exactly what I want with my life. But you . . ." I reach out and touch the back of his hand. "You know you can talk to me, right? I'm good at venting but I'm also good at listening."

Mason stiffens, shakes himself out of whatever he was lost in. "I'm fine." The way he says it is like a door closing. I withdraw my hand and he turns the ignition. "We should get back."

CHAPTER THIRTY-ONE

MAY 1999

Things have settled into a pleasant routine the last couple of months. After that painful week when Grace was guest-starring on ITD, crossing paths but never acknowledging each other, I accepted that our friendship was over. Actually, I truly accepted it at the end of February, when my birthday came and went without a card from her. We always get each other cards.

That was what it took to get me to move on.

I set aside my frustration and grief and put everything I have into fine-tuning the role of Skylar Vaughn. When I'm not in an episode, I take extra voice lessons and movement classes to keep myself limber, and the occasional improv class, which helps me stay loose on set. I also spend hours in the media library, watching classic movies and old episodes of *In the Dollhouse*, studying what makes key performances so special. I pore over every one of Skylar's lines, delving into her motivations, what she's trying to express and what she's trying to hide in each moment, adding more memories to the rich tapestry of backstory I already created for her. I grow to know Skylar like I would a real person. Even though my character started out more antagonistic and one-dimensional, I work like hell to humanize her, and my efforts must be evident, because I'm written into meatier storylines.

By the last several episodes of the season, I'm written into an A story with Ivy, which will end on a cliff-hanger, meaning there's every reason for my character to return. With any luck, I'll be promoted to series regular.

After that first scene with Ivy, we've done several more together, and every time I work with her, I learn something new. In one scene, where we have an argument, she tells me to think of us as percussion instruments creating a rhythm. In another, where my character mourns the sudden loss of a parent, she tells me to imagine myself as a dam holding in my grief, and to experiment with it bursting in unexpected moments. Our off-camera interactions are fleeting, but it's still a privilege to receive her knowledge and guidance.

Gracie mania is going strong in Owls Point, with the Main Street theater airing episodes of her show every Sunday to a packed house and stories on her in just about every magazine I pick up. *Rock the Dollhouse* has continued to be a smash hit, sometimes (but not always) overtaking *In the Dollhouse* in ratings. I tell myself I can't control who watches what, and the numbers don't matter, considering both shows are hugely popular, but I can't resist a sense of pointed satisfaction whenever I see ITD at number one. Ditto for when Gracie's second single, "Don't Be That Guy," doesn't knock Ricky Martin's "Livin' La Vida Loca" off its number one perch. It's not a pretty feeling, but it's an honest one.

While I've stopped hoping I'll get any correspondence from Grace, after many months without any white envelopes, I've also stopped dreading getting any additional anonymous notes.

All of which leads me to believe my earlier suspicions: the notes were part of some elaborate scheme or loyalty test, from Genevieve or other Dollhouse higher-ups, and I've passed by disregarding them.

This leaves me free to enjoy the Dollhouse in a way I've never been able to before. I've been doing the best work of my life, and I spend my off-hours with Jude, who's as sweet and doting as ever, and Tia, who's said nothing further about Project Understudy, but whose upbeat disposition always brightens my day.

The only thing that still nags at me is that I don't feel as elated as I should.

Devon says it's normal for any initial fizz of euphoria to settle into something more subdued and sustainable, whether it's a new relationship, a new job, or anything else. He says if I need that dopamine hit, I should get more sleep, exercise, and natural light. Despite doing all of those things, I can't muster any positive feeling beyond being generally pleased. I get that it's not healthy to be giddy all the time, but I wonder if I should be this emotionally muted.

Not long after celebrating my one-year anniversary at the Dollhouse (Jude, Tia, and I grabbed drinks at the Sterile Cuckoo but only a couple because I had an early call time the following morning), I get summoned to Genevieve's owl room.

This time, my nerves buzz less with dread and more with expectation.

Tea is served, along with a tiered tray of finger sandwiches and miniature pastries, which I take as another good sign.

"It would appear you've had quite the turnaround." Genevieve assesses me from over the rim of her porcelain cup. "Most trainees so close to expulsion end up buckling under the pressure."

I hesitate sipping from my own cup, the china so delicate, looking like it might crumble between my fingers. "I'm glad I found it in me to keep pushing myself."

"Yes, we've all been pleasantly surprised to see what you've done with Skylar Vaughn. In the hands of a lesser actor, she would've remained a forgettable tertiary character. But the show's directors and network executives are happy, as am I, and you've been getting positive buzz in the media."

My smile is placid, belying the exhilaration zipping through me. "That's gratifying to hear. Skylar is a great character to play, and I'm glad I've been able to do her justice."

"No need for false modesty, Ramona."

"I'd be lying if I said I wasn't working my butt off." Emboldened, I take one of the finger sandwiches from the tray's lowest tier. It's been ages since I was this hungry, and I take a big bite—egg salad and watercress, yum—before devouring the rest in a second bite.

"I want you to know your hard work hasn't gone unnoticed."

"Thank you." This calls for another finger sandwich. Ooh, smoked salmon.

"And since I'm a firm believer in rewarding hard work, you should know you're being considered for a role in the first of what we hope will become a series of *In the Dollhouse* films."

"You're finally making an ITD movie?" I can't keep the excitement out of my voice.

Genevieve flinches. "I do wish people would stop using that acronym. There's something reductive and lazy about it. It's only one extra syllable to say the full name of the show."

"*In the Dollhouse*, of course, you're right," I quickly correct myself. "Are you still planning on filming it in black, white, and red?"

"With the musical sequences in full color, yes. The working title is *Dollhouse Daze.*"

"It would be an honor to be part of it."

"It certainly would." Genevieve fingers the owl brooch pinned to the lapel of her suit; today's Chanel is white double-breasted with black piping. "The script is going through rewrites at the moment, but I believe Skylar Vaughn could play a substantial supporting role to Tabitha Noelle."

"How is the story going to fit in with the IT—*In the Dollhouse* canon?"

"Our writers are making sure it's relatively stand-alone, so that anyone can enjoy it whether or not they've seen the show while also satisfying dedicated viewers. The storyline will involve parallel worlds." Catching herself, Genevieve straightens up. "Of course, this is all strictly confidential."

"Of course."

"If I give you this part, I'm going to want a few things from you."

"Anything."

"I want you to get your teeth bonded and whitened."

"Done."

"I want you to get hair extensions. And for your hair to be lightened to platinum."

"Will do."

"I want you to lose fifteen pounds, though I'll make sure you work with a nutritionist and trainer to do so in a healthy way." A pointed glance at the sandwich on my plate, my third.

"No problem." I push away my plate, my appetite instantly vanished. While part of me wants to protest and repeat what I told her last time about being happy with the way I currently look, the last thing I want is to cause any friction and be robbed of this rare opportunity.

"This movie will take your career to a new level. Are you sure you have no hesitations?" she prods.

"None at all. I'll do anything that's required of me." Because if I don't, she'll find somebody else who will. I shudder to think what else I would've acquiesced to if asked, how quickly I would've buckled. Yet I judged Grace for being as compliant as I'm willing to be right now. And I gave Jude a hard time for his honesty over the same issue. Which reminds me . . . "What about Jude? Will he be in the movie, too?"

A shrewd smile plays across her lips. "How fascinating that you covered your own interests first before enquiring about your boyfriend. But to answer your question, yes, he will be in the cast, though his role won't be as robust as yours. We do think the romance between you and Jude will help the film, and since you two have a higher profile as a result of the show, we'll be sending you both to Los Angeles and New York City in the coming months, to be seen out and about together, and to build on the fan investment in you as a couple. It will be a hectic schedule, since you'll also be shooting." She waits for my reaction.

"I'm sure Jude and I will be able to handle it. It sounds exciting." And exhausting, though I try not to let any of my qualms show.

"It certainly will be, though that level of pressure and scrutiny can take its toll on a relationship. If you're seen arguing in public, it'll be photographed and written about, which can cause further strain. Which is to say, you mustn't exhibit any conflict in public, and if you fail at that, you must ensure your resolution is made equally public."

"Jude and I never fight." Almost never.

Genevieve sits back and assesses me. "Depending on how this shoot goes, and how you handle the publicity, we may make you a series regular on *In the Dollhouse*. Before you give me that hopeful smile, know that a lot will be expected of you this summer. If you think you've worked hard up to this point, you have no idea what awaits you."

Her final words stay with me as I return to the dorm and find a white envelope waiting for me in my mailbox.

My heart sinks. Maybe I should toss it away without reading it. It can only cause more stress, likely meant to mess with my head more than to help me.

My fingers tighten around the envelope, crushing its edges. I want to tear it to pieces, burn it, bury it, do anything other than read it. The smart thing to do would be to leave it sealed and get rid of it.

But curiosity tugs at me.

CHAPTER THIRTY-TWO

Ivy's Diary

MAY 5, 1999

After so many years spent fooling an audience from behind a screen, I wonder if I've developed a secondary expertise of fooling myself, too. It's taken me all these years to truly begin to see things as they really are.

My source continues to come through. Most recently, he's brought me bags of shredded paper, which I'm keeping in my attic. It's tedious and time-consuming reconstructing sensitive documents, but from what I've gathered so far, they're patient assessments quantifying why a Project Understudy candidate might be promising ("background of poverty," "troubled household," "abusive formative years") or not ("healthy self-esteem," "absence of childhood trauma," "extensive circle of friends/family"). There are other papers that contain scientific and medical terms I can't decipher. The next step is to find someone to help me make sense of these other documents, someone to analyze the science, and to find myself a lawyer not affiliated with Dahlen Entertainment. I have several upcoming media engagements in Manhattan, which may afford me the chance.

The more of these confidential records I piece together, the more vindication I feel, but also the more trepidation. I still believe someone may be following me, so I'm cautious when speaking with my source in public, and when he has something new to give me, he only visits in the middle of the night. Otherwise, I continue to be on my best behavior.

For a time, I thought it might be Timothy's paranoia rubbing off on me. Now I realize he was thinking more clearly than I ever was. The truth was just too much for him to bear. I will never shed my guilt over betraying him the way I did. At the same time, I must take care not to meet a similar dark fate.

When I found out Timothy was dead, I wailed. I never heard such a sound come out of my mouth before or since, so much despair pouring out of me all at once. My body shook with sobs as I cried until my throat was raw and eyes swollen shut. "Let it out, let it out," said someone trying to console me. As if there was a way to purge myself of the grief. But no matter how much I let it out, my body was an endlessly refilling well of tears and sorrow.

The ache of losing Timothy remains with me, like a ghost limb.

Oh, and the blame. In the ensuing years, I've blamed the Dollhouse for taking Timothy away from me. But in the moments where I can look at the cold, hard truth, I can't deny that it was my fault.

The rest of 1986 passed in a dark blur of grief. Production was halted on both ITD and my new album; they knew better than to ask me to work at such a time.

I was brought into the medical wing weekly, to make sure I was eating enough and not in danger of harming myself or others. Whenever I had these appointments, I kept an eye out for any janitors, even managed to surreptitiously ask a couple of them if they knew a man named Caleb, but none did.

I also continued my regular counseling sessions, but there are only so many ways you can say you're devastated. I felt like one of Genevieve's china teacups, ready to shatter at the slightest hint of pressure. Most days, I didn't leave the house, wandering through the rooms as if I was haunting them, a blanket draped over me like a cape. On better days, I could get lost in books or mindless television. On worse days, I would drop to the floor of whichever room I happened to be in, cocoon myself in my blanket, and lie there crying until sleep came over me.

There was an outpouring of support from fans during that time, with letters and flowers coming in droves. In the past, I'd been too busy to read my fan mail, but now I had the time and needed the sympathy. I pored over the messages, which reflected my heartbreak and anguish. How was it that strangers were able to connect so deeply to this man through the fictional characters he played, to mourn his loss so acutely? Yet they did, and our shared pain brought me an odd sense of comfort. I wanted the world to grieve with me, and I had a mountain of letters affirming it was.

There were also gifts from fans: books on bereavement, keepsakes like picture frames, charms, figurines, and candles. But one package contained something different: a film script, sent by the screenwriter herself, though it was attached to a studio, too modest to be one of Dahlen Entertainment's competitors. The attached note said she'd written the script after suffering the loss of a loved one and always imagined me as the female lead. It was called *Colorbound*, about a young couple in Hawaii, a photographer and professional surfer, who become engaged, only for the man to be diagnosed with a terminal illness and die before they can wed. I wept as I read the script, seeing so much of myself and Timothy in the main characters, painfully identifying with their love cut short.

I brought the script to Genevieve and told her I wanted to do this movie.

"We never lend our talent out to other studios. It would set a bad precedent. Besides, it's a tropical version of *Love Story*, nothing special."

Normally, I would've played the obedient doll and buried my frustrations so deeply they'd be forgotten. But not this time.

I told Genevieve I had no interest in returning to the show or finishing my album if I couldn't do this movie. They could threaten to sue me, ban me from the industry, you name it. None of that mattered. The loss of Timothy had hollowed me out, left me indifferent to the world and my fate within it. The only thing that had brought any modicum of inspiration into my life since he died was this script. If Genevieve couldn't understand and respect that, she could go ahead and replace me with one of my look-alikes.

I braced myself for pushback, but instead, she calmly said she'd consider everything I said and would get back to me in a few days.

In early 1987, I was given six weeks off to shoot *Colorbound* in Hawaii. I poured my heart into that movie, and it's the work I'm proudest of to this day. After that, I returned to the set of *In the Dollhouse* and completed shooting the fifth season of the show. Timothy's absence was written as an unexplained disappearance, and so while Tabitha Noelle grieved the loss of Hayden Close, it wasn't fully satisfying to channel my loss through hers because she had one thing I did not: hope that she'd be reunited with her love. It was slightly more satisfying recording the rest of my album, which I insisted be comprised of melancholy ballads for which I provided the lyrics and the title: *Little Doll Blue*. The first single off that album, "Not So Lucky After All," went straight to number one.

That summer *Colorbound* made the round of European film festivals, and I debated once again whether I wanted to continue playing Tabitha Noelle, whether I wanted to remain in the Dollhouse at all.

Then my life was threatened on a private jet. I spent the rest of that flight shaking, my thoughts in shambles. Had Timothy received a similar threat? In my case, my sense of self-preservation overrode my desire for autonomy. What if Timothy refused to acquiesce at the cost of his self-preservation?

Was he silenced or did he silence himself? I may never know the truth.

When I returned to Owls Point early the next morning, I remained in shock. After showering and changing clothes, despite it being a warm morning, I made a fire and sat close to the hearth, wrapped in an afghan. This did not ease the cold in my bones. My teeth would not stop chattering.

There was a knock on my door. I don't know what time it was, but I was probably late for rehearsal.

"Ivy, let me in." It was Genevieve.

The moment I opened the door, she rushed inside and swept me up in a hug, the most physical affection I'd ever received from her.

"They told me what they did, those monsters. The way they threatened you is entirely unacceptable," she raved. "It's all my fault. I put my trust in certain people and gave them too much responsibility. I asked that you be persuaded to sign on for more seasons of *In the Dollhouse* but not in such an appalling fashion. Rest assured, everyone involved has been terminated."

I gazed at her, as if trying to recognize her through a thick fog. She hadn't known about the threat on my life? She hadn't been behind it?

Genevieve steered me to the sofa and bade me to sit. "In all the years we've known each other, have I ever treated you with anything but respect and maturity? Have I not always acted in your best interest to ensure you had the career of your dreams? Do you really think I would stoop so low as to have your life threatened?" She pinched an earlobe, consternation tightening her features. "The unfortunate truth is that I am unable to manage every aspect of running the Dollhouse Academy and Dahlen Entertainment, and I gave more power to certain executives than I should have. It turns out we have opposing ideas on how to manage operations, and in some cases, they have gone over my head. I'm sorry you got caught up in their schemes, but they're gone now, and your safety here is assured."

I took in everything she told me, trying to make sense of it. Genevieve Spalding was the most powerful woman I'd ever met. There was no way she would relinquish control of her entertainment empire. Was it really possible she had no part in the threat against my life?

Looking at her face as she sat in my cottage, earnest, full of remorse, I had to believe her. Because if I was wrong for putting my faith in her, I'd be left with nothing.

After that ill-fated flight from Rome and Genevieve's visit to the cottage, she delayed ITD production by a few days so I could get myself together. Then I returned to work. I shot the next season of the show and was given a break from recording music that autumn and winter. Instead, I did my first tour of Asia and Australia, playing multiple nights in stadiums holding over a hundred thousand people. It should have been gratifying to be adored on such a scale, but I felt nothing except sorrow, which I channeled through the songs from *Little Doll Blue*.

By this point, I had been off the pills for nearly a year, since the *Colorbound* press junket and its aftermath. To be sure, it was counterintuitive. If there was a time I needed to be numbed from personal horrors, it was then. But a masochistic part of me wanted to see what life would be like without their chemical enhancement.

It was horrendous. The headaches and fatigue went away after a few weeks, but the gnawing sense of irritation and doom persisted. Everything struck me as dismal and futile, though I pretended otherwise.

At any moment, I could've put an end to my misery, either by returning to the pills or taking more extreme measures (which I would've done if it guaranteed a reunion with Timothy). I don't know why I cast aside both options. Instead, I continued on as I was, enduring a meaningless reality devoid of hope or joy. Why did I put myself through that? Probably to punish myself for not being able to save Timothy. It was also a way to feel closer to him, to experience the world the way he had before he made his exit from it.

If he was indeed responsible for taking his own life, I understood all too well why he did. I don't know how I endured such bleakness for nearly a year. If anything, the depth of my desolation made me lean more toward the notion that Timothy died at his own hand, without interference from the Dollhouse.

By mid-1988, it was clear that my career as a performer wasn't making me happy, but then again, nothing was. And no one.

In late May, a week before my North American *Little Doll Blue* tour was about to begin, I went to see Genevieve.

I told her this tour would be my last, as would the next season of *In the Dollhouse*. I was done. I had nothing left to give.

Naturally, Genevieve saw through me. "Have you stopped taking your supplements? Much as we miss him, you don't want to follow the same dark road as Timothy. Perhaps we need to make an adjustment to your dosages."

I lied and told her I was taking the supplements, that I didn't want any adjustments, that this had been on my mind for a long time.

Genevieve tried a different tack. "You seemed to quite enjoy working on that last film you did. What if we found you another project? We could have something developed and written specifically for you."

No. It wasn't about finding the right project. It was about leaving everything.

Her forehead creased. "Perhaps it's a case of exhaustion. We can send you away on a lavish vacation, you'll spend a week or two on a private island and come back good as new. Unless you believe you might benefit from a stay at Epiphany Bay?"

I said I didn't want any of it. It was challenging enough when I had Timothy, and I'd tried to continue on without him, but I couldn't do it anymore. I'd given myself fully to the Dollhouse for eight years, and now I wanted to leave.

For a long time, she said nothing and only stared at me, narrowing one eye, and tilting her head sideways ever so slowly. Her shoulders heaved with a long, deliberate breath and she finally said, "Very well. You're right. You've given us eight years of exceptional work. If you've decided you have absolutely nothing left, I will respect that. Since this will be your last tour, I hope you'll give a little more to make it special. Your fans need to remember you at your best."

That was an easy promise to make, now that I could see a way out.

"We'll figure out how to write Tabitha off the show, but for now, focus on the tour," she continued. "The only other thing I ask is that you not say anything to anyone else about stepping away from show business. I'll talk to our PR team about how best to announce it publicly."

I said I would do everything asked of me but would appreciate having all my work obligations fulfilled by the end of the year.

"That is feasible. It should give us enough time to figure out a series of graceful exits for you. By 1989, you will be a free woman."

I hadn't the faintest idea of what I would do with this newfound freedom, but the promise of it filled me with a heady ebullience.

The night before I set off on my North American tour, Genevieve called. "I want to wish you safe travels. And to let you know, if at any point during the tour you change your mind and decide to stay on, call me on my private line, at any time. There will always be a place for you at Dahlen Entertainment."

Is that what her grand scheme was? To give me enough leeway so I might come around and rediscover my passion for performing?

If that was Genevieve's plan, it looked, for a while, like it might work. During the first leg of the tour, which began on the West Coast, I connected with audiences in a way I never had before. It was bittersweet, absorbing their collective love while silently bidding them farewell. Every night, a smaller crowd backstage shared personal stories of how my music and my work on *In the Dollhouse* inspired them and helped them through difficult times. How was it possible they all saw something so special in me? Why was I chosen to experience this (for better or worse) extraordinary life? And was I sure I wanted to permanently step away from it?

As our tour buses zigzagged their way around the United States, I watched the country go by—deserts, mountains, expanses of empty fields and endless skies—and wondered what was waiting for me on the other side of those Dollhouse gates. The entire world, yes, but the breadth of it was daunting, the idea of traversing it solo more so. I was already deeply lonely; how much more would my loneliness be magnified without having a clear purpose and structure to my days? What if, after a year or two of experiencing aimless freedom, I missed Owls Point and wanted to return? Genevieve said there would always be a place for me at the Dollhouse, but new rising stars were proving their worth in various Dahlen productions. And while I was hardly old at twenty-four, these up-and-comers were mostly in their late teens and likely more spirited, impressionable, and eager to please than I was.

By the middle of the tour in July, I was straddling the line between wanting to remain at the Dollhouse and wanting to leave. We'd just stopped in Austin and were staying in a hotel for the night. I was put up in a luxurious suite, and as I slipped into a fluffy bathrobe, I couldn't decide whether I was more eager to soak in the Jacuzzi or sleep in a bed that wouldn't be jostling back and forth. Then the phone rang. It was Genevieve.

"Everybody is raving about the tour, Ivy. They're saying you've never sounded better. I only wish we had the hindsight to book you in South America, too. I appreciate you showing such immense grace under pressure. From what I hear, nobody would know how distressing it is to you."

I told her that it was actually a pleasure getting on stage every night, though I didn't add that perhaps it was such a pleasure because I knew I wouldn't have to do it for much longer.

"Is there any chance you may have reconsidered leaving? You know, there are other options. We could discuss an extended hiatus. If a week or two isn't enough time for you to recover from the stress that's been put on your shoulders, maybe a couple of months would do the trick. Even a six-month hiatus isn't out of the question."

Every part of my body tensed at the thought of having my hard-won freedom curtailed like that. As much as I was enjoying this tour, it would still be my last.

"Certainly, Ivy, the final decision rests with you. You can't blame me for trying."

I mentally began making plans for my life beyond the Dollhouse. The cold months in the Northeast never suited me, so I'd move somewhere more tropical, perhaps Miami or one of the Hawaiian Islands. I'd use the money I'd saved up to support the good causes Timothy and I had discussed and would start a children's hospital charity and build an animal sanctuary. I would also create a nonprofit for suicide prevention. Maybe I'd even open my own bookstore. How thrilling it was to dream about this next chapter of my life.

The last leg of the tour had us going up the Eastern Seaboard, finishing up Albany, New York, before returning to Owls Point. Before I knew it, we were on our way to the final show.

We were driving from Syracuse to Albany in the middle of the night, and I was fast asleep in the bedroom at the back of the bus. All I remember is being jolted awake by a loud noise, then being thrown off the bed and against the wall as the bus violently lurched to one side. That's when I blacked out.

I came to four days later in a hospital intensive care unit. Every inch of my body flamed with pain, and I couldn't even open my mouth to speak. A nurse told me I had just come out of a medically induced coma. I couldn't speak because of my broken jaw, which had to be wired shut. My other injuries included several rib fractures, a broken arm, a fractured tibia, a broken nose, and brain swelling.

The nurse told me I was lucky to be alive.

You ever get sick of people telling you how lucky you are?

Initially, I learned about the accident by watching the news. According to reports, the tour bus driver fell asleep at the wheel and crashed through the highway's guardrail, at which point the bus flipped and went down a thirty-foot embankment. Astonishingly, everyone else on the bus survived the accident with minor injuries, even the driver, who walked away with only a concussion, a few bruised ribs, and a sprained wrist.

It was a fresh agony, this ongoing physical pain, which was relieved now and again by the drips connected to my arm. The days dragged and bled into one another as I slept in fits and starts. Other than doctors and nurses, nobody came to see me in the first few days after I came out of the coma. I was in a private room with a bodyguard stationed outside. Nobody sent gifts or flowers, likely because Dahlen was keeping my whereabouts confidential.

After I'd spent a full week in the hospital, a nurse was in the middle of taking my vitals when a strange woman arrived, dressed in an oversize black caftan, a headscarf, and large dark sunglasses obscuring much of her face.

When the nurse saw her, she returned my chart to the foot of the bed and said, "I'll give you two some privacy." She closed the door on her way out.

At first, the woman said nothing and did nothing but stand beside my bed, staring down at me. Had I seen her somewhere before? She looked familiar, though it was hard to tell with those sunglasses on.

The phone rang. I picked it up, keeping an eye on my strange visitor.

"Is she there?" The person on the other end of the line had a deep distorted voice, like the kidnapper in a TV movie.

I asked who I was speaking to, and who this woman was.

A moment later the woman removed her scarf and sunglasses.

She was me. Several doubles had filled in for me in recent years, but I had never seen one up close since the sneak peek Genevieve had given me of Leonora before she'd had the final procedures done to resemble me. I didn't know if this woman was Leonora or someone else, but she could have been my identical twin.

"You'd never know she wasn't you, right?" said the voice on the other end of the line. "Hand her the phone."

I was too stunned to protest and did what I was told.

The woman listened for a few seconds, murmured something into the receiver, and handed it back to me.

"Listen closely, Ivy," said the voice. "Not to me, to her."

A moment later, the woman gave me a bashful smile and said, "I wrote this next song about someone special who is no longer with us." Then she launched into the chorus of "Not So Lucky After All."

I let out a strangled gasp.

Nausea seized me. I leaned over the side of the bed but could only dry heave.

The woman hurried to my side, retrieved the receiver, and placed it in my hand.

"Ivy, you've had many chances to come to your senses, but this is your last one. It was a miracle you survived the bus accident—and a complication. So, we'll give you a choice: either you continue in your role as Ivy Gordon, or this woman takes your place."

It was unthinkable. How could a stranger take over my life? And what would happen to me if I stepped aside?

"You're in a very delicate state with your recovery. Something could go wrong at any moment. Fortunately, your fans wouldn't have to mourn you. After a certain recovery period, you'd reappear. Good as new."

My skin broke out in a clammy sweat. How ironic that my jaw was wired shut, that I had no choice but to speak through gritted teeth. I muttered that this was lunacy, there was no way the public wouldn't see through the ruse. And even if they did, the people who knew me, my coworkers and friends and family—

"What friends? What family? As for your coworkers, they'll welcome your return and praise your professionalism. Nobody will know it isn't the real you because your therapy sessions provided enough fodder for your replacement to learn all about you. And we'll chalk up any gaps in your memory to the accident—you did suffer a brain injury after all. So come on, Ivy, are you going to continue being part of building something with Dahlen . . . or are you finished?"

How long did I have to decide?

"You have to decide right now. There's a nurse standing by to administer your evening sedative. You must be in a lot of pain. If you'd like to be put out of your misery for good, that can be arranged. Otherwise, say the word and you'll make a full recovery. The nurse also has some new contracts with her. It could be months until you're well enough to work, but our writers have ideas on how to rewrite the new season of *In the Dollhouse* to incorporate your untimely hiatus. And the new record can wait until you're back on your feet—we've been thinking an album of holiday classics could be lucrative. But that's getting ahead of ourselves. We're going to need an answer from you. Is this where we part ways, or will you be staying on with us?"

Had Timothy received a similar offer?

"Timothy ended his own life. We considered replacing him but decided it would pose too much of a risk—surely you would've sniffed out the imposter. We won't have that problem in your case."

How simple it would be, to say a few words, allow a nurse to inject me, and drift off to sleep. If I couldn't have true freedom, wouldn't this be the next best thing?

And yet, from somewhere deep within me, a fresh desire emerged, like a drowning person thrashing to the surface of the water.

I wanted to live.

Even if it meant sacrificing my autonomy, even if it meant being a willing prisoner in Owls Point, even if it meant having champagne problems poured down my throat. A limited life was better than no life at all.

I chose to stay, and once again, I signed the contracts. I even begged to have my doubles retired, vowing to resume any publicity appearances required of me with no complaint.

Dahlen may have thought they could train copies of me to look and act and talk and even sing like me, but no facsimile could ever replace the very essence of me, the nuances and charisma that brought me to such heights of success. There was only one Ivy Gordon, and from now on, only one woman who would play her: me.

And that's what I've done. Along the way, I've found ways to embrace my work, because the alternative was a void I didn't want to face. Yet however much I've changed, I've remained the Ivy Gordon everyone thinks they know and believes they love.

Of course, the Dahlen executives found a clever way to punish me for my crisis of faith. The rumors of my dying in the tour bus accident and being replaced with a double came from within the Dollhouse, a gossipy urban legend that haunts me to this day. My recovery involved having facial reconstructive surgery, which changed my appearance slightly, and this was used as the basis for the claim that I was swapped with a look-alike, along with a made-up story from a former wardrobe assistant about my shoe size being smaller, and other so-called testimonials from former *In the Dollhouse* crew members. How bitterly ironic that the press never suspected a thing when decoys took my place, yet my own authenticity has repeatedly been brought into question. Over the years, the rumors have been periodically revived in tabloids as a way to keep me in line when I was perceived as being difficult. The threat has been effective. It's kept me in line.

To this day, Genevieve swears up and down that she had nothing to do with these attempts on my life, or with Project Understudy spinning out of her control. I don't know why I've believed such an obvious lie. At the same time, even today, even as I persist chasing it, I wonder if I can handle the truth.

CHAPTER THIRTY-THREE

You can be replaced at any moment. In ways you can't even imagine.

This latest note disturbs me more than the others. Do these "ways I can't even imagine" have something to do with Project Understudy? That makes me more concerned about Grace and Tia's well-being than my own. Come to think of it, it's been over a week since I've seen Tia.

She's not in her room, but her schedule is on the dresser, so I hurry over to where she's currently having a voice lesson. I wait for her outside a Gothic building, pacing the flagstones until she comes out.

"Ramona!" She greets me with a dazzling smile and a big hug. "I was just thinking about you. We've both been so busy, we should grab a coffee sometime and catch up." When did she completely lose her southern accent?

"You're absolutely right." I link my arm through hers. "In fact, we should do that right now, but let's skip the coffee so we don't waste any time." Instinctively, I check her face for any changes and stop short.

Tia's lips are noticeably fuller and there are dark yellow patches under her eyes. It's her nose. Actually, it's not *her* nose. It's Grace's new nose. The resemblance between the two is striking now.

"You had a nose job?" I peer more closely into her face and recall Tia saying she didn't care for her old nose anyway. "And lip injections?" *To look more like Gracie?*

"Yeah, it's no big deal." There's a defensive note in her voice telling me to rein in the vinegar.

"You look gorgeous!" I say. "I mean, you were gorgeous to begin with, but your face now . . ." *Is no longer your face. You lost what made you special.* "They did an *amazing* job."

"You think so?" She brings a self-conscious hand up to her nose, then lowers it to her mouth. "I'm still getting used to it. But it's been fun when people mistake me for Gracie. I just tell them I'm her stunt double." She checks her watch and groans. "I wish I could hang out, but I have modern dance in fifteen minutes."

"Skip it," I insist.

"It's Lady Edna. You know how she is if you miss one of her classes. Are you okay? You look a little . . ."

"I'm not okay. I am a little . . . no, a lot . . . this is important. I need you to come with me and . . ." I lean in and quickly whisper, "It's about Project Understudy."

That makes her snap to attention. We haven't discussed Project Understudy since that day she told me about it in the hedge maze. That's where we go now, despite it being a bitterly cold late spring day.

Once we're seated, I take out my collection of anonymous notes and hand them to Tia. I explain how long I've been receiving them.

When she finishes reading, she says, "It's awful that you've been getting these. Have you reported them to the administration?"

"No," I say, frustrated that she's missing the point.

"Maybe you should. I can see why you're shaken up . . ." She looks thoughtfully at one of the owl topiaries before turning to me. "But what does it have to do with Project Understudy?"

"I mean, this last one sounds pretty sinister. And isn't the whole point of what you're doing to replace someone?"

"I mean, maybe in some press events and performances, but—"

"But you're being groomed to take over as Gracie, right?" The name feels sticky on my tongue. "Not as Juniper York, but Grace herself."

"Yeah, so what?"

I feel like I'm tiptoeing around mousetraps. "Don't get me wrong, you look beautiful, but don't you think it's a little . . . extreme to have surgery to look more like one of the Dollhouse's stars?" Her eyes flash, but the words keep tumbling out of my mouth. "Are you going to be satisfied filling in as Grace's double, living off the crumbs of her fame and success? What kind of career do you expect to have as someone else's shadow?" I put a hand on Tia's shoulder, and she recoils like I've struck her. "We both came here with such big dreams. Don't you feel like you're shrinking yours?"

"I did at first." Tia chews on the inside of her cheek and stares in the distance.

"What changed? What about all those things your mom said about working hard and dreaming hard?"

The wistfulness in her eyes hardens. "Mama also used to say a granted wish doesn't always look like you expect it will." Tia removes my hand from her shoulder, gently but resolutely. "I still want to be somebody. If that means being somebody else, so be it. I don't see it as shrinking my dreams, I see it as playing the role of a lifetime. We've got to keep Gracie everywhere for her to remain a top star, and these days that's more work that one person can handle."

I want to see it her way, I do. And yet . . .

"Don't you understand?" she presses on. "This way both Gracie and I get to succeed. It doesn't have to be just one of us. I get a piece of that spotlight, too. I get to live that glamorous life I always wanted. I'll never have to water down shampoo bottles and bathe with slivers of soap. I won't have to eat rice and beans for a week straight—or worse, ketchup sandwiches. I won't have to stoop so low as to shoplift lipstick and nail polish. As long as I'm here and doing well, I'll never have to worry about those things again. Don't you want that security, too?"

"Of course. But you're making a big sacrifice for it. Are you really going to dedicate god-knows-how-many years of your life pretending to be someone else?"

"Isn't that what we're all here to do?" She stands and hands me back the papers. "Whatever they have planned for me, I'm committed to playing my part. I'm committed to being in the Dollhouse. I belong here. If you're having doubts, maybe you should take a closer look at yourself and whether you belong here."

She walks away and I don't follow.

After my conversation with Tia, I don't know what to think or what to do with myself, so I go for a walk. Why did I push her so hard? What if this last note has nothing to do with Project Understudy? And yet, how could it not?

This time, it's not so easy to put the notes' warnings out of my mind. The more I try to brush them aside, the more they keep swarming me. I need to talk to someone else about this. Only one name keeps circling my mind. Mason. It may be a huge a risk sharing my misgivings with him, but he might also be able to give me some clarity.

Fortunately, we're done taping the latest season of *In the Dollhouse* and I have a few days free before preproduction on *Dollhouse Daze* begins.

Hopefully, I'll be able to track down Mason quickly. The first place I check is the lake. He's not here. The question is, do I stay and see if he turns up or . . . or what, hang around outside of Genevieve's house in a trench coat and dark glasses, waiting for him to come out? Wander the vast grounds of Owls Point on the off chance I'll run into him? No, my best option is to stay here and wait.

I sit on the fallen log and take out the script I know I won't be able to give my full attention to. In the distance, I hear the thump of sneakers hitting the paved jogging trail that winds around a wooded area behind the beach.

Over the course of the next few hours, a handful of people filter in and out, mostly couples whose romantic interlude I've interrupted.

I'm pacing around the log, wondering how much longer I should wait, when Mason finally comes into view.

"You're not out here waiting for me, are you?"

That's when I remember I was supposed to meet Jude for drinks and accidentally stood him up.

"Listen, can we not do the back-and-forth right now?" I ask. "There's something serious I need to ask you about." I'm between two land mines, either one of which could blow up in my face. One is confirming something evil about Project Understudy, the other is having Mason tell Genevieve I'm investigating it.

Mason gestures to the fallen log by the water. "Step into my office."

I take a seat and clutch my messenger bag containing the anonymous notes close to my chest. "How do I know I can trust you?"

"You either do or you don't." A barely perceptible shrug.

"That's reassuring."

"If you have to be persuaded to trust someone, that's not trust, it's bullshit. I try to avoid bullshit as much as I can—probably one reason I didn't make it further in this business."

It's also why I find it so easy to talk to Mason. He tells me the truth, even when I don't want to hear it. "If I ask you about something confidential, can you tell me everything you know about it but also swear not to tell anyone I asked?"

"You mean you'd like me to put my job in jeopardy and reveal secrets about an intentionally clandestine entertainment behemoth while protecting you if there's any fallout from revealing said secrets? Yes, of course, that sounds totally reasonable."

Ignoring his baffled smile, I continue. "This might be putting my job in jeopardy, too, but there are things more important than that. I need to know if we might be . . . in danger."

At this, Mason's face turns somber. I take a long breath in.

I can't take any more speculation torturing me.

"What do you know about Project Understudy?" The words come out rapid-fire, a series of verbal darts that hit Mason between the eyes.

He freezes, his mouth forming a small O, then casts sharp glances over each shoulder before scanning the rest of the beach.

"Genevieve threatened me with expulsion if I ever brought it up again, so you're not the only one taking a risk by discussing it."

"All right then." Mason measures out his words carefully. "What do you think you know about Project Understudy?"

"I'll tell you, but you can't ask me how I found out."

"Because you don't want to implicate your friend Tia."

"That's right." A small shiver goes through me. So, he does know about it. Of course he does. But how much? "I only know what she's told me, which isn't a lot. And I'm wondering if it has something to do with this." I show him the most recent note, give him a quick overview on the others, along with my suspicions, beginning with Gino Rinaldi and concluding with what Tia shared with me.

He listens without interrupting, periodically rubbing his forehead and temple as I speak.

"Up to now, I was usually able to dismiss the notes as a stupid prank, but I'm starting to feel like there's more to it. And for some reason I keep coming back to Project Understudy," I say. "What can you tell me about it?"

There's an extended period of silence as he looks intently down at the sand, then up at me, alternating between the two. Somebody like Mason will not respond to prodding or impatience, so I wait, hopeful he'll tell me the truth and that truth won't be devastating.

Finally, he speaks. "I really shouldn't be telling you anything. The program is kept highly confidential so it doesn't get out to the public— understandable, since the doubles are supposed to distract paparazzi, over- zealous fans, potential stalkers. But there's also concern not everyone who knows about Project Understudy is on board with it from an ethical standpoint—deceiving the public, sacrificing personal identity to ensure the ongoing success of singular Dollhouse talent . . ." Mason studies the tree trunk we're sitting on, picks at a section of bark in the space between us. "I've been taking a more active role with the program, and if I'm com- pletely honest, I'm not sure if I'm entirely on board with it, either."

My stomach plummets. "Is there horrible shit going on behind the scenes? Something with the medical tests and supplements?"

"Of course not. I just couldn't imagine giving up that much of myself for Dahlen's greater good." There's a faint snap as a piece of bark sails onto the sand.

"But what about Gino Rinaldi? During his meltdown, he was ranting about Project Understudy."

"As far as I know, everything DahlenRex does is to keep everyone at the Dollhouse healthy. And the doubles aren't trained to permanently take the place of Dahlen's top stars, but if someone like Gino was already unstable, I could see how the pressures of Project Understudy made him think the worst and triggered his breakdown. These doubles are well compensated for their discretion and dedication, but it's hard work. Now that Gracie is the next big thing, it makes sense that she'd have her own double. You may not consider it an ideal career track, but Tia isn't getting herself into something she can't handle. There have always been rumors that DahlenRex is experimenting on trainees to develop new drugs, but your friend is hardly in jeopardy." His roving eyes finally lock on mine. "Maybe I'm reaching a point where I don't have many years left in me working in this business, but that has more to do with me and not this place. I've been here a long time—too long probably, but long enough that I'd know if something dodgy was going on. And I wouldn't stay if it was."

It's exactly what I needed to hear. I needed permission to set aside my percolating dread, stop worrying about my friends, and continue enjoying my steady rise in the industry. I should be relieved, but I don't like how quickly I'm running to embrace these explanations.

Despite Mason not giving me any reason to disbelieve him, despite my *wanting* to believe him, I'm not able to fully step over that line. I don't think he's lying, but . . . could there be more to Project Understudy than what he's aware of?

CHAPTER THIRTY-FOUR

JULY 1999

I keep my promises to Genevieve, which are written into my *Dollhouse Daze* contract. I get my teeth bonded and whitened, get extensions for my newly platinum hair, and lose fifteen pounds. This means more exercise and fewer carbs, avoiding crunchy foods or beverages that can stain my teeth, and adopting a new hair routine involving brushing, braiding, and a host of expensive products.

As determined as I've been to unearth the full truth about this place, every time I tried to think rationally, a fog of contentment settled over me, making it easy to dismiss my worries. There was only one way I could guarantee a clearer mind.

And so, I spent the last two months weaning myself off all the pills I was taking. Which isn't to say I was able to avoid withdrawal entirely; I fought off headaches, lethargy, and insomnia for weeks. And every pound I lost was an uphill battle, since my appetite increased as my dosages decreased.

Worst of all, the numerous doubts that had been subdued and pushed to the periphery of my mind are now front and center, bellowing the same refrain over and over again.

Something isn't right here.

A new worry that looms in the weeks leading up to the beginning of film production: Will I be able to perform well without the pills? Fortunately, I'm only involved in one of the movie's musical numbers, whose choreography I can handle. But what about the acting? What if my nerves get the best of me again?

I've tried to put in place some safeguards against this. I meditate daily. In the month before we start shooting, I take a movie acting boot camp and spend hours a day working on my sides, studying recordings of my performances, taking careful notes on the feedback I get from the instructor and other students. I also, grudgingly, return to Breaking Down Barriers, which turns out to be as ridiculous as I expected, but also useful. It makes me drop my inhibitions and vocalize my fears, which turn out to be similar to everyone else's: variations of not amounting to anything, of disappointing loved ones, of failing.

I remind myself that talent and hard work is what got me to the Dollhouse and those are the things that will ensure I do well in this movie. If I did it before without chemical intervention, I can do it again now.

With all this time spent detoxing, dieting, exercising, and preparing for the film, I don't see much of Tia. The peace between us is tenuous, but I'm determined not to have two friendships disintegrate back to back. When Tia and I do hang out, we still talk about our work, though we never mention Project Understudy.

While I'm happy to make time to see Tia, I have less and less time to spend with Jude, which bothers him more than it does me. Jude loves my new look, which comes as no surprise after the way he raved over Grace's makeover. Part of me wishes he didn't love it so much. I sense myself pushing him away, first by limiting our time together, then by limiting our intimacy. It's been over a month since we had sex, and I've given him all kinds of excuses, like wanting to channel all my energy into my work, which isn't a total cop-out. Under different circumstances, at this point I'd suggest Jude and I take a break, but I can't risk adding more friction to the *Dollhouse Daze* shoot, especially since he and I have scenes together, as well as upcoming publicity obligations. I have enough to worry about now that I've gone chemically au naturel. Like how to get more info about Project Understudy and how to pull off filming a scene with Grace when we haven't spoken to each other in months.

Grace must really be a big deal now, because the film production is working around her touring schedule and even letting her skip out on the table read. Which means there's no telling how the two of us will act alongside each other, in any sense.

The scene with Grace is on the first schedule I receive. It will be shot at a large greenhouse on campus.

My call time is 10:00 p.m. and when I arrive on set, there's already a swarm of people there. Even though it's similar to being on a TV set, there's a bigger crew and a different energy in the air. With everyone bustling about, it's like we're human cogs in a larger machine, each with our assigned job.

I'm in my Dollhouse uniform for this scene and my hair and makeup are standard. To be honest, I'm getting a little tired of the plaid skirt and red tie.

As the makeup artist is finishing up, there's some cursing and yelling coming from outside.

"Where the hell is she? Every minute she's not here is costing us money!"

Grace is going to be an hour late, though nobody is sure what's causing the delay.

Normally I can pass the time by reading a book or going over my sides, adding in more backstory and character flourishes (I recently decided Skylar Vaughn is allergic to strawberries). In this case, I'm too distracted by all the movement around me, the various apprehensions plaguing me, and my growling stomach. Instead, I spend the next hour watching people run in and out of the greenhouse, listening to the crackle of walkie-talkies, and ignoring the tantalizing smell of grilled sausage and peppers from a nearby catering van.

After an indeterminate amount of time, a sickly looking girl with

Grace's haircut stumbles past me. She's in dark sunglasses, sweatpants, and a torn T-shirt, and I cringe away from her rank body odor as she goes by.

An assistant comes scurrying after her, apologizing on her behalf, saying she's recovering from a severe case of food poisoning but will be ready to go in an hour.

I clap a hand over my mouth: this *is* Grace.

There's no way this transformation is due to food poisoning. Grace looks nothing like the cool charismatic star I saw months ago. Could she be sick with something more serious? Could it be the stress of her new-found fame and success? Could she be on drugs?

Could she be *off* drugs?

I don't know what to think.

When Grace returns to set an hour later, I'm stunned at her makeover. While there's only so much the wardrobe department could do to hide her gauntness, they've made her look more chic than scrawny, putting her in a sequined shift dress the exact shade of her hair, which of course matches her Diva Doll lipstick. I try not to think about how much focus she's going to pull from me in this scene solely because of her eye-grabbing appearance. It just means I'll have to work that much harder, which has become my mantra of late.

In the scene, Juniper is trying to keep Skylar out of the greenhouse because it contains a portal to a parallel world, which Juniper hopes will return her to her original dimension. Skylar, unused to being told no, barges past Juniper into the greenhouse. Their argument continues inside until the portal is open and mayhem ensues.

We run through the first part of the scene several times, adjusting our blocking until the AD is satisfied. Grace only looks at me when she's playing Juniper; otherwise, she keeps an air of professional detachment. We're dismissed, and Grace looks ready to scurry off.

Before she can, I grab her arm, then quickly drop it, shocked at how frail it feels.

"Can we talk?" I ask. "We're doing this scene together—it would be nice to . . ." I make vague gestures with my hands.

"I can't. I . . ." She stares over my shoulder, as if searching for an excuse. "I have something I need to do."

"Cut the crap, Grace. We're both waiting for the same thing. I don't understand why you can't give me a few minutes." There's a garden shed about ten feet away from the greenhouse that appears unoccupied. I motion to it. "Can we just . . . ?"

She looks like a little kid being sent to the principal's office but grudgingly follows me into the shed. When I pull on the string connected to a naked bulb hanging from the ceiling, it's a relief to find the space empty apart from garden tools and a few cobwebs.

We stand six feet apart in the musty air, the lightbulb string dangling between us. While it's tempting to mimic her hostile body language (her sullen slouch and crossed arms remind me of her Times Square billboard), I keep my arms loose at my sides. Going into attack mode won't help matters.

"Grace, what gives? We've known each other half our lives—longer. Why would you let one stupid fight overshadow that? Why completely cut me out of your life?"

Her eyes burn into me and her jaw twitches. "It wasn't a stupid fight. It opened my eyes to how things really were between us. I was nice to have around when you could feel superior to me, but as soon as I started doing well for myself—not just well, better than you—you couldn't handle it. Genevieve said your jealousy would only hold me back and poison whatever progress I was making, and I could see she was right."

Something dark and thorny rises in my throat. "She wasn't right. I mean, of course I was jealous, I admitted that. But we've both been jealous before and gotten past it. I don't know why we couldn't do that this time." I take a step forward, reassured when she doesn't retreat. "As for feeling superior to you, I don't know where Genevieve got that from, but it's not true."

"Oh, come off it, Ramona. Like, cut the bullshit for two seconds. We both know I'm the better dancer of the two of us, but you always considered yourself the better actor. Not that you thought I was bad or anything, only that you were better. Can you admit that for once in your life?" She shifts her weight from one foot to the other and the light flashes off her dress's ruby sequins.

I open and close my mouth once. Twice. There's no point in lying, no matter how much I want the lie to be true. "Okay, yeah, I did think I was a better actress."

"And singer?"

"And singer," I admit.

Her mouth contorts into a triumphant smirk though her eyes reflect disappointment. Sometimes, being right is equal parts wonderful and terrible.

"Did you really think I'd try to sabotage you by sending you those notes?" Her tone is simultaneously hurt and pitying.

"No. I was awful to accuse you, and I don't know why I did." The shame of it makes me wince. "I obviously underestimated you, Grace. When you guest-starred on ITD, you blew me away. And your music—I mean, it's not the kind of stuff I listen to, but your voice is incredible." Her face softens. "This place has proved me wrong. It's made me question a lot of things. Like whether I'm cut out for this business. Whether I'm actually as good as I thought I was." As a performer *and* a person.

"You've done okay for yourself, so that should be answer enough. Is that why you chose now to make up? Because you have the boyfriend and the career?"

"No! God, no. I've been trying to reach you for months. Didn't you get any of the stuff I sent you?"

Her eyes narrow. "I haven't gotten anything from you."

"What the fuck? I sent you a white rose and gummy bears, a birthday card, all kinds of notes. You really didn't get any of it?"

Grace slowly shakes her head.

I ball my hands into fists, then release them. If she wasn't actively snubbing me, that changes things. "Maybe the Dollhouse thought I was a distraction." There's more I want to say, but I don't want to scare her off.

"Maybe." Her eyes are on me but still look far away.

My voice is soft and tentative as I ask, "Grace, are you okay?"

"Why, because I lost so much weight?" Her arms tighten across her chest. "Looking a certain way is part of the job."

"I get that. I mean, look at me. It'll be a miracle if my lines don't get drowned out by my growling stomach." I take another baby step toward her; she doesn't move. "And yeah, you're the thinnest I've ever seen you, but it's more than that. You look . . . not just exhausted—which I'm sure you are—but you look, I don't know . . . *extinguished* somehow."

A prick of fear in her eyes before they fill with tears. "It was wild at first. Everything is nonstop, all the time. But then it feels like it'll never actually stop, and I have to hold on for dear life." Her chin trembles. "I hardly get a say in anything. The show is pretty good, but I hate the music. *Hate.* I'm just their puppet. And nobody tells you how lonely it is."

There's a sharp rap on the shed door. "Gracie? Ramona? You're needed on set."

Grace dabs at the corner of her eye with her pinky. When I try to move toward her, she says, "Don't worry about it. That's what last looks are for."

"Do you think I give a shit about your mascara right now?" I try to keep her inside for another few seconds, but she's already opening the door.

We return to the set, get our final hair and makeup touch-ups, and start our scene. There's a new poignancy as Juniper tries to protect Skylar from entering the greenhouse and triggering the portal to another dimension.

"Please, you have to stay away. Don't make the same mistake I did," Grace says as Juniper.

Just then, the skies open up and unleash a fierce thunderstorm.

The director doesn't call "cut" though, so I keep going.

"I need to see what's inside," I shout over a clap of thunder.

"Cut!"

The director confers with members of the crew and before long, production is shut down for the night.

In all the confusion, I lose track of Grace, and when I go to look for her, I'm told she's already left the set.

The following morning, a PA tells me we'll be shooting around Grace for the rest of the week, though I'm not given a reason why.

On Thursday night, when I return to the dorm after a long day on set, there's a sunflower and bag of Skittles in my mail cubby. My eyes well with tears as I vacillate between feeling hopeful at a reconciliation with Grace and uneasy about her absence.

On Friday, I come home to my roommate pacing up and down the hall.

"Hey, Nicole. I feel like it's been weeks since—"

She cuts me off. "You have a visitor. She said there's absolutely nowhere else you two could talk, so . . ." A peeved nod toward the door of our room.

Inside, Grace sits on my bed, poring over a script.

"I wish we could have a cheesy Hallmark moment, but we've got some serious shit here," she says. "Come sit. You're gonna want to read this." She barely looks at me as I cross the room.

When I sit down, I see it's not a script on her lap but a thick stack of photocopied handwritten pages, a border of leaves around each one.

It's only when I begin to read that I realize the significance of the decorative border.

Not leaves.

Ivy.

CHAPTER THIRTY-FIVE

Ivy's Diary

JULY 7, 1999

"Your life is no longer your own," said that distorted voice on the phone when I was in the hospital. "You are now living a borrowed life on borrowed time. Never forget it can be handed over to someone else in an instant."

I haven't forgotten. I've held on tightly to my life ever since.

It helps that I love my work.

When I returned to Owls Point from the hospital, Genevieve had me stay at her house for several months, with armed guards stationed outside.

"I thought I did a thorough job of ridding the company of bad operators, but evidently I have not," Genevieve said.

Once again, I convinced myself she had nothing to do with the attempt on my life. If I didn't believe in her, I would have no one.

When I had recuperated and the guards were removed, she said, "If you still want to leave, I understand, but I cannot guarantee your safety outside the compound. Much as I've tried to subdue them, it appears I have some powerful enemies. However, I *can* guarantee your safety within the compound. I'm putting additional security measures in place, and you've seen for yourself that there have been no major incidents on the property. Any hazards you've faced have always been outside of Owls Point."

She was right.

And after nearly losing my life for the second time, I found I no longer anticipated the idea of being free of the Dollhouse. Instead, I feared that freedom, feared the dangers that lurked beyond the gates.

Now I know for certain it's not safe here, either.

I haven't been imagining it.

I *was* being followed.

She came to me in the middle of the night. There was a knock on my bedroom window, and it took me a moment to realize I wasn't staring at a reflection in the glass, but at a second person. How eerie to face such a faithful copy of myself.

I hadn't been seeing things, there *was* still a double of me at the Dollhouse. She climbed through the window, and we sat at the foot of my bed.

"Project Understudy never went away," she said. How did she mimic my voice so perfectly? "It only became more clandestine. After all these years, Ivy Gordon remains one of the Dollhouse's biggest stars. Dahlen has to protect its assets. I guess I'm a type of insurance policy in case something happens to you."

It shouldn't have surprised me. Over the years, I wondered whether Project Understudy surreptitiously continued without me. After all, Dahlen had other assets to protect. I hadn't suspected that I was inadvertently still a part of the program.

I asked if she was the same woman I met in the hospital.

"I don't know," she said, distress creasing her forehead. "My memories are . . . blurring together. I'm not even sure how many years I've lived in Owls Point. I do know I've spent a lot of time in hospitals getting surgeries and recovering from them."

I felt like I'd been pushed off a cliff's edge and sent into free fall. What kind of surgeries?

"That's the tricky thing." The woman rubbed her jaw thoughtfully. "I'm not sure which were mine . . . and which were yours."

It couldn't be possible. Had she had brain surgery?

"No, but I spend a lot of time in that water tank wearing that strange helmet. They leave me in there for hours, and when I finally emerge, it's always with new memories. I think they're trying to give me only the best ones, but that doesn't always work. I end up knowing dark things, too, and personal things I feel I have no right to know."

Like what?

"Like how Timothy once burned a pot of chili because we got distracted making love in front of the fireplace. Or how my mother intentionally braided my hair a little too tight for auditions so I'd 'be more alert.' Or how the actor who played my dad on *Fish Out of Water*, a man older than my own father, whispered in my ear that he was in love with me on our last day of shooting."

I felt like a windowpane that had been shattered. There was no way this woman could have those memories. They were moments I never discussed with my therapist or anyone else, and I certainly never wrote them down before now.

"So many other memories," she continues. "How I yelled at Stevie for eating my favorite Monopoly piece—the top hat—and how bad I felt about that after he died. How Aunt Janet dog-eared the raciest pages of her books and I'd take them into the bathroom and—"

"That's enough. Please stop."

"I think you need to leave here," she said.

It sounded like both of us need to leave, I told her, but she only shook her head.

"I'm starting to forget who I was, but I do know I can't go back to being that person. It would be impossible. I've made the commitment to be Ivy Gordon, and I think I can do an outstanding job of it. They told me it will be my turn to step into the spotlight soon."

When?

"All they say is soon."

Who is 'they'? Is Genevieve part of this?

"I have no dealings with Genevieve." But she looked away when she said it. "Ivy, I want that spotlight, desperately—I feel so strongly that you are a part of me now—but I don't want you hurt again. You've survived two attempts on your life, but you won't survive a third. I don't want to see you become a victim of Project Understudy."

How curious, that she saw me as a potential victim instead of herself.

Then again, we've both been victimized by this place, along with many others.

It's time for me to become a survivor.

It's time to leave the Dollhouse.

CHAPTER THIRTY-SIX

Holy fucking hell.

I stare at the diary pages, mouth agape, unsure of what to think.

"This can't be real," I say, looking over at Grace. Waiting for her to roll her eyes and tell me of course it isn't.

But she only gnaws at her thumb's cuticle, her eyes cast down.

"Grace, come on. What is this?" As much as I want to grab her and force her to look at me, she's obviously in a fragile state. Any sudden movements will scare her off. Instead, I remain still and wait.

When she finally speaks, her voice is devoid of all emotion. "It's exactly what it looks like, Ivy Gordon's diary. She gave it to me herself. Made me swear I wouldn't show anyone else and would return this copy after I read it . . . but I had to show you first. It's pretty fucked-up, huh?"

I'm touched that she thought to share it with me, but still flabbergasted by what I just read. "Do you seriously think it's legit? I mean, it would be a stretch to believe the Dollhouse could create such convincing doubles of its biggest stars, but okay, maybe that's feasible," I reason. "Still, there's no way in hell they've been able to *implant memories* into those doubles. That's just . . . forget unbelievable, it's *impossible*. And if Ivy believes such a thing, she's got to be disturbed and delusional."

"She's not." Grace swivels her head and pins me with a look that's both desperate and resigned. "Deep down, you know she's not."

Grace is right.

Ivy does come across as nervous and suspicious in some of these entries, but more than anything she seems honest and vulnerable, not mentally unhinged. And while Timothy was clearly disturbed, maybe he had reason to be. It reminds me of that expression about how it's not paranoia if they're really out to get you.

"You know I'm the last person who'd believe something so out-there," Grace says. "But think about it. DahlenRex has become a pharma giant and a leader in medical research. If anyone is capable of something like this, it's Dahlen. I didn't believe it at first, either, but then Ivy showed me a couple of the reports, and I didn't understand all of it but . . ." She winces and shakes her head. "It's easy to get the gist of what Project Understudy is up to, based on what I've seen. There's already a girl training to becoming my double."

"You met Tia?" I gasp.

"Yeah, apparently, it's one of the ways they've updated the program. They have me working with her so I can teach her all about being 'Gracie.'" She puts air quotes around her new name, then frowns. "Wait, *you* met Tia?"

"She moved into Gale House after you left."

"Are you friends with her?"

My hands flail as I consider how to downplay my relationship with Tia. "I mean, you know—we live under the same roof, and she *is* really outgoing."

"It's fine, you're allowed to make other friends." She lets out a bitter laugh. "Like you said, it's not like I've been around for you. And Tia is so sweet. Sweeter than I could ever be. She's also really talented. At first, I thought it would be great to have someone who could take some of the pressure off, who could fill in for me so I can catch my fucking breath once in a while." Her face twists into a grimace. "But then it became a different kind of pressure. Like, she's so good at being Gracie, if I'm not careful, she'll get to do the job full-time. She'd probably be better at it, too."

"Hang on. You're not talking about actually staying here, *willingly*, after what you read in this diary. If Dahlen is going to such lengths to keep their star factory profitable, we're not safe here. If what's in these pages is really true—"

"Then it's too late for me. But not for you. That's why I showed you the diary. Figured I could do one decent thing after being such a shitty friend."

"I haven't been so great in the friend department, either." I grit my teeth but make myself say it again. "I was jealous of you, like, to an embarrassing degree, and I hate myself for it."

"Well now you know how much superstardom sucks, so you can stop being jealous."

"Not all of it sucks, though, right?" I offer a tiny smile.

"Of course not. Playing Juniper York is a dream. And once you're famous, it's amazing how much free stuff you get—on top of how much you get paid—not to mention all the pampering. To a ridiculous degree, down to stupid shit like how many ice cubes you prefer in your drink." Her expression grows wistful. "Remember when we first got here and met Vanessa Sanchez—"

"You mean your new best friend?" I can't help interjecting. At her bewilderment, I add, "You two seemed all buddy-buddy when you guest-starred on that ITD crossover episode."

"All she ever talked about was hair stuff and what skin products I use. Anytime I tried to bring up foster care, she changed the subject to, like, leave-in conditioners. It was pretty lame." She allows a moment of disappointment then shrugs it off. "Anyway, remember how she said she never gets sick of people telling her how much they love her? It's kind of like that. I may get tired of everything else about this business, but I'll never get tired of that. When you have hundreds—thousands—of people freaking out over your very being . . . there's nothing like it. But it's not only just an ego thing. I think I've done some decent work, at least on-screen. We both have."

"Better than decent. We've done some great work here."

"And with any luck," Grace's voice hitches, "I'll continue to do great work here."

"You're not seriously going to stay. There has to be a way you and me can get out of here safely. Not to mention Jude. Oh god, and Tia."

"They'll never let me leave."

"Don't say that. At least let me talk to Ivy."

"Yeah, good luck. When I did the show with her, she was nice enough, but I didn't have one real conversation with her. Even when she stopped by my house to give me this"—she motions to the photocopied pages—"she said maybe three sentences to me."

"Let me see what I can do."

But Grace's eyes glaze over again. "Maybe I should go back on the supplements. Ivy was dumb to go off them, and so was I. They make everything so much easier, like they're covering your whole little world in Bubble Wrap. Are you taking anything?"

"I was for a while, but I stopped."

"It sucks to see the world as it really is, doesn't it?"

"Yeah, but it's necessary. Listen, Grace—"

"I gotta go." She stands and hugs the pages to her chest. "I guess I'll see you on set . . . but I kinda hope I don't."

CHAPTER THIRTY-SEVEN

I barely get any sleep, my mind a whirlwind. Part of me wishes Grace could've left me the copy of the diary, so I could spend all night rereading it.

I think of those emergency alert messages broadcasting "this is only a test," and that if it had been an actual emergency, further instructions would've followed. Part of me is desperate for this to be another Dollhouse loyalty test, the greatest one of them all. But denial will get me nowhere.

This is not a test.

So, what now?

I haven't received any further instructions. I can't even fully wrap my mind around the diary. Despite Grace's certainty, I still need Ivy herself to confirm she wrote it and that its contents are authentic. In which case, I may also need her help in ensuring that Grace and I make a safe exit. And Jude and Tia.

It's going to be a lot to ask from a woman I've never spoke to one-on-one for more than a minute.

Fortunately, the following day, I have an 8:00 p.m. call time to shoot a scene with Ivy, as well as the greenhouse scene with Grace that was interrupted by the storm.

I get to the makeup trailer a half hour before my call time and am relieved to see Ivy in one of the chairs, getting foundation sponged onto her chin.

"Hi, Ramona." Ivy gives me a smile in the mirror.

"Hi . . ." I take the other makeup chair, staring intensely at her but not returning the smile.

"Pardon me, ladies, I left some brushes in another trailer," says Missy, the makeup artist, a petite woman with curly orange hair tied back in a handkerchief. "Back in two shakes."

The moment she leaves, I turn toward Ivy and whisper, "I need to talk to you, privately."

At first, she's taken aback, but the polite mask quickly glides into place. "I'm sorry, that won't be possible."

No way. I'm not letting her brush me off like this. "Ivy, this isn't just my career and my friend's career at stake, this is our *lives.* You really can't—"

"Sorry to keep you waiting." Missy steps back inside.

"I read the diary," I say to Ivy.

Alarm flashes across Ivy's face. "Actually, Missy, could you give us a few minutes?"

She glances at her watch. "I guess so, but the schedule is *really* tight today and—"

"It's tight every day." Ivy shifts her body to face the door, drapes an arm over the back of her chair. "We just need five minutes to finish up some girl talk. If anyone gives you a hard time, blame me."

Missy steps out and closes the door behind her.

Ivy turns back to me. "Grace promised me she wouldn't show it to anyone else."

"She and I have been best friends for more than half our lives. I'm not just anyone."

She sighs. "Go ahead."

"Did you write that diary?" I brace myself for her response.

A shrug. "I suppose I did, yes." She looks flattened, the kind of tired a good night or even week of sleep won't cure. "I really did count on Grace to keep it confidential."

"Seriously?" I take a breath to steady myself. Losing my temper won't get me any answers. "How much of it was true?"

Her chest rises and falls with a long sigh. "I've dedicated my entire life to artifice. That diary was the only place I could truly be myself. I didn't have the strength to leave, but writing each entry somehow brought me closer to doing so. The notebook was a gift from Timothy. He thought I would find the ivy border corny, but I loved it. Even though I never wrote a word in it while he was alive." Another quiet sigh. "It's all true. I'm still in shock over that little visit I received. I can't wrap my mind around her knowing the things she knows. But, Ramona, I'm not crazy. You have to believe that. Timothy wasn't, either." Her eyes grow shiny. "I don't want to end up like him."

I don't want Grace to end up like him, either.

All the air leaves my body. Even though it's the answer I've been expecting, it still feels like an icy tidal wave rushing over me. "Why should I take you at your word?"

"I can give you more than my word. My double was somehow able to get a copy of her medical records. This isn't everything, but . . ." She unbuttons her blouse, reaches into her bra, and brings forth a folded-up piece of paper. "I've been carrying it with me to remind me the clock is ticking, that I can't stay here."

I unfold the paper, which contains something called an aquatic image summary for Leonora Schoonhoven. There are a series of dates followed by: "transfer successful." At the bottom of the page, it says: "Craniotomy: TBD." There's a lurching inside me followed by an urgent need to flee.

"Ivy, if it's all true . . . That means I can't . . . I can't stay here. None of us can. We need to get the fuck out of here."

"Keep your voice down, Ramona." She takes the paper back, refolds it, and hides it away again. "And stay calm. No one is going to do anything dire to any of us today. We need to be careful about how we make our exit."

"You have to help me get Grace out. And my friend Tia. And my boyfriend, Jude."

"Are you sure they want to leave? All of them?" Her eyes rove the room. "You are still—and I mean no offense here, but you're unimportant enough that you could possibly be released from your contract simply by performing badly. Same goes for Jude. Gracie is trickier. She's the next . . . well, she's the next me. She seems so hungry for stardom—even though she showed you the diary, that may have been more for your sake. She may not be ready to go. I'm not familiar with your friend Tia."

"She's in Project Understudy. One of Grace's doubles."

Ivy sucks air through her teeth. "I'm not sure about those two. But you might still have a chance if you can get yourself fired from the movie."

"What if all that does is make them send me to Epiphany Bay? What if they force drugs on me—I've stopped taking the supplements, and it's nice to think clearly, though it also sucks." It takes all my strength to keep my voice at an insistent murmur. "I need to get out of here. Please help me."

"I don't know if I can. You have no idea how much it took out of me, living my life and then reliving it all on the page. I'm sorry I didn't share this with any of you sooner. I myself didn't know the worst of it until very recently."

"Don't be sorry, be useful. Find a way to get us out of here."

There's a rap on the door. "I really need to get back to work, ladies."

Ivy's face wavers between helpless and determined. "Give me a couple of days. In the meantime, act normal and find out if any of the others even want to leave."

"*Days?* I can't wait that long."

"You must. And don't do anything rash."

When I come out of the makeup trailer, a harried-looking PA says, "They're waiting for you in wardrobe."

Once I'm camera ready, I head to the set, my limbs numb and my brain on the brink of short-circuiting. I don't have it in me to tank my scene with Ivy, though I flub enough of my lines that the director gets testy with me. Still, we get through it and move on to the greenhouse scene with Grace.

When we first see each other, we exchange smiles, mine expectant

and hers defeated. It's all we have time for before we need to begin
shooting.

Once again, we sneak off to the shed as soon as we have a break between setups.

"I talked to Ivy," I say. "She needs to know that we definitely want to
leave. I'm, like, a thousand percent sure. You?"

"Are you kidding?" She shudders. "I already wanted out, but now I
super-duper want out."

"You're really sure?" I can't keep the dubious note out of my voice.
"The way you were talking about it yesterday . . . You'd be giving up a lot."

"Oh yeah, a lot of money I'll never have time to spend and fame that'll
turn me into a prisoner. And, you know, the possibility of having my
identity and my life taken from me. I haven't been at this long, Ramona,
but I can already see how it's gonna go. I can't imagine how Ivy lasted here
as long as she did. It's scary how isolated you can end up." Her eyes do a
frenzied sweep of the room. "What if it's already too late for me? What if
the only way out for me is—"

"Stop it. It's not too late. We'll both get out. Ivy said she'll help us."

"How? In all these years, she hasn't been able to help herself."

"Right, but you read the diary. She's been collecting dirt on Project
Understudy and probably has some kind of leverage by now."

Grace cocks an eyebrow. "Yeah, I'm not feeling especially optimistic
about that."

"I'll be optimistic for both of us then. You tell Ivy that you're with
me and keep being Gracie until we have a plan in place. I'll keep being Ramona. But I'll need to borrow that photocopy of Ivy's diary in the
meantime."

"You could just leave now and probably be okay." There's a shuffle as
she toes the ground.

"As if I'd leave without you."

As I head for the door, Grace puts a hand on my shoulder to hold me
back. When I turn around, her face is flushed and there's a fierceness in
her eyes.

"You know, you've apologized to me a bunch of times since our fight, but I never . . . and I am. Sorry, that is."

"I know."

"I just don't want you to think I stopped giving a shit about you," she says.

"You wouldn't have brought me Ivy's diary if you did."

"Still, I don't understand why you're being so nice to me—*beyond* nice—after I was a complete and utter asshole to you."

"Because I love you, silly." A lump forms in my throat.

"But I don't deserve it."

"Come on, Grace, it's not about deserving love, it's about needing it."

"Yeah, but I wasn't there when you needed me."

I try to hold them back, but a few stray tears escape. "It's okay. You came back. And you'll do better next time."

"I will." She gives my hand a squeeze and sniffs, blinking hard. "I promise, I will."

I believe her.

My sleep last night was fitful, but fortunately, I'm not on today's call sheet, which gives me all day to find and persuade Tia and Jude. I grab my messenger bag with the diary pages and set off.

Tia isn't in her room, but I get a lucky break as I leave Gale House and catch her coming up the walkway in workout clothes, drenched in sweat. Her smile is polite, far from the beaming grins she used to give me. I rush over and block her path.

"Tia, wait. I know things have been weird with us, but I need to talk to you." My words come out in a breathless jumble. "I'm not being dramatic when I say it's life or death."

She regards me with reluctant concern. "I have to be at the medical wing in an hour, and I still need to shower."

"That's okay." I do a quick scan of our surroundings. There's a trellis with a stone bench beneath it about twenty feet away and I motion to it.

The pages are in my hand before I sit down, the stone beneath me warm from the summer sun. I riffle through the entries before passing them to her. "This is a copy of Ivy Gordon's diary. I've marked the spots I think are most important with Post-its if you don't have time to read the whole thing. But read as much as you can."

"You actually got a copy of Ivy's diary? Oh my gosh, how?" Some of Tia's old bubbliness resurfaces through her new patina of jadedness.

"Just read it."

She huffs but takes the pages, her face blank.

"So?" I prod when she finishes.

"So . . ." She hands me back the entries. "So, I think it's bullshit."

"It's not bullshit, Tia. Ivy wrote this diary. She told me so. It's supremely bizarre and disturbing, but the stuff in these pages is true." I pause for a reaction, but she remains unmoved. Why is she being like this? Is it whatever drugs they have her on? "Aren't you afraid of what they might do to you? I'm not even part of Project Understudy, and I'm scared for you. And Grace." When this doesn't elicit a response, I add, "I'm leaving the Dollhouse. You should come with me."

She does a double take, as if I told her I was moving to Mars. "You can't be serious. We beat out so many other people to be here and we're actually *making it*. You'd be insane to walk away now. There's *no way* I'd find anything better out there than what I have in here."

"But is it worth losing yourself? Losing your memories?" I feel like we're speaking different languages.

"I'd love nothing more than to lose my memories." Her eyes flash and her twang returns as her words grow more heated. "They're sad, and the ones that aren't sad are boring. Nothing special ever happened living in Fame. My life didn't get exciting until I came here."

"And you'd rather stay and take on Grace's memories? They're not all happy, she's been through a lot of shit."

"If this procedure is real—which sounds crazy as all get-out but whatever—and if they can pick the best memories to give me . . . well, I'm all for that. And if they give me some of her crappy ones, too, maybe that'll give me extra motivation. Being Tia got me this far, but if being Gracie will get me further . . . I'll be whoever I need to be." The firm set of her mouth tells me she means it. There will be no convincing her otherwise.

"Can I please go shower now?" There's something heartbreaking about the cordial way she asks. I hope she's able to hold on to that sweetness.

Tears sting my eyes. "I'll miss you."

"Me, too." But she doesn't look at me when she says it, and the quick hug she gives me is perfunctory. "Good luck out there."

I watch her walk up the steps and into the dorm without a backward glance.

That leaves Jude. Maybe I'll be able to get through to him. He and I have lunch plans, so I arrive at the dining hall early, waiting by the entrance. It's a humid, sweltering day, and perspiration drips down my spine even though I'm in the shade.

"You must be melting out here." Jude leans down to kiss my cheek. "Why didn't you go inside?"

"I was thinking we could get some salads to go," I suggest.

"It's like ninety degrees out. Are you trying to get heatstroke?"

Great, he hasn't even seen the diary and he's already looking at me like I'm a lunatic.

"There's something I need to talk to you about in private," I say.

A nervous smile. "Sure." He looks like he wants to say more but instead moves to open the door to the dining hall for me, ever the gentleman.

We get our salads and find a picnic table near an athletic field. There's a large group of sweaty trainees running drills as an instructor blows a whistle and shouts at them.

I remove the pages from my bag and, after giving him the background on the diary, hand them over.

Fortunately, Jude is a fast reader, and I'm only halfway done with my salad before he pushes the stack of pages away. "I never would've suspected this. Clearly Ivy needs help. Or the whole thing is made up." He gives a quick headshake. "Ramona, I don't get why you'd think this is real."

"Because *it is*. What don't you get? Is everyone here medicated to the point of not giving a shit about anything important?" I don't mean to sound so shrill, but between Tia's and now Jude's understated reactions, my frustration is volcanic at this point. "The Dollhouse is training people to take our place if we become disobedient. They're drugging us up, they're performing god-knows-what kind of procedures on the trainees, and they tried to kill their biggest star! Twice! Why am I the only one who finds this fucking alarming?" The exercising trainees, now doing lunges, swivel their heads in my direction. I grit my teeth and lower my voice. "Jude, this is no joke. I'm getting out of here, and I think you should come with me."

"No fucking way." It's the first time I've ever heard him use profanity.

I grip the edge of the picnic table, my knuckles white. "Why are you being so blasé? This diary is real. Ivy told me so. Don't you believe it?"

"I mean . . . not really?" He waves at the manuscript as if it's a pesky fly. "I'm surprised you do. The stuff in here is nuts. Implanting memories? There's no way."

"I've seen other proof. A medical transcript."

"That can be fake, too."

"Okay, but Project Understudy is real. Are you comfortable with the idea of being possibly *murdered* and swapped out if one day you decide you're tired of being on the same show for years and years, or making whatever movies they want you to make?"

"Are you kidding? I'd be happy doing *In the Dollhouse* forever. And all the best movies are coming out of Dahlen, so I'm sure I'd be happy making any ones they want me to make."

"You say that now, but after years of being run ragged, you might feel differently—I mean, I've been here only a year and I'm already so worn out."

"That's you. That's not me. I'm in it for the long haul." Jude gives me a pitying look. "Actually, I've been wanting to talk to you, too. I feel like we've been growing in different directions and—"

"Yeah, we should've broken up months ago." I don't have time for something needlessly drawn-out. Though his wounded look tells me I could've been a bit less callous. "I didn't mean to sound harsh. It's just . . .

you should be with someone as . . . dedicated to this as you are. I used to think the only thing I wanted to do with my life was to be a performer, but I'm starting to wonder if I had tunnel vision." Jude's face is still puckered, like he hardly recognizes me. It's okay, we all make mistakes. Live, learn, get the T-shirt. "But you're different. You're talented *and* you're obviously going to stick with this. I wish you only great things." I feel like I should hold out my hand to shake, but I refrain.

"You, too, Ramona." He manages an expression that falls just short of a smile before getting up from the table, taking our empty salad bowls with him.

CHAPTER THIRTY-EIGHT

The next couple of days are agony as I wait to see if Ivy will keep her word. What a bittersweet bookend to how it all began, when Grace and I were desperately waiting for our Dollhouse Academy acceptance packets. Now a darker anticipation twists my stomach as I wait to find out if we'll be granted a safe exit from here.

By Wednesday, the third day, there's still no word from Ivy. We're shooting at the studio today, and my call time is 5:00 a.m., an hour earlier than it was originally, based on the new time hastily scrawled above the crossed-out 6:00 a.m. I leave my dorm at a quarter to five, only to find a club car waiting for me with Ivy at the wheel and Grace sitting beside her.

"Get in, we've only got an hour," says Ivy.

Grace splays out her hands as if to say, *your guess is as good as mine.*

A few minutes later, we're at the hedge maze.

"Let's do this by the owls," Ivy says.

"Do what exactly?" Grace's eyes dart between her and me.

"Give your testimony."

Ivy hurries us to the center of the maze, a large satchel bouncing against her hip, from which she pulls out an expandable tripod and a camcorder. "A while back, on a visit to Manhattan, I was able to sneak away and meet with an attorney. He already has my diary and a video corroborating everything I wrote in it, along with Leonora's medical transcripts and other documents. I wanted some sort of security net. Having your testimony will hopefully help extend that security net to both of you."

"Hopefully?" I ask.

"There's more to it," Ivy assures me. "I can't get into specifics right now, but I need you to trust me."

Grace and I exchange a look: What other option do we have?

"When I start recording, I want you to talk about everything unusual you encountered since the moment you got here, in detail. The medical tests, the supplements, the counseling sessions, Project Understudy, my diary, anything else that comes to mind. Ready?"

Not really, but when the red light appears on the camcorder, we begin to speak. Haltingly at first, then we become more animated as we get into the flow and recall more and more details.

"That should do it," Ivy says sometime later, switching off the camera. "I'll FedEx this to my lawyer and set up a meeting with Genevieve. Expect to see a red flyer in your mailbox soon. In the meantime, keep acting like everything is normal."

I get the red flyer the next day. The meeting with Genevieve is at noon.

Taking no chances, I arrive ten minutes early. A familiar British voice buzzes me in at the gate.

"And how is the glamorous life treating you?" Mason asks when he opens the front door.

"Do we have to do this right now?" My voice is weary, but my body feels electrified at the sight of him.

"And there I was, thinking you missed my sardonic charm." He puts a hand over his heart.

Instead of being lured into his verbal hopscotch, I say the first thing that leaps into my mind, which takes us both by surprise. "I did miss you, actually. Your sardonic charm, but also the rest of you." Before I can stop myself, I reach a hand up and stroke the stubble of his cheek. "You still look tired. Probably working too hard."

Mason blinks rapidly, his mouth open for a moment before he forms words. "It's what's expected of us, isn't it?"

"It is." I offer a small, sad smile. "But sometimes you need to subvert expectations. Will you please let Genevieve know I'm here?"

Before he can say anything else, there's a buzz from the security gate. Grace and Ivy are here, the latter armed with a thick accordion folder.

The three of us are ushered to the owl room. Mason gazes at me similarly to how Jude did when we were parting ways, like he doesn't quite recognize me—only coming from Mason it feels like a compliment.

Genevieve is standing in the center of the room, hands on hips. A sunbeam hits her like a spotlight, glinting off her diamond brooch. Some people never forget how to find their light.

"What a trio," she says. "The luminary"—she motions to Ivy—"the supernova"—a nod at Grace—"and you . . ." The sun catches the silver of her hair as Genevieve tilts her head. "We're still figuring out where you fit in our little galaxy, aren't we?"

Presumably, Genevieve sees herself as the sun around which we all orbit. "It's all just dust and gas," I say. "Sooner or later, we all burn out, anyway."

The red lips part to show teeth. "Let's have a seat. I've just had the most delightful tea sent from Beijing. It's made from the peel of blood oranges." She directs us to a small round table with four place settings. The usual porcelain tea set has been swapped for silver, a matching cup gleaming at each of our place settings. No fragile things at this table.

When the tea sits steaming in our cups, its spicy citrus aroma infusing the air, Genevieve fixes us with an appraising look. "All right then. To what do I owe the pleasure?"

"The three of us . . . We want out," Ivy says.

"Out of what exactly?"

"All of it. This movie. The shows. The albums. The tours. The contracts. The Dollhouse. All of it." Her tone is steady, but when I glance over to her, I see Ivy's hands are trembling in her lap. Fortunately, she's sitting directly across from Genevieve, who can't see.

"You think it's as simple as coming over here and boldly proclaiming such a thing?" Genevieve purses her lips to let out a steady stream of air over her teacup.

"I didn't expect any of it to be simple, which is why I've spent years looking for my way out, using any tool I could find to chip away at the bars of my cage."

"How very dramatic of you, Ivy. You live a life millions of people only dream about."

"They wouldn't if they saw the nightmare it really is." Ivy places the accordion folder on the table. "This is what I've put together. It's not just my account of what I've been through, though that's in there. I've also collected half a dozen witness testimonials, copies of medical records, surgical case reports, and detailed chemical analyses of the various so-called supplements you've been plying us with. My attorney—not one of your Dahlen thugs, one who's actually working toward my best interests—has all of this, along with samples of five different medications prescribed here. If you let me, Ramona, and Grace leave, voiding our contracts and assuring us there will be no retaliation, monetary or otherwise, everything my lawyer has will remain locked away with him. If you try to stop us from leaving or any harm comes our way, my lawyer has explicit instructions to release everything to a number of top news outlets." Ivy lifts her chin, remaining perfectly composed. In her lap, the nails of her right hand are digging into the skin of her left.

Genevieve handles the accordion folder as if it's a dirty diaper. As she reads, her stiff posture falters. "How could you possibly have gotten ahold of such confidential material?"

"I learned a few things from Timothy. Like how important it is to treat everyone like human beings, including the custodial staff. How they see more than anyone gives them credit for. How they catch moments of carelessness. You wouldn't believe what kind of messes are left behind. Lost key cards. Passcodes written down and thrown away. Documents that should've been shredded but weren't." A vein at Ivy's temple throbs, and she starts to sink her teeth into her lips then thinks better of it and relaxes her mouth. "We'll stay on and finish the movie. And Grace is willing to play her remaining concert dates. But that's it. You'll have to get your brilliant writers to write me and Ramona out of *In the Dollhouse*. What you do with Grace's show is . . . not our problem. None of it will be our problem anymore."

"Is that what you think?" Genevieve murmurs, sifting through the paperwork.

Ivy sits taller and swallows hard. "You knew everything, didn't you." Her voice is concrete, rigid and flat. "You knew everything happening with Project Understudy, about the threats on my life. You must've been behind all of it."

"Of course, my dear," Genevieve says without looking up, her tone unruffled. "Do you think anything happens here without my knowledge?"

"So you lied to me," Ivy says.

"I did what I needed to do in order to hold on to my biggest star."

Ivy clenches her jaw. "And you worked me to the bone and when that wasn't enough, you created doubles to look like me and sound like me, and when *that* wasn't enough, you gave them my memories so they could *be* me."

Genevieve's eyebrows rise. "Do you really believe our medical facility is capable of such a feat? I was concerned about your paranoid tendencies, my dear, but if you believe this, you're more far gone than Timothy ever was." She looks from Ivy, who's clutching the edge of the table, to me and Grace. "And if she's got you both believing such nonsense, all three of you should be booked into Epiphany Bay."

"I met one of them," Ivy says through gritted teeth. "She knew things it would be impossible to know. And those documents mention brain surgeries and aquatic imaging—"

"That implant memories into other people?" Genevieve waves around one of the pages. "Show me where. Because I only see reports detailing high-tech scans for physiological irregularities and the occasional surgery for an aneurism, stroke, or brain tumor." There's a rustle of papers as Genevieve returns the documents to the folder. Her nostrils flare, and I brace myself for her to spit fire. But instead, her words are icy. "Whatever you think you have collected here, I could still have my lawyers tie you up in court for years, which would be a nuisance for all of us. You three have proven nothing today except that you are disloyal and don't deserve to be here. I'll let you all leave, on certain conditions." She glowers in my direction. "We'll finish the movie, but Ramona, you'll be recast. You've been underwhelming in the dailies. Frankly, it's a wonder you made it this far. Once you leave here, you're welcome to work in theater, but consider your career in film and television over. You can go and pack your things right now. A contract termination agreement will be prepared for you over the next few hours, and once you sign that, you'll be free to leave. I trust you are competent enough to make your own travel arrangements. Your last paycheck will be mailed to your sad little home in Brooklyn."

This verbal assault leaves me momentarily winded. Stunned tears spring to my eyes but I'll be damned if she'll see me cry. "What about Grace and Ivy? I won't leave without knowing they'll be—"

"They'll be fine," Genevieve interrupts, then casts a disgusted look at me. "I expected more from you. I really thought you would rise above the others. And you handled those notes I sent you—"

"You sent me the notes?" It shouldn't be a surprise at this point, but it feels like another blow.

"Well, not personally, but they were sent at my behest. And you used them as I intended, as motivation, not the deterrent many before you found them to be. But not everyone is cut out for this work, as you have nonetheless come to prove. Now"—a single clap of her hands—"since Ivy and Grace accomplished a great deal more than you, there are more logistics and terms I need to work out with them. Go on now, let the big girls talk." She makes a shooing motion.

There's a ringing in my ears as I leave the owl room. I walk in a daze to the front door, all background sound muffled to the point where I don't notice Mason trying to get my attention until he grabs my arm in the foyer.

"Ramona. Are you all right?"

I'm woozy and my thoughts are muddled, and I am very much not all right, but . . . "I will be. Walk me outside?"

He puts an arm around me as he escorts me to the gate. "I'm guessing I won't be seeing you around."

"Not around here." I lean against his shoulder.

"Is lover boy coming with you?"

"No, he's staying. We broke up. It was long overdue. The tears aren't for him, they're for me." I wipe at my wet face. "It's so stupid, I chose to leave. I just didn't expect her to be so brutal."

"What did you expect from Genevieve, balloons and a cake?"

An unexpected laugh bubbles out of me. I stop walking and step in front of Mason. "You've been a good friend to me."

"I've been a dick."

"People aren't just one thing. You should leave this place, too. There's some dark shit going on here. Really dark."

Mason nods. "I'm becoming aware of that. It's going to take a bit of maneuvering for me to make a clean break, but I'm working on it."

"I hope you'll come find me in Brooklyn."

"It's not out of the realm of possibility." Mischief dances around his eyes.

"You don't belong here."

"I never felt like I belonged much of anywhere. I think that's how a lot of us ended up here. You're pretty lucky you're finding your way out."

"I hope you do, too." And before I can give it another thought, I rise up on my tiptoes, slide my arms around his neck, and kiss Mason square on the mouth.

At first, he stiffens, then he relaxes into me, tightening his arms around my body.

As we kiss, I envision two scuba divers floating in the deep, sharing a single tank of air, our heartbeats becoming synchronized.

CHAPTER THIRTY-NINE

"Don't be nervous, *Sarah*," I say.

"I'm not nervous. You're nervous."

My best friend and I are at a grocery store a few blocks from the Mag, getting fruit for props in a play that I wrote, and Sarah Madison directed. Tonight is opening night.

I'm still not used to Grace's new name or her new look. When she returned to Brooklyn from Owls Point at the end of last year, her lips were deflated, her hair was dyed black and cut short, and she'd put on some much-needed weight ("if I ever try to give up carbs again, shoot me"). She also got another new nose and had her jawline adjusted, which turned her face from heart-shaped to square. And she not only looked like a different person, but thanks to surgical alteration, even the pitch of her voice was lower. At first, I didn't truly believe it was Grace.

"Tell me something only Grace would know."

"Seriously?" she snorted. "Okay fine. At the beginning of sixth grade, the kids started calling you 'Bosom Lady' after one of the shoulder ties of your romper came loose and you accidentally flashed everyone during recess."

I flinch, the nickname still painful to hear after all this time, but it's a memory I never shared with anyone else. This had to be Grace.

In addition to drastically changing her appearance, one of the stipulations of Grace's release from the Dollhouse was that she change her name.

"I wanted Madison as my first name," she said. "You know, like—"

"The mermaid in *Splash*. Duh."

"They said it wasn't generic enough, though they did let me use it as my last name."

Back in the grocery store, I assess the pyramids of fruit. "Did we decide the conference room scene worked better with an orange or a banana?"

"I don't think fruit is going to make or break this play. Don't make that frowny face. Just get both."

Once we're done buying produce, we head back to the theater, where we still have a few hours before the show.

We stop at pedestrian crossing even though the light is green and gaze up at the billboard on the side of a parking garage.

"You'd never know it wasn't really me," she says with awed disbelief. "We've walked by this thing like a thousand times and I still can't get over it."

The billboard for the new season of *Rock the Dollhouse* has Juniper York slouching against a chain-link fence. And she's not alone.

"You miss him?" Sarah asks.

"Not even a little." Jude isn't the one I miss from the Dollhouse. But I haven't heard anything from Mason since I left. "Jude and Gracie make a much better couple than Jude and I ever did."

"You think they're an item in real life or it's just a publicity stunt?"

"Who cares?"

Even though Reed and Alonso change the channel anytime a commercial for *Rock the Dollhouse* comes on, Sarah and I watch the show when they aren't around. How could we not? It's fascinating to see how seamlessly Tia took over as Gracie. The Dollhouse spared no detail, even surgically lengthening her earlobes (whereas Sarah had hers shortened). And to distract from any speculation about her face, they gave Gracie a noticeable breast augmentation, which created a frenzy in the tabloids.

"You think Tia actually has your memories?" I ask.

"If she does, I hope they didn't give her the worst ones." She shudders and looks at the sky. "And she won't have my best ones because those are still to come."

"Look at you being all glass-half-full." I sneak one more look at the billboard. "Do you miss it?"

"A little. Not the Dollhouse itself, but . . . you know."

"The endless adoration."

"And I'd be a liar if I said I didn't miss the money." In giving up her name and likeness, Sarah also had to give up any of Gracie's future earnings. "You think Dion is doing okay?"

"I hope so. I just read *Overruled* got renewed for two more seasons." Though neither of us have been able to watch it anymore—or *In the Dollhouse*. It's sad to have our favorite show, and by extension, a large part of our formative years, now tainted. At least we still have Mary Tyler Moore.

"Come on, let's go," I say. "We still have a lot to do for opening night."

When I returned to Brooklyn, after swearing them to secrecy, I told Reed and Alonso everything about the Dollhouse. I braced myself for a litany of I-told-you-so's from my uncles (well, at least from Reed), but they didn't come that first day I was back, or the second, or the third.

Finally, over dinner on the fourth night, I asked, "Aren't you going to gloat even a little about how you were right?" I helped myself to seconds of Reed's mediocre tuna casserole (the noodles were burnt at the edges and raw in the center; I relished every crunchy bite).

Reed put his fork down. "What kind of monsters do you think we are that we'd gloat over that?"

"We're just happy to have you home safe and sound, *chica*." Alonso gave my wrist a tender squeeze. "This one over here"—a nod to Reed— "was a nervous wreck for over a year. So was I. It didn't stop us from bragging like hell about you to anyone who came into the theater, but it was stressful, always worrying about you."

"Be honest, Ramona," Reed said. "The Dollhouse might've offered to make your biggest dreams come true, but is anything better than the Kimono Zone?"

I grinned at my uncles draped in vibrant silk, tasting tears at the corner of my mouth. "There's no place like the Kimono Zone."

For the first couple of weeks I was home, I wandered around in a mental fog, like I couldn't fully wake up. I helped around the apartment and the theater, took walks in the neighborhood, read books, and tried to sift through the rubble of last year. What should my next step be? I wasn't feeling the pull of performing anymore.

One day I spotted a catalog for adult education classes that had been left out on the kitchen table, most likely intentionally. I paged through it and stopped at the description for Beginner Playwriting.

I don't know why I hadn't thought of it before. I'd already been flexing my writing muscles when coming up with song lyrics for the Mag's live coming attractions. Plus, all the years I'd spent inventing rich backstories wasn't just a way to improve my acting, it was also fulfilling a creative need in me. Instead of keeping those stories hidden away in my subconscious, I could bring them onto the page, take one-dimensional characters and expand them, breathe nuanced life into them.

The writing workshop was tough—just like with acting, nobody is going to like everything you do, and you need to set aside your ego to embrace constructive feedback and improve. Which is what I did as I wrote several one-act plays. Bolstered by the positive notes from my instructor, I followed that class with an intermediate playwriting class in which I tackled my first full-length play. I finished it in a month and then spent two more months intensely revising it, at which point I showed it to my uncles. It was called *Soused*, about a modern-day mermaid navigating life on dry land in a big city, battling alcoholism, heartbreak, and depression (my much darker take on *Splash*).

Alonso and Reed loved the play and talked about staging it at the

Mag. That was right about when Sarah came home, which diverted our attention for a while as she dealt with her own Dollhouse PTSD. Adjusting to a new appearance and identity was a lot, but it turns out my best friend's superpower is emotional resilience.

It was only a couple of weeks until she turned to me and said, "So, what's next? They let me audit classes on theater directing and choreography while recovering from my surgeries, and since I'm contractually bound to stay behind the scenes from now on, I think that's something I could be good at."

I gave her a copy of *Soused* and told her my uncles were interested in putting it on at the Mag. "We'll need to find someone to direct it."

"I'm inexperienced but I'm cheap. I'll do it for zero dollars."

"I think we can work with that. But read it first to make sure you like it."

Her response after reading was, "I fucking love it. Let's make it happen."

We both signed up for theater production classes, putting our new knowledge to practical use, working odd jobs to help my uncles with the bills (they insisted we invest our Dollhouse earnings), promising we'd get our own place soon (though neither of us were in a hurry to leave the Kimono Zone). We also helped out at the Mag, where I'm recognized from time to time as "that girl from *In the Dollhouse*" and Sarah is recognized never. We no longer perform live coming attractions, but I still enjoy writing them for fun. (*If you poison a town's water, you're a son of a bitch / How do we get justice? Erin Brockovich!*)

A few months ago, I also got a part-time job as a personal assistant to Eugenia Barrett, a cantankerous Pulitzer Prize–winning playwright in her sixties who chain-smokes, listens to nothing but Kraftwerk, and claims to have had an affair with Georgia O'Keeffe (she often boasts that one of O'Keeffe's lotus paintings was inspired by her anatomy). Eugenia read *Soused* and said, "Too earnest but better than the dreck I was writing at your age." When I invited her to opening night, she said she'd rather not leave the comfort of her Tribeca loft to schlep all the way to Brooklyn.

But then again, she couldn't be coaxed into attending the Tony Awards, either, despite her last play being nominated for six of them (it won four). Instead, we watched the ceremony from her place while eating copious amounts of sushi, Eugenia providing a running commentary on the industry and juicy gossip about the presenters and nominees.

I have so much to learn from this woman.

While I've had plenty to keep me busy the last year, my thoughts frequently return to Mason and Ivy. Is Mason still at the Dollhouse, still being overworked? As for Ivy, she released a new album earlier this summer, which knocked Britney Spears's *Oops! . . . I Did It Again* off the top spot on the Billboard charts (for a single week, before Eminem took them both over). She's been doing a ton of promo for the album and for *Dollhouse Daze*, which is predicted to be a massive hit and the beginning of a new film franchise when it's released next month. Meanwhile, *In the Dollhouse* will be airing its eighteenth season later this year.

The question is: Did the original Ivy Gordon ever leave the Dollhouse? Whenever I catch her on TV or in tabloids, I scrutinize her image for any signs that it's a decoy. I hope it is, and that the real Ivy finally made her escape. I hate to think of the alternative. She said her lawyer would release all the damaging Dollhouse material if something ever happened to her, but as long as there's an Ivy Gordon out there, those documents will remain sealed. When I'm at my most optimistic, I imagine the real Ivy got a makeover like Grace did and is now living as a different person, under a new name, with a new face. Sometimes, when I pass a woman on the street about her age and height, I pretend it's Ivy beneath the different exterior.

Back at the Mag, it's showtime. The lights are dimmed and the curtain is drawn. I expect to feel a stab of envy that I'm not the one up onstage, but instead, a quiet pride engulfs me as the actors begin reciting lines I've written. The show is a bit raw, and some of the scene changes aren't as smooth as they could be, and when the orange rolls off the table during the conference room scene, it creates a moment of levity I wish I'd intentionally added to the script. After the first act, I become so immersed in what the characters are doing I momentarily forget I created them.

Wild applause snaps me back to the moment.

I think of what Tia said, about how a granted wish doesn't always look like you expect it will.

After the show, a smaller group of us gather in a large storage room that my uncles converted into a backstage area, Sarah and I standing side by side, grinning like idiots. Alonso approaches us, a bouquet of flowers in each arm, sunflowers for me and white roses for Sarah.

"I told him he could leave the flowers upstairs, but he insisted on giving them to you here," Reed grouses, proffering two plastic flutes of champagne. "It was a marvelous show. Brava to you both, and to your talented cast."

"It was a triumph," says Alonso, kissing me on the cheek. He glances over my shoulder and his eyebrows shoot up. "Who is that handsome devil who just came in? He's staring at you."

I look over at the doorway.

Mason.

We meet in the center of the room.

"You're so committed to being the cool guy, you'll even wear a leather jacket in July, huh?" I ask, though I can barely hear myself over the blood pounding in my ears.

Mason doesn't answer, he just sweeps me into a hug. His lips brush against my ear, his breath warm as he whispers, "You never gave me back my flask, you little thief."

"You didn't have to come all this way," I demure. "I could've mailed it to you if you asked nicely."

He pulls back to give me a look like he wants to devour me. "Pretty please?" But he doesn't wait for me to answer before pressing his mouth against mine.

When I come up for air, the first thing I see is Alonso, excitedly elbowing Reed and pointing at me. I ignore my uncles and turn back to Mason.

"So when did you finally leave?" I ask.

"Late last year. The thought of starting a new millennium at the Doll-house was too grim." He offers a quick headshake. "I told Genevieve I wanted to return to England and try my hand at theater over there again. Which is what I planned on doing, but once I got back to London, I got a job in A&R at a record label instead, which I quite enjoyed. As luck would have it, the label is opening a New York office, and since I have loads of experience working stateside, as of two weeks ago, I live here."

"You've been here two whole weeks?" I can't keep the accusation out of my voice.

"I did come to the Mag looking for you when I first arrived, but when I saw the poster for your play, I figured opening night would be a better way to surprise you. And not distract you from the production. Which is outstanding, by the way." I wait for him to add something snarky, but he just smiles. "I actually have another surprise for you." From inside his jacket, he pulls out a small clothbound notebook embossed with ivy leaves and a sealed envelope. His face grows serious.

"Did she make it out?" I ask.

"I don't know."

"When did she give this to you?"

"Not long before I got out. After you left, I had a feeling something was off." He sucks air through his teeth. "For months, anytime I saw her, she seemed skittish, even scared. One night, I was asked to hand deliver some legal papers to her house. When I did, I told her that I wasn't sure what was going on at the Dollhouse, but I'd be leaving soon. I asked if there was anything I could do to help her. She made me wait while she wrote this letter and gave it to me along with the diary, making me swear to pass it on to you and Grace in person. Apologies for the delay."

I tear open the envelope, hungry to read the letter inside.

There's a lump in my throat when I finish reading. My heart goes out to this woman who has lost so much of herself. I hate to think of Tia willingly embracing a similar fate. "Did you read the diary?" I ask Mason, my thoughts in a whirlpool.

"Yes, which is what finally got me out of Owls Point," he says. "I'm sorry I couldn't come see you right away. I was a mess and needed to sort myself out first."

"No, I get it, I—"

"Ramona!" calls a husky voice several feet behind me. It's Sarah. It's still disconcerting how different she sounds. "Did you know—oh, hey, Mason." She gives him an appraising look. "Glad you finally escaped."

"Have we met?" he asks her.

"That's Grace. Only she's Sarah now." At his startled expression, I add, "I'll explain later." I turn to Sarah, holding out the letter. "You need to read this."

As she reads, her jaw drops open in slow motion.

Her eyes are shiny with tears when she hands me back the letter. "It could've been so much worse."

"We're lucky we left."

"So lucky."

"We need to find a way to get this out there," she says.

"We will."

"How?"

"I don't know yet," I say. "But we'll think of something."

"Let me see that letter again."

We huddle over it together as we read.

Dear Grace and Ramona,

We've never met, yet I have memories of you both.

I don't know what's become of the other me, the original. There are whispers that she left in the middle of the night, that she was taken away. Some say we both entered the medical facility and only one of us emerged back out. I want to believe she's still alive, but I can't say for certain.

If she was still alive, wouldn't she have taken her diary with her?

Or did she intentionally hide it where she knew only I would find it?

I live in her house now. I act in her show. I sing her songs. I know her so well, I've almost forgotten who I was before I became her.

Their technology isn't advanced enough to properly filter the memories, so I remember her entire life, before and after coming to the Dollhouse. I have read this diary, and over the last few months, I've added my own entries, filling in more details about Ivy Gordon.

Whether or not the original Ivy is dead, I think we should get justice for her. Maybe we can't beat Dahlen in court, but we can still get her story out there. When the time is right, I hope you'll help me do that.

You may be wondering, who am I?

My own story doesn't matter. There's less and less of me every day, and soon, there will be nothing left at all.

Only Ivy.

THE END

ACKNOWLEDGMENTS

Caroline Bleeke, thank you for bringing out the best in my stories, masterfully pruning the superfluous, and for letting me get a little dark and weird sometimes.

Philippa Sitters, thank you for your unwavering enthusiasm, support, and guidance.

Rosie Gurtovoy, thank you and everyone else at Peters Fraser + Dunlop working on my behalf.

I'm grateful to everyone who read early versions of all or part of this book: Stephanie Wrobel, Heather Chavez, Kerry Kletter, Natalie Jenner, Elissa R. Sloan, Elle Marr, Erin Foster Hartley. Thank you to Mike Coleman and Kelly Calabrese for sharing your showbiz inside knowledge, as well as James Gushue for answering my industry questions on the fly.

Thank you to the brilliant folks at Flatiron and Macmillan, including Sydney Jeon, Cat Kenney, Brittany Leddy, Katy Robitzski, Maria Snelling, Drew Kilman, Mary Retta, David Litman, Shelly Perron, Frances Sayers, Bob Miller, Megan Lynch, Malati Chavali, Emily Walters, Jason Reigal, Omar Chapa, Keith Hayes, and Kelly Gatesman.

The idea for this novel was sparked by my personal fascination with stories of former child actors. For years, I consumed their memoirs, essays, and interviews, not realizing I was actually doing research for what would eventually become this book. Valuable resources include: *The Coogan Chronicles*, an excellent podcast hosted by former child performers Chris Marquette and A. J. Trauth, particularly their interviews with Vanessa Chester, Madeleine Zima, Lauren Frost, and Andrea Bowen; personal essays by Mara Wilson; Alex Winter's 2020 documentary *Showbiz Kids*; *You Look Like That Girl* by Lisa Jakub; *I'm Glad My Mom Died* by Jennette McCurdy; the ingeniously titled *Coreyography* by Corey Feldman; *Melissa Explains It All* by Melissa Joan Hart; *High on Arrival* by Mackenzie Phillips.

As ever, I'm grateful to librarians, booksellers, book clubs, fellow authors, bookstagrammers, and every member of the reading community who has supported my work, as well as the staff at Porter Square Books, RJ Julia, and Inkwood Books for hosting me in person.

Thank you to the talented voice actors who have brought my audiobooks to life: Brittany Pressley, Alejandro Antonio Ruiz, Amy McFadden, Dan Bittner, Fred Berman, Hillary Huber, Johnny Heller, Katharine Chin, Ramón de Ocampo, and Suzanne Toren.

Lauren Whitney, thank you for showing me a kinder side of Hollywood, and for sharing that story about Jim Carrey and the tap shoes.

Terry Montimore, I wouldn't get to do this without you. Thank you for answering that salty 4:00 a.m. email from the pink-haired kook. I don't think I'm going to be hungry for dinner, either.

ABOUT THE AUTHOR

Margarita Montimore is the author of *Acts of Violet*, *Asleep from Day*, and *Oona Out of Order*, which was a *USA Today* bestseller and a *Good Morning America* Book Club pick. After receiving a BFA in creative writing from Emerson College, she worked for more than a decade in publishing and social media before focusing on the writing dream full-time. Born in Soviet Ukraine and raised in Brooklyn, she currently lives in New Jersey with her husband and dog.

RECOMMEND

The Dollhouse Academy

FOR YOUR NEXT BOOK CLUB!

Reading Group Guide available at
flatironbooks.com/reading-group-guides